No Longer the Property of Hayner Public Library District

R̶ MAR 0 1 2010 ̶D̶

By_____

W9-BVP-137

IF YOU WERE MY

Man

HAYNER PUBLIC LIBRARY DISTRICT
ALTON, ILLINOIS

OVERDUES .10 PER DAY, MAXIMUM FINE
COST OF ITEM
ADDITIONAL $5.00 SERVICE CHARGE APPLIED TO
LOST OR DAMAGED ITEMS

HAYNER PLD/ALTON SQUARE

· Also by Francis Ray ·

INVINCIBLE WOMEN SERIES

Like the First Time
Any Rich Man Will Do
In Another Man's Bed
Not Even If You Begged
And Mistress Makes Three

AGAINST THE ODDS SERIES

Trouble Don't Last Always
Somebody's Knocking at My Door

THE GRAYSONS OF NEW MEXICO SERIES

Until There Was You
You and No Other
Dreaming of You
Irresistible You
Only You

GRAYSON FRIENDS SERIES

The Way You Love Me
Nobody But You
One Night With You

SINGLE TITLES

Someone to Love Me
I Know Who Holds Tomorrow
Rockin' Around That Christmas Tree

ANTHOLOGIES

Rosie's Curl and Weave
Della's House of Style
Welcome to Leo's
Going to the Chapel
Gettin' Merry
Let's Get It On

IF YOU WERE MY

Man

Francis Ray

ST. MARTIN'S GRIFFIN

New York

This is a work of fiction. All of the characters, organizations,
and events portrayed in this novel are either products
of the author's imagination or are used fictitiously.

IF YOU WERE MY MAN. Copyright © 2010 by Francis Ray.
All rights reserved. Printed in the United States of America.
For information, address St. Martin's Press, 175 Fifth
Avenue, New York, N.Y. 10010.

www.stmartins.com

Library of Congress Cataloging-in-Publication Data

Ray, Francis.
    If you were my man / Francis Ray. — 1st ed.
        p. cm.
    ISBN 978-0-312-57369-0
    1. African Americans—Fiction.   2. Widows—Fiction.
3. Myrtle Beach (S.C.)—Fiction.   I. Title.
    PS3568.A9214I4 2010
    813'.54—dc22
                                                    2009033884

First Edition: March 2010

10   9   8   7   6   5   4   3   2   1

FRAY

b19063776

This book is lovingly dedicated to the awesome readers who made the Invincible Women series a success. You make all the solitary hours at the computer worthwhile.

ACKNOWLEDGMENTS

I would like to thank Lieutenant Doug Furlong, Myrtle Beach Police Department, Myrtle Beach, South Carolina, whose help was invaluable regarding S.O.R.T., the Special Operation Response Team, of the Myrtle Beach Police Department.

I'd also like to thank the Dallas SWAT team for their assistance on procedure. The paramedics at Dallas Fire Department Station 40 were extremely helpful with emergency care information.

Leo Cortez, manager of the fantastic Pappadeaux seafood restaurant in Duncanville, Texas, for his help in the day-to-day operation of the restaurant. Pappadeaux has the best seafood and the friendliest waitstaff in the state!

Any mistakes are my own.

IF YOU WERE MY

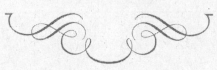

Man

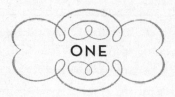

ONE

Rafael Dunlap was running late.

He didn't need to check his watch again to know he should have been at Fontaine fifteen minutes ago, which fortunately wouldn't present a problem for the men waiting for him. They were off duty and reportedly in one of the best-stocked restaurant bars in Myrtle Beach.

Rafael would see for himself . . . if he could ever find a parking space. Coming off a grueling workweek, they were all entitled to relax and have a little fun.

All except Rafael.

As a hostage negotiator with SORT, the Special Operations Response Team for the Myrtle Beach Police Department, he never knew when he might be needed. Unfortunately, unlike in the movies and on television, a negotiator couldn't go on for hours on end. The emotional and mental strain was too much.

On occasion, he had remained as the sole negotiator when

necessary, but he'd always known backup was there if it was needed. He had days off, but ever since he had taken the position five years ago, he accepted that he was never completely off duty, except for those rare times he visited his family in Charleston or went on vacation.

Rafael saw a parking space and whipped his vintage black Mustang into the spot. Parking was at a premium after five on any night, but especially on a Friday at the popular seafood restaurant near the Atlantic Ocean, which was one of the reasons Rafael had only been there a couple of times. While he didn't mind waiting for a table at a good restaurant, waiting for a table *and* a place to park as well was a bit much, especially when he was on a date.

Getting out of the car, Rafael slipped the keys into the pocket of his gray slacks. As he started up the gentle incline and smelled the fragrance of roses, camellias, and honeysuckle edging the wooden walk, the sweet perfume kept his mind on women.

He hadn't been on many dates lately. Work and family took up most of his time. A slow smile curved his mouth upward as he thought of his four brothers.

The Dunlap clan was about to get bigger. His brother Alec was heading for the altar, and his other brother Patrick was about to become a father for the first time. Both of his brothers and the women they loved couldn't wait for the happy events. Sam and Simon were already married. Although he was extremely happy for them, Rafael couldn't see himself as a married man or a father.

The boisterous laughter of a group of women ahead caught his attention. Bits of the conversation drifted back to him.

"Girl, that man is hot."

"But he kisses like a fish."

"Yuck."

Rafael's smile widened. Get a group of women together for

over fifteen minutes and the conversation usually turned to men. Not that men were any different.

The conversation between him and his male friends might start with work, but as the evening lengthened and the alcohol content increased, the topic of women always came up.

"Allow me," Rafael said, stepping past twin four-foot flower-pots filled with blooming pink camellias, trailing petunia, and ivy to open the half-glass door leading into the seafood restaurant.

The women turned, and their frowns morphed into interested smiles.

"Thank you," they chorused sweetly, giving him a slow once-over they didn't try to hide.

"My pleasure," he said, still holding the door.

The women traded naughty looks. Rafael could just imagine what they were thinking. A slow flirtatious grin spread across his face as he followed the women inside, where the hum of conversation, tinkling glasses, and Cajun music greeted him. The main dining room was a bustle of activity with the waitstaff in white shirts, black pants, black vests, and white aprons hurrying to and from the full tables.

Gas lanterns flickered on the large square posts throughout the dining room. Three-foot brass chandeliers hung from the recessed wooden ceilings in the area up front. In the back, the chandeliers were crystal. A bragging-rights string of mounted fish hung on a post. Beneath the fish were photographs of men in fishing gear wearing big smiles as they showed off their catch for the day.

He noticed that while some of the diners were dressed casually, others wore dressier clothes. Clearly, the restaurant was more about food than fashion.

While waiting to be seated, a few of the women kept throwing interested looks at him. He looked back. Perhaps it was time to end his solitary existence.

"Rafael, over here!"

Shrugging his broad shoulders in regret, Rafael turned toward the bar area off the main dining room. He spotted the six men he was meeting immediately. Sitting almost shoulder to shoulder, they had two high square tables grouped together. Rafael pulled out the lone empty red leather chair and took his seat.

"I see you're all way ahead of me." Each of them had some kind of alcoholic beverage. Tomorrow they'd all be back at work, but they obviously planned to enjoy tonight to the fullest. They were all on S.O.R.T.'s thirteen-member team with him, and all good men.

"What will you have?"

Rafael looked up to see a full-figured waitress with curly red hair dressed in a collarless white blouse, black slacks, and white apron. Her pretty round freckled face beamed a welcoming smile. "Iced tea."

Her eyebrows lifted over arresting green eyes. "Straight?"

He laughed. "Yes, to both."

Catching the double meaning, her laughter joined his. "Got it. Be back shortly."

"Is there a woman you can't charm?" asked Charlie Gibbs, the entry man. At six feet two, he had a massive chest and the muscled arms that could get the team through a barricaded door in seconds. He had saved their butts numerous times.

Rafael grabbed a handful of beer nuts. "I'm sure there is."

Douglas Hayes, who worked entry as well, grunted. At forty-three, with traces of gray at his temples, he was the oldest member of the team. He had a droll sense of humor. "Modest, isn't he?"

"Here you are." The waitress placed the large glass on the table. "Your next order of appetizers will be out shortly. Anything else?"

"No, thanks, Clarice." Ronald Diaz, the sniper of the unit, picked up his Jack and Coke, giving Clarice a lazy once-over as he did. There was nothing lazy about him when he picked up his rifle, though. Then he was steady, patient.

"Yell if you need me."

Rafael grabbed his tea. "How much time do you guys spend here?"

Tim Henderson shotgun and breach man, picked up a shrimp and swirled it in cocktail sauce. He was the jokester of the bunch. "Not much for the rest of us, but Gibbs and Diaz are regulars. They were trying to catch the owner's attention, for all the good it did them."

"Struck out, did you?" Rafael said, a smile curving his mouth.

"They never got to first base," said Tim gleefully.

Diaz scowled, sipped his drink. "When I tell women I'm the sniper for the unit, they melt. With her I didn't even get up to bat."

Rafael looked at Diaz, who dated almost as much as he did. He had the easygoing manner and charm women went for. "Both of you?"

"And every man that we know of, but, man, that is one hot woman," Gibbs confirmed, reaching for his bourbon.

"Hot doesn't even come close to describing her," Al Barron, the other sniper on the team, pointed out. At five feet eleven, he had the lean build of a runner, and the gray, unblinking gaze of a cat.

"Barron, you're married," Rafael teased, although he knew Barron doted on his wife and their two young children and wouldn't dream of cheating.

"I know it, but it doesn't keep me from giving props to a fine woman when I see one," Barron said with a Western twang, an impish grin on his broad face.

"It would if Wanda was anywhere nearby to hear you," Gibbs told him.

The men laughed. Barron looked a bit sheepish as he glanced

around, as if expecting his wife to appear and chastise him. The men laughed harder.

"You'd think a woman that sexy would be tired of sleeping alone after three years," lamented Diaz, clearly still wishing the owner had gone out with him.

Rafael sipped his tea. "How do you know she is?"

"Because I asked Clarice," Gibbs said. "Not if she was sleeping with anyone, but if she ever dated." He shoved his hand though his sandy hair, his disappointment obvious. "Seems she didn't date before she married Martin Fontaine either. Story is, he had to work hard to get her to go out with him. She saved his life after he had a heart attack and stopped breathing."

"You think if I fell over, she'd rush over and give me mouth-to-mouth?" Willie Stubbs asked, a dopey grin on his long, freckled face. He handled transportation for the unit.

The men at the table rolled their eyes. "Be sensible."

"I am." Stubbs picked up his beer and took a long swallow. "I haven't been out on a date in months. You're the only people I drive around. A man's gotta have hope."

"She's out of your league, man." Henderson slapped Stubbs on the back and said in his usual joking manner, "But don't feel bad. I bet lover boy here couldn't get to first base either."

The men around the table stared at Rafael. He casually picked up more nuts. "She's probably not my type."

"She's every breathing man's type," Gibbs commented. "But she turned us down flat. That's one door I won't be getting through."

"Shows she has taste," Rafael said.

The men traded looks. Diaz turned in his seat to face Rafael. A slow smile bloomed on his olive-hued face. He and Rafael had a friendly rivalry where women were concerned. "Then I suppose you could do better?"

Rafael shrugged. It was well known that he could have a date every night if he wanted one. Lately he hadn't been very interested. The satisfaction of being with a beautiful woman had lost its thrill.

There was no challenge, no surprise. Or perhaps it was simply that with the weddings of his niece and then his two older brothers and the engagement of another, there hadn't been much time for dating.

"I hate to bet on this, since my mother raised me better, but I'm sure she'll understand." Gibbs pulled out his billfold. "Ten dollars says you can't do any better."

More money hit the table. "Since Simon's basketball team needs new equipment, I'll take those bets," Rafael said, pulling out his wallet to cover the money on the table.

"You'll lose," Gibbs told him. "You can't do any better than Diaz and I could. Like I said, she hasn't been out with a man since her husband died three years ago."

Rafael grinned slow and easy. "Then I say she's overdue. If she's not dog ugly."

Diaz looked over his shoulder. Longing stole over his handsome face. "You can see for yourself."

Rafael glanced around. Air stalled in his lungs. The woman standing there was stunning, with flawless skin the color of cinnamon.

A white blouse with the collar turned up framed an exquisite face with alluring dark chocolate eyes, high cheekbones, a pert nose, and a pouting lower lip that begged to be kissed. Often. Her slim-fitting black skirt stopped just above her incredible knees. Her legs were shapely and endless.

She stopped at the curved fifty-foot rosewood bar to speak with the bald-headed bartender who had the shoulders of a linebacker. She laughed softly. Even with the noise of the crowded bar Rafael heard the alluring sound. He decided then and there he'd hear it again . . . while they were in bed.

Leaving the bar, she stopped at the tables and booths in the bar area, greeting customers. Each time she moved away, the wistful gazes of most of the men followed. Finally, she stopped at their table.

"Welcome to Fontaine, gentlemen." She met the stare of each man with a polite smile. "Is the food and the service to your satisfaction?"

The men chorused their agreement. Clearly, they were smitten.

"I have a problem," Rafael said, waiting for her to face him. When she did, the impact was lethal. His pulse hammered, but nothing showed on his face. He wasn't a cop for nothing.

She took two steps to bring her closer. She stopped inches away. Her fragrance, something exotic and sensual, drifted to him, tugged at him. "Yes?"

Standing, Rafael held out his hand. "My name's Rafael Dunlap." After only the briefest hesitation, she took his hand. The contact was barely the touch of their palms. Still, Rafael felt his heart rate increase. He studied her incredible face for a reaction, and was disappointed to see none. "Go out with me and we can discuss it."

Not one luscious black lash moved. Her expression remained polite. Rafael couldn't recall a woman being totally unresponsive to him. He wasn't sure he liked it.

"Please excuse me for a moment." Leaving their table, she went to the hostess station several feet away. Rafael watched her every step. He admired the erect posture, the way the black material hugged her perfectly shaped hips. Without conceit, he told himself that he'd be doing the same before the week was over.

Selecting a menu from the stack at the hostess station, she returned and handed it to him, a smile curving her sensual lips. "As you will see, I'm not on the menu," she said sweetly. "Gentlemen. Please come again."

She hadn't taken two steps away before the men at the table burst out laughing. Gibbs and Diaz, overjoyed that she'd rebuffed

Rafael as well, got up from their seats to slap Rafael on the back, joyfully ribbing him about finally striking out and being glad they were there to see it as they raked up the bills on the table.

Rafael wasn't bothered by their teasing or by losing the bet. She might not know it, but she had just issued a challenge he wasn't about to refuse. Before long, she'd purr his name.

Nathalyia Fontaine, manager and owner of Fontaine, moved to the next table, startlingly aware of the man watching her. She couldn't for the life of her explain how she knew, especially since her experience with men was so limited, that it was him and that he still watched her. She just did. She'd stake anything on it, and life had taught her early on not to gamble. If nothing else, she was a cautious woman.

Keeping the pleasant smile on her face, and her shoulders erect, she stopped at the next table, welcoming a large group of businessmen and businesswomen celebrating the end of the workweek and enjoying the happy hour specials.

Pleased with their response that they were enjoying themselves and that the service was excellent, she moved on to the next table and the next, all the while feeling those incredible black eyes on her.

They were heavily lashed, piercing. When he'd looked at her, it was as if she were the only person in the universe. She had never been the focus of such intensity, and she wasn't sure she wanted to be again.

Continuing to circulate, she forced the man from her mind. Fontaine prided itself on offering exemplary food and service in a friendly atmosphere.

She spotted four regulars at a table on the patio and returned their wave. The two couples were in their seventies and had been coming since her late husband, Martin, founded the restaurant in 1986.

Fontaine was the only thing she should be thinking of. Martin had taught her everything he knew about the restaurant that had been his life's work. She continued to learn after his death.

It was her duty and her pleasure not only to keep the restaurant open, but to see it prosper and thrive. He had entrusted her with his legacy, and she didn't plan on letting him down.

A man, no matter how attractive, wasn't going to get in the way. She'd seen firsthand with her weak and gullible mother and sisters how a lying, deceitful man could ruin your life. There were good ones like Martin and Jake, the bartender, but finding one was the problem. She had no interest in searching.

Nathalyia started back to her office. She wanted to look over the work schedule. Her assistant manager made the schedule, but occasionally Nathalyia checked it afterward. Martin had taught her to hire competent people, but it never hurt for them to be aware that the owner did spot-checks.

She stopped at the end of the bar near the take-out station and casually glanced toward the man's table. Their gazes met. The sizzling sensation she'd been trying to ignore zipped though her again. Quickly she looked away.

It must have taken her at least thirty minutes to circulate, yet he had watched her all that time. He hadn't even pretended not to.

"You all right?" Jake asked.

Nathalyia barely kept from jumping. Keeping a pleasant expression on her face, she met the concerned gaze of the bartender. Jake Sergeant had worked at Fontaine longer than anyone else, including her.

Jake was a good man, but a serious one. Nathalyia was sure it had something to do with his tour of duty in the armed services and the resulting scar on his face. He had the wide shoulders and muscled body of an athlete and a bald head that suited his direct, no-nonsense manner. He had always been her husband's right-hand man, and since Martin had been gone, she'd learned she could depend on Jake as well.

"Fine," she finally answered.

Jake glanced toward the table where Rafael sat, then stared at her. She fought the urge to fidget. Pulling a chilled bottle of Ty Nant from beneath the counter, he placed the bottle of water on a napkin.

"Thanks." Picking up the bottle from the gleaming counter, she headed to her office. She had work to do.

Men had come out of the woodwork after Martin died. A few might have been interested solely in her, but most had seen dollar signs. Too many men were users, and she wasn't interested in finding one who wasn't. She was happy with the life she had.

The last customers were shown to the door a little after one o'clock Saturday morning. If possible, Nathalyia always came out to bid the last guest good night or to gently encourage those lingering to go home. Tonight it was a group celebrating a birthday. She followed another tradition by stopping at the bar to talk with Jake and Clarice.

"Looks like our Nathalyia has another admirer," Clarice stated, a wide grin on her attractive freckled face. "He wasn't able to take his eyes off you."

Nathalyia fought the urge to avoid Clarice's teasing gaze. "Some men are rude."

"Determined," Clarice said, propping a rounded hip on the barstool. "Just tell me how you could have turned down such a mouthwatering specimen of manhood?"

"How did you know?" Nathalyia asked, surprised.

Clarice grinned, quick and easy. "The men at his table kept ribbing him. The thing is, he didn't seem to mind. He just kept staring in the direction he'd last seen you when you went to your office."

"I'm not interested," Nathalyia said, reaching for the bottle of water a silent Jake had placed on the bar. So she'd felt something hot and smoldering just looking into his eyes. So what?

Clarice slid off the stool and placed her hands on her ample hips. "That man was a walking, talking hottie. If he had asked me out, I might have had to ask Jake to forget his promise to lock me up if I even thought of dating again." Wrinkling her nose, she sighed dramatically. "I'm off men."

"And I don't have time for them," Nathalyia said firmly.

"I know," Clarice said, blowing out a breath. "I admire you for your strong will. It gives me hope to hang on. It's been six long months since my last disastrous date. A record for me, and a long dry spell." She tossed a sexy smile at Jake. "I might jump you."

He grunted and continued tabulating the liquor. Clarice folded her arms under her generous breasts and made a face at Jake. "It's a good thing I don't take offense easily."

Used to their bantering, Nathalyia continued on her final inspection of the restaurant after all the customers had left, just as Martin had taught her. He'd started the restaurant with a bank loan, his Creole grandmother's secret spice recipes, and faith. He'd succeeded, as he'd known he would.

With no close family, he'd entrusted Fontaine to her. She wished there could have been a child, but that had been impossible. Sometimes, she felt as if she had let down the first person who had loved her unconditionally.

Almost immediately, she could hear him say, "You saved me in more ways than you will ever imagine. You gave me peace. That's all a man can ever hope for."

Stopping at the big picture window, Nathalyia gazed out at the Atlantic Ocean. Loneliness settled around her. The staff and people on the beach would go home with or to someone; she'd go home to an elegantly decorated but completely empty house.

Her arms wrapped around her stomach. Martin, ever mindful of her, ever loving, had secretly purchased the three-story house for her. She hadn't known of its existence until his will was read. He hadn't wanted her to be saddened by remaining in the house they'd shared. He had been a wonderful man. The years had dulled the ache of his leaving, but also made her loneliness more acute.

Chastising herself, she turned away. She shouldn't want more. She was financially secure, had a job she loved, and good friends. She'd come a long way from the cramped two-bedroom apartment she grew up in with her greedy, grasping mother and her two older sisters. Never in her wildest dreams had she ever allowed herself to imagine she'd have so much. She should be satisfied.

Suddenly she thought of the mystery man who had asked her out. His voice had been seductive and cloaked in velvet. Since she didn't recall ever seeing him before, she probably wouldn't see him again. Why wasn't she relieved?

"She's lonely," Clarice said softly.

"She's just having her quiet time like she always does, just like her and Martin used to do after closing," Jake told her without stopping restocking the bar.

Clarice, standing beside him, wanted to punch him. However, considering Jake's massive shoulders and muscled body, she'd probably hurt herself more than him. "How can you say that? Just look at her."

Jake threw a quick glance at Nathalyia, then at Clarice, before continuing. "We need to finish this."

"Is work all you ever think about?" she asked, staring at his shiny bald head, slick as the polished brass on the footrail of the bar.

She'd always thought men with shaved heads were wired or trying to hide the fact that they were going bald. Jake had changed her mind. He was solid—in more than body mass. He was comfortable with who he was. His shaved head was just an extension of his days in the army. So was the three-inch scar on his left cheek.

"It's better than interfering in other people's business," he finally said.

Strange words for a bartender, but not for Jake. He never gave advice, just listened to the customers—which, more often than not, was what the other person needed. "It's not interfering, it's concern," Clarice clarified. "Martin has been gone over three years. Perhaps it's time for her to think about dating."

"Stay out of it, Clarice," Jake told her, stopping to stare at her.

Since Jake often used that firm tone with her, his blue eyes piercing her, she let it glide right off. "The guy from tonight maybe."

"It takes longer for some women," he said.

Her eyebrow shot up. "You wouldn't be aiming that remark at me, would you?"

"If I have something to say to you, Clarice, I'll say it," he told her, holding her gaze.

"See that you do," she said, letting go of the mild hurt that he thought less of her because, until lately, she had been one of those women who wasn't happy unless she had a man in her bed.

It wasn't her fault—exactly—that the men she fell for were the scum of the earth. If a man had a sob story and was reasonably good-looking, they somehow found their way into her life, where she tried to fix them, help them.

It always ended with her getting the shaft. One of those occasions had actually turned out for the best because she'd ended up working at Fontaine.

Since she'd taken a few psychology courses in college while getting her degree in elementary education, she knew a shrink would say she was searching for acceptance because of her weight and growing up without a father. She'd tell the shrink to take a flying leap.

"Ernie, tell Mrs. Fontaine it's time to close," Jake told his fellow bartender.

"Sure thing, Jake," the young man said. He put down the polishing cloth and came out from behind the bar.

"You usually give her all the time she needs," Clarice pointed out, her eyes narrowed.

"She has to get up early tomorrow for the street fair," he told her, going back to counting the liquor.

"I'd forgotten about that." Clarice sighed. "I'm supposed to help her."

Jake frowned at her. "See that's all you do."

Clarice grinned. "I'm not making any promises."

"Jake says it's time to close, Mrs. Fontaine."

Nathalyia turned at the sound of Ernie's voice. He'd been with them six months and was working out well. She prided herself on the low turnover at Fontaine. Happy employees often translated into happy customers. "Thank you."

After one last look out the window, she started back to the bar. Sending the new hire for her had been Jake's subtle way of reminding her of who she was, of her responsibility—as if she'd ever forget. He was too sharp to have missed her looking at that man. Jake didn't have to worry.

She might be lonely, but she wasn't stupid. She didn't have time for a man.

Saturday morning, Rafael entered his precinct in a good mood. He'd learned during his time as a police officer not to waste a single moment bemoaning life. Bad things happened, so he tried to live each moment to the fullest.

Rafael had almost lost his brother Patrick two years ago when he'd been shot. It was one of the scariest, most helpless moments he'd ever experienced in his life . . . until his older brother Alec entered a hostage situation to save his now fiancée, Celeste de la Vega, and four other hostages. Rafael knew from experience just how precious life is and let few things affect his happiness.

That was one reason he planned to pursue Nathalyia and find her weakness. He didn't doubt he'd find it. She had been smart to turn him down. His line certainly hadn't been one of his best openings. As the beautiful young owner of Fontaine, men had to be in her face all the time. He just had to come up with a way to show her he wasn't interested in her money.

Just in her.

He'd done a bit of checking—nothing invasive—and learned she owned a home in the exclusive gated community of Navarone Estates and the restaurant outright. Nathalyia Fontaine was a very wealthy woman, though that wasn't intimidating to him. Although he had nowhere near her fortune, he wasn't hurting. If a woman cared only about money, he wouldn't waste his time on her. His gut instinct told him Nathalyia wasn't like that.

"Hey, Dunlap. Hate that I missed it last night," Patrolman Owens called, swinging his hands with a pretend bat. "Ouch."

"She cut him off at the knees," Diaz commented happily.

"Never thought I'd see the day." Gibbs put his arm around Rafael's shoulder and hung his head. "I initiated the bet, but I'm not sure I'll ever recover."

Rafael smiled. The ribbing didn't bother him. It was simply his turn. "Glad I could provide everyone with some entertainment."

Diaz stared at him, then shook his head of curly black hair. "Does nothing ever get to you?"

"Not if I can help it."

"Hold that thought," the SORT commander, Captain Louis Coats, said. "Our unit has to fill in for the unit working the traffic tie-up on 117."

Rafael's eyebrows lifted. "Doing what?"

Captain Coats handed Rafael a colorful flyer with balloons running along the sides. His team members crowded around him. He quickly read the flyer. A slow grin spread across his face. "I live to serve."

Gibbs snatched the flyer out of Rafael's hand, then narrowed his eyes. "You can't be thinking of trying again."

"What?" Officer Cannon, the gas expert who had been home with her husband the night before, grabbed the flyer.

"Well, I'll be," Henderson said. "You've never lacked self-confidence, so I guess we shouldn't be surprised."

"Am I missing something here?" Captain Coats asked.

"Fontaine restaurant is the main sponsor of the charity event today," Diaz explained with a dimpled grin. "Dunlap struck out with the owner last night."

"Dunlap, I don't have to remind you that when you're wearing the uniform, it's police business only, do I?" Commander Coats went strictly by the book.

"No, sir." Rafael turned to Stubbs, the driver of the tank, the name they'd given the old bread truck that had been converted to transport the team. "We don't want to keep the citizens waiting. Let's roll."

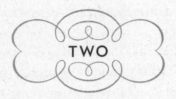

TWO

*Nathalyia had been up since six A.M. to ensure the day went flaw-*lessly. She wanted to be there to meet the crew to set up Fontaine's booth, then have time to check on all the other vendors who had promised to participate in the street fair.

The street fair was the main fund-raising event for Helping Hands, a charitable organization that gave financial assistance to families with children who had life-threatening illnesses. Martin had founded the nonprofit ten years before they met, after a staff member's child was diagnosed with sickle-cell anemia.

The day was turning into one of those perfect sun-kissed days Myrtle Beach was famous for. The early morning breeze had quickly given way to higher temperatures. People who had worn light jackets and sweaters had them tied around their waists. Seeing the large crowd enjoying themselves as they strolled the aisles sampling the various food items, Nathalyia didn't feel the least bit tired after only a few hours of sleep. There was a ten percent increase in vendors over last year. Attendance was up as well. She felt exhilarated.

This was one task Martin hadn't had to ask her to do. She'd taken over the annual fund-raiser for Helping Hands two years before she lost him. Instead of a banquet, she'd suggested a street fair where the children could come and enjoy themselves with clowns, puppet shows, and a petting zoo.

For the parents and other adults, there was a wide range of free and for-purchase food items, with most or all of the money going to Helping Hands.

"If the brisk sales keep up, we're going to sell out of Fontaine's hot sauce again this year," Clarice said, arranging more of the slim bottles on the nine-foot-long wooden counter in front of their booth.

"Good." Nathalyia checked the progress of the shrimp gumbo being tended to by two of her staff. Part of the draw to get people over was to pass out free food. Martin was fond of saying that if he could get them to taste his food, they'd come back for more. "The hot sauce might be a dollar more than at the restaurant, but people feel good about donating that extra dollar to charity."

"And there's the extra bonus of being able to purchase the five-dollar raffle ticket for four dollars," Clarice said, eyeing the growing number of tickets in a hamper behind them. "Everyone likes a bargain."

"Yes, that's what I'm counting on," Nathalyia said, moving to help fill up the small plastic containers with gumbo and hand out certificates for one dollar off any food purchase at Fontaine.

"Hi, Clarice."

"Hi, Officer Diaz." Clarice greeted the policeman with a warm smile and handed him a gumbo sample. "Is your friend from last night here?"

Ronald scooped up a shrimp, then grinned, showing even white teeth. "Yeah, he's in my unit. For all the good it will do him."

Clarice cut a meaningful glance at Nathalyia, who was selling tickets for the raffle. "So he's the kind to give up easily?"

Ronald's speculative gaze went to Nathalyia and frowned. "I've known him since we were in the academy together. He can be dogged when he wants something. But this time I don't think he has a choice."

"No guts, no glory, I always say," Clarice said with a careless shrug. "Fontaine is having a raffle drawing at five. The tickets are five dollars each. The prize is dinner for two and an exclusive tour of the restaurant with the owner. Maybe he'd like to purchase a few? Excuse me, Officer, customers are waiting."

Officer Diaz returned from his break to find the line in front of Rafael's table even longer than when he'd left. Besides giving out information about the department and personal and home safety tips, they handed out officer ID cards with stats and a photo. As usual, Rafael handed out more cards than all of the other team members put together.

The last hostage situation a few weeks ago with Rafael as the main negotiator had been picked up by the local media and included his picture and footage of him and his family leaving the scene. Since then he had become even more popular and in demand.

None of the members of SORT minded. They admired his ability to keep the smile he now wore while women asked silly or personal questions and passed him phone numbers that he'd never call.

Officer Diaz waited until the commander placed an orange cone behind the last woman in Rafael's line. He should wait, but what the heck. He stepped beside Rafael. "Guess who I just saw looking hot as ever."

Rafael's head snapped around. His usual smiling eyes were hard. "You're talking about a lady."

Ronald frowned at Rafael's unexpected reaction. The only times he'd seen that unbending expression on Rafael's face were when they were in tense situations. Never where a woman was concerned.

"Excuse me," the woman waiting said, her eyes shooting daggers at Ronald. "Officer Dunlap and I were talking."

"Sorry." Rafael turned to her. "As I was saying, we don't make personal visits, but this pamphlet will give you information on personal and home safety tips."

The tall, slender woman dressed in a halter top and shorts took the pamphlet, handing Rafael a piece of folded paper. "Hands-on has always worked better for me."

"I'll keep that in mind. Goodbye," Rafael said, wearing the same smile he'd worn patiently all day.

The redhead reluctantly moved away and another young woman eagerly took her place. "I saw you on television. Could you please sign your card for me?" Her pretty smile widened. "The name is Patience Johnson."

"I'd be delighted."

Ronald couldn't resist as Rafael grabbed a pen and bent to sign his name. "There's a drawing at the Fontaine booth in twenty minutes." He waited until Rafael looked up. "Five-dollar tickets. Guess what the prize is?"

Rafael's black eyes narrowed. "Since you can't wait to tell me, it could only be one thing." He straightened and held out the card to the woman, unobtrusively looking at his watch. "Thank you."

She sighed, pressed the card to her chest. "My book club members won't believe this. Thank you."

"It's dinner for two with the owner," Ronald said as soon as the woman moved away. "I would have purchased you a ticket, but I didn't want to see you lose and be reminded of striking out."

"I'll bet." Rafael greeted the next two women and quickly moved each along until he was finished. He turned to the commander standing nearby. "Since I've been good and didn't take a break, I'd like permission to do something for me."

"Just remember you're in uniform," Commander Coats told him.

"I'll go with him to remind him," Diaz offered.

"Me, too," Gibbs added.

"If I go, will it make it three?" Cannon asked. "I missed it last night."

The commander held up his hand before the next person could ask. "Why don't we pack things in, and then we can all go?" The team quickly complied.

"Clarice, I think you've mixed them up enough," Nathalyia said, standing by the half-full drum to draw the winning ticket.

Clarice continued to turn the handle. "I want to give everyone a chance."

Nathalyia frowned at Clarice. She'd been turning the thing for the past five minutes, all the time straining her neck in an attempt to look over the crowd gathered in front of their booth.

"It's ten past five," a man in the front of the small crowd yelled, waving his tickets.

"You're right." Nathalyia placed her hand over Clarice's, effectively stopping her, then spoke to those gathered. "I want to thank each of you for purchasing a ticket for a chance to win dinner for two at Fontaine's and a tour of the restaurant. Thanks to projected sales for today, as well as corporate and private donations, I think we're going to greatly surpass the funds raised last year, which were close to a quarter of a million dollars."

She paused as people applauded. "Thanks to you, families with a critically ill child will receive much-needed financial assistance." Nathalyia reached for the latch.

"Wait!"

She turned to see the man who had tried to pick her up the night before at the restaurant pushing his way through the crowd. She was surprised to see him wearing a police uniform and annoyed when her pulse sped up. With him were several other men in uniform. She recognized a couple as Fontaine regulars. "Is there a problem?"

Rafael made his way to the front. Nathalyia was even more beautiful in daylight. She looked sinfully sexy in the hot pink top that lovingly cupped her full breasts. "I wanted to purchase tickets for the raffle."

"The raffle is closed," the slender man in front who had spoken earlier told him, his voice filled with annoyance. He was wearing sandals with socks, a Hawaiian shirt, and a straw hat. Clean-shaven, he appeared to be in his late sixties.

Rafael kept his gaze on Nathalyia. "Since the aim is to raise money, it would make sense to sell more tickets."

"It certainly would," Clarice said, stepping forward and reaching for the roll of tickets. "How many?"

"But it would also decrease the chances of winning," the irritated man pointed out. "I bought twenty dollars' worth of tickets. The sign said the drawing would be at five. Policeman or not, fair is fair."

"You're right, of course," Nathalyia said, turning to the drum, her fingers fumbling with the latch.

"Let me get that for you." Rafael opened the latch, then stepped back.

It hadn't been fast enough. She felt the heat of his muscular body, the pull. Commanding her fingers not to tremble, Nathalyia reached inside and dug deep to give herself time to catch her breath. He was without a doubt the most gorgeous man she'd ever seen, with sculptured cheekbones and incredible long black lashes over beautiful black eyes. His mouth was made for sin. He was definitely off-limits. She swallowed hard.

The easygoing smile he'd sent her tempted her to smile back. He enticed her to throw caution to the wind, to brush her lips across his. No man had ever made her feel this hot, edgy way. She didn't like it one bit.

Confident that she was in control once again, she pulled the ticket. "The winning number is one-nine-five-five-five-five-one-two."

A high-pitched scream went up in the back of the crowd. "That's me! That's me!" An elderly woman in slacks, a blouse, and a floppy straw hat pushed her way to the front.

Rafael instantly turned to the woman. "Excuse me. How much for the winning ticket?"

"What?" she asked, blinking up at him from behind silver-rimmed eye-glasses.

"I'd like to buy your ticket," he explained, pulling out his black leather wallet.

"There's nothing about selling the ticket," Nathalyia said, a bit frantic. He made her nervous. Her stomach fluttered, and that was reason enough to avoid him.

Rafael grinned. "The ticket is the property of Mrs.—"

"Evans," she supplied, straightening her hat.

"Evans, and if she chooses to sell it, it is her right." Rafael pulled out two twenties.

Nathalyia's lips pressed together in annoyance. "But I'm sure she'd rather dine at Fontaine. She and a guest can order anything on the menu."

Rafael plucked more money from his wallet. "Or she can have a hundred dollars."

"Appetizers and dessert are included," Nathalyia said, determined to win.

"One fifty," Rafael amended.

"A bottle of wine to complement her dinner selection," Nathalyia added spontaneously.

Rafael looked in his wallet, then at Nathalyia. She sensed victory until his fellow officers stepped forward, drawing out their wallets and handing him money. "Two hundred fifty."

Mrs. Evans looked at Rafael, then apologetically at Nathalyia. "Sorry. Wine gives me a headache. With the senior discount I get at your restaurant, I could eat several times and have my tea and a dessert." She handed over the ticket. "But if I was a few years younger, I'd hold out and ask you to take me since it's dinner for two."

Rafael smiled down at the older woman, enjoying the twinkle in her hazel eyes. "It would have been my pleasure."

She pressed her hand to her chest, then looked at Nathalyia. "You're a lucky woman."

Nathalyia said nothing.

"Thank you," Rafael said. He gave Mrs. Evans the money and waited as she took out a wallet from her fanny pack and carefully placed the $250 inside. "Do you want an officer to walk you to your car?"

"Do you think that's necessary?" she asked, glancing around nervously as two other older women approached. "These are my friends."

One of the women waved a stout walking stick. "Just let some thug try to hassle us. I retired from teaching high school a few years back. They don't want to mess with me."

Rafael smiled. "It pays to be proactive. An officer can be there for backup."

Stubbs stepped forward. "I'm the driver for the unit. Officer Stubbs. Ladies, whenever you're ready."

Mrs. Evans looked at Rafael, then at Nathalyia. "Be glad I'm not younger." Then she turned to Officer Stubbs. "Let's go, young man."

Rafael stepped forward and presented the winning ticket to Nathalyia. "Would tomorrow be too soon?"

Nathalyia could barely keep from gritting her teeth. He had her trapped, and from the smile on his incredibly handsome face, he knew it. It had been thoughtful of him to think of the woman's protection, but Nathalyia wanted nothing to do with him. He made her nervous, restless. Despite her best efforts he got to her, and he knew it.

"We have large crowds and groups on Sundays after church," she finally answered him. "It will have to be early Monday—if you're free."

He quickly glanced at an older man in a police uniform. "Sir, can I come in two hours late on Monday?"

"Yes," the man answered without hesitation, a small smile on his angular face. The jovial expressions of the other police officers surrounding him widened.

Grinning, he turned back to her. "How does eleven sound?"

She nodded abruptly. She might as well get it over with. "I'll see you at eleven."

"In case you've forgotten, my name is Rafael Dunlap."

She remembered too much about him. "Nathalyia Fontaine."

"Until Monday at eleven, Nathalyia." Bowing his head, he turned and left. The other policemen followed, slapping him on the back with congratulations.

Nathalyia swallowed, swallowed again. The way he said her name sounded like a caress, the erotic sound vibrated though her body. Her skin tingled. She didn't have time for all these crazy feelings, or for a man as persistent and compelling as Rafael. It appeared as if she didn't have a choice.

. . .

Rafael was fifteen minutes early Monday for lunch at Fontaine, and he hadn't come empty-handed. He realized Nathalyia would probably be the most difficult challenge in his lifetime. Her defenses were already up. He had to go slow and show her he was interested in her and that he was worth getting to know.

"A beautiful bouquet," said the hostess. "Table for two?"

"Yes, I have an eleven o'clock appointment with Mrs. Fontaine."

"Oh, she's expecting you." The young woman smiled. "Please follow me."

"Thank you." Rafael followed her to a table in the middle of the restaurant. On the paneled walls were fly rods and reels, a rustic wooden steering wheel, and an anchor. In an arch near the glass-enclosed kitchen was a twelve-foot canoe. Marble lined the aisles. There was a casual elegance about the restaurant.

The young woman stopped at a table in the middle of the restaurant, pulled out a leather and wood side chair at a linen-draped table, and handed him a menu. The place was already beginning to fill up. People surrounded the table on all sides. Nathalyia clearly didn't want them to have a quiet conversation.

When he didn't immediately take his seat, the young woman glanced from the flowers back to him. Her smile became a bit strained. "Enjoy your lunch."

"Thanks, I plan to." Placing the bouquet of orchids on the white tablecloth, Rafael took his seat, wondering how long she planned to let him wait or if she'd even show.

He glanced around to see the woman who had been with her yesterday and who had also been their waitress on Friday night, coming toward him. He came to his feet when she stopped at his table.

Smiling, she extended her hand. "Clarice Howard. I was with Nathalyia on Saturday."

"Hello, I remember. You were also our waitress Friday night," he said. "Are you taking Nathalyia's place?"

"I guess it's no secret that she wasn't too happy with how things turned out with the drawing, but she takes her responsibilities for Fontaine seriously." Clarice folded her arms. "She'll be here."

Relief swept through him. He wasn't sure what his next plan would have been had Nathalyia sent a replacement. Loud laughter erupted. He looked around to see a large group of men and women. All of them had cocktails.

Clarice frowned and unfolded her arms. "This table is not very conducive to conversation, is it?"

"Exactly what she planned," Rafael said. There was no sense in beating around the bush.

Clarice grinned. "We'll just have to unplan." She reached for the menu. "I think you'll enjoy the new location better. Follow me."

Picking up the vase of orchids, Rafael followed Clarice to a far corner of the room with a wall of glass looking out to the ocean. With the various flowering green plants inside and out, it was like being in the tropics. Although there were four tables in the area, all were empty.

"This is Nathalyia's a favorite spot, and mine, too." Clarice placed the menu on the table and pulled out a chair facing away from the ocean.

Rafael placed the bouquet on the table. "Thank you, but aren't you concerned she might not like you changing her plans?"

"Nope. She might be annoyed with me for a bit, but when she thinks about it, she'll realize that regardless of how you obtained the ticket, or what transpired before, the reputation of Fontaine is at stake," Clarice pointed out.

"That's the second time you've mentioned her in connection with the restaurant."

Clarice nodded. "Glad you're listening. The restaurant is the most important thing to her in the world. Its continued success is paramount to her. Nothing else comes first."

Rafael understood responsibility, and the subtle warning. He had his work cut out for him. "From what I've seen, she's doing a fantastic job."

"She's good at what she does, but . . ."

"But what?" Rafael urged.

"Nothing. Can I get you a drink?"

Sensing he wasn't going to get any more information, he said, "Iced tea."

"The same drink you had the other night." Her gaze ran over his tan dress slacks and white shirt. "I don't think I've ever met a policeman in here who always orders a nonalcoholic drink."

Since she had helped him, he explained. "I'm a hostage negotiator. I never know when I might be called, so I seldom drink."

She nodded. "Seems I was right about you."

"What do . . . ?" He broke off as she moved away. She'd heard him, but apparently wasn't going to explain that comment. He took his seat.

When they returned to the station Saturday after the street fair, Diaz had told Rafael that Clarice had asked about him and told Diaz about the raffle. Now she'd changed their table. It appeared he had an ally. He was going to need all the help he could get.

Rafael saw Nathalyia the moment she stepped out of a door near the kitchen. His breath caught. His body tightened in response. No woman, and there had been quite a few, had ever affected him this way. She was grace and beauty in motion. He wanted her and he planned to have her. She paused as if fortifying herself, then continued.

She stopped by the bar, spoke to the same bald-headed bartender she'd talked with Friday night, then turned to the table where he'd first been seated. She stopped, her head lifting, searching for him.

Their gazes met, clung. His heart thumped. Her slim hand went to the triple strand of large pearls at her throat briefly, then she continued toward him. He hadn't pegged her as the nervous type.

There was only one explanation. She felt the attraction between them just as he did, though she obviously wasn't pleased and planned to fight her feelings. He wasn't about to let that happen.

He stood when she was a few feet away and reached for the back of the chair next to him. She hesitated. Her gaze went to the chair across from him.

"Good morning, Nathalyia," he greeted her to put her at ease. This morning she wore a fitted short-sleeve black dress with a wide belt low on her hips. Her lustrous black hair was in a sleek braid fastened with a black bow at the base of her slim neck. His fingers itched to take her hair down and caress her scalp with his fingertips while he leisurely kissed her glorious mouth.

"Good morning, Officer Dunlap," she returned, her voice formal.

"Rafael, please." He picked up the orchids. "These are for you."

She looked startled, then pleased as she took the flowers. "For me?"

He was surprised by her reaction. As beautiful as she was, she must have received dozens of flowers in her life. "Yes. I know Saturday was exhausting and certainly wasn't easy, yet you did it to help families and their children."

"It was my late husband's idea to help families, and my pleasure to carry on his work," she said, her finger gliding over the tip of one thick white petal before her gaze returned to him. "Helping needy families has its own reward."

"I agree." He stepped behind the chair, giving her another hint.

Placing the flowers on the table, she sat.

"You have quite an extensive menu here." He took his seat and picked up the menu. "I can see why the restaurant is so popular."

"Thank you." Her shoulders relaxed the tiniest bit. "My late husband loved to experiment with new dishes and spices. If it didn't work, he'd take it off the menu." She smiled. "I finally convinced him to stop putting items on the permanent menu until he was sure they would stay."

"Are you a good cook?" Rafael asked. He wondered if she was aware of how many times she'd mentioned her late husband.

"I like to think so."

"Do you have any dishes on the menu?" he asked.

"Two, actually." A tentative smile touched lips painted raspberry. "The bread pudding with bourbon sauce and the caramel pecan cheesecake have been on the menu for some time now."

"Here's your tea, Officer Dunlap," Clarice said. "Nathalyia, your bottled water and strawberry lemonade. I can take your order if you're ready."

Nathalyia glanced up at Clarice, then toward the bar.

Clarice smiled. "I have it covered. You know Jake wouldn't let me neglect my tables even if I wanted to, which I never would."

"Sorry," Nathalyia said, picking up the glass of strawberry lemonade. "Thank you for this, and for taking the order for Officer Dun—"

"Rafael."

"Rafael," she said slowly, as if testing the words. "Are you ready to order?"

"If you don't mind, I'd like to go with your suggestions." He folded his arms and leaned across the table. "I don't have any food allergies, and I love food."

"All right, but I need to know your preference."

Her, hot and willing in his bed. "I'm listening."

As if she'd read his mind, she twisted in her seat. "We have cold, hot, and oyster appetizers," she told him. "Salad? Gumbo? Would you like your main dish fried, from the grill, or one of our Cajun specialties? We also have steak, chicken, and fish. The mahimahi is the chef's special today. Which would you prefer?"

You, any way and every day, he thought. One thing was for certain, he wasn't about to say oysters. "Hot appetizer, salad, gumbo, fried seafood, and for dessert we can share the bread pudding and caramel pecan cheesecake."

"I suggest the crab cakes, a small Fontaine's Greek salad, a cup of shrimp gumbo, followed by the seafood platter with dirty rice and broccoli."

"I'll turn your order in right away." Clarice moved away.

"Is the street fair the only event you have as a fund-raiser for Helping Hands?" he asked, truly interested. He knew a few families who had children with life-threatening illnesses and had seen how emotionally and financially difficult it had been for them.

"Yes." Her hand touched an orchid petal. "I was going over the final tallies just before you arrived." She smiled, warm and open. "We're up over twenty-five percent from last year."

"Here are your salads and hot bread with butter." A young server set the food on the table and pulled a pepper mill from beneath his arm. "Pepper, sir?"

"No, thank you," Rafael said. The server nodded and picked up the deck tray and left, easily weaving though the tables. "I'll say grace."

Once again, Nathalyia looked startled. "Of course."

Rafael bowed his head and blessed their food. Looking up, he reached for his cloth napkin. "I didn't mean to embarrass you."

"You didn't." She placed her napkin in her lap. "I was just surprised."

He picked up his fork and grinned across the table at her. "You thought I was a heathen?"

His remark drew a smile from her. "Not at all." She cut wedges of bread for both of them. "Have you been on the police force long?"

He accepted the bread and spread butter on it. "Eight years. The last five with S.O.R.T., an acronym for the Special Operations Response Team."

She paused from eating her salad. "What do you do?"

"Negotiate."

She stared wide-eyed across the table at him. "You're a negotiator?"

He shrugged. "I like to think I do a better job than I did with you Friday night."

She glanced away. "It wouldn't have made any difference. I'm too busy to think about dating."

A waiter arrived to take away his empty salad plate and placed a cup of shrimp gumbo in front of him. "Anything else, sir?"

"No, thanks." Rafael picked up his spoon and looked back at Nathalyia. "The service here is fantastic. I have a feeling it isn't just because you're sitting here."

Pleasure spread across her face. "Thank you. The cornerstone of Fontaine is exemplary service and extraordinary food."

Rafael ate another bite of gumbo. "I can attest to both. Back to dating, you don't have time to go for a walk, a boat ride, a movie?"

"No." She motioned that she was finished with her salad. More than half remained. The waiter removed her dish and served her gumbo.

He'd met few women who were so dedicated to their jobs. "What does your family think about you running the restaurant?"

The hand reaching for the bottled water paused. "I'm an only child. My parents died when I was young."

She was lying, and not very good at it. What was she hiding?

"How about your family?" she asked to end the silence as she bent her head to eat her gumbo.

"I have four brothers, all policemen," he told her. "We're extremely close. The oldest, Sam, lives here. The next two are in Charleston where they met their wives." His lips quirked. "Alec, my older brother, met his fiancée there as well. They're having a Christmas wedding."

Interest shone in her beautiful eyes. "They all met their wives in Charleston? Were they on vacation?"

"Patrick, next to the oldest, moved there and purchased our niece Brooke's condo when she married. Incidentally, she met her husband there as well." He finished his gumbo. "I guess she started the wedding craze. Simon, the next brother, went there to help the police department with their high burglary rate. He met his future wife when her home was robbed."

"And Alec?" she questioned.

Rafael waited as the waiter placed the huge platter of seafood in front of him. There were fried shrimp, catfish filets, dirty rice, and broccoli. He noticed she had a single filet of grilled catfish with a floret of broccoli. "Are you on a diet?"

"I'm not very hungry," she said, picking up her fork. "I told the kitchen what I wanted earlier. How did Alec meet his fiancée?"

She'd only eaten a few bites of the gumbo. She wasn't frail. Her skin looked healthy.

"You're staring."

"Trying to figure out if I should slide some of this onto your plate," he admitted.

"I told you I'm not hungry." She took a dainty bite of fish. "About your brother?"

Her fork shook the tiniest bit. She was nervous. He couldn't imagine a successful businesswoman being nervous—unless she was dealing with something she had never faced before.

"Alec met Celeste while he was building a gazebo for Simon and his wife at their house while they were on their honeymoon. Celeste was redecorating the master suite at the time."

"Your family sounds wonderful. How did you all become policemen?"

Since she was really eating, he didn't mind answering her questions. He didn't usually talk about his family to his dates. It seemed too personal.

"Our daddy was a policeman. He was a great guy and a wonderful father. We lost him ten years ago. Our mother followed six months later." He looked out at the distant ocean. "She missed him so much. I remember her saying that we had each other so she wouldn't worry about us."

He felt a warm hand on his and jerked around, but it was already gone. Her unexpected gesture was comforting. He started to tell her thank you, but she'd looked down to her plate again. She might have regretted reaching out to him.

He'd always miss his parents, but they had a special love and he tried to understood what his mother meant. They were buried the way they wanted: with his mother's coffin on top of his father's, as if in the embrace they had shared so often. "What about your parents?"

"Both gone. An automobile accident." Lifting her head, she reached for her water, raising it to her lips and effectively obscuring her face.

He'd meant the emotional ties. She'd given him another lie. What was she hiding? If he really wanted to, he could find the answer. Since they had down time when their unit wasn't needed, all of the officers on his team had desk duty.

Rafael conducted background checks on applicants to the

police department. He had access to computer banks all over the country. He could have a complete file on her in less than twenty-four hours.

"You're a very fortunate man, Offi— Rafael," she amended.

He heard the wistfulness in her voice. Instinctively he knew her childhood hadn't been happy. "I saw a carnival setting up their stands on the way over here. How about we go when you can get away?"

A strange expression crossed her face. "I'm already going— with the families of the children of Helping Hands. I was able to contact the owner and get him to have a private night for Helping Hands. The children will have special badges that will allow them to go to the head of the line for rides and have any food free—if they have their doctor's permission."

"Those small carnivals don't make that much," Rafael mused. "He's donating all that food?"

"Not exactly, but it's taken care of." She leaned back in her chair. "Last year I was able to take them to the circus."

It clicked. Nathalyia was footing the bill. "You're one special woman."

She blinked. "I—"

"Do you need a volunteer?" he asked.

"If you weren't trying to date me, would you have asked?"

A fair and smart question. "I honestly don't know. Simon has a teenage basketball team and I usually donate money. I do know that I'd like to help." The words were barely out of his mouth before his cell phone played "Bad Boys," the theme song of the television show *Cops*.

"Excuse me." He pulled out his cell, already knowing what the call would entail. "Dunlap." Rafael listened. "ETA fifteen minutes." He disconnected the phone, rising to his feet. "Please excuse me. I have to go."

She came to her feet as well. He thought he saw a flash of regret in her open face. "I understand."

He briefly touched her bare arm. Her skin felt like warm silk. "Lunch was wonderful. Thank you." He strode from the restaurant.

Nathalyia stared after him, then turned and began clearing the table. Expertly, she stacked their plates, glasses, and flatware.

Frowning, Clarice rushed over. "Did he say something off-color? Why did he rush out of here?" Clarice asked, hands on her hips.

"He got a phone call. He said he had to leave."

"Oh, my God!" Clarice palmed her mouth.

"What?" Nathalyia swung around.

"He didn't tell you what he does?"

"Yes, he—" Nathalyia's eyes rounded. Her hands shook, causing the plates and glasses to rattle. "I thought the call might have been one of his brothers."

Clarice took everything from Nathalyia's unsteady hands. "Maybe it was, but I don't think anything but police business would have gotten him away from you."

Nathalyia bit her lower lip. "We were just talking. You don't think he's in danger, do you? He didn't look concerned."

"Rafael struck me as the kind of man who can take care of himself. Don't worry." Clarice put the service pieces on the table and picked up the bouquet. "You take your flowers and go to your office. He'll be back later, and you can finish your meal, have dessert, and show him around the restaurant."

Nathalyia clutched the orchids closer and went to her office, praying each step of the way.

THREE

Rafael turned into the drive of the gated community and was waved on by a policeman standing near a patrol car halfway blocking the entrance. With onlookers and residents trying to get into the estate, the patrolman had his hands full, but no one was getting though until everything was under control.

There was no telling how long that would be. Domestic situations were unpredictable. James Powell had taken his wife hostage and was threatening to kill her. Rafael would do everything in his power to prevent that from happening.

Rafael knew that an officer had already gone door-to-door to ask residents to remain inside until the standoff was over. A few residents would comply, but there were many who would come outside to try to see what was going on. Just like the man across the street standing behind a bright yellow Mini Cooper.

Rafael pulled up behind a patrol car, shut off the motor, and went to the trunk of his car for his bulletproof vest. No shots had been fired, but the angry husband was reported to have a handgun.

Fastening the vest as he went, he quickly approached the command center. The challenge of a negotiator was to get the person to stop and think. It didn't always happen. "Any change?"

"It's been quiet," Lieutenant Hines answered. He was the shift supervisor. Rafael's unit was on its way. The goal was always maximum control with minimum force.

The two-story stone-and-brick house resembled a small castle with a turret. The lawn was green, the shrubbery neatly trimmed, the borders edged with colorful flowers. The house looked deceptively peaceful.

Hines shook his head. "You'd think people would learn." He snorted. "It's the same old stupid story with a few variations. Powell came home early from a business trip to find his wife in bed with his younger brother, Broderick, who's out of work and staying with them. The brother ran when the husband lunged for the wife."

"That's says a lot about Powell's brother," Rafael said as he studied the windows of the house. They were all covered with closed wooden blinds except the four narrow ones in the turret.

"Apparently, the husband has a license for the gun. He either had it on him or went to get it when he saw what was going on," the supervisor said. He glanced at the back of a police car several lengths behind them. The top of a man's dark head could be seen.

"The mailman was driving by when Broderick—that's the brother—ran naked out of the house. He called nine-one-one. That was thirty minutes ago. A patrolman was here in five minutes. When he went to the door, he was told, and I quote, 'Back off or I'll kill the cheating bitch.' We called your commander."

"Are we patched in?"

Hines handed Rafael the cell phone. "Yes, but Powell won't answer."

Rafael's gaze went to the car with the brother inside. "The husband's hurt. Angry. I wouldn't answer the phone either."

"What next?" the supervisor asked.

"Let me talk to the brother." Rafael went to the car and opened the door. A slim black man lifted his close-shaven head. He had a blanket wrapped around his shoulders. A knee poked out.

"It wasn't my fault," he said, licking his lips. "She came on to me."

Rafael kept his expression carefully blank. He didn't have to think about the impossible happening and any of his brothers' wives making a pass at him. He'd walk. "Mr. Powell, it's my business to get your brother and sister-in-law out safely, not to point blame. I just need to know something about him, what kind of man he is."

Down went the man's head. "He's a hard worker. Always has been." His head came up. "Vanessa always talks about how much time he spends at the office or on the road."

"Is Vanessa his wife?"

"Yeah."

Rafael would bet anything Vanessa had no problems spending the money those long hours brought in. "Any children?"

"James Jr. J.R., we call him. He's from James's first marriage. Anita died in childbirth."

"How old and where is he?"

"Seven. He's at a special overnight camp for asthmatics. Maybe it will get him to lose some weight. He's too fat, just like James."

The man didn't have one ounce of backbone or morality. "What's your brother's temperament?"

The man shrugged. "He's cool—until now." He shook his head. "I've never seen him like that. Yelling and waving that gun, crying." He hunched into the blanket. "I thought he was going to kill me. I'm his brother."

A brother who cheated with his wife. "So you ran."

"I didn't know what else to do. James is good with that gun. It's her fault," he shouted, then looked away. "He loves her. Gives her anything she wants. He'll calm down."

"And if he doesn't? If he's too hurt to think clearly?" Rafael asked, getting a pretty good picture of the selfish man sitting in front of him.

The man gulped, shook his head. "Lord, I never thought. Never. What's gonna happen when Mama finds out?"

Rafael pulled out his cell. The man's eyes bugged. "If I called her, what would she say?"

"You wouldn't do that."

"I'm trying to save two people's lives. You had a hand in this," Rafael told him.

"You haven't seen her. She's built, ten years younger than James is, and likes showing off her body in those skimpy clothes, teasing me when he's not around. I couldn't help myself."

Disgust rolled through Rafael. "What would your mother say?"

"What she always says," he spat. "She's always on James's side. James made something out of his life. James is successful. James makes her proud. It's always about James. If I could get a break, I'd be the man, too."

"A real man doesn't bed his brother's wife." Rafael closed the door, and went back to the car to call the house again. After twenty rings, he hung up, just as his team pulled up behind the cruiser. The members piled out as the field supervisor gave his commander an update.

Rafael didn't want to use the bullhorn. The neighbors would find out soon enough, but he didn't want James Powell thinking about the humiliating situation for too long.

Rafael's hand clenched. He'd tried that once, with disastrous results. The man had killed his girlfriend and the man she'd been caught with. His last words on the phone had been, "I can't live with everybody knowing and laughing behind my back."

Rafael punched in the number with one hand and picked up the bullhorn with the other. "Answer the phone or I'll call the one person who has always been proud of you."

Silence.

"You have five seconds. Perhaps your—"

The phone was picked up. "You better not call Mama! She has a heart problem!"

"Help me!" a woman screeched.

"Shut up, bitch! I trusted you, loved you. I should kill you!"

"J.R. is probably expecting a call from you and his stepmother tonight, James," Rafael interjected, trying to get James to stop and think past his rage.

"From me at least. All she talks about is his weight. How could I have been so stupid?"

"Please don't kill me. He took advantage of me," the woman moaned.

"Shut up or I'll kill you now."

Rafael wanted James to focus on his son and not his wife's betrayal. "James, think about your son. You said your mother had heart problems. Who will take care of her, your son?"

"My own brother, man. I gave her the best of everything. She never had to work after we got married. I can't let her get away with this."

"Then what happens to J.R.? If your mother can't take him, he'll have to go into foster care if you're in jail."

"I won't be in jail," he said quietly.

A chill raced though Rafael. His hand tightened on the cell phone. "James, listen to me. I won't snow you and say I know how you feel. I don't. I do know that there are enough children without parents in the world. I do know that no one can love and support him like you can or understand his asthma."

"Just leave me alone and let me think," James demanded.

"Let Vanessa come out, James. You have to think of J.R."

"I swear I'll be a better mother, I swear!" she wailed.

The sound of a gunshot, coupled with a woman's scream, splintered the air.

"Tear gas," his captain ordered. Cannon stepped forward with the tear-gas canister on her shoulder.

"Wait," Rafael said. He didn't want to escalate the situation. James was at a fragile point. "She's screaming and crying, but not in pain," he said, then into the phone, "James, put the gun down and let Vanessa come out. Then you come out behind her."

"No, leave me alone or I'll really do it this time," he warned. "My mama tried to warn me about her, but I wouldn't listen. Is he the first? How many times have you cheated on me?"

"Please, James, please!"

"Send Broderick back in here."

"You know I can't do that," Rafael said. "Let Vanessa come out, and then you."

A shot was fired from one of the turret windows. The bullet lodged in the back tire of the patrol car. "Send him in!"

"Rafael," Captain Coats warned. "We need to go in."

Rafael lowered the cell phone. "If that happens, the chances of James and his wife coming out alive aren't good, and we both know it."

"That's all we need," the captain stated, as he looked up to see a news helicopter hovering overhead.

Rafael shook his head. "His brother says he's a good shot. He wasn't trying to hit us." He held the cell phone to his mouth. "James, we're running out of time. A news camera overhead is going to pick up everything that happens. You have to decide. What is the image you want your mother and son to remember of this day? Your son and mother need you. Send your wife out, and I'll meet you halfway. I want your son to go to sleep tonight knowing he's going to see his father the next day and the day after."

"This hurts, man! I want her to pay!"

"If you do what you threatened, you, your son, and your mother will pay with her," Rafael told him. "You haven't come this far without overcoming obstacles. I'm sure you can figure this out as well." He could only hope James understood his innuendo.

There was a long stretch of silence, then, "Get out of my house."

"She's coming out!" Rafael yelled, seconds before the front door swung open, and immediately slammed shut. A slender naked black woman ran screaming down the walkway. Two policemen rushed to intercept her, leading her to a waiting ambulance.

"James, we're waiting."

"Kids are going to tease J.R.," he said, his voice tormented. "I can take it, but . . ."

"He'll have you to help him deal with it," Rafael said. "I was fortunate enough to grow up with my father, a man I admired. J.R. will be able to say the same thing about you."

"You're sure you're going to meet me?" a hint of fear crept into his voice.

"The moment you open the door with your hands raised, I'll start walking," Rafael promised.

"Man, I know you have snipers. I hope you aren't lying to me. I've seen cops get trigger-happy."

"I'm not, James." Somewhere unseen, Diaz was in position to take James down if things went bad. There were at least fifteen other officers there.

The front door opened slowly. Rafael clicked off the cell phone and stepped around the car. James, stocky and balding, appeared to be in his midfifties. He had on a white shirt and black dress pants. His face was haggard. He swallowed, blinked.

"You made the right decision." Rafael started toward him.

"You bastard!" Vanessa shrieked. "I'll take everything for this! You tried to kill me!"

Panic flashed in James's eyes and was quickly replaced by rage. He started toward her. She screamed.

Rafael tackled James, pinning him to the ground and handcuffing him. "Stay down, James. Too many guns are here. Remember your son."

The haze seemed to clear from his eyes. "And she knows it."

Rafael pulled James to his feet just as other policemen arrived. He was read his rights. "Call your lawyer so he can make bail. You want to be the one to tell J.R."

James nodded as they led him away.

"Another one completed," Captain Coats said from beside Rafael and the shift supervisor. "But you had me worried."

"Me, too." Rafael took off his vest. "When I don't, it will be time for me to quit."

Early on, Rafael had made a habit of going back to the station to file a report on a hostage taking, then heading home to relax with some jazz music and quiet. Negotiating was emotionally and physically draining.

So why had he taken the turn leading to Fontaine instead of continuing to his house?

Since it was a Monday night, it only took one circle of the parking lot before he saw a car pull out. Quickly parking, he switched off the motor and sat there.

No one knew better than he that life could turn and bite you on the butt in the blink of an eye. He'd seen it happen too many times to friends, on and off the force, and to total strangers, as he had today.

He didn't understand why people cheated and lied. Whatever pleasure or gain they thought they were getting out of it didn't last. Affairs had ended several marriages of his comrades, and not one of them had married the person they were cheating with.

The child always paid the price, just as J.R. would initially. His father had to be forcibly restrained when he was informed his son had been turned over to social services until his grandmother could fly in from Virginia the next morning.

Getting out of the car, Rafael made his way to the entrance and went inside, waiting behind two couples. He wasn't sure what he'd say when his turn came. Nathalyia had been cautiously warming up to him when he'd received the call from his commander.

"Rafael."

He turned to see Clarice. Her green eyes filled with concern, she quickly crossed to him. "We caught some of it on TV." She grabbed his arm and led him to the bar area. "I have a quiet table open. I'll tell Nathalyia you're here just as soon as I get you something stronger than tea."

He eased into the chair, feeling tired and anxious. "A beer, I guess."

"You got it." Clarice went behind the bar and drew beer into a glass, then returned to place it on the table. "I'll be back to get your food order in a bit."

Rafael wrapped his hands around the cold beer he really didn't want. Clarice had obviously wanted to do something, and it wasn't unusual for people to feel the need to help out. He didn't need a beer. He needed—

He rose to his feet as soon as Nathalyia came around the corner of the bar. He didn't like seeing the worry lines in her face. They weren't there this morning. "Hi."

"Hi, yourself." She took the seat he pulled out next to him without hesitation. "Are you all right?"

He smiled to reassure her. "Couldn't be better."

"The man shot the police car you were standing by."

Automatically, Rafael's hand covered hers, felt hers tremble, and he saw the fear in her eyes. "He was hurt and angry because of what had happened."

Nathalyia bowed her head for a moment. "The news on TV kept showing the wife running from the house—with a warning and her strategic areas covered."

"Maybe it will help the husband in divorce court," he said, then glanced around at the group of men loudly commenting on a football game on one of the five TV screens in the bar area. "You mind if we go outside for some fresh air?"

She hesitated for a moment, then nodded. "Of course." She stood and motioned a watching Clarice over. "Rafael and I are going out for a bit. Please let David know."

"I will. You know we can handle things."

Nathalyia looked beyond Clarice to the bald-headed bartender intently watching them. "Reassure Jake, will you?"

Clarice grinned. "Count on me."

Nathalyia turned to Rafael. "Ready."

Taking her arm, Rafael led her outside, aware that they were being watched by several members of her staff.

They strolled along the boardwalk near the ocean in silence. Unlike during the day, there weren't any bicycles or mopeds on the walk. A quarter moon hung over the calm ocean. It was a quiet, beautiful night.

"This is nice." She stopped and leaned against the iron rail, looking out at the boats with the lights on. "I seldom get a chance to come out here."

"Managing Fontaine must keep you pretty busy, but from what I've seen, you're up to it."

She smiled at the compliment. "Martin taught me."

"Your late husband?"

"Yes." She threw a quick glance at him. She didn't have any experience, but she didn't think men wanted to know about deceased husbands. She wasn't sure when she'd stopped trying to push Rafael away and began thinking about the possibility of getting to know him better. Yes, she did. It was when the bullet lodged in the police car a few feet from where he was standing.

"He was a smart man, but you had to put what he taught you into practice," Rafael said easily, bracing his arms on the railing beside her. "A couple of friends of mine inherited businesses, but they couldn't make it work. You have a large staff and they all appear happy."

"Martin always said—" She flushed. "I'm sorry."

He turned and leaned back against the rail, facing her. "For what?"

"I seem to bring up Martin's name in almost every sentence."

"Shows you cared for each other, respected each other." He frowned. "I've seen too much of the opposite."

"You helped that man today," she said. "You helped his little boy." Her mouth tightened in anger. "I couldn't believe a newswoman had the nerve to try and interview a seven-year-old child."

"What people do for their own selfish gain no longer surprises me," he told her.

"That makes me a bit sad," she said.

"Don't be." He straightened, lightly taking her arms in his hands. "The other side of that is the courage and generosity I see in far more people. There will always be those who try to get over or get by, but there will also be those who will stop to give a stranger a hand, to help those in need, just like you do. Every day you make a difference."

"So do you," she said. She had been frantic with worry.

His hands fell. "Just doing my job. I read that the restaurant is coming up on twenty-five years next summer. Quite a feat in today's economy."

"Thank you." He didn't want to talk about his job. She wasn't used to carrying on conversations with men outside of work or church. "Have you talked to your family yet?"

A lazy grin spread across his gorgeous face. She almost sighed. He had to be the most beautiful man she'd ever met. He also had the type of lean, muscular body that drew a woman's attention and made her think about how it would feel being held in his strong arms.

"Yes. I've spoken with all of my brothers, their wives, and my future sister-in-law. Alec was off today, so he was in Charleston until his permanent transfer comes though. I'll miss him when he leaves."

"Your mother was right; you go take care of each other." Rafael had the kind of family she'd always wanted and was destined to never have.

"That we do. It's great knowing your family will be there for you," he said.

The only thing Nathalyia's mother and her older sisters had wanted to do for her was demean her and take what little money she had earned working. None of them ever worked, just schemed to live off welfare and gullible men.

"My only family are the people at the restaurant," she said, the lie rolling easily off her tongue. Only Martin had known the ugly, embarrassing truth.

"I'm sorry." He gently took her into his arms, rocked her. The gesture was comforting rather than sexual.

She wouldn't feel like a fraud, a liar. In a way, she was right. Her father might as well be dead because he'd never acknowledged her, and her mother had never wanted her. Reluctantly, she pushed away and stepped back. Being in his arms was as incredible as she had imagined. For those short moments she'd felt a strange peace. "I better get back."

"All right. What time do you finish up tonight?"

"Probably around twelve if we're lucky." She started back. He fell into step beside her. "We close early on Monday and Thursday because Friday through Sunday we're so busy. It gives us all a little time to regroup."

He lightly touched her on the arm to stop her on the walkway to the restaurant. "I'd like to drive you home."

"I drove," she said, feeling a twinge of regret. She enjoyed talking with him, being with him.

"I can follow you," he suggested.

The request didn't surprise her, but it was time to be sensible. Rafael made her heart race and her mind think of naughty possibilities. "Thank you, but that won't be necessary." She extended her hand. "Good night, Rafael. I'm glad you're all right."

He was slow to take her hand. She hoped he didn't feel her racing pulse, but from his narrowed gaze she didn't think she was that lucky. "I don't mind waiting, or I can come back."

She shook her head. "Closing time is controlled chaos, and tonight the cleaning crew is coming in to do the floors. I'm finishing up the time cards for payroll, so I'll be busy doing paperwork."

Taking a card from his pocket, he wrote a number down and handed it to her. "I live about thirty minutes from here. If you change your mind, all you have to do is call."

"I won't." She reached for the door, then turned back. "You haven't eaten."

"I'm not hungry."

"If you're tired, I'll put a rush on it," she told him.

Smiling, he lifted his hand toward her cheek only to open the outer door instead. "I'm fine. Thanks for asking."

"All right. Good night." Trying not to be disappointed, she turned to go inside.

"Wait," he called.

She swung back around to see him wearing a mischievous grin. She grinned back before she thought not to. "Yes?"

"I didn't get all that was promised." His gaze strayed to her mouth.

Heat pooled in her lower body. She tried not to think of his hot, sinful mouth on hers.

"I didn't have my dessert and the tour."

She might not have much experience, but Rafael wanted more from her than dessert and a tour. "I can meet you here at nine in the morning for the tour, and I'll box a variety of desserts for you to take with you."

He frowned. "I know it's my fault and you're busy, but I'm hoping you can fit me in."

Her mouth went dry. Her mind strayed where it shouldn't have.

"How about around eleven tomorrow night? I don't want to interfere with you running Fontaine. And . . ."

"And," she prompted, when his wicked smile blossomed again.

"I can keep working on you to let me follow you home."

Too tempting and too dangerous. "I'm perfectly capable of taking care of myself."

"I'm sure you are. There's another reason." Reaching out, he brushed an errant strand of hair behind her ear. She shivered.

Everything about Rafael enticed and excited her, and made her remember she was a woman without a man.

"Rafael," she prompted again before her wayward thoughts got her into trouble. "I have work to do."

"If I follow you home, I might be lucky enough to find out if you kiss on the second date."

She blinked at his boldness and tried not to stare at his lips. There was nothing she could do about the wild fluttering of her heart. "We aren't dating."

"Depends on your perspective, I guess. In any case I'm patient when something is important to me." He opened the door. "I've kept you long enough. Until tomorrow night."

His voice shouldn't make her skin tingle. He was so close she felt the heat coming from him, caught his masculine scent. She wanted to lean closer. She quickly stepped back. "Good night."

She slipped inside the restaurant before his incredible face and intense black eyes made her do something silly. Several employees, including Jake and Clarice, stared at her as she went to her office.

Clarice gave her a thumbs-up. Jake just stared at her, his gaze searching. She appreciated that he watched over her. He didn't have to worry. Despite a few lapses with Rafael, she had no intention of letting her emotions get in the way of what was best for Fontaine.

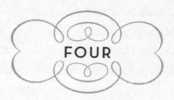

FOUR

Nathalyia felt good the next morning. She'd had a restful night and was more in control of her emotions. Her self-assurance probably showed in the wide smile on her face, the jubilant way she greeted the staff, the little bounce in her steps. She wasn't going to fool herself. She was looking forward to seeing Rafael, but it wasn't going any further than that. What woman wouldn't be flattered by the attention of an attractive, self-assured man?

"Good morning, Jake, Clarice," she greeted as she stopped at the bar. The staff was still coming in. The faint sounds of the kitchen staff making preparations could be heard, but the bar area was empty.

"Morning." Clarice grinned. "Don't you look happy and even more gorgeous than usual. Would a certain hot police officer have anything to do with it?"

Nathalyia felt her face heat. "It's just such a beautiful day."

"Are you expecting anyone for lunch?" Clarice persisted.

Jake stopped polishing the bar. "Don't be nosy, Clarice."

Clarice frowned at him. "She has to eat, doesn't she?"

"Before this goes any further—I am not expecting a guest for lunch." Nathalyia told them.

"You're not seeing him again?" Clarice asked, clearly disappointed.

"That's none of your business," Jake told her, his hands on his hips to emphasize his annoyance.

Clarice waved his words aside. "Nathalyia knows it's concern, not nosiness."

She did. Although they didn't socialize outside the restaurant, she liked the honest, outspoken Clarice. So did Jake, but he'd deny it until his last breath. He'd resigned himself to always being alone.

"Rafael is coming later tonight for his tour and dessert," Nathalyia told them. If he hadn't had her so flustered, she would have insisted the tour be earlier. She thought of his comment about kissing on the second date and barely kept from blushing again.

"That's more like it," Clarice said, giving Jake a friendly pat on the back before moving off.

"Go on and say it," Nathalyia said to Jake. His strong face was set in forbidding lines.

"You're a grown woman." Jake opened the Sub-Zero refrigerator, pulled out her bottled water, opened it, and handed it to her.

She took a sip. "That fact has never stopped you before."

"This is different, and we both know it." He tossed a white cotton dish towel over his shoulder.

"Yes." Her hands closed around the bottle. "He admires how I handle the restaurant. He doesn't freak when I mention Martin, which I do a lot. In fact, he praised him."

"Men can be devious," Jake pointed out.

She smiled at him. "There are also wonderful men, like you and Martin."

"He was one of the best." Jake glanced at a picture of a group of men in fishing gear on a boat that hung on the wall. "He saved my sanity."

"He saved me." She smiled. "If he were here, he'd tell us to stop being sappy and get on with life. He hated people who spent time bemoaning life instead of living it."

"Is that what you're going to do?" he asked, watching her.

"I admit a part of me would like to know him better, but as I said, I don't have time for a man." She tipped the bottle to him and continued to her office.

Clarice came to stand beside Jake. "Did you change her mind? She wasn't smiling when she left."

"I don't know." Jake watched Nathalyia all the way to her office before turning to Clarice. "This is your fault."

"Yes, it is, isn't it."

He glared at her. She smiled. "Don't give me that look. I left you alone so you could get it off your chest, but she's lonely and I like Rafael."

"We know your taste in men," he said gruffly.

The smile slid from her face. "Yes, we do." She turned away. He caught her before she had gone two steps. "Let go of me. I'm two seconds away from tearing into you and if I do that, I'll be fired."

His fingers flexed on her arm, but he didn't free her. "You know I didn't mean it the way it sounded."

"You mean like I'm a brainless sl—"

His large hand covered her mouth. She bit him. "Ouch!" Shaking his hand, he staggered backward.

She eyed him. "Your hands are as tough as leather. It's a wonder I didn't lose a tooth, so stop pretending I hurt you so I'd feel better."

"I don't want you mad at me," he said, letting his hand fall to his side.

She didn't want to be mad at him either. He was the first man she'd spent time with that she trusted, liked, even depended on in some ways. "Those pictures still need hanging at my place."

"You know I don't like hanging pictures. I tried it here and the wall had to be repaired," he reminded her.

"Noted, so you'd better be careful. The walls are thin at my new apartment, but it's closer to work and larger than my last one. We don't have to be here until ten in the morning. I'll expect you at eight." She walked off and Jake watched her go. How could a woman know him so well and not have a clue that he loved her?

If Rafael answered one question about his lunch date with Nathalyia, he answered fifty. It seemed the entire station had heard about the date. He didn't really mind. If his team members hadn't pitched in to help him, he might have struck out again. He still might.

It wasn't a pleasant thought. There was no telling how long it would have taken to get past her defenses. She was a cautious woman in some ways, and totally captivating. He could easily lose himself in her dark, sexy eyes.

He pulled his cell phone from its case on his belt and considered calling her. It was almost three and he was getting off in a couple of hours. He could swing by the restaurant and grab a bite to eat. Maybe they could go for another walk and he could work on getting her to let him follow her home after the tour of Fontaine.

He readily admitted to himself that he wanted his mouth on hers, wanted the freedom to let his hands roam over her incredible body. He blew out a breath. She was rightly cautious, but definitely interested. He was willing to let Nathalyia set the pace and learn he could be trusted. He smiled. Well, up to a point.

"You're the talk of the station. Again."

"That's our little brother."

Rafael looked up to see Alec and Sam. Both of his brothers had their arms crossed, indulgent smiles on their faces. Rafael placed the cell phone on his desk. "What can I say? Women like me."

Alec, two years older, with dark, piercing eyes and a muscular build, sat on the edge of Rafael's desk. "Modest, but I hear you had to work hard to get this one to go out with you."

"You heard right," Diaz commented from the next desk over. "If it hadn't been for me, he never would have known about the raffle, let alone won it."

"We all pitched in to help," Gibbs pointed out. "I just don't see why she chose Dunlap over me."

"Look in the mirror," Henderson commented, then burst out laughing.

"Sit and spin," Gibbs pointed out, then went back to filing cases.

"Boys. Boys." Cannon's sigh was long-suffering. "You can't imagine what it's like to work with testosterone-driven men all day. I can't imagine why my girlfriends envy me."

"You know you love it, Cannon," Barron drawled in his Texan accent. "It took you three tries to be accepted into the unit."

"Same as you," Cannon replied sweetly.

Rafael chuckled. "As you can tell, I need a break after being with them all day."

Sam nodded. He was second in command at the station. At sixty-two, his hair remained jet-black, his broad shoulders square. His voice could lull or flay the hide off an insubordinate officer or a hardened criminal. "It's about time women stopped falling over themselves for you."

"Shows she's cautious and selective," Alec said. "A woman worth having is worth fighting for."

"Whoa!" Rafael put up both hands. "Put on the brakes. I just met her."

Sam walked closer and pitched his voice low so only Rafael and Alec could hear him. "You went to see her instead of going home last night."

"That's what I get for calling Helen." Rafael hadn't wanted Sam's wife, who mothered all of the Dunlap men, to worry. Without fail, she always called him after he had to negotiate. She was his rock as much as his brothers were.

When he'd lost three people in a hostage situation last year, they'd talked for hours on the phone. She'd been the same attentive way six months ago when a suicidal woman had taken Rafael over the roof of an office building with her. His safety harness had saved them, but they'd been badly bruised from bumping against the concrete wall. The woman had quickly changed her mind about dying, and frantically clung to him.

Alec clasped Rafael's shoulder. "You knew she'd worry. Celeste called me to check on you as well. She said to tell you she's sending you a batch of cookies."

Celeste, Alec's fiancée, was gorgeous and a fabulous cook. "You really lucked out, Alec."

"Don't I know it." His eyes grew serious. "You made our future possible."

Rafael knew he referred to the hostage incident. "Your going in made the difference."

"You both did." Sam pointed to the cell phone on Rafael's desk. "You were about to make a phone call."

Rafael almost squirmed. "I was thinking about calling Nathalyia."

"An unusual and beautiful name," Alec said. "I've been to Fontaine and know it fits the woman."

"You've seen her?" Rafael asked. "What did you think of

her?" he asked before he could stop himself. He didn't discuss the women he dated with his brothers, or anyone else for that matter.

The odd look on his brothers' faces said they were aware of his deviation. "She was very friendly the times Helen and I went there," Sam answered.

"You've been there, too?" Rafael asked.

"It's a popular restaurant." Alec stood. "Just think. You could have met her months ago if you weren't so set on not eating at restaurants that don't have valet parking."

"But I would have been on a date so it wouldn't have come to anything," Rafael felt compelled to point out.

"You never know." Sam slapped him on the back. "By the way, I'm proud of the way you handled the standoff with the hostage yesterday. You made the right call."

"Thanks." Even as an adult, Rafael enjoyed receiving praise from his brothers, especially Sam.

"We'll see you for Sunday dinner," Sam said. "You can bring a date if you want."

Rafael's brows drew together. "I've never brought a date to dinner with just the family."

"As far as I know, you've never called one from work either," Alec pointed out as he stood to his feet and leaned over. "Don't look so stricken. It happens to the best of us."

Waving, Sam and Alec left the office. Rafael stared after them and then put the phone away. He and Nathalyia were just having fun. Nothing more.

Rafael knew something was wrong the moment Clarice met him at the door and seated him in one of the back booths and slid in on the other side. "Is Nathalyia all right?"

"One of Nathalyia's children with sickle cell had a crisis. The little girl wanted Nathalyia, so she took off."

Rafael came to his feet, pulling his car keys from his pocket. "Which hospital? Maybe I can help."

Clarice stood and gently touched his arm. "She didn't tell me."

"Can you call her?" he asked.

"Only if it's an emergency," Clarice told him. "Nathalyia left instructions for me to take you on the tour and give you the option of taking the dessert tonight or stopping by tomorrow after eleven."

He didn't like the idea that she might need him and he wasn't there. She hadn't given him a choice. "Do you think she'll come back by closing time?"

"She'll be at the hospital as long as Carmen or the family needs her," Clarice told him. "Her children are the one thing that takes priority over Fontaine."

It didn't surprise him. "She's a fantastic woman."

"On that we agree." Clarice held out her pad. "Give me your number and I'll call you if she comes back tonight."

Rafael quickly scribbled down his cell and home phone numbers. "Thank you, but I think I'll wait for a little while."

"Anything else besides the usual iced tea?" When he hesitated, she smiled. "If you're thinking of a dessert, I'll put it on your bill. Fontaine will still owe you a dessert."

He took his seat. "The bread pudding. Nathalyia said she came up with the recipe."

"She did, and it's delicious." She grinned. "You probably can tell I like desserts."

"I can tell you're a good friend."

She stared at him. "I'm glad I was right about you. I'll be back in a jiff with your order."

Rafael checked his watch and leaned back against the booth.

Dealing with a family with a critically ill child was heart-wrenching. He'd already guessed that Nathalyia had a soft spot for children. He wished he was there to offer her support, to help the family in any way he could. All he could do was wait.

Nathalyia pulled into her parking space at Fontaine with a flourish. Despite its size, her husband's Rolls-Royce handled as well as her Volvo. Getting out, she hurried to the back door. The restaurant was due to close in ten minutes.

Punching in the code, she entered and went to the office to put away her handbag. She glanced at the pile of invoices she'd been working on when she received the frantic call from Carmen's mother, and kept walking. She wanted to make her last round of the night.

She turned in to the bar and came to a complete stop. Her heart did a crazy dance.

"Nathalyia." Rafael slid out of the booth and came to her. "How is the little girl?"

"Sleeping," she said, staring at him. "You're still here?"

"I wanted to make sure you were all right, but I can see by your expression that you are," he told her.

"Yes, I—"

"Boss. It's almost closing time," Jake called.

Nathalyia looked beyond Rafael to Jake's hard face. He was reminding her of her responsibility to Fontaine. "Excuse me, I need to make final rounds."

"Sure. I'll wait."

"You don't—"

Rafael took his seat and picked up his glass of tea. "You'd better get going."

She didn't have time to argue with him. She moved to the next table, and the next. Twenty minutes later she showed the last couple to the door. Tonight had been their first date. She thanked them for selecting Fontaine and gave each a $10 coupon to use on their next visit. Smiling at each other, they promised to return.

Nathalyia watched the couple walk away. The man's hand moved from the woman's shoulder to her waist as he opened the outer door. She smiled up at him.

Nathalyia hoped it worked out for them. Anything important carried risks. She thought of Rafael. It was difficult not to. Besides his heart-stopping good looks, he was a caring, thoughtful man.

Clarice approached with her usual smile. "I'm glad to hear that Carmen is resting."

Nathalyia didn't have to ask how she knew. Clarice had an easy way with men. She was also a risk taker. Nathalyia was neither. "Did you take him on the tour?"

"Nope." She grinned. "Seems he didn't want a substitute. He knows exactly what he wants." She elbowed Nathalyia. "Give him a chance."

"Clarice," Jake called.

Clarice rolled her eyes. "The master calls," she said loud enough for Jake and the other bartenders to hear. They laughed as she rounded the bar. Jake's expression remained stoic.

Nathalyia started for the booth Rafael sat in. She'd never met a man as persistent as he was or one who made her restless, made her body want.

He stood. "I ordered you a water and strawberry lemonade. Clarice didn't think you were hungry."

Add thoughtful to the list. "Thank you." Nathalyia sat near the edge of the booth's seat. She had a feeling that if she scooted in farther, Rafael would slide in beside her. She was having enough trouble resisting him without his hard, muscled body pressed next to hers.

"Drink up and then tell me about Carmen, if you feel like it," he said, pushing the drinks closer to her.

Nathalyia sipped her strawberry lemonade. "She's beautiful. She has an iron will that both parents agree comes from her late maternal grandmother. When the episode began, she was angry because she hadn't had a crisis in seventy-eight days, and if it was a bad one it would keep her from the carnival. She wanted me to promise her that, no matter what, she could go."

She looked up. Tears glistened in her eyes. "I told her whenever she felt better, the first thing I'd do was take her to the carnival. Thank God the crisis wasn't major. The pain can be—" She bit her lip.

Rafael got up and nudged her over with his body. When he was seated, he curved his arm across her shoulders and gave her his handkerchief. "She's sleeping, Nathalyia, and probably dreaming of all the wonderful things she'll do at the carnival."

She dabbed her eyes. "I told her about the rides, the food. She'll have a wheelchair so she won't get tired Friday night, and plenty of water to keep hydrated. Before I left I talked with her parents about a trip to Disney World next summer for the entire family. Her eighteen-year-old sister is a college freshman and takes care of Carmen while their parents work at night. They're a good family."

"You're a good woman." He pressed his lips against her temple. "Drink."

She picked up the glass, but instead of drinking the lemonade, she looked at Rafael. She'd brushed him off, tried to get out of having lunch with him, constantly quoted her husband, stood him up, and now cried on his shoulder, and he still looked at her as if he wanted to gobble her in one greedy bite.

She had to admit, she wouldn't mind a little nibbling on him herself. She didn't have Clarice's experience with men, but

Carmen's sudden illness had reminded Nathalyia of her husband's philosophy of living life to the fullest with a minimum of regret.

She didn't want not getting to know Rafael to be one of her regrets. "Do you want to wait and follow me home, or should I call you when I'm ready to leave?"

"I'll wait."

Homes in Navarone Estates started at three million dollars and went up sharply from there. Many who lived there were politicians, sports figures, entertainers, and entrepreneurs. The exclusive community had twenty-two homes on the fifty-acre gated estate.

The homes, built on only one side of the street, faced a wooded park with a running and bicycle trail. The property of ten lucky owners backed up to a man-made lake. Rafael drove through the manned gate behind Nathalyia, but he didn't miss the guard stepping out to write down his license plate.

Rafael wholly applauded the man's action. A woman, even a careful woman like Nathalyia, couldn't be too careful.

Nathalyia, driving her late husband's Rolls-Royce, continued down the street past two- and three-story homes until she came to a curve. She'd shyly told Rafael she drove it once a week to keep the battery from dying.

Directly ahead was a magnificent three-story mansion with landscaped lighting and palm trees blowing in the night breeze. She went up the long driveway on one side of the house. Rafael heard a gate disengage, then heard it closing after she drove through.

He stopped on the street. The front door was at least fifty feet from the curb. Getting out, he went to the massive fifteen-foot-high door. He glanced up at the eye of the camera. He'd bet anything it was a live feed. She'd told him she had to go around to the back and disengage the alarm system.

More lights flickered on. Through the grillwork of the leaded glass door, he could see a domed ceiling, a massive chandelier, artwork, and a graceful wrought-iron double staircase. He saw her hurrying toward him and thought the house suited her.

"Sorry it took me so long."

"It's fine. It gave me a chance to admire your home." Stepping inside, he saw the living room with yellow and white walls, silk-covered furniture, and the immense lighted pool beyond. "The elegance suits you."

She flushed and closed the door, glancing around. "It's too big, but it's what—" She stopped abruptly.

"Your late husband wanted," Rafael filled in for her.

"Restaurateurs have odd hours. He wanted me safe."

"I won't keep you. You must be tired."

He easily read the regret on her face. Her emotions were so transparent. Her husband had been right to protect her. The world would chew her up and spit her out.

He wouldn't let that happen. "Good night." He leaned over to brush his lips across her cheek. He'd planned to tease her afterward about kissing on the second date. The compelling scent, the soft-ness of her skin, had him wanting more. His mouth moved to cover hers. Desire hit him before he could draw in his next breath. He pulled her into his arms, his tongue teasing and his teeth nipping.

She tensed momentarily, then her lips parted. His tongue slipped inside. She tasted hot and sweet. Her slim arms slid around his neck. His tongue swept across hers, again and again, compelling her to follow. With a little whimper she melted against him in sur-render.

The kiss heated and tested his willpower to keep it light. He desperately wanted to cup her hips and bring them closer still, wanted his hand to feel the fullness of her breasts, and wanted to savor every luscious bare curve.

Suddenly, she pushed out of his arms and stumbled back. Breathing hard, her eyes wide, she stared at him.

He glimpsed the surprise in her eyes, the wariness, and the lingering desire before she glanced away. If he didn't know better, he'd have thought she'd never experienced passion before. Studying the erratic pulse in her throat, he decided it was an intriguing possibility he definitely planned to explore.

"You said the carnival is Friday?" he asked to get the conversation started again and to put her at ease.

"Yes. Friday night," she said after a moment. "I plan to be there around six to ensure things are in order and the badge for each child is ready. Things start at six thirty."

"I could pick you up at the restaurant at five thirty and take you back or home," he offered.

She stared at him. "All right. It will be back to the restaurant. I've missed few closings."

She was as dedicated as Clarice had said. "See you Friday. Good night, Nathalyia."

"Good night, Rafael."

After one last lingering look, he left. Once outside, he motioned for her to lock the door. Smiling, she did, then waved through the window, and frowned when he frowned. The glass was pretty, but it allowed too much of the house to be seen.

The door opened. "What is it?"

"The glass door."

The smile returned. "It bothered Jake, too. He insisted it be changed. It's bulletproof and shatterproof."

"It still allows too clear a view inside the house."

"I'm seldom in here. My bedroom and office are on the second floor so I can look at the lake and ocean," she explained, then hastened to add, "The gates at the back of the house on the lake are locked and patrolled."

"Jake again."

"Part of the security provided by Navarone Estates. I'm as safe as if you were here."

The idea sent heat splintering through her. Her breasts felt tight and achy. She licked her suddenly dry lips. Rafael's gaze followed. His breathing accelerated.

Her heart thundered. She wanted to reach out to him, to taste him again, savor him on her tongue. She clenched her hands instead.

"Good night, Nathalyia." He spun on his heel and went down the sidewalk.

Nathalyia closed the door, then shut off the lights in the entryway so he couldn't see her. At the moment she couldn't move. Her knees were too shaky. Not only did his kisses excite her, but just thinking about being in his arms did the same thing.

It looked as if she did kiss on the second date—if the man was Rafael.

Standing outside Clarice's second-floor apartment Wednesday morning, Jake wiped the fine beads of perspiration from his forehead. "Get a grip, man," he ordered himself.

He'd faced the enemy in the Gulf War and hadn't faltered. He had more medals than he knew what to do with. His hand touched the left side of his cheek, a reminder that he hadn't escaped unscathed. But the man who had put it there never saw another sunrise.

His hand lifted to knock. Instead, he ran his hand over his face again. He didn't know squat about women. His faithless wife proved as much.

He never had a clue she was cheating, both before he left for combat and after he returned. He just thought she didn't want him touching her because of the scar. He blew out a breath. He wasn't going there.

It had taken him a long time and numerous late-night talks with Martin for Jake to finally let go of the anger and the "poor me" attitude. He'd lost good friends in the war and a wife, but he was still living. Martin helped Jake see that his life wasn't over and he was dishonoring those who hadn't made it by wallowing in self-pity.

His cell phone rang. Without looking, he knew who it was. He accepted the call. "I'm here."

Instead of an answer, the door opened. Clarice stood there with an exasperated look on her pretty face. He couldn't remember falling in love with her; he had just looked up one day when she was going on about another jerk who hadn't panned out and accepted that he loved her.

"You're five minutes late. Breakfast is getting cold." Reaching out, she pulled him inside her new apartment.

"Breakfast?"

She rolled her eyes. "Do you think I'd invite you over this early and not feed you?" she asked, and held up her hand before he could answer. "Of course, you do. You think I'm scatterbrained, irresponsible."

He frowned at her. "Why would you say such a thing? You're smart, but your heart is too soft. Hanging a few pictures for a friend doesn't call for breakfast."

"It's more than a few." She grinned. "You might demand more than breakfast."

She turned away, which was a good thing. He knew exactly what he'd demand: Clarice in bed for a week, maybe two. It would take a lot of loving to satisfy him. He'd wanted her for a long time.

"Come on, Jake, and have a seat," she called from the kitchen. "And since I'm not subtle, what do you think now that all the furniture is arranged?"

He looked around the cheery apartment decorated in blue and green, her favorite colors. He'd helped her move since her brothers were "busy." He thought they should look out for her more.

He'd been the one to help her find an apartment when hers had become overrun with gang violence. Although there had been two shootings, her brothers weren't concerned for her safety. However, they had no problem stopping by to ask for money or to borrow her car.

Men should take care of women, not the other way around. His mouth tightened. If they weren't her brothers—

"You don't like it?" she asked, coming back into the room to stare at him.

"Sorry. I was just thinking." He glanced around again. "I like it. You did a good job."

She appeared relieved, which surprised him. In most things, Clarice was self-assured and pigheaded. "Thanks. I wasn't certain. I asked Nathalyia about the color scheme. She always looks fabulous."

"So do you," he said, then could have bitten off his tongue.

Clarice stared at him, then laughed. Taking his arm, she led him to the kitchen. "Laying it on a bit thick, aren't we, Jake? I forgive you for yesterday."

He took the seat she waved toward. On one hand he was glad she didn't think he was serious, but on the other it showed that she'd never view him as anything other than a friend. Why should she?

He was fifteen years older, towered over her, and was scarred for life. He should just be happy that she had never seemed to notice the scar.

"Breakfast smells good," he finally said.

"I can cook my behind off." She put biscuits in a basket.

With her back to him, he studied that behind. That would be some feat.

On the table she set a platter of pork sausages, scrambled eggs, and fried red potatoes with one hand and a woven basket of biscuits with the other. She took the chair beside him that he pulled out. Bowing her head, she blessed their food. Picking up his plate, Clarice filled it.

"I usually have cold cereal," he told her as he reached for the spoon for his cheese grits, which were already on the table.

"I know we're supposed to watch cholesterol, but I can't abide turkey breakfast meats. When I eat an egg, I want an egg." She prepared her own plate.

"I feel the same way." He bit into a golden biscuit. "You can cook!"

"Told you." She grinned. "If you ever want to drop by for breakfast, you can, you know."

Somehow, Jake kept his expression friendly. "Exactly how many pictures do you have?"

She laughed and slapped him on the shoulder. "Ouch!"

He was out of his seat instantly, her hand in his, searching for injuries. "Did you hurt yourself?"

"No." With her other hand, she poked his chest. "Solid, just like I thought. You have one incredible body, Jake Sergeant."

He dropped her hand.

She rolled her eyes. "Sorry. I didn't mean to embarrass you. As you know, I don't always think before I speak."

"That's all right." He took his seat and picked up his fork.

She reached across the table and briefly covered his hand with hers. "You're sure? I've got pictures that need hanging."

Somehow, he smiled. She had no way of knowing how her words affected him. "Then I guess we better finish breakfast so we can get to it."

Grinning, she picked up her fork. "That's the bossy Jake we all know and love."

Jake kept eating. She was slicing his heart to pieces and she'd never know.

FIVE

Hold out, Rafael, he told himself Thursday morning. You'll see her tomorrow.

On the back porch of his house, he looked out at the churning ocean and sipped his first and only cup of coffee for the day. The house sat on a prime piece of real estate, but, more important, the rambling two-story structure had belonged to his parents. They'd left it to him. He didn't take the responsibility lightly.

He and his brothers had grown up in the four-bedroom house. His father had moonlighted to help make the payments. He'd wanted a better life and home for his family, and had done everything he could to ensure that it happened. His wife and partner, the woman he'd loved more than life, had been a stay-at-home mother and had made every penny count.

How many times had Rafael come out on the porch to see his parents walking on the beach holding hands? They'd all helped to build the sleek nautical railing so their mother could look out and always see what her adventurous sons were up to. Occasionally, he'd found his parents on the porch together.

His father would be reading the newspaper and his mother one of her many romance novels. They had the kind of love his brothers were also blessed to have. Rafael had long ago decided that he'd walk alone. No woman or child should fear the ring of the phone or doorbell.

Rafael glanced at his watch. Again. Eight thirty-three A.M. Nathalyia should be up. He imagined her awakening from sleep, her skin soft and warm, and her arms reaching for him. He hardened instantly.

Returning inside, he dumped the coffee into the sink. He didn't ever recall going through such mental acrobatics over a woman or of wanting her this much. He'd certainly never been this impatient to see one. He enjoyed women, made sure they enjoyed him, then he moved on.

He forgot them, as he was sure they forgot him. And during the time they were together, he kept them compartmentalized. They didn't intrude on his thoughts.

He wasn't able to do that with Nathalyia, and it bothered him. He was the type of man who liked answers, a man who wanted everything laid out. He didn't like puzzles or deviations.

He rinsed out the mug and put it in the dishwasher, and glanced at his watch again. He wasn't due on duty until ten. This restlessness was odd for him. He wasn't obsessive, but he always knew what came next, even if next was nothing.

If he went by Sam and Helen's house, she would cook him one of her special breakfasts. She'd also realize something was bothering him and, because she loved him, she would try to find out what it was so she could help.

So going over there was definitely out. He didn't feel like exercising or running on the beach. What he felt like was seeing

Nathalyia, holding her, kissing her. Muttering, he picked up the phone and paused. He didn't know her home number.

He hung his head. For a man who dealt in facts, he hadn't done very well.

His cell rang. He threw it a nasty look since the ring tone wasn't his commander's or one of his family members'. He always plugged in his phone up to charge before he went to bed and unplugged, then turned it on when he came to the kitchen for his coffee.

He walked over and picked it up. Seeing a number he didn't recognize, he reluctantly accepted the call. "Whatever you're selling, I'm not buying."

Light laughter filtered though the line.

He straightened. "Nathalyia."

"Good morning, Rafael." Laughter still resonated in her voice.

"Morning." He laughed, then opened a drawer and reached for a pen. "What are your cell and home numbers? I was about to call you and realized I didn't have either number."

She gave him the information he requested. "I just wanted to make sure you're still picking me up tomorrow."

"I'll be there." He leaned against the counter and crossed one leg over the other. "How are things?"

"Great, thank you," she said. "I haven't seen or heard anything on the radio or television I have in my office, so I'm assuming you haven't had to use your negotiating skills again."

He didn't want her worried. "I've been doing boring but necessary desk work."

"I know what you mean," she said. "When I go in today, I have to reconcile inventory and order supplies for several special events scheduled later this month."

"Since both of us are going to have a day we're not looking forward to, why don't we do something to get it started right?" he suggested.

There was a slight pause before she asked, "What do you have in mind?"

Unfortunately, not what she was probably thinking and what he wanted. "There's a great coffee shop a couple of miles from the restaurant. We can grab a Danish and juice."

"I'd like that."

"Great." He reached for his car keys and gave her the address. "I can meet you there in twenty minutes."

"It might take me a bit longer," she said, worry in her voice.

Rafael thought of his clotheshorse niece, Brooke, and could easily imagine Nathalyia trying to decide what to wear. "No problem. I'll go on and grab us a table. I'll see you when I see you. Bye."

She laughed. "Bye."

Disconnecting the call, Rafael headed for the garage, a wide grin on his face. The day was definitely going to begin right.

Nathalyia hadn't planned to dress up to go in to work today, but that was before she knew she had a date with Rafael. And it was definitely a date.

She went quickly to her closet. She didn't want to overdress, but she wanted to look nice. The red shawl-collar knee-length lightweight sweater with a matching T-shirt caught her attention. She quickly unbuttoned the gray blouse she had planned to wear and slipped the tee and the sweater on.

Exchanging the small silver earrings for red crystal ones, she was almost ready. Luckily, she already wore black pants and had planned to take her black handbag.

Reaching up, she removed the pins from her hair, brushed it out, and applied red lipstick. She stared into the mirror at her flushed cheeks, the excitement in her eyes.

"I certainly hope you know what you're doing."

Dropping the lipstick into her purse, she ran lightly down the stairs to the kitchen, grabbing the car keys from the hook as she passed. In less than a minute, she was driving through the estate gate and heading to meet Rafael.

Twenty-seven minutes after she hung up from talking with Rafael, Nathalyia parked her car near the coffee shop. Battling the wind that was blowing her hair in every direction, she hurried down the sidewalk. What had seemed like a good idea, leaving her hair down, was proving to be a problem. Perhaps she could slip into the ladies' room and comb her hair while he was getting their food.

Opening the door, she stepped inside to see a long line of people in front of the curved thirty-foot glass case. She didn't see Rafael or an available table. Uncertain of what to do next, she bit her lower lip.

"Over here."

Rafael stood by a table in the back waving at her. Her heart thumped. The man was absolutely gorgeous. There was definitely something about a man in a uniform that got to her. A bit breathless, she made her way to him. "Good morning. Sorry I'm late."

"You're fine." He held out a chair for her. "You look fantastic."

Her hand fluttered to her hair. "Thank you, but the wind was blowing—"

One of his hands captured hers; his other hand brushed lightly over her hair. "There. You look perfect."

There went her crazy heart again. She searched her mind for something to say and looked at the table. "You already ordered."

He sat back in his seat. "I took a chance on orange and apple juice, an apple Danish, and a cinnamon roll. The line was starting to get long. I can get you something else if you'd like."

"This is fine. Which would you like?"

"I'm easy," he told her. "And today you're eating."

She usually didn't eat breakfast because she wasn't hungry. She reached for the apple Danish and orange juice. "Have you been here before?"

"First time." He took a large bite of the cinnamon roll. "How about you?"

"The same." She took a small bite of the Danish. "I don't usually eat breakfast, but this is pretty good."

"Stick with me," he teased, finishing off his pastry and picking up his apple juice. "Is everything set for tomorrow night?"

"Yes." She sat back in her seat. "I can't wait to see the children's faces."

"How many are coming?" he asked.

"Seventy-nine at last count," she told him.

"I haven't been to a carnival in years," he mused. "How about you?"

"This will be my first," she confessed, trying to seem matter-of-fact instead of a bit embarrassed. There hadn't been any time for fun things when she was growing up.

"But you're going to ensure that the children in your program have a chance to go at least once," he said. "You're a special woman."

Now fully embarrassed by his compliment and very much aware of him, she twisted in her chair. "I want them to have fun, to forget for a little while and be like every other child, to give the family an evening of fun."

"How about you?" he asked, leaning across the table. "What do you do for fun?"

The simple question caught her off guard. She'd never been carefree as a child or as an adult. "Different things," she finally answered, reaching for her juice to break his gaze. "How about you?"

"Sailing, bowling, clam digging, riding my bike, sitting here with you," he told her.

Pleased, she lifted her head. "I'll have to add this to my list."

"Like I said, stick with me." He grinned at her. "The best is yet to come."

She wanted to believe him. It almost scared her how much.

Nathalyia really tried to concentrate on checking time cards for the payroll, but she kept thinking about Rafael. He was spontaneous, easygoing, and patient. He was fun.

She leaned back in the chair behind her desk. She couldn't remember a time when she hadn't had some type of responsibility, a time when she could just forget about everything and just have fun.

Except now—with Rafael.

Because her late husband became tired easily and had frequent bouts of angina, they seldom did anything not connected with the restaurant before or after they were married. The restaurant took up most of their time and energy anyway. She hadn't minded.

She'd grown to love and respect Martin. If they didn't share a passionate love, it was honest and unshakable. His well-being was always first and foremost to her. He'd cared deeply for her and had been the first person she could always count on, no matter what.

He'd been persistent and very open in his pursuit of her. He wasn't above joking with the regulars that he knew she was too young for him, but she had saved his life, so she was responsible for him.

One night after the restaurant was closed and they were sitting at a table looking out at the ocean, he had taken her hand. He'd told her she was his salvation and he was going to keep at her until she realized he just might be hers.

Nathalyia picked up their wedding photo on her desk. Six months later they were married. Afterward she did everything in her power to show him she cared and that she would see that Fontaine continued to prosper.

She'd done a lot of soul-searching before she'd agreed to the marriage. There had been no childhood dreams for her of finding the perfect man and getting married. All she'd ever wanted was what she'd never had—to be wanted and safe. Martin fulfilled those dreams. She hadn't thought there might be more.

Until Rafael entered her life.

She'd had exactly two dates before meeting Martin. Both turned out disastrously. When the dates came to pick her up, her sisters had put her down in front of them and then left with them for a "real" date. She'd been in the twelfth grade. Her hope had been that she wouldn't have to go to the senior prom alone. Dateless, she'd skipped the prom.

The humiliating experiences had made her even more determined to leave after graduation and get a degree at Coastal Carolina University. Unfortunately, the cost of living in Myrtle Beach was so high she couldn't afford the tuition. She'd gotten a job at Fontaine and never looked back.

The knock on her door brought her out of her musing. She glanced at the clock on her desk. Five twenty. It was probably Clarice. Each time she saw Nathalyia today, she'd given her the thumbs-up sign.

"Come in, Clarice."

The door opened and Rafael entered, sinfully sexy in a chambray shirt and jeans that molded to his muscular thighs and legs. He smiled. Butterflies fluttered in her stomach.

"Hi. Clarice was busy and waved me on back. I hope it's all right."

"Of course." She stood on unsteady legs and went to the wooden coatrack for the lightweight navy jacket that matched her slacks.

"Let me help you." He took the jacket from her and helped her slip it on.

"Thank you." She didn't know why she felt so nervous. "I'll get my bag."

His hand on her arm stopped her. "What's the matter?"

"Nothing."

He tilted her chin upward. "You have a very easy-to-read face. Is it the restaurant or something else?"

Lying crossed her mind, but she quickly dismissed the thought. "Something else."

"Ah." He pulled her into his arms and stared down at her. "Would it be this?" He tenderly brushed his lips across her forehead. "Or this?" His lips moved to the corner of her mouth to nibble and excite. "Am I getting warmer?"

Clasping her hands behind his neck, she nodded, then moved her lips to his. With the first brush of warmth, her body relaxed, she sighed. Then as his tongue touched hers, her blood heated, and desire shot through her. Her arms tightened even as he pulled her closer, his mouth devouring hers.

Too soon, he lifted his head. "Feel better?"

She stared up at him. "How did you know?"

"Because kissing you again has occupied a great deal of my thoughts since I followed you home Tuesday morning." He smiled. "Yesterday didn't count."

"Definitely. No comparison," she said. Her mouth gaped at her gaffe.

Rafael laughed aloud, hugging her to him. "Nathalyia, you'll keep me on my toes."

"I didn't mean— Oh, my. I just—" She burrowed into him, too embarrassed to face him. How could she explain it was the brevity of the kiss when he had walked her to her car after they left the coffee shop, not the technique? Words failed her.

His hand swept up and down her back. "I know what you meant. I shouldn't tease you." His face grew serious. "I think this is new to you."

She wasn't sure if that was good or bad. She'd seen the openly lustful way women looked at him at the coffee shop. There was probably a long list of women before her.

The thought angered her—which was odd. She promised herself that she'd never be jealous of others the way her mother and sisters were. It had only made them miserable.

"You don't know how rare a woman you are," he said. "You're stunning, elegant, wealthy, honest. You could be just about yourself, but you're not. You care about others and prove it in so many ways. I'm glad we met."

Slowly her head came up. He seemed to understand her so well, and she hadn't a clue about him.

"What?"

"My copy of the dating manual must have been misdelivered," she said, finally looking at him and trying to be casual. "I'm an open book to you."

"I'm not playing games. I'm not trying to use you. I like being with you."

"Just being with me?" she asked. She wasn't that naïve.

"You do ask the tough questions." The backs of his fingers gently brushed against her cheek. "I want to take you to bed, but I'll wait until you're ready."

There it was. He was too experienced not to be aware of how her body reacted to his, hot and hungry. Yet he hadn't pushed, hadn't let his hands roam enough to make her nervous. He was patient with her. He wasn't pushing her. He was willing to wait. That was as good as she was going to get.

"We'd better get going or we'll be late." Pushing out of his arms, she started for the door.

Somehow he reached the door ahead of her and opened it. "I'm right behind you."

Rafael helped Nathalyia and the other volunteers as they checked the families in and clipped the laminated badges on the children in her Helping Hands program. Some of the children were obviously ill, while others appeared as healthy as their siblings or any other child.

What was so amazing to Rafael was that Nathalyia knew the name of each of the seventy-nine Helping Hands children. Clearly, they were more than just statistics to her. Many of them wanted hugs. Nathalyia gladly obliged. By the time the last family had checked in, it was a quarter to seven and Nathalyia kept brushing away tears.

His heart clenched. He handed her his handkerchief. "I'll say it again. You're amazing."

She shook her head, brushing moisture from her eyes. "Not me. The children. The youngest, Ty, is four. He was diagnosed with leukemia when he was two. He's a walking miracle. He's been through so much in his short life. But so have his parents."

Rafael hugged her closer. "Is he the one who wanted to hug Aunt Nathalyia and wanted to ride the Ferris wheel first?"

"Yes," she answered. "He's been in remission for six months and is an adorable handful."

Rafael heard the happy laughter coming from the midway, saw many children tugging their parents toward rides, while others were already lined up for cotton candy or corn dogs or waiting for their chance to play a game of skill. Tickets weren't needed. Everything was free. "I want to help."

Nathalyia slid his handkerchief into the pocket of her navy slacks. "You are helping."

"I meant financially. You made a lot of people happy tonight." He looked around again at the children. "Patrick and Brianna are expecting their first child. I pray he or she is healthy, but some parents' prayers won't be answered."

Her fingertips brushed across his cheek. It was the second time she had voluntarily touched him. "You're the one who's amazing. I knew you'd understand."

Taking her hand, he kissed her palm. "Let's go watch your kids have fun."

Rafael was awed by the stamina of many of the children in the program. Like Nathalyia, he fully intended for them to have fun. When she held Ty up so he could have a better chance of putting a wooden ring around the neck of a bottle and he missed, Rafael reached for the young boy.

Rafael patiently showed Ty how to hold the ring over the target, and then held him over the rows of glass soft-drink bottles. The usual rules were suspended for the children in the program.

"You can do it, Ty," Nathalyia encouraged.

His parents, a couple in their late twenties, yelled encouragement as well. The little boy looked over his shoulder at Rafael, his bottom lip tucked between his teeth, and said, "I might miss."

"Then we'll try again," Rafael told him. "You can do it."

The little boy looked back at him, then twisted his head.

Sensing he was trying to see his parents, Rafael turned him back around. They each gave Ty two thumbs-up, along with Nathalyia.

"I'm ready."

Rafael held Ty over the bottles. The little boy reached his hand out, moving it first one way, then the other, before he stopped and dropped the wooden ring. The ring hit the top of the bottle and bounced off.

"Here's another one, Ty," Nathalyia said, coming to stand by them.

Ty took the ring, his face scrunched in determination. "I can do it this time."

"I never doubted it," Nathalyia said. "Your parents and I know you can."

"You ready, Ty?" Rafael asked.

"Yes, sir."

Rafael held Ty over the bottles. Almost immediately the little boy released the wooden ring. With a clink it dropped down over the top of a bottle.

"I did it! I did it!," he yelled.

"Yes, you did," Nathalyia said, applauding and cheering.

Chuckling, Rafael set Ty on his feet. Ty's parents were there to hug and congratulate him as he pointed to the stuffed elephant he wanted.

Nathalyia caught Rafael's hand and squeezed. "Thank you."

He nodded toward Ty, now clutching the stuffed animal. "That's thanks enough."

"Nathalyia," called a small, timid voice.

Rafael looked around to see a little girl with a special badge in a wheelchair. She was a beautiful child with large brown eyes and looked to be around six years old. She was ten. Rafael remembered checking Carmen in, the joy on her face. She'd made it to the carnival just as she'd wanted. She hadn't let sickle cell rule her life. Her older sister had brought her since both parents were at work.

Nathalyia knelt, placing her hand on the little girl's small one. "Hi, Carmen. What's up?"

Carmen looked up at Rafael, then leaned over to whisper something in Nathalyia's ear.

Nathalyia glanced up at Rafael. "I'd say your chance is excellent. Why don't you ask him?"

Rafael hunkered down on the other side of the wheelchair. "Hi, Carmen. I'm a pretty easy guy. Ask away."

"I'm next. Selma says she can't hold me over far enough." She glanced over her head at her older sister. "When it's my turn, can you help me?"

"Say please," Selma said.

"Please," Carmen added.

"Start picking out your prize," Rafael said with a wink.

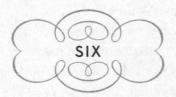

SIX

Rafael was a hit with the children. If Nathalyia had any lingering doubt that he had volunteered just to score points with her, she had quickly dismissed it.

The moment they arrived, he wanted to know how to help. It was he who had gotten the registration tables set up and then affixed the banner. Although he had to be tired after working all day, he hadn't complained when a line formed for him to help out at the ring toss.

His laughing comment had been, "I hope they have enough prizes."

Nathalyia had planned that each child could go home with at least one prize. With Rafael's help, many would go home with two or three.

The last happy and tired family left the carnival at nine thirty. Nathalyia waved the last volunteer off a short while later, then turned to Rafael, who had been beside her almost all evening. The only time he wasn't was when he was helping a child or taking one through the scary house or on a ride they weren't sure about.

"I know I keep saying it, but thank you."

"None needed." He caught her hand. "But I do have a couple of requests before I take you home."

She was intrigued and hoped one of those requests involved long, deep kisses. "I'm listening, but I'm going back to the restaurant."

He frowned. "It's close to ten. You've been on your feet for four hours straight."

"I used to be a waitress, remember," she told him. "What are the requests?"

He wasn't willing to let it go. "That was a long time ago. I'm sure you have people who can take care of things."

"I do, but it's my restaurant, my responsibility," she told him patiently. "I like being there at close. Now, stop stalling."

"You can be stubborn when it comes to Fontaine."

"Very."

His arms slipped around her waist. "Guess it's a good thing I understand responsibility and independence."

"Rafael, get to the point."

He kissed her on the forehead. "We never got to go on a ride together where you'd be scared and close your eyes and cling to me. Nor did we get around to your eating cotton candy, getting sticky, and me kissing it off. Nor did I have a chance to win you a stuffed animal so you'd be proud and happy."

Her heart sighed. "I've seen the Pavilion Amusement Park in Myrtle Beach several times. It gave me the idea for the carnival. When I was a teenager I wanted everything you mentioned, but that was long ago. Besides, they're closing up and I have to get back to work."

"You aren't the only one who can make a deal with the owner." Grabbing her hand, he started toward the carnival rides.

Surprised and pleased, Nathalyia allowed Rafael to lead her toward the Ferris wheel in the middle of the carnival. From the center of the Ferris wheel, lights exploded in various patterns. After helping her into a seat, Rafael sat beside her and closed the latch. The attendant checked the bar, nodded his approval, and went back to the controls.

Nathalyia clutched Rafael's arm at the first sudden jerk of the wheel, then she laughed. "I can't believe I did . . ." Her voice trailed off as they rose higher and she could view the surroundings. "Oh, my. It's beautiful."

Rafael curved his arm around her shoulders. "You're supposed to be scared."

She heard the teasing laughter in his voice and leaned into him. "Is this better?"

"Much." He wrapped his other arm around her and held her closer.

They went around three times before Nathalyia was satisfied enough to move to one ride after another. She was spending as much time as possible with Rafael holding her.

Rafael slowly walked Nathalyia to the front door of Fontaine. It was thirty minutes before closing. A steady stream of people passed them. "I'll wait in the bar until you're ready to go home."

"I hate to keep repeating myself, but Jake can take me home."

"I'm taking you home." He leaned over and whispered in her ear. "I'm looking forward to my good-night kiss." He straightened to open the front door and ushered her inside. "Just let me know when you're ready." Not giving her a chance to argue, he went to the bar.

As he expected, the bar was a beehive of activity. There were only a couple of empty seats at the bar and one table open. Not wanting to take up a table in case there were late arrivals—which he hoped there weren't—he took a seat at the end of the bar where he'd have a clear view of Nathalyia heading to her office.

She stopped, waved, and continued on. He waved back, looking forward to the time when they'd be alone and he'd have her in his arms again.

"What can I get you?"

Rafael's gaze moved to the bald-headed bartender he knew was Jake, who had the muscular build of a man who took care of his body. Rafael didn't know what the connection was between the two, but from the hard look in Jake's blue eyes, he wouldn't have any problem rearranging Rafael's face if he stepped out of line with Nathalyia.

"You drinking or not?"

"Iced tea," Rafael answered.

The bartender's eyes widened a fraction. The order obviously surprised him, but Rafael could see Jake couldn't decide if Rafael was trying to be funny. "I seldom drink liquor," Rafael explained. He and Nathalyia were getting along well. He didn't need any waves. From the distrustful way Jake stared at him, he could cause a tidal wave of problems.

"Hi, Rafael." Clarice stopped beside him. "You abandoning me?"

He smiled into her mischievous face. She'd pulled her shoulder-length red hair into a ponytail. "I didn't want to take up space if there were any latecomers."

"Considerate, but unnecessary." Clarice looked at Jake. "He drinks iced tea, Jake."

"I can handle the bar," he said, and moved off.

Clarice stuck out her tongue at Jake's retreating back, then turned to Rafael. "His bark is worse than his bite." She leaned over. "I'm on your side; he isn't."

"I figured as much. Thank you, but do you mind if I ask why?"

"Nathalyia is a fabulous boss and a dynamic businesswoman, but you know what they say about all work and no play," Clarice told him. "She needs to have a little fun."

The glass of iced tea hit the bar with a thump. "Table eight is trying to get your attention."

"I can handle my tables," she said with the same bite. "He's had enough. I was on my way to the kitchen to get him a cup of coffee."

"What's keeping you?"

"Jake, you try my patience." She reached over and patted his scarred cheek. The burly man jerked his head back and looked ready to bolt. "It's a good thing I know why you're so grouchy." She looked at Rafael. "Duty calls."

Rafael stared at her as she continued toward the kitchen. "She's something."

"Isn't one woman enough?" Jake snapped.

Rafael knew a jealous man when he saw one. He casually picked up his tea and sipped. "I can admire a woman without lusting after her."

"I'm watching you." With that warning, Jake moved off.

"You're the cause of that," Jake muttered as they neared Clarice's car in the back parking lot. Fontaine had closed for the night.

"That" was Rafael and Nathalyia leaving together. Clarice watched the taillights of the Mustang disappear around the corner of the restaurant. Clarice didn't care what Jake thought. It did her heart good to know that there were still good, caring men out there. Which meant there might be a man out there for her.

"I know you heard me."

Continuing to ignore Jake, Clarice kept walking. Although he was peeved with her, he walked her to her car as he did every night she worked.

She hadn't once thought he wouldn't. Jake was a man with a strong code of right and wrong, a true Southern gentleman where women were concerned, the kind of man she'd met precious few of.

"Just because he's a cop doesn't mean he can be trusted."

Clarice threw an impatient look at Jake and stopped. He looked angry, but there were lines of worry in his strong face.

Nathalyia was a grown woman, and although he didn't like her dating Rafael, he was powerless to stop her. Without thinking, Clarice gently touched Jake's arm. This time he didn't jerk back.

In her experience, it was rare to find a man who truly cared. Her father had left soon after she was born. Her two brothers didn't come around unless they needed money. Men wanted to use her, not protect and love her.

"Jake, I agree that my track record is a disaster, but you have to admit, we haven't seen her this happy in a long time."

"He could be biding his time."

"Or he could genuinely care about her. I think he does and wants this to work out for them. I think she does, too," Clarice told him.

"He just better not hurt her." Jake's expression hardened. "I'm watching him."

Clarice wanted to give Jake a comforting hug. He had his mind made up, and nothing she could say would change it. "Why don't you trust him?"

"It's been my experience working the bar that a lot of men who look like him play the field." Anger flared in his eyes again. "He was looking at you."

She laughed. "Rafael was just being friendly. He has no interest in me. Look at me. Why should he want me when he has Nathalyia?"

"There's nothing wrong with the way you look," Jake snapped.

She frowned. "Rafael really has you steamed. Tell you what. I'll hold him while you beat him to a pulp if you're right. If I'm right, you take me for a ride on that snazzy motorcycle of yours."

She rolled her eyes at the panicked look in his, the same look he'd given her when she'd first brought it up when he'd walked her to her car last month and she'd seen the gleaming red and black motorcycle. "I've seen people riding motorcycles that are heavier than I am."

"I told you, it's not that." He stuffed his hands into his pockets. "I just don't like people riding on my motorcycle."

"I'm not 'people,'" she told him. At her car, she manually unlocked it and opened the door.

"I thought you were going to have the automatic lock fixed?" Jake said, holding the door as she got inside.

"It was more than replacing the battery in the key like I thought. The apartment deposit took precedence." She started the motor. "And before you lecture me again, I always have my key out and I look around to check my surroundings when I approach my car and my apartment."

"It's better to be safe than sorry. Night." He closed the door.

Clarice lowered the window. Thank goodness it still worked. The one on the passenger side didn't. Jake would have a fit if he knew. "Good night, Jake. Nathalyia will be fine, and I want my ride."

He stepped back. "Drive safely."

Clarice backed out and drove away. Jake watched until she was on the street, then slowly walked to his Trans Am. It was a good thing she didn't know he cared or his slip about the cop watching her might have made her suspicious or, worse, uncomfortable.

Although it was rough being around her when he was unable to tell her how he felt, at least he was near her. As for his taking her for a ride on his bike, he'd like nothing better. But that would mean she would have to hold on to him, press her lush body against his. It would be sheer torture, physically and emotionally.

Head down, he walked to his car. Perhaps he should cruise by Nathalyia's house. He discarded the idea almost before it formed. She wouldn't appreciate it, and it would solve nothing. All he could do was watch and wait. But if the cop messed up, he'd answer to him.

"I don't think your bartender likes me," Rafael said, his arms around Nathalyia's waist as they stood in the foyer of her house.

"I'm sorry. Jake and Martin were very close friends. I think Martin asked him to look after me."

Rafael stared down at Nathalyia's beautiful, trusting face and felt protective, an emotion he'd never experienced before to this degree with a woman he'd dated. He could easily see why her husband wanted to ensure she was taken care of after he was gone. He could even see Jake's point, and was glad he was there to watch out for her.

"Don't apologize. He can try to scare me off all he wants." He gathered her closer. "I'm not going anywhere."

"I'm glad." She lifted her mouth to his, her body curving naturally into his. He felt the warmth, smelled the floral scent mixed with spices she always wore, felt her tremble in his arms.

"I better let you get some sleep." He eased her away from him. He was more than ready to take her to bed, but she wasn't there yet. He sincerely hoped it wasn't too much longer.

"I had a wonderful time on the rides. Thanks for indulging me."

After the Ferris wheel she had wanted to ride the Tilt-A-Whirl and the carousel. She'd been as gleeful as the children had been earlier. "Since we never made it to the concession stands or the games, how about we go bowling tomorrow night? Before you say no, I can pick you up around seven and have you back by nine."

"I don't know how to bowl," she said with a frown.

"I can teach you," he told her.

He could see the possibility of his doing just that take root in her mind. She looked up at him through a sweep of her lashes. "You'd have to stand extremely close to show me."

"Yes, I would."

She leaned into him. "Then how can I refuse?"

A few minutes after ten the next morning Rafael punched in Nathalyia's cell phone number and waited for her to pick up. He couldn't keep the wide grin off his face.

"Hello."

His smile widened. "Morning, Nathalyia. I was thinking that you never got your corn dog or cotton candy last night."

"I got my rides," she said, laughter in her voice.

"Doesn't count as the true carnival experience," Rafael said. "Would it be disloyal to Fontaine if you ate food from another restaurant on the premises?"

"You're at the carnival?"

"The mall," he answered. He'd been waiting at the door when it opened. He'd come up with the idea while shaving. "Should I bring them to you or can you meet me?"

"I haven't agreed to anything."

"Couldn't slip that one by you, huh?"

"No," she said, chuckling, "I'm Fontaine's event coordinator, and I need to return several phone calls this morning."

"Come on, Nathalyia. You probably didn't eat breakfast again. I'm already the talk of Corn Dog World. We could sit in the courtyard and enjoy the beginning of a beautiful day."

"It had better be the best corn dog ever," she said.

"If not, we'll find another place and keep trying. See you in fifteen."

Nathalyia was waiting for Rafael on the covered patio when he pulled up. The man was built and a great kisser to boot. He made life interesting and fun. Slamming out of his car, he waved and hurried to her. She eyed the large drink and paper bag. "Corn dogs for breakfast."

"It's a first for me, too." He nodded to the small white wrought-iron table behind her. On top were plates and flatware. "I see you have things ready."

"Of course." Nathalyia took the bag from him and placed one corn dog on her plate and two on his. Beside each plate were small containers of ketchup and mustard.

"I'm saving the cotton candy for another time." He leaned over and whispered in her ear. "When I can leisurely kiss it from your mouth."

Heat zipped though her. Her eyes went to his mouth.

"Don't look at me like that or I'll get us both in trouble." He pulled out a chair.

She sat because her legs were trembling. Taking the chair next to hers, he scooted closer and put the corn dogs on one plate. "Mustard or ketchup?"

She had never had one before and didn't care that much for

hot dogs. Rafael, not the food, had caused her to leave the work piled on her desk. "Mustard," she answered, her voice breathy.

Dunking the corn dog in the mustard, he held it to her mouth. She took a small bite. He watched her the entire time.

"Good?" he questioned.

She nodded. "Good. You're saved."

Chuckling, he dabbed the corn dog into the mustard and took a huge bite. He pushed the drink toward her. "Have a sip."

It finally dawned on her that he planned for them to share. She drank the strawberry lemonade, leaving traces of her lipstick on the rim of the paper cup. He picked up the cup and placed his mouth exactly where hers had been. Her stomach muscles tightened. "I think it's you who's going to get me into trouble."

His eyes heated. "Tonight can't come fast enough for me."

"Me, either." She took the corn dog from him, took a bite, dabbed it in mustard, and offered it to him. "When do you think you might find that cotton candy?"

The bowling alley was like nothing Nathalyia had ever seen. She should have known it was different when Rafael pulled up in front of the valet stand and then, at a door covered with red quilted leather, they were welcomed by a hostess.

Inside, the décor was ultramodern in shades of red, black, and orange. Instead of a concession stand there was a sushi bar and a restaurant. There was the sound of bowling balls hitting and rolling down the lanes, then slamming into the pins, and laughter filled the air.

After they'd put on their bowling shoes and secured their lane, Rafael patiently showed her how to hold the ball and how to follow through on her swing.

"I might regret this," Rafael said, then shook his head. "A pink bowling ball."

"I won't tell anyone if you don't," she told him with a grin.

He curved his arms across her waist. "See that you don't."

She wanted to stay there in his arms, basking in the approval in his beautiful black eyes. She might have been embarrassed if there hadn't been an announcement at eight P.M. that no one under seventeen would be allowed to remain. There had been shouts of approval. Couples were more affectionate, but no one went overboard. "I promise."

He tilted his head downward, then stopped inches from her waiting lips and released her. Regret stared back at her. "You make me forget."

"Is that good or bad?" she asked.

"Let's say it's a first," he said slowly, as if he wasn't sure how he felt about it.

"It's a first for me as well." She tilted her head to one side. "Just like the corn dog breakfast this morning."

His smile returned. "Like I said, stick with me."

She had every intention of doing just that. Pushing herself out of his arms, she went to the bowling lane and picked the ball up the way he had shown her earlier. She glanced around at the bowlers on either side of her. Bowling pins went crashing down for a strike. Yells went up. Fists were pumped.

"Everyone has to learn. Come on and show me what you can do with Ms. Pinkie," Rafael told her and stepped back.

Staring at the pins, she breathed deeply, took four steps, and released the bowling ball, trying to follow through on the swing and keep her arm straight. She grimaced as the hot pink ball bumped before rolling toward the row of pins, then slowly curved to the left.

"No. No," she said. The ball kept going, clipping a pin just before it plopped into the gutter. Disappointed, she turned to Rafael. "I know, I was horrible."

"The first time I went bowling it was on a school field trip. It took me three tries before I hit a single pin." He glanced at her ball as it came back. "You have another try. Put more speed on it and keep your eye on the center pin."

Nathalyia picked up her ball, went over the steps in her head, and tried again. The ball stayed in the center of the lane this time, maintaining speed instead of slowing down, hitting the center pin, knocking all the pins down.

Nathalyia screamed with glee. Pumping her arms, she ran to Rafael. "I did it! I did it!"

"I'd say you and Ms. Pinkie are off to a good start."

Rafael circled the parking lot on returning to Fontaine. With Nathalyia sitting beside him, he didn't mind. He enjoyed being with her. "We could always go back for another game."

"Don't tempt me. At the end I finally managed to hit at least one pin each time I bowled. All I need is more practice."

Leaning over, he kissed her on the cheek. "I'd like nothing better than to tempt you, and I know exactly what I'd like to practice."

She looked up at him through a sweep of lashes. "There should be a free parking space in the employee parking area." She pulled a placard emblazoned with Fontaine written in bold letters out of her purse and hung it on his mirror. "Since you're picking me up and dropping me off, your car qualifies."

"Thank you." He reached over and lifted her chin. "I'll only use it when I return with you. By then all the employees should be here already."

"I wouldn't have given it to you if I had thought differently."

Rafael drove around to the back of the restaurant. A large sign read EMPLOYEE PARKING ONLY. He pulled into one of two remaining parking spaces.

The area was well lit, but the lights were low enough that the interior of his car remained in the shadows. In his rearview mirror, he didn't see any movement. He hadn't done this since high school, but he didn't hesitate.

He moved his seat back, then picked Nathalyia up around her waist and sat her in his lap. She came willingly, her arms circling his neck; her mouth, a scant inch away, beckoned. He was unable to resist. His mouth took hers, hot and hungry, as he'd wanted to do all night. Her mouth was just as hungry. He felt her tremble, the restless movements of her body against his.

She had to feel the bulge in his lap, just as he felt the hardness of her nipples pushing against his chest, begging for his hand, his mouth. Her trust helped him resist taking things further.

His phone vibrated in his pocket. Muttering under his breath, he sat her back in her seat. "Sorry."

He flipped open the phone and accepted the call, closing his hand over Nathalyia's as he listened to his commander.

"I can be at the station in less than twenty minutes," he said, then disconnected the call.

"Is it dangerous?" she asked, her gaze direct, her voice tremulous.

"No." He palmed her face, stared into her wide eyes. "I'm backup. I can't discuss the case, but there's no danger to me or the other negotiator."

She pressed a quick kiss to his lips, then reached for the door. "Call me, no matter how late."

He caught her arm. "I'll walk you to the back door."

"I'd argue if I knew it wouldn't make you late. Come on."

Rafael climbed out of the car, meeting Nathalyia at the back bumper of his Mustang and caught her hand, felt it tremble. His arm curved around her shoulder, drawing her closer, kissing her temple. "I won't be in any danger. I promise."

Silently, they went up the steps. She punched in the code on the lock, heard it disengage, and opened the door. "Call. No matter how late," she repeated.

"I promise."

She touched his cheek and slipped through the door, closing it behind her.

Nathalyia kept the radio and the television on in her upstairs bedroom once she arrived home. The news had picked up Rafael's case. A man had botched an ATM robbery, and when he was surrounded by police cars a couple of blocks away, he threatened to kill himself.

The alleged robber, as the newscaster kept calling him, had been in his battered Ford for the past three hours with a handgun. All the news reported was that there was a hostage negotiator on the scene. She had no way of determining whether it was Rafael or someone else and he was still backup. At least he and the other policemen weren't in any immediate danger.

The music on the radio was abruptly interrupted for a live report from the scene. She rushed to turn up the radio on her night table.

"Moments ago, the alleged robber threw his handgun out the window and emerged from his car with his hands raised. He was promptly surrounded by several policemen, handcuffed, and taken away in a police car. The standoff is over. No shots were fired."

Saying a prayer of thanks, Nathalyia plopped down, then pounced for the ringing phone. "Rafael?"

"It's almost two. Why aren't you asleep?"

"I couldn't."

"Nathalyia, there was never any danger."

"I know in my head— It's just—" She plucked at the hem of her pajama top and wondered how she could ask him to come over. She just needed to see him.

"Get some sleep," he said. "I usually spend Sundays with my brothers and their families."

She wouldn't see him today. Her arm wrapped around her waist. Loneliness settled over her like a heavy cloak. When had seeing him become so important? "They'll want to see you even more after tonight."

"Since all I did was hang out in the command center, I doubt it." There was a slight pause. She heard a door close, then the purr of an engine. "Tonight was no big deal except that it kept us apart."

"We'll just have to resume practice when we see each other the next time."

A sharp intake of breath came over the receiver. "Nat."

She liked the way he shortened her name. She might not have that much experience, but she recognized the desire in his gravelly voice. "I guess I shouldn't have said that."

"It was exactly the right thing to say."

She relaxed. "Thanks for calling me."

"I didn't want you to worry. I'm as safe as if I were there with you."

"I wish you were," she said. The words just slipped out and she didn't know if she wanted to take them back or not.

"You don't know how much I wish I were, but it might be best that I'm driving home instead of to your house."

"Probably." She wanted to be with him, just relax, and not worry about anything. "How does your schedule look for Thursday evening? You can come over here around seven. I can grill outside on the patio."

"Great. I can take you back to the restaurant and then pick you up later."

"I don't think they'll miss me for one night," she said, then groaned inwardly. What if he thought she planned for them to spend the night together?

"Since I won't overstay my welcome, how about we work around your schedule and go check out your competition for dinner Friday, and a movie Saturday?"

Saved. "I'd like that."

"Now, let's discuss Monday, Tuesday, and Wednesday."

SEVEN

"Domino!" Sam shouted with glee. "Simon and I win again."

Alec frowned at Rafael sitting across from him. "If my partner had his mind on the game, perhaps we'd make a better showing."

Rafael shoved his dominoes into the pile on the card table. "I told you I didn't feel like playing."

"You're usually the one wanting to play," Alec pointed out. "What's different today? It couldn't be the standoff last night. It went off without a hitch."

Rafael could feel the stares of everyone in the room. He loved them, but he wasn't ready to discuss the restlessness he felt.

"Rafael has had a tough week." Helen nudged his shoulder. "I'll take this hand. Alec and I will take that smirk off Sam's face. Sorry, Simon."

"You can try." Sam began shuffling the dominoes. "Give her your seat, Rafael."

Rafael slowly stood. Almost immediately, Helen slid into the seat. "We're running low on drinks and ice. Patrick, do you mind making a run?"

"Sorry, Helen. Can't," Patrick said, then kissed Brianna, who was sitting on his lap. "We're keeping score."

"I can go," Maureen offered.

Simon caught her hand and pulled her closer. "If we get trounced I'll need moral support."

Laughing, she leaned into him, kissing his cheek. "Then how could I possibly leave you."

"I'll go," Celeste offered.

"No!" came the response from everyone.

Celeste lifted a delicate brow. "Just because my last trip to the convenience store didn't turn out as planned, there is no reason to suspect this one won't."

"I'll go." Rafael fished his keys out of his pocket. Perhaps a drive would clear his head.

The door had barely closed behind him before Sam leaned over and kissed Helen. "You still got it. He doesn't have a clue."

"He's finally found a woman he can't forget." Helen pulled the dominoes to her.

"It's about time." Alec picked up his dominoes. "I wonder if he'll have sense enough to call her or at least drive over to the restaurant."

"If he's not as stubborn as his older brother, he might," Celeste commented.

"Ouch!" Alec said, then grinned. He'd fought hard to resist falling in love with Celeste, and to his everlasting delight had failed miserably.

"I hope he brings her back," Brianna said, standing to press her hand into the small of her back.

Patrick came to his feet immediately and began to rub her back. "Better?"

"Much," she said, leaning against him.

Helen glanced around the room. "Let's hope Rafael has the same good instincts as his brothers."

"Amen to that," Sam said and picked up his dominoes. Then he grinned. "You're about to go down, Helen, my love."

Helen picked up her hand, then looked up at Maureen. "Stick close to Simon. He's going to need you."

"What are you doing here?"

The mere fact that Rafael asked himself the question signaled he was in trouble, for he had absolutely no answer. He turned into the parking lot of Fontaine behind two other cars. At least he had the presence of mind to call Helen and tell her he had to make a short run before he came back.

"We already beat Sam and Simon once, so take your time," Helen said gleefully, then hung up.

Simon was indulgent with Helen, but he was also competitive, as were the rest of his brothers. The domino game would be fierce, which meant no one would miss him.

Rafael turned into an aisle, trying to find a parking spot. There was none. He grabbed his cell and called the restaurant. There was another car ahead of him and one behind. It wasn't likely that he'd get a space any time soon. He might have been tempted to use the employee parking placard, but that lot was full, too.

"Fontaine, please hold."

Rafael's fingers tapped impatiently on the steering wheel.

"Fontaine, how may I assist you?" came a cheery voice.

"Nathalyia Fontaine, please," Rafael requested. A couple passed his car and got into a truck just ahead of the car in front of him.

"Ms. Fontaine is on the floor and unavailable. I can take a message if you'd like, or you can call back in an hour."

The car ahead of him whipped in as soon as the truck backed out. He didn't doubt the woman was following Nathalyia's orders. Customers came first. "Is Clarice available?"

"Employees aren't allowed to take calls unless it's an emergency. Is this an emergency?"

Depends on your definition, he thought. The urgent need to see Nathalyia, to hold her and kiss her, was new to him. "No, it's not a true emergency, but it is important. If you'll please just tell either of them Rafael called, I'd appreciate it. I can't find a parking space."

"I will, sir."

Rafael ended the call. He'd make one more round and then he was leaving.

"Excuse me, Ms. Fontaine, but you're needed."

Nathalyia glanced around at the sound of Clarice's anxious voice, the firm hand on her arm. She had been about to approach the next table. She couldn't read anything in the waitress's face. "Certainly." She allowed herself to be led away.

None of the employees disturbed her while she was making rounds unless it was extremely important. She frowned when Clarice led her outside. "Where are we going?"

"Rafael called. He can't find a parking space." Clarice released Nathalyia's arm, searching the crowded parking lot. "The hostess just told me he asked for you, then me. You have your cell, so you can call him."

"It's in my office." Nathalyia never carried it with her when she made rounds. Martin had thought it disrespectful. She started back inside.

"Wait!" Clarice caught her arm. "Isn't that his car?"

Nathalyia saw the slow-moving black Mustang and started

toward it. She reached the edge of the walk and looked back. Clarice waved her on. "We won't miss you for an hour or so."

Nathalyia bit her lower lip in indecision. The restaurant had always come first. Yesterday she'd put work aside for the impromptu breakfast and later to go bowling.

"Nathalyia."

Her head came back around. Rafael stood by the car with the driver's door open. She went to him. He didn't say a word. He didn't have to. The hot desire in his intense gaze said it all. Her body trembled. "I can't stay long."

Quickly rounding the car, he opened the passenger door. She slid into the seat. In a matter of seconds Rafael was behind the wheel and they were driving away.

Rafael tossed a glance at Nathalyia. She stared straight ahead, her hands clasped in her lap. His hand covered hers, felt them tremble.

"I don't want to, but I'll take you back if this is going to upset you."

"No." Finally, she looked at him. "I'm not the spontaneous type. At least I didn't used to be."

He stopped at a traffic light and shifted into park. "My sister-in-law sent me for ice and drinks and I ended up at Fontaine."

"And you couldn't find a parking space," she said.

"Nor was the woman who answered the phone willing to get you or Clarice," he complained, then pulled through the light.

"I have rules," she said. "I'm here now."

"Which might have saved my sanity. You look beautiful."

"Thank you." Some of her worry fading, she turned to him. "Did you pick up the drinks and ice?"

"Yes."

"Is that where we're headed now? To your brother's house?" she asked.

He shoved a hand over his head. "I can't see any help for it."

"But you're not pleased with the idea because I'm with you," she said, her hands linked in her lap again.

Rafael remembered her elegant fingers in his hair, her slim arms around his neck, her slender body pressed against his. Need and heat zipped though him. "I don't want them making more of this than there is."

"I see." She twisted her hands in her lap. "I can stay in the car."

"No." He reached over to squeeze her hands. "No," he repeated, then his voice softened. "It's probably for the best. I don't want you going back looking any different than when you left. If we went somewhere else, I wouldn't be able to keep my hands off you. We'd definitely do a lot of practice. I'm having a hard time now keeping my hands off you and that tie on your dress."

He pulled up in front of a two-story frame home painted white with blue trim and shutters. The lawn was neatly trimmed, with beds of red rose bushes. "We're here. The trucks belong to my brothers."

"Rafael, I don't mind waiting for you."

"I do." Unable to resist, he slid his hand around her neck and kissed her. "It won't be bad, and we won't stay long."

Nathalyia didn't know what to expect when Rafael opened the front door of his brother's house, calling out to his family as he ushered her inside the comfortably furnished house. Conversation came to an abrupt halt when they entered the screened back porch.

"I can see why it took you so long." A slightly older version of Rafael came to his feet, a welcoming smile on his handsome face.

"Hello, Mrs. Fontaine. I'm Sam Dunlap, Rafael's oldest brother. This beauty is my wife, Helen."

"Hello," Nathalyia greeted, wondering if he recognized her from the restaurant or if Rafael had mentioned her. "I've heard so much about you."

Sam's brow lifted at her admission. She didn't have long to think about it because Helen and the rest of the people in the room stepped forward.

"Welcome," Helen said, her smile warm and bright as the sun shining outside. "We've eaten at your restaurant and enjoyed it immensely."

"Simon Dunlap, and this is my better half, Maureen. It's nice to meet you."

"Patrick Dunlap, next to the oldest." He hugged the beautiful pregnant woman by his side. "My wife, Brianna."

"Alec Dunlap, and this is Celeste de la Vega, soon to be Mrs. Dunlap."

"It's nice meeting you. I didn't mean to interrupt," Nathalyia said.

Helen laughed, taking Nathalyia's arm. "Sam is probably glad. Alec and I were trouncing him and Simon. Let's go into the kitchen and get dessert." She winked at her husband. "It's apple strudel."

Nathalyia had no choice but to follow. Rafael placed the ice in the sink and the drinks on the counter. "You need any help?"

Helen pushed him out of the kitchen. "He's a work in progress in the kitchen. Nathalyia, if you don't mind, please get the dessert plates. They're in the third cabinet." Helen uncovered a glass baking dish containing the apple strudel. "Celeste, you know where the spoons are."

"I got the napkins." Brianna laughed and faced Nathalyia. "If I lift anything heavier, Patrick becomes annoyed with me."

"I'll get the ice cream." Maureen opened the freezer.

Nathalyia placed the plates on the counter. "Is there anything else I can do to help?"

"No." Helen expertly cut the strudel into large squares. "I'm just glad I didn't cook bread pudding. Yours is fabulous."

Nathalyia relaxed the tiniest bit. "Thank you. It's my own recipe. The cook had to sign a confidentiality clause. He's been with Fontaine for five years."

Helen nodded in approval. "That's smart."

Maureen scooped the vanilla ice cream on top of the apple strudel and handed the plate to Nathalyia. "Very. Restaurant competition is fierce. Nathalyia, you're obviously doing something very right."

"Thank you."

"Serve the first one to Sam," Helen said with a smile. "It will help soothe his ego since he lost three straight games of dominoes."

"If not, there are always other ways." Brianna clapped her hand over her mouth, then lowered her hands. "Blame it on the hormones."

"For being right?" Helen questioned, her expression innocent.

The women burst out laughing, Nathalyia joining them.

Less than an hour later Rafael reluctantly parked in the employee parking space in back of Fontaine. "I wish it were dark so I could kiss you."

"So do I," Nathalyia said, then smiled. "I enjoyed meeting your family."

His hand curved around her neck to keep it away from the tantalizing tie of her dress at her slim waist. "They like you, too. None of them could believe you couldn't play dominoes."

"It's one of the fun things I'm adding to the list you're going to teach me."

His eyes darkened. "I know what I'd like to be doing with you that's at the top of that list."

"Unfortunately, not now or tonight." She reached for her door handle. "Goodbye."

His hand closed over hers. "I wish you didn't have to go back inside, but I understand that you do."

She looked toward the restaurant, then stared at him longingly. "I wish I didn't have to either."

His hand clenched hers instead of moving to the gearshift and putting the car into reverse. She might leave with him, but she'd regret it later. "That makes leaving you easier, and makes me look forward even more to tomorrow night."

The corners of her mouth tilted upward. "I'm sure I'll be equally terrible as I was at bowling."

He brushed his thumb across her lower lip. "Then we'll just keep on practicing."

Her teeth scraped over his thumb, and bit down. His breath hissed though his teeth as desire shot through him. "I'm holding you to that." She opened the door, and was gone.

Rafael got out of the car and watched her walk across the parking lot and up the back stairs. He admired the way the silken material hugged her glorious body and showed off her great legs. At the back door, she punched in the code, waved, and then slipped inside. Tomorrow night couldn't come soon enough for him.

On Monday night, Rafael and Nathalyia had gone roller-skating. Tuesday evening, they had played miniature golf. Wednesday they had gone paddleboat riding. Rafael was aware as he kept glancing at the miniature clock on his desk on Thursday afternoon that he had purposely chosen things that would require him to hold her or be very close to her.

He accepted he wanted her as close as possible when they were together. He also got a kick out of introducing her to new things. She enjoyed what she did, but she wasn't competitive.

He glanced at the clock again: 5:30 P.M. In thirty minutes he was off. He was going home to shower and change and then go to Nathalyia's house. He was looking forward to being with her when they didn't have to watch a clock.

He didn't anticipate the evening ending in bed, but he did anticipate lots of practice in what was becoming his favorite pastime—kissing Nathalyia. Her mouth could be both sweet and seductive.

At 5:47 P.M. Rafael moved the cursor to shut down his computer. Sometimes the machine was slow. He wanted to be walking out the door at 6:02.

"Listen up."

Rafael's head came up at his team commander's order. *No. No!* his mind shouted.

"We've been assigned to help with crowd control at the Oyster Festival. We leave in forty minutes," Captain Coats told them and then turned to leave.

Rafael followed him into the hallway. "Captain."

His commander turned. "Dunlap."

"Is the entire team needed?" he asked.

"Isn't that what I just said?" the commander answered.

Rafael was not backing down. One more man wouldn't make that much difference. The commander was a reasonable man. "I have plans."

The commander folded his arms across his thin chest. He peered at Rafael from beneath bushy gray eyebrows. "You're probably not the only one with plans, nor is this the first time you've had to cancel."

He didn't want to cancel. He wanted to be with Nathalyia.

His commanding officer studied him. "The restaurateur?"

There was no way around answering the question. "Yes, sir."

His arms fell to his sides. "I'll tell you what my commander told me when I was dating Maria before we married. Absence makes the heart grow fonder." He looked at his watch. "We leave in thirty-seven minutes."

Rafael watched his commander leave, then pulled out his cell to call Nathalyia.

"Hi, are you on your way over?" Nathalyia asked.

"No." He blew out a breath. "My team is going to help with crowd control at the Oyster Festival. My commander just told us."

"Oh."

He heard the disappointment in her voice. "I tried to get out of it, but no go."

"Doesn't your team act as a unit?"

He looked at his team members making their own phone calls. They were there for one another. Period. "Yes."

"I was looking forward to you coming over, but if your team needs you, then that's where you should be," she told him. "How long do you think you'll be?"

"I have no idea." He walked to his desk to shut off the monitor. If anyone understood responsibility, it was Nathalyia. "I'll call if we finish before the restaurant closes, but tonight is out. I'm sorry you went to all the trouble for nothing."

"Don't worry about it. Thanks for the call. Be careful."

"I will. Bye." He hung up and went to get ready.

Saturday morning Rafael wasn't in his usual good mood, and he knew the reason. Picking up the dry cloth, he slid it over the hood of his newly washed car. Nathalyia had had to cancel last night and tonight. She'd sounded tired. She took on too many responsibilities at the restaurant, but he wasn't about to suggest she hire someone to help out. He didn't want her to think he thought she couldn't handle things or for her to think she should stop dating him and spend more time at the restaurant.

Finished, he picked up another cloth to polish the chrome. The vintage Mustang had been a high school graduation present from his family. It had been a chick magnet. He sighed. There was only one woman he wanted riding in his car.

"You keep it looking good."

Rafael started, then glanced around at the sound of Helen's voice. She was already out of her car and coming down the driveway toward him. He'd been so deep in thought he hadn't heard her drive up. "Hi, Helen. You want a cup of coffee?" he asked, then smiled. "I'm getting better at making it."

"Maybe next time." She looked at the house. "Your parents loved this place, loved each other, their sons."

Something about her voice had him stepping closer. His hand closed over her upper forearm. "Are you all right?"

She turned and stared up at him. "I'm fine. I'm beginning to wonder about you, though."

"Me?" He frowned. "I'm fine."

"Rafael, don't be afraid to follow your heart."

His frown deepened. "What are you talking about?"

"Nathalyia."

His hand came to his side. He stepped back. "We're just having fun."

Her smile was sad. "Then why have you been so restless and preoccupied lately? I watched you after I drove up. You were just standing there staring into space, looking miserable."

He shrugged and tossed the cloth on the hood of the car. "So I like being with her. It's no big deal."

Helen kept her gaze steady. "It is if you let fear rule you."

"Fear?" he said, then his expression cleared. Helen was intuitive. Perhaps he had said or done something that alerted her to his feelings about long-term relationships. "My job is too dangerous. I won't leave a woman and child behind."

Helen touched his cheek with trembling fingertips. "It's not fear for them. You fear for yourself."

Rafael was stunned. He'd always considered Helen to be on target, but she had missed the mark this time.

"Your mother's death affected all of you. You felt the pain and loss the deepest. You were angry at first, then you seemed to want to cram life into every second. You dated more than ever. You didn't want to care about anyone that deeply again and lose them."

"You're wrong," he told her fiercely. "If your theory is right, which it isn't, it wouldn't make a difference because, although I enjoy Nathalyia, it won't last. It never does."

She shook her head. "You feel differently about her. Could you face not seeing her again?"

His heart thudded. His gut clenched.

"The answer is on your face." Her hand palmed his cheek. "I love you, Rafael. One day you'll have to face your feelings, and when you do, I pray you'll make the right decision." On tiptoe, she brushed her lips against his cheek. "Sam is barbecuing for our Sunday dinner. I'm making a huge peach cobbler. If you want to bring Nathalyia, there'll be plenty of food. See you tomorrow."

Rafael watched Helen get into her car and drive away. She was wrong. Just because he wasn't ready to end things with Nathalyia didn't mean anything. Picking up the cloth, he bent to polish the chrome on his car.

Fate was conspiring against them, Nathalyia thought as she served a couple their order of the fried catfish and oyster platter on

Saturday night. Two servers were out sick, another had an ill child, and a fourth had car trouble. She and Rafael hadn't been able to go to dinner on Friday night, and the movies tonight were out as well.

"Is there anything else I can get you?" Nathalyia picked up the deck tray and stand.

"More butter for the baked potato."

"Bread," the woman requested. "I love your bread."

"Thank you. We make it here. I'll get those right out." Nathalyia headed for the kitchen, checking on customers as she went. She didn't see anyone with bored or annoyed looks and counted herself lucky. She had an excellent staff, but they were all busy trying to keep up, and the pace didn't show any signs of letting up.

It was a little past ten and people were crowded by the hostess stand or in the bar waiting to be seated in the main dining room. Business was good, and while she was grateful, she wanted to see Rafael. That wasn't going to happen.

She'd called him that morning and canceled. She just hoped he didn't get tired of waiting on her.

Clarice came through the swinging doors of the kitchen carrying a tray loaded with bread and salads. Nathalyia had changed her assignment to the dining room. As she had expected, Clarice had no trouble adjusting.

"Rafael came in five minutes ago," Clarice told her in passing.

"What?" Nathalyia glanced in the direction of the bar. She didn't see him. "I told him not to come."

"Guess he didn't listen." Clarice continued past her.

Nathalyia glanced toward the bar again, then went to the kitchen for the bread and butter. She placed the items on a tray, then went to the table and served them. "How is the food?"

"Delicious as usual," the young woman said. The man, with a mouth full of food, nodded in agreement.

"Excellent." Nathalyia picked up the tray and headed for the bar. She could tell herself that she was checking on the guests on that side of the room, which she was, but she also wanted to see Rafael.

She hadn't seen him since Wednesday night, when he had followed her home. They'd shared a brief kiss and then he was gone, saying she had to be tired. She was, but she hadn't wanted him to leave.

She entered the bar area and frowned when she didn't immediately find him. People were two deep around the bar. Jake and the other two bartenders were extremely busy. Nathalyia walked farther into the bar. She scowled when she saw a female customer practically in Rafael's lap. Nathalyia's temper spiked. She began to work her way through customers.

"Excuse me," Nathalyia said tensely. The redhead glanced around, a frown on her pretty face.

Rafael took the opportunity to stand. "Hi." He turned to the woman. "Excuse us, please."

The women glared at Nathalyia, then took a seat at the booth where three other women were sitting.

Rafael reached out and caught Nathalyia's hand before the woman moved away. He uncurled her clenched fingers. "Never in a million years. Nat, you should know that."

She felt foolish. Jealously was new to her. She'd never been rude to customers—even when they might deserve it. "I thought you weren't coming."

Rafael looked around them. There was no way for them to speak privately. He had just needed to see her. "We'll talk later. Go take care of the customers." He sat back on the stool and began typing on the laptop in front of him.

She should send him home. They'd be lucky if they got out by two. "Order dinner," she told him and went back to work.

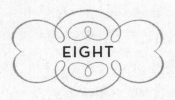

EIGHT

"Strawberry lemonade," Rafael requested. *Thank goodness Fontaine* was less than thirty minutes to closing. He was more than ready to leave. He could only play so much solitaire on the computer.

Jake's glance slid to the almost full glasses of iced tea and Pepsi inches away from Rafael's laptop. "I'm taking up space and not ordering the usual for the bar," Rafael explained.

"You could order water and it wouldn't matter. The boss wants everyone who comes in here to feel welcome, no matter what they order."

Rafael folded his arms. "That sounds like her."

"She learned it from Martin." Jake stared straight at him.

Rafael accepted the challenge and stared back. "We both know she didn't have to maintain his philosophy. She's her own woman."

"It doesn't mean she can't be scammed."

Rafael's eyes narrowed. "No, it doesn't, and that's why I'm sitting here and letting you try to intimidate me instead of telling you to take a leap."

Jake grinned. Evil twisted his mouth. "Try."

Rafael leaned in. "If the time comes, I won't *try*."

"Rafael. Jake." Nathalyia glanced uneasily between the two men. "Is everything all right?"

"Just a little discussion on what a fantastic owner-manager you are," Rafael said, turning to her. Unobtrusively, his hand closed briefly over hers, his thumb grazing across the top of her hand. "You have to be beat."

"I'm fine. You should go home."

"I plan to. After I see you home. Thanks for sending the food."

She frowned at him. "Which you insisted on paying for."

He lightly squeezed her hand. "It's a man thing. Go on. I'll be here when you finish."

"All right." She looked at Jake again before leaving.

Rafael watched her leave, then went back to his laptop. Jake could growl all he wanted. There was no way he was leaving. Helen's comment kept intruding on his thoughts. Could he face not seeing her again? She was dead wrong about him being afraid, but she was right about Nathalyia being different. He was nowhere near ready to stop seeing her.

Tonight—rather, this morning—he was getting the kiss he'd been thinking about.

She reached for him as soon as he came through the door later that night, curving her arms around his neck, pressing closer to his solid warmth.

Nathalyia was almost desperate for the feel of Rafael, desperate to taste him. It was as if she was starved and only he could appease her.

"I missed this," he rasped.

"Me, too. Our jobs keep interfering."

Leaning her away from him, he stared down into her exquisite face. "My sister-in-law is expecting me for dinner today."

"And Sundays are busy for us. I'm not sure that my staff will be in full force tomorrow. That is, today," she told him.

"We need time just for us." He brushed his mouth across hers.

"We're going to keep trying until we make it happen." She bit her lip. "Unless you don't want to try anymore."

He kissed her, causing her blood to sing, her heart to leap with joy. "Does that tell you what I want?"

Her mouth trembled. "I'm slow at times. Maybe you should tell me again."

He grinned and lowered his mouth.

Nathalyia breathed a sigh of relief when all of the staff checked in for Sunday service. She had never thought that she would want to get away from Fontaine. Finishing her rounds, she went to her office and called.

"Hi. Is everything all right?" Rafael asked.

She played with the pearls at her throat. "I'm at full staff. I can leave for an hour or two—if you can get away. We can relax on the patio."

"I'll be there in twenty minutes."

"I'll be waiting." Smiling, Nathalyia went to check her hair and makeup.

Rafael picked her up in sixteen minutes. Grinning, she rushed to his car. His smile was just as huge.

"You're early," she said, getting into the car.

"Anxious." He closed her door and went around to the driver's side.

"I hope your family doesn't mind," she said.

He twisted his mouth and pulled off. "I'm going back later. Helen is like a mother hen, but she understands."

"Good. I like your family. You're very lucky to have them."

He caught his second green light. "Thanks. I know it. We've always been close. Simon and Patrick moving to Charleston hasn't changed us. When Alec joins them in December we'll remain close."

"Celeste is beautiful. So are the rest of the women your brothers married," she said.

Rafael didn't choke at the mention of marriage, but he cut a glance at Nathalyia as he pulled into the entrance to her estate. No matter what Helen thought, this wasn't forever, but he couldn't imagine not seeing Nathalyia's smile, holding her, kissing her.

"If nothing comes up tomorrow, maybe you can come over and I can grill," she said. "You can park around back."

He slowly pulled though the iron gate. There was nothing calculating in her face or voice. He parked in front of her house, instead of doing as she directed, and turned to her. "I want to be with you so much at times I can't think of anything else," he confessed. "But this isn't forever."

The smile slid from her face. Her hands clenched in her lap.

He cursed himself under his breath and took her hands. "I'm sorry. I want to be honest with you. If you want me to take you back, I will, but I don't want to go a day without seeing you." She didn't lift her head. He prayed he wouldn't see tears when she did. "I wouldn't be in danger of getting calluses on my rear if I didn't care about you." Unsteady fingertips lifted her chin. She wasn't crying, but the smile he'd come to associate with her wasn't there either. "Please don't tell me to take you back."

"My bar stools are too well padded for that to happen."

He kissed her, rocked her. He hadn't lost her. The scary feeling receded. "You won't be sorry."

Her smile was tremulous. "I'm going to hold you to that."

Less than ninety minutes later Nathalyia waved to Rafael and entered the back door to Fontaine. His announcement that their being together wasn't forever shouldn't have surprised her. No one had to tell her that there had been a long line of women before her. Just as no one had to tell her that he didn't have to go to such lengths to be with a woman.

Entering her office, she put away her handbag and went to the window to stare out at the churning ocean. Sailboats were out in large numbers. She could accept him or walk away. Her arms closed around her waist. She simply couldn't. She was going to reach out for what she wanted.

There was a knock on her door. "Come in."

Rafael came though the door. Closing it, he didn't stop until she was in his arms, his hungry mouth on hers. Heat and desire fused their lips, their bodies. He kissed her as if she was all that mattered, as if he'd die if he didn't.

Lifting his head, he stared down at her. His unsteady hands cupped her face. His incredible eyes stared intently down into hers. "You matter to me. I don't want you to ever think differently. Believe that. Believe me."

Her hands circled his wrists. "I do because you matter to me."

His forehead rested on hers. "I'll be here to follow you home."

"This week is going to be hectic. We have private parties every night," she said.

"Then we'll steal time when we can. I'm not walking away."

"I think we're stuck with each other," she said, her voice shaky. She wanted this. She wanted him for as long as possible.

"Good." His mouth lowered to take hers again.

"Clarice, you're looking good these days," Douglas Franklin told her as she placed his second whiskey on the high round table in front of him on Friday night. "I never noticed how good before."

"Perhaps because you're always with a different woman every time you come in." Clarice picked up his empty glass. Douglas had a lean build and was a regular and an average tipper. Several times Clarice had heard him boast to his dates about his six-figure salary and his 735 Beemer. He dressed well, wore an expensive watch and rings. He wasn't handsome, but he wasn't ugly either. Unlike the men she'd dated in the past, he didn't need fixing. "Anything else?"

"Yes." He turned fully toward her and picked up his drink. She caught a glint of gold and diamonds on his thin watch. "How about you and me having dinner sometime?"

She was surprised and a bit flattered. Douglas's dates were all thin and pretty. "No, thank you."

"Pity. There's a new club that I wanted to check out." His gaze roamed over her. "I'd like to walk into Zodiac with a hot woman like you."

She felt herself weakening. She wasn't immune to flattery. "I'll come back in a bit."

Clarice went to check on the next table, and then to the bar to turn in the drink orders before she headed for the kitchen. She paused on seeing Rafael and Nathalyia going out the back door. Before it closed, he drew her into his arms. He'd been there every night for almost two weeks. Sometimes they went out; other times he waited on her and followed her home.

Clarice missed the impatience to be alone, missed the heady

excitement of being in a man's arms, the laughter, the intimacy. Perhaps it wouldn't hurt to go to a club. She'd heard the Zodiac was jumping.

Picking up the food orders, she served her other tables, then casually made her way back to Douglas's table. "Is everything all right?"

"How can it be when you won't go out with me," Douglas said, his expression downcast. "I'm a nice guy."

"I wonder if the women you date would agree?" she asked.

"Go out with me and see for yourself," he cajoled. "We could eat dinner first, then swing by the club. Come on, Clarice, say yes."

What woman could resist a man practically begging her to go out with him? "You only get one chance with me, Douglas."

"That's all I'll need."

"I'm off tomorrow night." She gave him her address. "I'll be ready at eight."

"You won't regret it, baby," he said, leaving a twenty to pay for a fifteen-dollar tab. "If the Zodiac is a bust, we'll go someplace else."

"I haven't been to a club in ages," Clarice said, a bit wistful.

He leaned closer. "I'm going to show you what you've been missing." Chuckling, he left.

Picking up the small tray, Clarice went to off-load the glasses. If he thought they were hitting the sheets on their first date, he was crazy.

Perhaps she shouldn't have accepted. She didn't have his phone number to cancel. She'd have to go and hope for the best.

In any case, she'd have to tell Jake that she was releasing him from his promise. She didn't have a chance to talk to him until it was almost closing time.

Seeing Nathalyia return wearing a bigger smile than when she'd left, and Rafael taking a seat in the bar to wait for her, Clarice's trepidation lessened. It was just nerves. It had been a long time since she'd dated.

She gave Jake a martini order for her customer and decided it was now or never. "Seeing Nathalyia's happiness, I've decided to go out with Douglas tomorrow night," she said.

Jake slowly faced her. His hard gaze drilled into her. "You told me to lock you up."

"I'm releasing you from your promise," she said, trying to keep things light. It didn't happen.

"Franklin is a phony," Jake told her, setting the drink aside. "He comes in here with a different woman each time. He tries to play it off like he's just playing the field, but I think he's striking out. All of his big talk is just that, talk."

"Thinking isn't knowing." She picked up the martini and placed it on her tray.

"I could actually lock you up," he warned.

Clarice couldn't shake the feeling that he might be serious. "Your objection is noted, but I'm going out. Nathalyia made me see that you have to take chances sometimes."

"Not with the likes of Franklin," Jake said. "You're making a mistake."

What he said was too close to her own fears. Her temper flared. "Just because a woman won't go out with you is no reason—" She stopped abruptly. His jaw clenched, and a muscle leaped in Jake's temple.

Conversation around the bar ceased. She'd spoken loud enough for everyone to hear. There wasn't an empty seat at the bar or at any of the tables.

Misery welled inside her. She wouldn't have hurt him for a thousand dates. She reached for him. "Jake, I'm sorry."

He shrugged her apology and her hand away. "We have customers to serve."

Helplessly, she watched him move to the other end of the bar. He wouldn't stay upset with her for long. They'd been at odds too many times to count, and this was no different. They'd always managed to get past their differences. They would this time as well.

A little over an hour later, when the restaurant was closed and Clarice was ready to leave for her car, she grabbed her purse from her locker and waited for Jake.

He'd gone to the back a little earlier and he hadn't returned. She waved to two of the waiters as they headed out the door. No one except she and Rafael were left in the main restaurant.

Clarice sent Rafael a tentative smile, then glanced away. She hadn't been able to look people in the eye since her outburst. Somehow, she'd make it up to Jake.

Nathalyia rounded the corner and Rafael came to his feet. "You didn't make your final round," Rafael said.

"Not tonight," Nathalyia said, looking past Rafael to Clarice. "Clarice, you can walk out with us."

Uneasiness crept over her. "I'll wait for Jake like I always do."

Nathalyia's expressive face saddened. Walking over, she closed her hands around Clarice's arms. "He already left. He asked me to see that you reached your car all right."

Clarice brushed ineffectively at the tears cresting in her eyes. "I said something stupid and hurt him, Nathalyia. I tried to apologize, but he wouldn't listen."

"Maybe he'll be ready to listen when you come back to work," Nathalyia predicted.

Clarice wished she believed that. Silently she headed toward the back door, her misery increasing with each step.

. . .

Clarice was ready when Douglas arrived. She'd purchased a new slenderizing black dress since they were going dancing. She usually liked to dance, but she couldn't get Jake's stricken expression out of her mind.

She'd called the restaurant three times that day and asked to speak to him. The answer was always the same; he was too busy.

Since she was sure everyone knew about their argument, she'd finally decided to let him have today. He wouldn't be able to ignore her when she returned to work tomorrow.

The doorbell rang and she rose from the sofa without much enthusiasm. She'd never felt less like going out. She opened the door.

"Hi, Clarice." Douglas entered the apartment, a grin on his face.

"Hi." Closing the door, she frowned on seeing Douglas in casual pants and a knit shirt. "You have to cancel?"

"No, doll face." He took a seat on the sofa and patted the seat beside him.

She didn't move. "We're supposed to be going to dinner and then dancing."

"Later, if you're all I'm hoping for." He stood, a look of annoyance on his face, and tried to pull her into his arms. "Come on, baby."

Clarice pushed him away. "What's the matter with you?"

"Me? It's you," he told her. "You don't have to play all shy. You know the score." He licked his lips. "I thought we'd stay in and have a little fun."

"You thought wrong." She opened the door. "Good night."

He stared at her. "If I walk out that door, I'm not coming back. A woman like you should be happy I even asked you out."

Clarice's temper flared. "If you don't get your sorry ass out of my apartment, I'm going to wipe the floor with you."

"Now, you just—"

She started for him. He circled around her and ran out of her apartment. She might have laughed if she hadn't been so mad, if she hadn't thought of Jake's face. She'd hurt him. She might have lost a good friend for a loudmouthed braggart.

NINE

Nathalyia invited Rafael to dinner Monday evening. She'd told Jake and David, the assistant manager, that she wasn't to be disturbed at home unless there was an extreme emergency. She'd grilled swordfish to be served on the patio near the infinity pool.

She had had guests before, but she never remembered being so nervous. The weather cooperated, and the food tasted as delicious as she'd hoped.

"Dinner was wonderful. You're an excellent cook."

"Thank you." She refilled his glass of iced tea. "There's key lime pie for dessert."

"After the two servings of bread pudding I ate yesterday, if I eat the pie today, I might have to lengthen my daily run," he said with a grin. "As it is, I'm so full, I can barely move."

"That would be a shame because I thought we might dance." Unable to resist any longer, she kissed him lightly on the lips. She loved the freedom to touch him, loved the way his eyes darkened with desire when she did, just as they did now.

His hand curved around her neck, holding her in place. "With an incentive like that, you can't keep me down. I'll even forgo dessert. I know something sweeter." His lips brushed across hers, then he slid his hands down to her, and linked her fingers with his. Standing, he pulled her into his arms.

Her body leaned against his. The heat and need built. "I-I haven't turned on the music." She picked up the remote control. Soft jazz floated through the air.

His lips brushed against her cheek, her chin. She shivered. Her head on his chest, she listened to the irregular heartbeat that matched hers. He made her feel sexy, desirable.

He lifted her chin with his fingertips. "Somehow you make every moment with you—more." He laughed, shook his head. "I'm usually better with words."

"I know what you mean. It's like everything is new, brighter," she said, smiling up at him.

She was such a wonder, so free and open. He kissed her. He only meant it to be a brush of his lips against hers, but she melted against him, pressing her sleek body against his. Need trampled through him. He gathered her closer, deepening the kiss, pulling her flush against him.

And as always, she came to him, giving him whatever he asked. That kind of complete trust was its own aphrodisiac. He wanted her passion, her fire.

His hand swept under her knit top, felt her bare skin, the heat, the silken softness beneath. He wanted more. He unclasped her bra, then covered one breast with his hand, ran his thumb over the distended nipple. She shivered, pressed against him, exciting him even more and giving him permission to continue.

Lifting her into his arms, he quickly went to one of the queen-size outdoor chaises in front of the pool and lay down with her. She was beautiful in the twilight. The sky was a beautiful mixture of pink and blue shades.

Her eyelids fluttered open. Desire stared back at him. With the sun setting, the gentle breeze blowing over them, he knew it was time. He kissed her again, his hands stroking her body, enticing her.

He deftly removed her top, watching as it revealed inch after incredible inch of her velvet-smooth skin. "You're beautiful," he murmured.

"I want to be for you," she said, her voice breathy.

His gaze went back to her face again. A small smile trembled at the corners of her kissed lips. Her hand lifted, brushed across his hair, lingered. She gazed up at him with complete trust.

No woman had ever looked at him that way. It made his chest tighten. He never wanted to do anything to hurt this woman. Yet, if he stayed, that's just what he'd do.

He was wise enough to realize that, while he might look at this as another in a long list of relationships, Nathalyia didn't. Their being together, her lying easily in his arms, wasn't something she took lightly or did often with other men. The thought of another man sent rage pulsing through him.

Her smile faltered. She brushed her fingertips across his forehead. "You're frowning. What's the matter?"

One day I'll leave, he thought, but he couldn't say the words. His forehead rested against hers. Somehow, she had come to mean more to him than any other woman.

A dangerous first.

Her hand stroked his back, comforting, reassuring, and letting him know she was there if and when he was ready to talk. She didn't push. Silence and his pensive moods didn't bother her. She gave him space and let him know she was there when he was ready.

An incredible first.

His head lifted. "You're a unique woman."

She laughed. "I hope that's a compliment."

He smiled. He liked that she made him smile. "You know it is." He kissed her again and pulled her into his arms. She came willingly, turning into him, pressing her soft body against his.

This time he didn't stop until both of them were naked. His mouth and hands moved with aching slowness over every incredible inch of her silken body—tasting, nipping, caressing. With each touch the need increased for him to plunge into her.

He'd never wanted so fiercely. His hands actually trembled as he put on a condom. Staring down at her, her dark eyes glazed with desire for him, his heart actually stopped, then pounded. She was the most beautiful woman he'd ever seen.

Unable to wait another second, he slid his legs intimately between hers and slid into her hot, silken heat—and met a barrier. Shock lifted his head. "It can't be."

"Rafael," she moaned, moving restlessly beneath him.

His hands clutched her hips in desperation. "Don't."

"I can't help it." She lifted her hips and he was lost.

His breath hissed though his teeth. Before he could breathe in, he surged forward, pushing through the thin membrane and completely joining them.

Her nails dug into his shoulders. She spasmed around him.

"Nat," he breathed, cursing himself for hurting her.

Her eyes opened. "Is it over?"

There was such disappointment in her voice that he wanted to laugh, to shout thanks to the heavens that he hadn't ruined this for her, that she wanted more. "Not by a long shot."

Fastening his mouth on hers, he began to move, surging in and out of her moist heat, letting friction and passion build with each thrust until she clamped her legs around his waist, her arms around his shoulders.

He brought them together again and again, until he felt her quiver, her breath shorten.

"Rafael," she cried, her voice shaky and tinged with uncertainty.

"Let go, sweetheart. I'm here."

He quickened the pace, measuring the length of her, loving her. Moments later she stiffened and cried out. Taking her cry into his mouth, he joined her.

He was unsure how much time passed before he was aware of his surroundings. He lifted his head to stare into her flushed face. He'd never felt such complete passion. Her eyes were closed but the blissful expression on her face, the sweet curve of her lips, reassured him.

Gathering her into his arms, he rolled over, holding her tightly. There were questions he wanted to ask. He didn't understand.

"I'm glad there was more."

"This was your first time." She stiffened in his arms. "Nat, I didn't mean to pry or embarrass you."

"He had health problems. The doctor warned against it," she whispered.

"Nat, you don't owe me an explanation." He stroked her hair and held her closer. The sun had disappeared. A few of the solar lights flickered on, giving the area a soft romantic glow.

"It's all right." She shrugged, her fingers stroking his back. "It might be hard for you to understand, but the affection and trust we shared was enough. He was a wonderful, funny man. People loved him and he loved people. His one regret was not having children to leave Fontaine to."

No matter how selfish it was, he was glad he was the first. "He couldn't have left it in better hands than yours."

Pleased, she lifted her head. "Thank you."

"I guess I should help you clean things up, but"—he rolled back on top of her—"I have plans for you."

"Good, because I have plans for you, too."

Clarice was nervous. She arrived an hour before her shift on Tuesday knowing Jake always came in early. He and Nathalyia were always among the first ones to show up, and the last to leave.

Jake had his back to her. It was broad, his shoulders muscled. The jeans he favored cupped his prime rear. She rolled her eyes. She must really be in bad shape if she was ogling Jake. He was almost like a big brother. In fact, he was more of a big brother than her two older brothers. She took care of them instead of the other way around. Jake had always taken care of her.

That might have changed after the other night.

His shoulders stiffened. Slowly he straightened, turned. His eyes remained hard.

Undaunted, she smiled at him. She and Jake had butted heads before. No big deal.

He turned his back on her. Unease crept through her.

"Good morning, Jake," she began cheerfully. "I know you're going to rub it in, but that guy was a bigger jerk than—"

"I'm busy here."

"I didn't go out with him," she said, rushing to get it out. She didn't want to lose Jake's friendship over a creep like Douglas.

"What you do on your time is your own business." He picked up another glass to polish.

She wasn't giving up. She tapped him on the shoulder, the way she'd done countless times. "You could give a little while I'm trying to apologize."

He faced her again. His eyes were cold and emotionless.

"Fontaine opens in less than an hour. Work or clock out and go home."

She gasped, firmed her trembling lips. "I won't beg."

"Work or hit the time clock," he repeated.

Without a word she turned, stopping a few feet away at the sink to begin washing the lemons and limes.

Jake turned away before he apologized. How could she keep talking about men to him like he was nothing? Easy. She didn't see him romantically. Her remark about his face said as much.

His hand lifted to the scar. He would have bet anything she didn't see him any differently because of it and he would have lost.

He kept his back to Clarice. He loved her. He had tried to stop but had just fallen deeper, harder. She was so much fun, laughing, joking. So insecure at times. So she wasn't skinny. So what? She was intelligent, honest, hardworking, and the prettiest woman with the deepest green eyes he'd ever seen.

"Hi, Clarice, Jake," Nathalyia greeted.

"Hi," Clarice said. She whacked a lemon with more force than was necessary, sending both halves skittering off the cutting board.

Nathalyia glanced at a stiff-backed Clarice, then at Jake, and noticed his lips in a hard, flat line. Going around the bar, she picked up her bottle of water.

Jake finally jerked his troubled gaze from Clarice to Nathalyia. Nathalyia had never seen him look so miserable.

"Morning."

"Do you have time to come to my office?" Nathalyia asked.

"Yeah." Placing the towel on the bar, he followed.

"Is there anything I can do to help?" she said as soon as he closed the door.

Tucking his head, he shoved his hands into the pockets of his jeans. "No. It's my fault for letting myself think I had a chance."

Nathalyia placed her hand gently on his arm. "I still think there is. I'd be the first to say that when you least expect it, sometimes something wonderful happens."

"Be careful, Nathalyia," Jake warned, lifting his head.

"Would it surprise you if I said I'm tired of being careful? For once I'd like to throw caution to the wind and just live," she said.

"You have Fontaine to consider. You have to remember that," Jake warned again.

"I know." She rounded her desk and took her seat. "Don't worry, Jake. I realize this won't last."

"But you wish it would," he said.

Her head came up. She was unable to keep the truth of his words from showing in her face. "I learned long ago that wishes don't count."

"Yeah. I guess we both did." He nodded. "I better get back."

The phone on her desk rang seconds after the door closed. "Mrs. Fontaine."

"I miss you."

Nathalyia's body actually tingled. Her nipples peaked. He hadn't left until dawn. "I miss you, too."

"What do you want to do tonight?" he asked.

"I think you know the answer to that," she said, bolder than she ever thought possible.

"Nat."

She loved the way he said her name. She loved everything about him. She straightened as realization hit. She loved him.

"First, a surprise. Be ready for something special around eight P.M. Bye."

"Bye." Nathalyia hung up the phone with an unsteady hand, then shut her eyes. What had she done? Rafael wasn't a forever kind of man. He'd told her as much. She should have realized her feelings for him sooner. She wouldn't have made love with him if she hadn't cared deeply for him.

And he could never know she'd fallen in love with him.

Rafael arrived at Fontaine at 7: 45 P.M. Clarice gave him the clearance so Nathalyia wouldn't see what he was up to. He and Clarice went into the private dining area and pulled together a floor-to-ceiling partition to create a cozy room. Clarice put a white tablecloth on the table while Rafael placed lit votive candles around the room. On the table, he placed a cut flower arrangement of white roses and white hydrangea.

"She is going to be so surprised." Clarice glanced around the room.

"Thanks for helping me set this up." He'd wanted to do something special for Nathalyia. She always gave to others. It was time someone did for her.

"After I bring her in, I'll give you a few minutes to say hi." Clarice giggled and continued, "Then I'll knock and come in with your food. Unless there is an emergency, you won't be disturbed."

"Thank you."

Her face looked wistful. "Maybe one day I'll find a man like you."

Before he could comment she left though the sliding door. Obviously she didn't know Jake liked her. If Rafael wasn't mistaken, Jake already wanted to be that man. He seemed even more annoyed with Rafael than usual. Perhaps Clarice would put a smile on the bartender's face. Nathalyia had certainly put one on his.

Rafael looked around the room to ensure he had everything ready. "Music." He took the mini tape recorder out of his pocket and put the gift-wrapped package by her place setting.

There was a brief knock and the door slid open. "Clarice, what—"

"Hi, Nat."

She was stunning in a teal-colored knit dress, and made his breath catch. Her beautiful eyes widened with pleasure. Behind her, Clarice closed the door. Taking her arms, he kissed her on the forehead. "I wanted us to have a quiet dinner. I couldn't think of a better restaurant than Fontaine."

She blinked rapidly, then glanced around at the candlelit room and the beautiful flowers on the table. "I've never seen the room lovelier."

"Please sit down." He pulled out a chair. When she did as he requested, he handed her a square box. "Open it."

Blinking rapidly, she slid the white satin bow off the box. Beneath the tissue was a crystal orchid paperweight. "Rafael, it's beautiful."

"It reminded me of you, graceful, elegant, and beautiful."

Rising, she kissed him. A knock sounded on the door.

"Clarice." Rafael slid back the door.

Clarice entered with a tray loaded with food. "Enjoy," she said, as she quickly set down the food and left.

Placing the paperweight carefully on the table, Nathalyia smiled up at Rafael. "This is so sweet of you."

"Apparently you bring out the best in me," he quipped.

Her fingertips leisurely grazed his muscled chest. "We'll see later tonight." She took her seat and picked up her napkin.

Chuckling, he pulled out his chair. "It's a good thing I'm cool under pressure." He picked up his glass of iced tea. "To tonight."

Still smiling, she lifted her strawberry lemonade. "Tonight."

Nathalyia sipped her drink and wondered how many nights they had left. Across the table, Rafael winked at her. She smiled despite the fear she felt. She was determined to take it one day at a time and enjoy every incredible moment.

Two weeks after she and Jake had their disagreement, Clarice barely kept from rolling her eyes as the woman at the end of the bar laughed loud enough for the entire restaurant to hear her. Each time she laughed, she'd flip the atrocious black wig with a red streak on each side, and look around to see who was watching. And every time she did, the thin-faced man at the bar with her would hunch his narrow shoulders deeper into his ill-fitting suit.

Clarice felt sorry for the man. Not only was the woman loud and obnoxious, she had ordered the most expensive items on the menu, and she'd also had two of Fontaine's special cocktails. Just one glass of the secret liquor was usually enough to make a person a bit woozy.

"Gimme another," the woman ordered.

"That will be your third," the man cried, shooting a worried glance at Clarice. "They cost nine dollars each."

The woman frowned, sneering at him. "No wonder no woman will go out with you if you're this cheap."

The man, clearly embarrassed, cut his eyes to one side, then looked down at his iced tea. A couple of guys at the bar laughed, whether a coincidence or not, and he seemed to shrink further. He had on a suit, whereas the woman had on a tiny denim skirt and an off-the-shoulder yellow blouse that showed a belly button in a bulging stomach that begged to be covered.

Clarice picked up the drink Jake placed on the end of the bar. She looked at him. He was still giving her the silent treatment. Two could play that game. Clarice placed the mixed drink in front of the woman and removed the empty glass. "Anything else I can get you?"

"Key lime pie," the loud woman answered, reaching for the drink.

The man's head came up. She stared at him as if daring him to defy her. "I need to go to the car to get more money."

Automatically Clarice glanced over her shoulder at Jake. It didn't happen often, but diners on occasion had used that excuse to get out of paying. "I hope you plan to come back," Clarice teased lightly.

The man flushed and pulled out his worn black leather wallet. He pulled out two twenties and a five. "I'll pay you."

Something about the sincerity of his words convinced her he was telling the truth. "I know. I can tell an honest man when I see one."

Sliding from the stool, the man left. His companion sucked on the straw in her drink. "I'm still waiting on my pie."

"Your friend might want a dessert as well. I'll return when he does," Clarice moved away, checking her watch as she did so.

Ten minutes passed and the man hadn't returned. The woman finished off her drink and glanced around. "Where's the ladies' room?"

Clarice nodded her head toward the far back wall. "Through the swinging doors."

The woman slid off the stool, pulling her brown imitation leather purse from the hook beneath the bar. "I want my pie waiting for me when I get back."

Clarice watched her walk off, then turned to wait on another customer.

"Watch that one," Jake said from beside her.

"Way ahead of you," Clarice said, forgetting she was annoyed with him. They stared at each other. She wanted to smile, but decided to be as stubborn and as stiff-necked as he was. She turned away to see the woman trying to sneak out, using several women leaving as cover.

"Runner." Clarice came around the counter like a shot. She couldn't tear into Jake like she wanted, but she could and would let the loud woman have it. Not wanting to create a scene, she followed the woman out the front door.

Clarice wasn't surprised to find Jake beside her. The woman glanced over her shoulder, saw them, and took off running. Jake sprinted off after the thief.

Clarice knew she wasn't in any shape to follow, so she walked to the end of the wooden walkway leading to the parking lot and the beach beyond, positive Jake would catch the woman. Clarice admired the way he moved, easy, graceful. The sand didn't slow him down as it did the woman.

Jake kept gaining on her, even when she kicked off her heeled sandals and stuck them in her bag.

Clarice almost smiled. The woman didn't have a chance. Jake was in great shape. He caught the runner's arm. She swung at him with a balled fist and missed. Eyes narrowed, Clarice started for them. She had better not hit Jake. He wouldn't hit her, but Clarice wouldn't hesitate. In a matter of seconds, Jake was bringing her back.

"Let me go," she said, trying to twist free.

"I advise you to be quiet," Clarice told her. "We can handle this internally or call the police."

"Why are you after me? He's the one who didn't pay."

"The money he left more than covered the po'boy and iced tea he had," Jake said, leading her back.

"He was my date. He was supposed to pay for everything."

"So you felt like you could order anything you wanted," Clarice said, repugnance in her voice.

"Sure. He should be lucky I even stayed after seeing him," the woman sneered. "He lied to me about what he looked like. He was a total loser."

Clarice didn't say anything, but she had little doubt that the woman had done her own fabricating. "You can tell it to the boss."

Calculation entered the woman's dark eyes. "Maybe he and I can work something out."

Clarice, who thought she was shockproof after working in the bar for four years, discovered she was wrong. "The man who ran out on you doesn't know how lucky he is."

"At least I can get a date." Her nose turned up and she gave Clarice a disgusted once-over. "No man in his right mind would look at you."

Clarice stopped, ready to tell the woman off, but Jake beat her to it. "Your date just ran off on you. What does that say about you?"

The woman shot him a dirty look.

He opened the back door. "The boss takes a dim view of people who dine and dash."

Clarice caught up with them in front of Nathalyia's door. "Yeah, she had the last one arrested."

"She?" The woman balked, and began to try to break free. "Let go of me. Help!" she screamed. "Help!"

Jake frowned. Clarice pulled a handful of napkins from her apron pocket and slapped them over the woman's mouth.

The door opened abruptly. "What is going on out here?" Nathalyia asked.

"We caught this woman leaving without paying her bill," Clarice said, removing her hand since the woman had stopped struggling.

Nathalyia stared at the woman who stared back at her. The woman's snide smile grew.

"Hello, Nathalyia. Long time, no see."

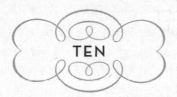

TEN

Nathalyia was stunned speechless. She hadn't seen her older sister Theresa in six years. She appeared harder, more wrinkled, and had bags under her calculating black eyes. She still dressed scantily, preferred bad wigs, and, as usual, tried to use people or get over on them.

"Nathalyia?"

She jerked her head up and around to see the query in Jake's face, the questions he was too polite to ask.

Nathalyia felt her cheeks flame, her hands clench. Ashamed and embarrassed, she fought not to show those emotions; her sister would take full advantage of any perceived weakness. "I'll take care of this."

Throwing Clarice and Jake a smug look, Theresa flipped her hair with a hand loaded with cheap rings and sauntered into Nathalyia's office.

Nathalyia closed the door on the puzzled faces of her two most trusted employees and friends. She turned to find Theresa giving her office a once-over, probably calculating how much each item cost.

Theresa picked up a crystal paperweight and hefted it in her hand. "So, you're the owner. Looks like our little Nat struck the big-time."

Nathalyia's eyebrow lifted at the word "our." "I was never a part of the family and we both know it."

Theresa carelessly dropped the paperweight on the wooden shelf. "Because you always thought you were better than any of us."

Nathalyia had heard it before. Just because she chose to live her life differently and not look for a man to take care of her or one she could spread her legs for, they called her stuck-up. "Leaving without paying your bill is a criminal offense."

The smug look disappeared. Theresa's lower lip began to tremble. "I've never done anything like this before. I was desperate." Her head lowered. "Things haven't been good since Mama died."

"What?" Nathalyia reached for the nearby chair for support.

Theresa's head came up. "Last year from complications of sugar."

"I didn't know she had diabetes," Nathalyia said.

Theresa shrugged carelessly. "She didn't find out until she had a sore on her foot that kept getting worse."

"Why didn't someone contact me?"

"How were we to find you?" Theresa asked, crossing the room. "Mama couldn't always eat the way she should because we didn't have the money. You left without letting us know how to find you. She might still be alive if you were there to help."

Nathalyia felt the accusation, the guilt. She hadn't left her address because she hadn't wanted them coming to her asking for money. Her hand cupped her churning stomach.

Martin had urged her to contact her family during his final months. He hadn't wanted her to be alone or to live with guilt if something happened to them. His family had been small, but close. He never understood why hers could never be.

"I'm sorry."

"We didn't land the big fish, like you. How did you do it?"

There was such greedy interest in her sister's dark eyes, such jealously. "We fell in love."

Theresa laughed as if the idea were idiotic. "Yeah, where is he?"

"He died three years ago," she told her.

Her sister's eyes rounded with greed. "You own all this?"

"The bank has a big chunk," Nathalyia lied. The restaurant had been debt free since Martin paid off the last improvement loan eight years ago. "I put in thirteen- fourteen-hour days to keep the place."

"I'd work if I could find anything. You know there isn't any work in Kingstree," Theresa said. "There isn't much of anything there. If the doctors were specialists, Mama might still be living if she'd had better medical care."

Nathalyia eased down in the chair. "I would have helped if I had known."

"Mama kept asking for you at the last moments. She wanted to see you before she died," Theresa told her, her voice hushed and strained. "Paula and I did what we could to help her in those final days, but we couldn't do much. Like I said, you could have made a big difference."

"Where is Paula?" Nathalyia asked. Paula was the oldest, and the meanest. She'd taken pleasure in taunting Nathalyia and in taking the few nice pieces of clothes she had been able to purchase.

"In Vegas for the past two months. She left soon after Mama died. She said she didn't want to grow old and die without seeing some of the world." Theresa laughed nastily. "She had to string on this fat old slob, a retired dockworker, to get out of town. She dumped him in Philly and is working her way across the country."

Nathalyia could imagine how her sister was "working her way" across the country. What a morally corrupt and dishonest family she had. If anyone found out— "It's against the restaurant's policy, but you can go."

"You're just going to turn your back on me again?" Theresa asked. Her voice trembled, her eyes huge in her dark face.

Nathalyia came unsteadily to her feet and shot a nervous glance at the door. "I'm not turning my back on you."

"Yes, you are, just like you did when you came to visit. I didn't hit the jackpot like you did. I want the same things any woman wants."

That was debatable, but Nathalyia wanted Theresa gone as soon as possible. "How are you getting back home?"

"The work bus," she said, referring to the bus that ran daily between Myrtle Beach and the tiny town that was slowly dying.

"How did you get on?" Nathalyia asked. The driver, employed by the city, wasn't supposed to let anyone on the free bus who didn't have a job in Myrtle Beach.

Theresa looked away. "I don't want to talk about it."

Revulsion rolled though Nathalyia. She went behind her desk for her purse. "I'll give you enough money to take a regular bus."

"Once I get home, then what?" Theresa cried in alarm. "The only reason I came here was to meet a man I'd met on the Internet. I was desperate. He lied about his big job. It's his fault for the mess I'm in, for running out on me."

Nathalyia pulled her purse from the bottom drawer of her desk. Seeing the designer bag increased her guilt. "I'll give you money to last for a few days."

"What will I do when it runs out?" Theresa caught Nathalyia's arm, her long nails digging into her flesh. "You're my only hope."

"You're hurting me."

"Sorry." Theresa released her arm. "I just don't know where I'll go or what will happen to me if you turn your back on me again like you did to Mama. You gotta help me!"

Nathalyia rubbed her hand over the area. Her skin burned. She couldn't tell whether Theresa was actually sorry or had intentionally hurt her. Theresa was a liar and a cheat. Nathalyia's uncertainty helped to convince her that she didn't want her unpredictable, amoral sister around. "Maybe you'll find a job."

"I told you—" Theresa stopped. Her eyes rounded. "That's it! You can give me a job."

"What?"

"I could work at the bar." She smiled. "I'd be better than that overwe—"

"Stop it!"

Theresa twisted her hands. "I didn't mean anything. I'm just so mixed up. I want a chance to be better." Theresa glanced around the room. "Look at you. You have all this and I have nothing. We're sisters. If you turn your back on me, where will I go? No one will hire me back home."

"Have you applied?"

There was the briefest pause. "Of course, but I had to take care of Mama for so long, and they wanted references. I have no other way of getting money. I can't even get food stamps." Her eyes narrowed. "The heif— The woman at social services acts like it was her money."

"What about from Macy or Karolyn and Kory?" Nathalyia asked, referring to Theresa's oldest daughter and her nineteen-year-old twins.

"They all deserted me," Theresa whispered, wiping her eyes. "I know I wasn't the best mother, but I raised them the way I was raised. Macy took off two years ago, and the twins joined the army as soon as they graduated. I checked with the enlistment office and they could send me money if they wanted, but they won't. The twins told me they couldn't. They don't answer my letters. I have no idea where Macy is. I have no one. Except you."

Nathalyia didn't like the sound of that. "Theresa, you can't work here. You tried to skip out on your bill. The employees know what you tried to do." Nathalyia was desperate to get rid of her sister.

"You own the place. You can hire me, and there ain't a thing they can do about it."

"You'd be embarrassed," Nathalyia reasoned.

"Once I might have cared, but not with the rent due and being low on food." She tucked her head. "Today was the first time I've had a decent meal in weeks. You gotta give me a chance to have a better life. We're sisters."

That was the crux of the problem. Nathalyia didn't want anyone to know they were related. She could give Theresa money for living expenses, but it would never be enough.

"Mama's dying wish was for us to be closer," Theresa pressed her point. "Don't turn your back on me the way you did before and let poor Mama die in misery begging for you."

The churning returned to Nathalyia's stomach.

"I can see how people knowing I'm your sister might be a problem, so we can tell them I'm an old high school friend. It ain't like we look anything like each other. Your daddy was high yellow, where mine was black as coal." Her eyes narrowed on Nathalyia's long black hair. "You got the good hair and the light skin. You always had it better than me and Paula."

"My skin and hair have nothing to do with anything. I worked hard." It was an old disagreement.

Theresa held up her hands. "I ain't knocking you. Like I said, I'm looking for my own chance. If you won't help me, I'll be out in the street in a week."

"I guess." Nathalyia didn't see a way out. She couldn't get it out of her mind that her mother had needed her and she hadn't been there.

Theresa grinned in triumph. "Thank you. You won't be sorry. We can be the sisters Mama always wanted. Maybe I can stay with you?"

"No." She'd spent eighteen years in the same household with Theresa—when she chose to come home—and couldn't remember a single day that they hadn't argued about something. "I have my own life."

Theresa grinned and elbowed her. "Got a man, huh?" She laughed at Nathalyia's blush.

Nathalyia thought of Rafael. He could never learn about Theresa, he just couldn't. His family cared for each other. Hers used her or anyone else to get what they wanted.

"You can count on me," Theresa continued, actually sounding as if she cared.

Nathalyia caught a whiff of her sister's strong perfume as she passed, and looked again at the wig and revealing clothes. "Do you have a white blouse and black pants or a skirt—that's not too tight or too short?" she added quickly. All of the clothes her mother and sisters wore were always skintight and embarrassingly short.

"No, and I don't have the money to buy them." She bit her lower lip, briefly bowed her head. "Maybe you could pick up a few things for me and take it out of my first week's pay."

Nathalyia wasn't surprised by the request. Theresa always spent other people's money and not her own. Nathalyia knew it would probably get worse as time passed. "Maybe there's a place at home you can try once you have a reference from here."

Horror leaped into her sister's eyes. "Mama wanted us to be close. I want that, too. It was the last thing she talked about on the day she died, that and how she wished you were there."

Guilt slammed into Nathalyia again. "All right. Report to my office at ten in the morning without the strong perfume, and wear a wig that isn't so flamboyant."

Frowning, Theresa touched her long black wig streaked with red. "This is my favorite. Men like it. They say I look sexy."

"You'll be working, not trying to attract men. We have a certain standard at Fontaine that I intend to maintain," Nathalyia told her, unwilling to back down on the dress code.

"Sure. I was just trying to help you," Theresa explained. "I thought they might spend more if they had an attractive waitress."

"That won't be necessary."

"All right. I better get going if I'm going to catch the earlier bus." Theresa started for the door. "Louis is gonna be surprised that I don't need him anymore to get on the bus. He better not try anything or I'll report him. I'm legal now that I have a job in Myrtle Beach."

Like a thief, Nathalyia quickly showed Theresa to the back door, looking over her shoulder. "Be here tomorrow at ten."

"I will. You can count on me," Theresa said with a wide grin. Slinging her bag over her shoulder, she went happily down the back steps.

Nathalyia watched until her sister rounded the corner of the restaurant, then she closed the door. The hardest part was yet to come, talking with Jake and Clarice. Neither of them would understand her decision. She didn't herself.

Theresa was trouble, always had been, always would be, but Nathalyia hadn't been able to reconcile the guilt that she felt for her mother's passing and not being there. Or the strong feeling that she might have been able to add to her mother's quality of life with proper food and care.

Perhaps Theresa really wanted a chance. Nathalyia couldn't live with herself if she turned her back on her.

Closing the back door, Nathalyia went to the bar. "Jake, please come with me to my office, and bring Clarice with you."

He stared at her and then nodded. Nathalyia returned to her office, feeling tense and on edge. She had just picked up the phone to call Rafael when a knock came at her door. She replaced the receiver. "Come in."

Jake held the door open for Clarice to enter first. Both looked worried. "Are you all right?"

Before coming to Myrtle Beach there were only a few people who took an interest in her. Now, with her long, hectic schedule, she had associates but not a lot of friends. The closest to real friends she had were standing in front of her. She idly wondered if they'd still want to be her friend if they knew what kind of family she came from.

"I'm fine, thank you." Feeling her hands wanting to fidget, she folded them together on the desk. "Was anyone else involved with the incident?"

"Just us," Jake answered, after sharing a look with Clarice.

"I know you must have a lot of questions, but I'd appreciate it if you'd just trust me on this."

"You let her go without calling the police," Clarice said.

"Yes, Theresa and I went to high school together." Nathalyia told the lie, realizing they'd forgotten to think of a last name.

Jake frowned. "She looks much older."

"Hard living and drinking," Clarice said. "She put away three Fontaine special drinks like they were water."

Nathalyia didn't doubt it. Theresa and Paula had been drinking since their early teens. They had begun stealing alcohol from their mother, who was a hard drinker and couldn't remember how much she had left in a bottle.

"She needs a job," Nathalyia said.

"You aren't going to say you hired that—"

"Clarice, be quiet," Jake said, staring at Nathalyia.

Clarice opened her mouth, no doubt to let Jake have it, then clamped her lips together.

"She starts tomorrow. I want you to train her," Nathalyia told them.

"And keep an eye on her," Jake guessed.

"Yes." Next to Rafael, Jake seemed to understand her better than anyone. "She starts tomorrow at ten. It would be best for all concerned if what happened today was forgotten."

"Whatever you say, boss," Jake said.

Clarice stared at her a long time. "I know you're the boss, but I have a bad feeling about this woman."

So did Nathalyia. Theresa had always been trouble. Nathalyia was taking a chance that Theresa really wanted a better life.

Jake grabbed Clarice's arm. "You can count on us. We had better get back. The lunch crowd is busy today."

"Thank you," Nathalyia said to him, aware that she might have his support, but not Clarice's.

The door closed, and all Nathalyia wanted to do was lay her head on her desk and bawl. Life was wonderful, and Theresa's sudden appearance could destroy everything.

Rafael was in a good mood, which wasn't unusual, but this time it was traceable to a woman. Nathalyia made him happy, and that shot holes in Helen's theory. He planned to tease her about it when they talked again.

"Dunlap is wearing that goofy smile again," Cannon announced to the office staff.

"Yeah, I've noticed," Hayes agreed.

Rafael ignored them and went back to checking background information for prospective employees on his computer.

"How long has it been?"

"Six weeks. Two weeks longer than usual," Cannon pointed out.

Since Rafael didn't talk about his dates or bring them around his friends or family, he wasn't sure how anyone on his team could possibly know his dating time schedule, but somehow they did. A month was long enough for the woman not to feel used, and enough time for her to realize it wasn't working.

"I'd ask what's so special about Nathalyia, but since I've seen her, I understand."

Rafael frowned. He didn't like them discussing her. His cell phone rang. "Lieutenant Dunlap."

"Rafael."

"Nathalyia, what's the matter?" he asked, getting up from the computer and moving to a quiet corner of the room. She sounded strange.

"Nothing. I just . . . never mind," she said.

He glanced at his watch. "I can take my lunch break and be there in twenty minutes."

"Just knowing you'd come if I needed you is enough."

"You feel all right?"

She laughed, but it sounded off. "I'm fine. I guess I'd rather be with you than in the office."

"I feel the same way. And I can still be there in twenty."

"I'm fine. You're still coming for an early dinner at the restaurant?"

"Not sure. We're on standby for assistance with felony warrants."

"Aren't those dangerous?"

"There's nothing to worry about. I'll call later and let you know."

"All right, but I'll bring something home with me if you can't stop by the restaurant."

"You're all I want," he whispered.

"If you were here, I'd kiss you."

"And I'd return the favor."

"Bye."

"Bye." He hung up and turned to see his team, arms folded, watching him. They were far enough away to have given him privacy for his conversation, but he didn't like the way they were all staring at him.

"Don't you have something better to do?" he asked them.

"Watching you fall in love is more interesting."

He was taken aback by Cannon's statement, then attributed it to her being a woman and a newlywed. His thoughts strayed to Helen. Women always tried to put love into everything. "That doesn't deserve a comment."

"I don't know, Dunlap," Diaz said, his face etched with concern. "You're my idol when it comes to women, but I think your wings might have been clipped."

The serious faces of his team stared back at him. "Nonsense."

"Are you bringing her to the card party at my place next week?" Barron asked. "Wanda is cooking."

He hadn't decided that he'd go. He'd rather spend the time alone with Nathalyia. "She might be busy."

"Ask her. She can get a taste of real barbecue, Texas style."

Barron was from Dallas. "I'll ask, but we're just dating."

"Yeah," Cannon said. "But remember, you heard it from me first."

Theresa was seventeen minutes late the next morning. Nathalyia had asked Jake to send Theresa back to her office when she arrived. When she hadn't shown up by ten ten, Nathalyia had gone to the front to wait for her.

Rafael hadn't been able to come over last night and she was restless. She wished she could have confided in him, but she was too ashamed. She might have hired Theresa under duress, but one thing Nathalyia would not allow was any hint that one employee received preferential treatment.

Nathalyia had hoped Theresa would at least make the effort to arrive on time for her first day of work. She should have known better. Theresa was irresponsible and shiftless. To Nathalyia's knowledge, her sister had never held down a full-time job.

All the other employees assigned to come in at ten were already there. Martin had always been a stickler for promptness, and Nathalyia had followed his example. She understood things came up, but employees knew to call. There had been no phone call from Theresa. Nathalyia briefly considered that Theresa might not know the phone number, but she was honest enough to realize that Theresa would have made no effort to find the number.

Nathalyia glanced at her watch. Nineteen minutes after ten. Hiring her sister might be the worst business decision she had ever made. She winced. She should view helping her sister as personal, yet somehow she couldn't. She had never felt a part of the Johnson family.

If Nathalyia didn't feel guilty about not being there for her mother, and just a little afraid that if she didn't help Theresa, she was vindictive enough to tell anyone who would listen that they were related just to embarrass Nathalyia and try to destroy her life, there was no way she would've hired her. One thing was certain, Theresa would not quietly disappear. Not when there was a chance of getting money.

Keep your friends close and your enemies closer.

Nathalyia saw Theresa coming from the bus stop. She had on a long black wig, a multicolored top, wrinkled white cotton pants, and heels. Despite her lateness, she made no effort to hurry.

Nathalyia didn't have to look around to know that although Jake and Clarice might be working to ready the bar for opening, they were surely keeping an eye on the clock and on Nathalyia. Once it became known that Theresa was a new hire, there would be talk of her tardiness and how it was handled.

Theresa entered the restaurant, chewing gum, wearing large, round sunshades and dangling red stone earrings that almost touched her shoulders. "Are you the welcoming committee?" she quipped.

Nathalyia glanced at her watch. "You're twenty-one minutes late. Your check will be docked accordingly. Be late again without calling and it will be your last."

The smile slid from Theresa's coffee-colored face to be replaced by anger. "I—"

"If you don't like the rules, this conversation is over, and I wish you well," Nathalyia told her. Martin had taught her to get in the first punch and make sure it was a good one. If Theresa thought she could walk over Nathalyia, she'd make her life hell and bleed her dry for money.

Theresa didn't say anything, but her eyes shot daggers.

"If you'll follow me, I have your uniform and there are some forms for you to sign." Not waiting for her to comply, Nathalyia went to her office. She left the door open. Halfway across the room, she heard the door slam, but continued until she stood behind the desk.

"I'll give you that one, but slam my office door again and you're history. I'm doing this to help you. Perhaps you should remember that you begged for a job." Nathalyia took her seat. "If that has changed, I can tear up these employment forms and give the clothes I purchased for you to charity."

"Why are you riding me?" Theresa flared.

"Theresa, employees follow strict rules. My staff knows this and abides by them without question. I won't allow you or anyone else to cause disruption within my staff." Nathalyia placed her hands on her desk. "Your choice. Follow the rules, be courteous to staff and customers, work hard, and there should be no problem."

"It wasn't my fault," she cried. "I didn't want to rush from the bus stop and get all hot and sweaty. The bus was late and I don't have a cell phone."

"Then perhaps you should take an earlier bus." Nathalyia refused to bend.

Theresa's mouth tightened. Clearly she had thought she would call the shots.

"What's your decision?"

"I'll stay."

Nathalyia kept her expression carefully neutral. She'd known what the answer would be. To Theresa, Nathalyia had become her big score. She nodded to the black pants and white blouse hanging on a coatrack by the door. "The employee locker room is across the hall. You can change in there. Please remove the earrings. Women wear studs or small hoop earrings."

Wordlessly, Theresa picked up the clothes and went to the door.

"Seventy-six dollars and seventy-eight cents will be deducted from your first paycheck for your uniform. Get rid of the gum, and please wear another fragrance tomorrow," Nathalyia told her. "Once you're dressed, come back here and I'll introduce you to Clarice and Jake. They will train you."

Theresa swung around. "Aren't those the two who hassled me yesterday?"

"They were doing their job. They're two of the best employees I have." Nathalyia picked up her pen. "I want you to have some idea of what to do before Fontaine opens"—she glanced at her watch—"in thirty-eight minutes."

Tight-lipped, Theresa closed the door. She didn't slam it, but Nathalyia knew she wanted to. She was learning—had to learn—that this new Nathalyia couldn't be bullied or walked on. Theresa would look for weakness and bide her time; Nathalyia was sure of that.

Theresa might say she wanted them to be closer, but most likely she was there to figure out how to get money from Nathalyia that she didn't have to work for. She'd soon learn she'd come to the wrong place.

ELEVEN

Clarice's face hurt from trying to keep her smile as Nathalyia intro-
duced Theresa Jones. Clarice would bet anything that Jones wasn't
her real last name. She didn't trust the woman or the half sneer on
her bloated face. Jake had better watch the liquor.

Clarice glanced toward Jake beside her and saw his rigid pro-
file. He hadn't relented. They were still on the outs. She needed
him with her on this. He was one of the few people she listened to
when her temper got the best of her. She had a feeling that the
new hire would test her to the limit.

"I'll leave you, Theresa, with Clarice and Jake. They're the
best, and I trust them completely. Welcome to Fontaine." Nathalyia returned to her office.

Obviously unimpressed, Theresa folded her arms and glanced
out the window. Clarice wanted to snatch the bad wig off her
head, then beat her with it. *Breathe. Breathe.*

"Clarice is the best person to train you, just as Nathalyia said.

Listen to her, learn from her, and you'll do fine," Jake said. His voice carried a bit of a bite.

Theresa's head whipped back around to stare at him.

"The slate is clean. What you write on it from now on is up to you," Jake said.

"Thank you." Theresa caught his arm. "I-I want to apologize for yesterday. There's no excuse, but I was desperate."

Clarice fought the urge to snatch Theresa's hand from Jake's arm. She just hoped he wasn't buying her load of crap the way Nathalyia appeared to be.

"Do your job and you'll be fine." Jake nodded to Clarice. "You're on."

Clarice bit her lower lip to control her emotion. Jake might be annoyed—all right, angry with her—but his faith in her hadn't changed. That meant more than wiping that smirk off Theresa's smug face. Clarice wasn't going to let him or Nathalyia down even if it killed her. "Theresa, you'll shadow me for the time being and we'll see how it goes."

"Yeah, sure."

Breathe. Breathe. Clearly Theresa was the type of woman who tried to charm men when it suited her and had little use for other women. "This way. I'll get you an apron." Clarice started for the bar, caught Jake gazing at her with approval. She smiled at him, but he had already turned away. Her gaze narrowed on his stiff neck.

"When is my break and lunch? Nathalyia said I eat free."

Clarice lifted her eyes heavenward. It was going to be a very long day.

Rafael took a seat at one of the high tables in the bar area of Fontaine at a little after seven. He wanted to check on Nathalyia. She hadn't sounded like herself when they'd talked yesterday or earlier today. Joy and laughter had been missing from her voice. Last night, after working with the narcotics unit to serve high-risk warrants, he'd gotten off work too late to go by her place.

"What can I get you?"

He glanced around to see a waitress he didn't recognize. Her cloying perfume made him want to lean back even as she inched closer, giving him a slow once-over. "Iced tea, please."

She propped her arm on the table and smiled in what he was sure she thought was a seductive pose. Her eyes, however, were coldly calculating. If he leaned back any farther, he'd probably topple off his chair. "You see anything else—"

"Theresa," Nathalyia interrupted, her voice terse.

The waitress straightened, but not before Rafael saw the surly expression on her dark face. "I'll be back with your order."

He caught Nathalyia's hand without thinking about it. She looked ready to blow. "No way," he said simply.

She shook her head. "Sorry, long day."

It was more than that, but she wasn't ready to confide in him. He didn't like knowing she didn't trust him enough to tell him what was bothering her. One day he hoped to change that. "I missed you, so I stopped in to eat and see you."

"What do you have a taste for?"

He laughed. She blushed. "Surprise me," he said finally.

The corners of her incredible mouth tilted upward in an easy smile. "All right."

"I don't suppose you can stop by later to share a dessert," he said, his thumb stroking the top of her hand.

"I'll try, but I doubt it," she said, glancing around the crowded restaurant.

"Then for dessert I'd like vanilla cheesecake with lots of whipped cream and strawberry topping to go," he said.

"I'll see to it personally," she said, a mischievous light dancing in her eyes.

Rafael watched her walk away. Quite simply, she got to him in the best possible way. He hoped she didn't skimp on the whipped cream. He knew just the places he planned to dabble it on her naked body.

Nathalyia turned in Rafael's order, then pulled Theresa to one side. "Your responsibility is to serve food and drinks and nothing else."

"I didn't mean to step on your toes," Theresa said. "I saw the way you two were looking at each other after I left. You should have said he was off-limits."

"All customers are off-limits, Theresa," Nathalyia told her, unwilling to discuss her relationship with Rafael.

"If that's a rule, you obviously broke it," Theresa accused.

"I'm not getting into a discussion about this, and I don't plan to have it again. You have customers waiting." Nathalyia walked off to continue her evening rounds. She could let Theresa upset her or try to think of how Rafael planned to use the whipped cream. She grinned as she came up with a few uses for the whipped cream herself.

Rafael's tongue slowly licked the mixture of whipped cream and strawberry topping from one taut nipple and then the other. Nathalyia arched her back and fastened her fingers in his hair. He moved with maddening slowness past her rib cage and over her quivering stomach to dip his tongue into the indentation of her navel.

She twisted beneath him, her body rubbing against his, making his erection harder. He wanted to be inside her, but first he wanted to savor her, to claim her. He never felt this possessive about a woman, never wanted to please one as much.

He wanted to taste every incredible inch of her skin before he took her. After tonight he didn't want her to ever doubt that she was the only woman he thought about, the only woman he wanted to be with.

His mouth moved down the sleek thigh of one leg, kissed the bend of her knee, her slender ankle, before doing the same thing with the other leg and moving back up.

Her breath hitched, her heart thudded as he loved her with such gentleness and single-minded concentration. Her body burned for him. She wanted him now. Each stroke of his tongue, of his hand, made the wanting almost unbearable.

"Please," she whimpered, her eyes closed.

"All you ever have to do is ask."

She felt his hands slide under her hips. His shoulders nudged her legs apart. Her hips lifted to receive him. The hot velvet lick of his tongue shocked her and sent pleasure sweeping through her. Her eyes snapped open and then she closed them again as wave after wave of exquisite ecstasy scattered her thoughts. She could only feel. She heard moaning and realized it was her. She wanted him inside her.

"Please, now." She tugged his hair.

With one sure stroke he filled her, loved her, pushed her closer to the edge. Her legs and arms wrapped around him and clutched him to her. His strong, deep thrusts thrilled her as he rode her. The pace quickened. They went over together.

It took a few moments for her mind to clear, and when it did, she pushed against Rafael's chest until he rolled on his back. Sitting up, she grabbed the can of whipped cream and straddled him. "My turn."

Rafael grinned. "I'm a lucky man."

. . .

Nathalyia practically floated into work the next morning—until she saw Jake's stony expression. "What's the matter?"

"Six pints of Grey Goose are missing."

"I'll give you one guess as to who stole them," Clarice said from beside him, and folded her arms.

Nathalyia felt her stomach muscles knot. "Did you see her in the cellar?"

Jake shook his head. "No, the bar was busy all day."

"We didn't have to see her," Clarice told them. "Just look at that bloated face and you can tell she likes to hit the bottle. I bet she'd too hungover to come to work today."

The front door opened and Theresa breezed in five minutes early. She saw the shocked, accusing expressions on fatso's face and wanted to laugh. She had surprised them, just as she had planned. "Good morning, everyone."

"Good morning, Theresa," Nathalyia greeted, closely studying her.

"Morning," Jake murmured.

From Clarice there was nothing but a cold, hard stare. Theresa could have cared less about the fat sow. "I remembered about the earrings." She shoved the strap of the large handbag up higher on her shoulder. A smart thief knew when to move on. Tonight she planned on taking home a couple of those steaks for herself and some shrimp to sell. The man who had bought the vodka said he'd take as much as she could bring him. "I took an early bus just like you suggested. I'll go put my bag up so I can be ready to start my shift." Still smiling, she walked away.

. . .

"*Keep the cellar door locked,* Jake," Nathalyia told him. "I won't speak to the entire staff unless it happens again."

"Already done," he said, his voice tight. "It should have been locked."

"Don't blame yourself. We both agreed it was too much trouble," Nathalyia reminded him.

"You're not going to question Theresa?" Clarice asked in disbelief, her hands on her hips.

"She'd deny it, and we have no proof. Enough regular customers know where the liquor is kept," Nathalyia said. "Or even another staff member could have taken the vodka."

Theresa hurried to them, tying her apron. She thought they were all stupid. The money she was getting from selling the vodka was paying for her manicure and a new wig she had her eye on. The money was chump change compared to what she was working on. Fontaine was a money tree and she was going to shake it. She just had to be careful. Her baby sister wasn't as gullible as she had been growing up, but she'd hit the jackpot and Theresa was getting her share one way or the other. "What do you want me to do first, Clarice?"

Clarice's lips pressed tightly together before speaking. "Start washing the lemons and limes."

"I'll get right on it." She hated fatso. *You had better not mess this up for me,* Theresa thought as she hurried away.

Nathalyia touched Clarice's stiff arm. "I can always count on you."

"But it's hard." Clarice shook her head and slowly followed Theresa. Jake walked behind her.

Nathalyia watched Clarice working with Theresa for a few moments to ensure they could get along before going to her office. Theresa had been at Fontaine less than twenty-four hours and problems had started already.

Was Theresa the thief? Nathalyia wouldn't condemn her without proof. Clarice was right, Theresa did like to drink, but she also liked money. Nathalyia wouldn't have put it past her to have sold the vodka. But if Nathalyia caught Theresa stealing, this time she was going to jail.

Rafael knew how he would have liked to spend his day off—in bed with Nathalyia—but since she was working, he decided the next best thing was to meet her for lunch, return for a stroll on the beach after sunset, and then enjoy a late-night supper. He could already envision feeding her in bed and then feasting on every incredible inch of her.

Nodding to the hostesses, he started for the bar. When he'd spoken to Nathalyia earlier she said she'd have Clarice reserve a booth for them. Waving to Jake, who still looked at Rafael as if he'd like to take his head off, he waited for Clarice to finish with her customer.

"Welcome back."

Rafael turned to see the waitress who had tried to come onto him. "Hello." He looked toward Clarice. After last night he didn't think Nathalyia would mistrust him again, but he wasn't taking any chances.

"Are you meeting our little Nat for lunch?"

Rafael's gaze jerked back to Theresa. He couldn't decide whether the words had been sneering or gleeful. "Yes, she reserved a table."

"I'll show you to your table and get you a drink. Iced tea. Right?"

"Yes." Rafael followed her to a booth in the back. She picked up the RESERVED sign and held it under breasts that sagged. He didn't think it was an accident. He slid in.

"Me and Nat go way back. Just like sisters. I'll get that tea."

"Wait," he called.

She swung back toward him. "Anything else?"

He ignored the suggestive overtone. "Then you knew her before she lost her parents?"

Her lips curled. "You'd be surprised what I know," she said and moved away.

Rafael let her go. Theresa didn't appear to be the type of woman Nathalyia would associate with. The waitress was too out there.

Clarice came over. "Hi. Sorry. You ready to order?"

"Theresa took it already."

"That—" *Breathe. Breathe.* Clarice blew out a breath. "Sorry."

"No problem," Rafael said, nodding toward Theresa at the bar. "Is she new?"

"Three days and it seems like three years. She and Nathalyia went to high school together. Customer waiting." Clarice took off.

Theresa sashayed back with his tea. "Here you go."

"You and Nathalyia went to high school together?" he asked, ignoring the tea.

Her eyes narrowed. "Who— Clarice likes to talk. Let me know if you need anything."

Rafael picked up his tea. She had gone from tempting to cool. There had to be a reason. He thought of the odd way Nathalyia had been acting. It started three days ago.

He scooted out of the booth and went to Nathalyia's office. If Theresa was giving her problems, he wanted to know. He lifted his hand to knock and heard voices.

"Lover boy is here. He thinks your parents are dead."

"What did you say to him?"

"I didn't tell him anything. Sisters help each other."

Sisters. Rafael turned and went back to his table. Nathalyia had a sister. He'd known she was lying about her family, but why would she deny her sister and then hire her?

Theresa reentered the bar area, grinning for all she was worth. Nathalyia was a few steps behind her. The smile on her face kept slipping. The wariness in her eyes, the distress, tore at his heart. He met her halfway and took her back to her office, wanting and needing to comfort her. The door had barely closed before his mouth was on hers, his arms locked around her.

She clung to him, opening for him, pressing closer. He felt the trembling of her body and wasn't sure that it was all due to passion. Lifting his head, he palmed her face. He'd respect her privacy. Obviously there was something major going on between the two women. "You're a strong, incredible woman."

"Sometimes I don't feel like it."

He kissed her lips. "No one can be strong all the time. If you ever want to lean on me, I'm here."

She placed her head on his chest and sighed. "I'm not used to leaning on anyone."

His arms tightened, then he held her away. Nathalyia didn't need interrogation or accusations. "Let's go have lunch. Later I'm coming back for our stroll in the moonlight, then tonight we're going to have a late supper and I'm going to do wicked things to your body."

She finally smiled up at him. "And I get to return the favor."

"I wouldn't have it any other way." His arm curved around her waist. He headed for the door.

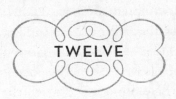

TWELVE

Three weeks later Nathalyia woke up with a smile on her face. She'd been doing that a lot lately. She couldn't remember a time in her life when she was truly happy and content . . . until Rafael came into her life. Not even Theresa unexpectedly showing up could dampen Nathalyia's spirits. It probably helped that there had been no more incidents of theft, and she and Clarice appeared to be working well together.

Nathalyia had loved Martin, but she could never quite get over the feeling that she was taking more than she was contributing to the marriage. She'd told him how she felt and, in typical fashion, he had tried to ease her concerns, hugging her, kissing her on the cheek.

That had been one of the reasons she'd felt she hadn't held up her end of the relationship. There had been no intimacy in the marriage.

Martin had told her up front that because of his heart problems there would be no sex. The smile on Nathalyia's face slowly ebbed.

To her shame, at first she had been glad. Then as she came to care for Martin and understand him, she had actually suggested they sleep together. It had been a bit awkward until they learned to relax in the intimate setting. Talking about the restaurant helped. With the medication and his heart condition, anything more was impossible. She had gone to sleep in his arms numerous times.

Then there were those times he'd wistfully mused that he wished there were children so she wouldn't be alone. During those occasions it had been her turn to comfort and reassure him. She firmly believed that he'd asked Jake to watch over her.

Throwing back the covers, Nathalyia got out of bed and crossed to the bathroom. Before she met Rafael, she was sure sex was overrated.

Nathalyia giggled. She'd definitely been wrong. Rafael hadn't been able to come over last night because of work, but they'd made plans for tonight. Her body shivered and tingled with delicious anticipation.

In her bathroom, she turned on the faucet over the deep tub and reached for her bottle of bath salts, only to remember she had used the last the day before.

Shutting off the water, she crossed to the built-in cabinets on the other side of the room and opened the door. Inside were the extra toiletries.

Moving aside the various bottles, she searched for the crystal bottle and saw the box of tampons with the date of the fourth in bold letters. Her hand paused. Her heart thumped. It was the nineteenth. Her cycle was annoyingly regular. Her entire body began to shake. She was two weeks late.

She couldn't be pregnant. Perhaps she was late because life had been so hectic lately, with dating Rafael and taking care of the restaurant. He'd always used protection.

Yet no matter how much she tried to explain away her late

cycle, her fear continued to grow. Reentering her bedroom, she quickly dressed and rushed to the garage.

In a matter of minutes, she was at the nearby shopping center and pulling up in front of the twenty-four-hour pharmacy. Inside, she read the overhead listings until she found the one she needed. Unsure of which pregnancy test to purchase, she grabbed two different brands and went to the counter. The young man at the counter didn't sneer as she feared; he simply rang up the merchandise.

The plastic bag clutched in her hand, she hurried out of the door and prayed all the way home. In her bathroom, she read the instructions, then opened the packages.

In less than a minute she was looking at a positive sign on one and "pregnant" on the other. Eyes closed, Nathalyia plopped down on the commode seat and put her head in her hands, tears flowing from her eyes.

She was pregnant.

How could she have let this happen? She'd never wanted to be like her mother and sisters, being pregnant and unmarried.

Regret hit her. She came from a line of weak, selfish, and, to her horror, fertile women. What was she going to do? The thought of trapping Rafael into marriage was abhorrent to her. That was her family's tactic, and it always failed.

Besides, he hadn't said anything about love. Neither had she. They were just enjoying each other. Apparently not doing it carefully enough.

What was she going to do?

Rafael dialed Nathalyia's private number in her office and once again listened to her recording. It was past twelve. She might be busy, but she always called him back within the hour. He'd been calling since nine.

Worried, he called the main number at Fontaine. A pleasant voice answered on the third ring. "Fontaine, seafood at its finest, how may I help you?"

"Nathalyia Fontaine, please."

"Ms. Fontaine isn't in today. Can anyone else help you?"

"Is she sick?" he asked, concern rushing though him.

"I'm not at liberty to say, sir," she answered.

"Thank you." Hanging up, he dialed Nathalyia's home number, paced in the narrow corridor of the police station as the phone rang, then barely bit back a curse as he heard the answering machine click on.

"Nathalyia, are you all right? Nat, pick up the phone. Nat!" Frustrated, he disconnected the call, then called Fontaine again. He cut the woman off. "Clarice, please. Officer Dunlap calling." He didn't like using his title, but he needed to find out if Nathalyia was all right. He'd had a nagging feeling since that morning that something was wrong.

"Just a moment, please."

He paced again.

"Hey, Rafael. What's up?"

"Why isn't Nathalyia at work? Is she all right? I can't get her on the phone," he asked, aware he wasn't giving Clarice a chance to answer any of his rapid-fire questions.

Still, there was a pause. "She didn't call you? You two have a fight?"

He might have been annoyed by her questions at another time, but he needed her. "No. Is she all right?"

"She called in this morning with a headache," she told him. "She spoke to Jake. I got the impression that she would be unreachable."

He relaxed marginally. It must have been a severe headache for her to stay at home. She lived and breathed Fontaine. "That explains why she didn't answer the phone. I probably woke her up."

"You're concerned about her. Knowing that will make her feel better," she said.

He hoped. He didn't recall ever dating anyone who'd been ill. "If she calls, let her know I called and will drop by tonight."

"I will. Bye."

"Bye." Rafael disconnected the phone, already thinking of ways to take care of Nathalyia. It disturbed him to think of her being ill and by herself. He had a large, extended family. She had no one. He went to his commanding officer.

"Problems, Dunlap?" asked the commander from behind his desk.

"I don't suppose I could leave early?" His shift wasn't over until eight that night.

The commander came around the desk. "You seldom asked to get off early before."

"Nathalyia is sick."

"It's that bad?" he asked, concern in his voice.

"A headache." When his commander's brows lifted he quickly added, "She didn't go in to work today and that's not like her."

Commander Coats, a married man, nodded. "I feel helpless when Maria is sick. She always took such good care of me and the children when they were at home. You can take off at six if things remain quiet."

"Thanks, Captain."

"I hope you don't plan to arrive empty-handed."

"Nope, I have things figured out," he said. "She's going to be surprised."

Rafael pulled up in front of Nathalyia's house and popped the trunk of his car. Shoving the keys into his pants pocket, he went to the back and lifted the cooler. Inside were shrimp and crayfish and a huge garden salad with lots of croutons, just the way Nathalyia liked it.

With his other hand, he picked up the single rose, the white bud tightly closed. Placing the cooler on the ground, he slammed the trunk, then he picked the cooler up and started up the sidewalk.

Not wanting to wake Nathalyia, he hadn't called her again. He had called Clarice to ask if they had heard from her a couple of hours after they'd spoken. They hadn't, which worried him until he recalled their last night together. It had been as near perfect as he could want.

He chuckled as he continued up the sidewalk. He'd never thought of being with a woman as perfect. He hadn't thought of a lot of things until Nathalyia. She was fun to be with because she enjoyed each new experience. Not just the intimate ones; she had just as much fun eating a corn dog, sharing a drink at the movie, learning a new sport or game.

Stepping onto the wide porch, he rang the doorbell, for the first time glad that the glass allowed him a clear view of the foyer. He was anxious for his first glimpse of Nathalyia, and at the same time hoping he wasn't waking her. He was debating whether he should ring the bell again when he saw her coming down the stairs. She wore a white silk robe, her hair was in disarray.

He had awakened her. Darn! He'd apologize, see that she ate, then be on his way.

She started toward him, her steps slow. He'd never seen her move that methodically, as if each movement was an effort. Perhaps he should insist she see a doctor.

Halfway there, she stopped, looked straight at him, then went still. Rafael almost looked behind him to see what had startled her. Her hand went to her disheveled hair. He relaxed. Just like a woman to worry about her appearance when she was sick.

"You're beautiful," he said, smiling, hoping to get her moving. He wasn't sure she could hear his words, but she could see him smiling. His smile faded when she kept staring at him.

"Nathalyia, honey." He set the cooler down, his concern deepening, his hand going to the iron frame of the door. "What's the matter?"

Her hands clenched, she glanced away, then she began to move toward him. His gut tightened on seeing her red, puffy eyes. She'd been crying. Had she been in that much pain? She was definitely going to the emergency room.

He listened to the methodical clicks of the locks disengaging. When the third one disengaged, he was though the door immediately, reaching for her. Holding up her hands, she stepped back.

"Don't."

The thin thread of sound, the distress in her voice, stopped him. "Honey, what's the matter? If your head hurt—"

"It's over," she said, her lower lip trembling.

"What? What are you talking about?" he asked, reaching for her again.

"Us. This."

Abruptly, he halted, staring at her. He heard what she said, but was unable to process it or understand the sudden vise around his chest.

"I've been spending too much time with you instead of taking care of the restaurant," she said, her voice quavering.

"Honey, we can fix that," he said.

"I don't want to fix it." Stepping around him, she opened the front door. "Goodbye, Rafael. It's been fun, but it's over."

He stared at her. The stricken look in her eyes didn't match the words she was saying. "Nathalyia, what is it? Talk to me. This is more than just our dating."

"Don't kid yourself. Leave. Or do I have to call the police?"

He lifted the flower toward her. "This was for you."

Her glance bounced to the flower, then away. Dropping the flower, Rafael walked out the door. Keep going, he told himself, but midway down the sidewalk he looked over his shoulder, then he was running back up the walk, opening the door, and rushing inside to lift a sobbing Nathalyia from the floor, holding her, kissing her, rocking her.

"Honey, I'm here. Whatever it is, I'm here."

Her hands clutched him to her, then they were pushing him away. "Please just go. Please."

He'd never felt so helpless. Lifting her in his arms, he placed her on the sofa. Despite her height, she looked small, alone. "If you don't want me here, is there someone else I can call?"

She shook her head, her face buried in her hands, her body trembling.

"You can call the police if you want, but I'm not leaving you on the sofa crying."

Her head lifted. Misery stared back at him, twisting his heart.

"I'm going to put you to bed and if you still want me to leave, I will." Not giving her a chance to argue, he picked her up. He felt the shivers that racked her body, but her skin was cool. She didn't have a fever.

While he climbed the stairs, she was placid in his arms. He didn't doubt the headache, since she'd been crying. The reason for it, however, eluded him. Was it the restaurant or something more personal? Had she been thinking of her dead husband?

Entering the bedroom, he felt her stiffen. She pushed against his chest. He stopped immediately, placing her on her feet. She quickly backed away from him. Fear stared back at him.

"I only meant to put you to bed, nothing else."

Tears rolled down her cheeks, made her voice thick and rough. "I want you to leave."

"Let me help you," he pleaded. "Please, just talk to me."

She wrapped her arms around her waist, turned from him. "You're not wanted here. Why can't you understand and accept that?"

"Perhaps because the other night, in this very bed, I held you in my arms, laughed with you, made love to you, heard your cries of pleasure, found my own satisfaction locked deep in your body," he said.

"Please, just go."

"I'll go, but this isn't over. We aren't over." He left the room. This time he didn't look back. In the foyer, he saw the rose and kept walking.

She'd see it when she came downstairs, remember him, remember the pleasure and good times they'd shared. He could only hope that the memories would be enough to help her deal with whatever was bothering her. Maybe she'd at least let him help her.

At the front door, he paused, then locked the door on his way out. The estates had a good security team, but that didn't mean they were invincible. He'd spend the night if he had to.

Placing the cooler in the back of the car, he got in and pulled up until the large trees near the edge of her lawn obscured his car. If she happened to look out her window or come back downstairs, he didn't want to upset her. Since security was aware he'd spent the night before, they wouldn't think it unusual for him not to leave.

Switching off the engine, Rafael looked at the house. The downstairs lights were still on. The master bedroom was in the back. He could only hope that she wasn't crying as he settled in for the night.

· · ·

Nathalyia was miserable. She couldn't stop crying. Part of her wanted to blurt out everything when Rafael carried her upstairs. The warmth of his body, his smell, his strength—all called to her . . . then she remembered the pregnancy test boxes in the bathroom. She panicked, thinking he might go into the bathroom and see them.

She curled tighter. She had been cruel to him, but it had been necessary. She hadn't expected him. She'd thought it was Jake checking on her. She had acquaintances, but no really close friends except Jake and now Clarice. It was difficult to balance being a friend and an employer.

She pressed her hand to her stomach. Her eyes shut again. She'd never thought about children. Unlike her mother and sisters, she might have been with one man, but the results were the same. She was pregnant and unmarried.

She had no idea what she was going to do about it. The only thing she was sure of was that she was not going to tell Rafael.

He'd looked so stricken. She recalled the rose he'd given her. Getting out of bed, she quickly went downstairs. She saw the white, long-stemmed bud on the terrazzo floor. Picking it up, she clutched it to her. It would be the last thing he gave her.

Fighting tears, she locked the door, bit her lip on finding it already engaged. Even when she had obviously hurt him, he'd thought to keep her safe. At least she had chosen an honorable man.

She flipped the light switch, throwing the entryway into partial darkness except for the light coming from the huge lanterns on either side of the double recessed doors, and headed for the stairs.

Rafael pushed away from the tree. He'd been too restless to stay in the car and had gotten out. He'd watched Nathalyia come down the stairs, held his breath as she'd stood over the rose. Emotions rushed though him on seeing her lift the flower to her lips and close her eyes.

He'd taken two steps toward her before he stopped. Obviously, she was dealing with something heavy. He thought it might be connected to her sister, but quickly dismissed the idea. Things had been fine between them these past weeks. She'd been happy. Their lovemaking incredible. It hurt that she wouldn't talk to him, but seeing her gently cradle the rose went a long way to soothing his jagged nerves.

Whatever was going on, her feelings for him hadn't changed. Tomorrow, he'd have his answer. After all, he was one of the best negotiators in the state. They were going to talk whether she wanted to or not. Getting in his car, he started the motor and drove off.

The next morning Nathalyia felt as miserable as she had when she'd gone to bed. She wasn't sure she had slept at all, but she must have, she thought, as she slowly got out of the car at Fontaine. The fragments of her horrific dream were still vivid in her mind. She and the baby she'd carried in her arms had no place to go, and Rafael had turned his back on them.

Nathalyia's trembling hand cupped her stomach. That wouldn't happen. She had successfully run Fontaine for the past three years. There was no reason to think that would change. Before she took another step she accepted that her pregnancy and the baby's birth would definitely change her life.

From hiring to ordering supplies to coordinating events, everything went through her. She had final approval on every aspect of the day-to-day operation of the restaurant—except ordering the alcohol for the bar. That had always been Jake's domain.

So far, she'd been well, and she prayed that she remained that way, but she was used to twelve- to fourteen-hour nonstop days. Several pregnant women who'd worked at Fontaine complained of morning sickness and being tired all the time.

Nathalyia would just have to face the situation, if and when it came. Deep in thought, she entered the restaurant. She had taken several steps before she realized people were calling her name. She glanced up. "Yes?"

The three waiters smiled and spoke. "Good morning, Mrs. Fontaine."

"Good morning," she managed, quickly lowering her head and continuing to her office. Her eyes were red, her lids puffy from all of the crying. She had on sunglasses, but she didn't want to answer questions from her concerned employees.

Inside the office, she rounded her desk and took her seat. She was exhausted and wanted nothing more than to return home. Aware that if she went, she might find it easier and easier to remain there, she put her handbag in the bottom desk drawer and reached for the menu she wanted to revise.

She had work to do. Feeling sorry for herself wouldn't get it done.

Time crept by while Nathalyia worked in her office. She kept having to go over information, recheck what she'd done. Every time her phone rang, she'd tensed, worrying that it was Rafael. It never was. She pushed the disappointment away. Yet she couldn't quite forget the rose she'd put in the bud vase last night and cried over this morning.

A knock sounded on her office door. She jumped, her head coming up, her back pressing against the leather chair. She was trying to figure out if Rafael would come to the office when she heard Jake's voice.

"Boss. Nathalyia."

She slumped in her chair in relief. At the moment she was in no emotional state to have another argument with Rafael. However, neither did she want to talk to Jake. She knew he must be worried about her.

Martin had taught her to be a creature of habit. That way she'd never forget, and the staff would be more likely to follow her good example. One of her rituals was to tour the restaurant before it opened. They'd been open for an hour and she was still in her office.

"Nathalyia."

Nathalyia recognized Clarice's voice. The knock came again. She could just imagine the two discussing their next course of action. They hadn't resumed their easy friendship, so for them to be together meant they were really worried. The bar was as busy as the main restaurant. Both of them were needed. Whatever happened, she didn't want her condition to interfere with Fontaine.

"Come in."

The door opened. Clarice came in, followed by Jake. Their faces were wreathed in frowns and concern.

"I'm fine," she told them, trying her best to smile.

"You don't look fine," Clarice said, and rounded the desk to stare down at her. "Rafael called to see if you came in and asked how you were."

Nathalyia's smile slid from her face. She clutched the pen in her hand. "What did you tell him?"

"That you were here, but I couldn't answer the second question." Clarice's frown deepened. "I'd say you weren't doing so hot."

Nathalyia busied herself with the menu she'd made almost no headway on. "Allergies. As for Rafael, we aren't seeing each other anymore, so please don't give out any information. I don't want to speak to him. Please tell the hostess."

"He do something?" Jake asked, his voice hard.

Nathalyia's head came up. Depends on how you look at it, she thought. "No. I just decided I was spending too much time away from the restaurant."

"But you two were great together," Clarice protested. "You were happier, more carefree, than I've ever seen you."

"Leave it, Clarice," Jake ordered. "She knows what she wants."

Clarice threw him an impatient look, and then spoke to Nathalyia. "The restaurant is doing great. You don't have to worry about anything."

"I appreciate your concern, but my first and only responsibility has to be the restaurant," Nathalyia said.

"A balance sheet won't keep you warm at night," Clarice pointed out.

Nathalyia's eyes widened.

Jake grabbed Clarice's arm. "We need to get back. The boss knows what she wants."

Clarice resisted his urging. "I'm not so sure." She bent down to eye level with Nathalyia. "Your eyes aren't red and puffy because of allergies."

Nathalyia swallowed.

· Clarice straightened. "We're here if you want to talk. Have you eaten?"

"I'm not hungry," Nathalyia answered, her voice barely audible.

"I'll bring you some soup." Taking Nathalyia's arm, she gently urged her to the sofa on the far side of the room. "Why don't you rest. I'll check on you, and if you're asleep, I'll come back later." Clarice took off Nathalyia's heels and spread the soft cashmere throw over her.

Nathalyia clutched the soft material, bit her lips, and closed her eyes.

"Whatever it is, we're here for you."

Taking Jake's arm, Clarice urged him out the door. "Something major is bothering her."

"If he hurt her, he'll answer to me," Jake promised.

Clarice shook her head, glanced back at the closed door. "My guess is that Rafael doesn't have a clue. He seems just as puzzled as we are."

"Well, something is bothering her," Jake said. "I haven't seen her like this since we lost Martin."

"I hate to ask, but do you think she might be feeling guilty because she might have found someone else?"

Jake looked uncomfortable. "How would I know? Besides, they're just dating."

Clarice rolled her eyes. "Men. There are none so blind as those who cannot not see."

Rounding the corner, Clarice saw Theresa hurrying away. "She was probably eavesdropping. I think she might be stealing my tips. If I catch her, I'm going to mop up the floor with her and that hideous wig she wears."

"Haven't you learned that fighting solves nothing?"

"I didn't start the fight with Evelyn at school," she protested.

"The results were the same. You lost your job."

Her chin lifted. "I quit and ended up with a job that pays better, has better benefits, and I can eat great seafood." She waited a beat. "Plus, I get to work with you."

"Yeah." His strong face softened. "Take Nathalyia the soup."

"We through fighting?" she asked.

"I guess," he said.

She gently touched his arm. "I'm glad. I didn't like being at odds with my best friend." Turning, she walked away and missed seeing the pain on his face.

THIRTEEN

Clarice returned with the soup a few minutes later. Jake was with her. They both fussed over Nathalyia so much that she couldn't take it any longer. "I'm pregnant," she blurted.

Fighting tears again, she stared at the stunned expressions of Jake and Clarice. "You think less of me, don't you?"

Clarice sat beside Nathalyia and hugged her. "Don't be silly. We're just surprised."

"He should have taken better care of you," Jake muttered, his fists clenched.

Nathalyia blushed and looked away. "He did."

Jake's gaze dropped to his tennis-shod feet. "You haven't told him, have you?"

"No, and you can't either." Panic entered Nathalyia's voice.

"Nat—"

"No," she repeated firmly. "I won't use a baby to trap a man. I can take care of this baby."

"But a baby needs more than just financial security," Clarice said. "Mama tried, but I missed not having a father."

"All men don't make good fathers," Nathalyia said. "I don't want him to know. You have to promise me."

"All right, but what if he sees you when you begin to show?" Clarice asked.

Misery and tears welled in Nathalyia's eyes. "He'd want to be a part of the child's life, but he'd end up hating me for trapping him into marriage."

"What if he thought it was someone else's baby?" Jake asked.

Clarice and Nathalyia turned to him, their expression shocked.

Jake stared at the floor. "There were a lot of troops in my unit and other men who had their sperm frozen before they left for combat duty. What if Martin had that done when he found out he was sick?"

"That's an absolutely horrible idea," Clarice said, clearly displeased. "What kind of woman would date one man and be artificially inseminated with her deceased husband's sperm? Rafael would despise her, and I wouldn't blame him."

"But it would serve the dual purpose of making him believe the baby isn't his, and once and for all make sure he'd never attempt to contact her again," Jake defended.

Nathalyia shook her head. "There has to be another way."

"I guess you could start dating another man and make Rafael believe the baby is his," Clarice suggested.

"I won't use anyone that way." She clenched her hands in her lap and sighed. "I'll take Jake's suggestion. I'll call and have him come to the restaurant tonight."

"Are you sure this is the way you want to handle things?" Clarice asked.

"It's the only way," Nathalyia said. *And Rafael would hate her forever.*

. . .

His team members were looking at him strangely. No wonder. No matter what, he could usually find the good in situations and make people think of a brighter day. It wasn't happening today, not with his emotions in such turmoil.

It wasn't only that a woman had dumped him. It might have been, initially, but there was more to it than that. Something was troubling Nathalyia. Something deep and important. Yet she didn't want to tell him about it. Instead, she chose to shut him out.

That hurt more than he could have imagined. He hadn't realized how much he wanted to be there for her until he couldn't.

His cell rang. Hearing the familiar ring tone he'd assigned to Nathalyia's number so he wouldn't let her calls go into voice mail, he quickly reached for the phone. "Hello. Are you all right?" The knowledge that she wasn't and there wasn't anything he could do about it had kept him up all night.

"Yes."

A lie. Her voice remained unsteady, hesitant. Whatever she called to say, he wasn't going to like it.

"I need to explain. Could you come to the restaurant about eleven?"

He had been right. They weren't going to talk at her house, which meant she hadn't changed her mind about them breaking up.

"Whatever it is that has made you change your mind about us, we need to talk. We can work this out."

There was the briefest pause. "I'll see you later. Goodbye."

Rafael slowly placed his cell phone on his desk. He didn't have a good feeling about this.

· · ·

Nathalyia replaced the phone, then went to get a bottle of water from the bar. There was no way she could make rounds. Opening the door, Theresa almost fell inside the room.

"Did I talk loud enough for you to hear?"

Theresa didn't have the courtesy to appear embarrassed. "Your secret is safe with me."

Catching her sister's arm, Nathalyia pulled her inside the office. "If you want to continue working here, it had better be."

Theresa pressed her hand to her chest as if offended. "I'd never say a word. Sisters have to stick together. You're just like the rest of us, after all."

Nathalyia wanted to deny it. She'd worked all of her life to be nothing like her amoral mother and sister.

"Rafael will walk away just like the men who had their fun with us did," Theresa told her. "Be smarter than me and get rid of it."

Nathalyia gasped in shocked horror. "I would never do that."

"You're just saying that because you still hope to catch Rafael. You'll think differently when you wake up puking your guts out or you're too tired to lift your head off the pillow," Theresa predicted. "The restaurant will suffer if you don't."

"No, it won't," Nathalyia said despite her fear of that very thing.

Theresa patted her arm affectionately. "You want to keep the baby because you think it will help you catch Rafael. It won't work, but I don't blame you for trying. He revs my engine."

Most men did. "You had better get back to work."

"Just trying to give you some sisterly advice. Wish someone had wised me up. I really thought Howard would leave his wife and marry me." Her lips compressed into a hard line. "The slimy bastard wouldn't even talk to me after I told him I was pregnant with the twins. He sure changed his tune when I threatened to tell his holier-than-thou wife."

"You didn't love him," Nathalyia pointed out.

Theresa lowered her head. "I thought I did. I was so tired of being poor, of never having enough. Howard had money. It was his responsibility to take care of the babies and me. He didn't even want to see the twins after they were born."

"Rafael won't be that way," Nathalyia told her, sure at least of that. Rafael would never desert his child.

Her eyes narrowed, Theresa's head came up. "If he's so great, why didn't you tell him? And why isn't he here?"

"Because I won't trap a man because I'm pregnant," Nathalyia snapped.

"Are you sure he'd marry you?" Theresa questioned, a hint of censure in her voice. "Men like hot sex, but take off in a hurry if you get knocked up. I know. Paula knows. Your daddy would cross to the other side of the street if he saw you or Mama coming down the same street."

Nathalyia felt the familiar stab of shame, the longing for someone to love her. Her mother had thought to trap Nathalyia's father, even going so far as to try to name her after Nathan Allen.

When it hadn't happened, her mother had spent the next eighteen years of Nathalyia's life telling her what a no-good bastard her father was, and what a mistake it had been for her to get pregnant with Nathalyia. She wondered what type of mother she would be.

"You better think again about having the kid. Nobody has to know," Theresa coaxed. "Like I said, you won't be able to take care of this place and a brat."

"I'm keeping this baby *and* running my restaurant. We'll be fine."

Theresa reached for the doorknob. "I'll stick by you when the gossip starts. At least you're smart enough to keep it from Rafael and save yourself the grief of him running out on you."

· · ·

Theresa had barely kept from laughing her head off until she was in the hall. Miss Goody-Goody had learned she wasn't any better than the other women in her family. She just had to figure out how this could help her. One thing, marriage to that cop couldn't happen. Nathalyia would be easier to manipulate and con if she was alone and miserable.

She frowned. She needed to get rid of Jake and Clarice, but she hadn't figured out a way to have them fired. She would. Maybe push fatso into losing that temper and hitting her. In the meantime she would keep playing on little sister's sympathies and reminding her how she let Mama die begging for her. How Mama wanted them to be close. What crap! She couldn't believe Nathalyia fell for that big-ass lie.

Their Mama never thought of anyone but herself. The day she died she was cursing the nurse because she was late with her pain shot. Medicare took care of all the medical bills, not that Theresa would have paid one cent if they hadn't. She wasn't going out like that, poor and helpless. Neither was she jumping into bed with any horny bastard for money, no matter how old or ugly, like Paula. Nathalyia was going to give her what she deserved. Everything.

Nathalyia could deny her all she wanted. It would give her more ammunition to blackmail her stupid self. She'd do anything to protect her old fart of a dead husband's reputation and the restaurant. Theresa could think of some pretty wild tales that the newspapers would love to print. Maybe she would get on TV.

In the meantime she was bringing in more money with her sideline than she thought possible. She wouldn't work one minute at the restaurant if she didn't have plans. Served Nathalyia right to get screwed thinking she would. Yeah, her time was coming, and little Nat was going to pay though the nose.

· · ·

Nathalyia rehearsed what she planned to say to Rafael over and over, but no matter how she seemed to phrase it, she sounded like a heartless slut. She wanted—no, needed—to end this tonight before she lost her courage. She would have preferred that Rafael not hate her, but she didn't appear to have a choice.

There was the briefest knock on her door before it opened, and Clarice came in. "Rafael is here. Theresa is in his face, as usual, but unlike usual, he's not being nice in deflecting her advances. Clearly, he has someone else on his mind."

No matter how petty, Nathalyia was glad he wasn't the least bit tempted by Theresa. "Please ask him to come to my office."

Clarice hesitated. "You sure about how you're going to play this out?"

"No, but I can't think of anything else," Nathalyia answered.

Clarice nodded. "I'll go get Rafael."

The door closed. Nathalyia stepped behind her desk to make their conversation less personal.

This time there wasn't a knock. The door opened abruptly and Rafael was there—handsome, arousing. It was almost as if he had wanted to catch her off guard. It worked. For long moments, she couldn't hide the naked desire in her eyes. She was achingly aware when his narrowed that he had seen her reaction. The same desire stared back at her.

Her hands clenched in her lap. "Thank you for coming."

He quickly crossed the room, but instead of stopping in front of her desk, he came around it to hunker down beside her and take her hands in his. "I'll always be there for you."

How she wished it were true, but she knew otherwise. She slid her hands free. He was too close and compelling. She wanted to reach out and brush her hand over his hair, cup his strong jaw, lay her head on his broad shoulder. "Please have a seat."

For a second it looked as if he might not comply, then he went to the chair positioned in front of her desk. He didn't sit down. "What changed between the other night and yesterday morning?"

He clearly didn't intend for there to be any small talk. Perhaps that was for the best. However, she discovered she couldn't just blurt her pregnancy out. "I didn't plan for this to happen this way. I just want you to know that."

"Just say it." He crossed his arms across his chest.

She'd never seen him so impatient with her. One of the things she had liked and admired about Rafael was his easygoing manner. He took things as they came and made her laugh and enjoy life. Her throat clogged. That wouldn't happen this time.

"Nathalyia," he urged, clearly approaching his limit.

"I'm pregnant," she said. She watched the words sink in, his eyes widen, and his hands come to his sides. She had wanted to see joy spread across his face, not disbelief. Or was it horror?

"It's not yours," she said and watched helplessly as anger slowly crept across the face she once simply loved to gaze at.

"There's another man?" he asked, moving toward her, his voice incredulous and filled with fury.

"No," she rushed on to say. She swallowed, looked away. "It's rather complicated."

"Considering that it can happen only one way, I don't think so."

His sarcasm helped her to gain her composure and continue. "That's where you're wrong. Martin wanted children. Before he became ill, he had his sperm frozen. The week before I met you I went to the clinic and was inseminated."

His stare grew colder with each passing second.

"It was wrong and thoughtless of me to go out with you after the procedure, but you caught me at a weak, reflective moment."

His gaze dropped to her belly and then lifted. She shrank back from the growing anger in his face.

She deserved the condemnation she saw in his eyes. "I'm sorry."

"Are you sure it's his and not mine?"

She hadn't expected that question. She thought he would just leave. "We always used condoms. Besides, I'm further along."

"Then you've been to the doctor?"

"Why all the questions?" she asked. "The baby isn't yours."

"I just never figured you'd be the type of woman to use a man. Or did you just want to know how a real man could make you feel?" he tossed in.

She gasped. "Goodbye, Rafael."

Without another word, he turned and walked out the door. This time he didn't stop.

Nathalyia slumped in her chair, placed her head on her desk and cried.

She'd done it, and she'd never felt more lonely or hopeless.

Rafael didn't stop until he was in his car, but he didn't attempt to start the motor. He was in no condition to drive.

It was over. She might care about him, but obviously she still loved her husband. There was no way to compete.

Nathalyia was pregnant with her dead husband's baby. He'd heard of men freezing their sperm, of course. He couldn't get over the initial shock, then the unexpected rush of joy when she first said she was pregnant. But hearing her say the baby wasn't his was a sucker punch.

It had flashed though his mind that the baby should have been his. He shook his head and put the key in the ignition. Crazy thought.

The car roared to life. He checked his rearview mirror, backed up, and pulled off. Of all the things he had tried to come up with that were bothering her, he'd never thought of her being pregnant, and certainly not by her deceased husband.

Jake knew how upset Nathalyia was when she didn't make her usual rounds and didn't protest when he suggested he drive her home in her car after the restaurant closed. Brushing away tears that tore at his heart, she'd gotten her handbag from her desk and quietly followed him out of the restaurant.

Clarice was waiting for them. He'd walked her out earlier so she could park beside Nathalyia. For once she hadn't argued. She was independent and opinionated, but tonight she'd been so worried about Nathalyia. Clarice was also angry because Theresa had overheard them and hadn't seemed to care that Nathalyia wasn't feeling well.

He was a bit torn. He wanted Clarice there if Nathalyia needed help getting to bed, but he didn't want her driving home so late by herself. Opening the passenger door of the vintage Rolls, he helped Nathalyia into the car and turned to Clarice. "Maybe I should just follow you home."

"We've had this discussion." She went to her Maxima and climbed inside.

Aware that she wasn't going to change her mind, he drove to Nathalyia's house. Parking in the garage, he helped her out of the car. Clarice joined them at the back door.

Punching in the lock code, Nathalyia opened the door and shut off the alarm. Each movement seemed to be an effort. "T-Thank you. I can manage from here."

"Sure you can," Clarice said, catching her arm. She knew where Nathalyia's bedroom was located. Every year Martin, then Nathalyia closed the restaurant and gave a big July Fourth party at their house for the employees and their families. "I'll just tag along. You know Jake isn't budging until you're tucked in bed."

"Martin wanted me to take care of you," Jake answered dutifully.

Nathalyia bit her lower lip. "I feel as if I've dishonored his memory."

Jake went to her. "Martin loved you. He'd never think that. You know how much he wanted children. He would have welcomed the child."

"Thank you," she murmured.

"Bed," Clarice said.

Nathalyia turned and went through the large kitchen to the staircase. She paused. "He hates me, and I can't blame him."

"He's hurt, but he doesn't hate you," Clarice said. "Let's get you into bed."

"I won't be able to sleep," Nathalyia said, but she began slowly climbing the stairs.

"Then you'll just get off your feet and rest." Clarice curved an arm around her waist.

Jake watched them slowly climb the stairs. What a mess. Nathalyia was wrong not to tell Rafael, but it was her decision. He hadn't appeared the type of man to turn his back on his child or a woman he cared about. Jake had pushed him, but he'd never backed down. Nathalyia hadn't given him much choice.

Caring about a woman could tie a man up in knots. He knew that. He'd loved Clarice for so long. It had snuck up on him. He hadn't realized he was falling for her until he'd seen her kissing some jerk who had picked her up after work. He'd wanted to smash the guy's face in.

His hand rubbed over his own face, felt the scar that ran the length of his left cheek. At the time, the doctors had said how lucky he was that the knife hadn't been lower and cut his jugular. He'd never been handsome, so he'd agreed with them—until he was released from the army and returned home.

He drew stares wherever he went. He was an oddity. He'd drank a lot in those days, and chose to do his drinking in a back booth at Fontaine. He'd known Martin before he left for his second tour of duty. If Martin had a free moment, he'd stop by his booth and quietly lecture him about getting on with his life. Finally, it had settled in, and he'd started to live again.

Clarice came down the stairs. Jake met her and saw tears sparkling in her beautiful green eyes. "Oh, Jake, she's so unhappy."

"Hush now." Without thought, he took Clarice in his arms. He realized his mistake instantly. He felt her warmth, the lush softness he'd craved for so long. He needed to step back while he could. Her cheek and breasts were pressed against his chest and tested his willpower.

"I feel so helpless." She lifted her head to stare up at him.

Jake looked down into eyes sparkling with tears and forgot all the reasons he needed to release her. His fingers flexed, tightened on her arms. His gaze locked on her mouth.

Her lips parted as if she wanted to speak. The temptation to know the pleasure of her mouth was too powerful to resist. He brushed his lips across hers, then settled. His tongue gently swept inside her mouth. He gathered her closer as he deepened the kiss.

Her tongue touched his. Fire and need exploded inside him. He wanted her. His hand swept down her back, settling on her hips, bringing her against his hard arousal.

Her soft moan jerked him back to reality. He pushed her away, saw her lips still moist from his kiss, and wanted nothing more than to drag her into his arms again.

Clarice wasn't for him. "I'm sorry." Turning, Jake practically ran from the room.

Clarice stared after him. A slow smile formed on her lips. "Well, I'll be."

FOURTEEN

Rafael slammed the front door of his house. He was in a foul mood, and it wasn't about to get better anytime soon. He couldn't get Nathalyia's words out of his head no matter how hard he tried.

"It's not yours."

What kind of woman did something like that? How could she have gone to bed with him after having that procedure done?

You caught me at a weak, reflective moment.

Rafael stripped off his shirt, heading to his weight room. He picked up his gloves, barely laced them up before he was hitting the punching bag. He'd been a convenient substitute, as he'd told her. Only, at the time, he hadn't felt that way.

He had been with enough women to know when they were faking. Nathalyia certainly wasn't. Two more quick jabs to the bag.

So she had wanted to experience the real thing! *Thump. Thump.* So he'd been a convenient stud. His anger escalated. He'd been with women before who just wanted the sex. He accepted that because that was all he wanted. He didn't want lasting love, or the tears when it was over.

He stopped, remembering the tears sparkling on Nathalyia's face; and rolling down. Why? Hormones? For a man who thought he knew women inside out, he was batting zero on this one. He didn't have a clue.

The phone rang on the small desk. He jerked his head in that direction, his heart thumped. He didn't lie to himself. He wanted it to be her, but somehow he knew it wasn't. Nathalyia wasn't the indecisive type. Obviously she'd thought long and hard before she told him.

Jerking off a glove, he started to the phone. He guessed he should be glad she told him now instead of stringing him along or, worse, trying to make him believe it was his.

Something twisted in his gut at the thought of her carrying another man's child. He couldn't be jealous of a dead man. How stupid would that be?

He snatched up the phone just before the fifth ring when it would have gone into voice mail. "Yeah!"

There was the briefest pause. "You all right?"

Rafael stared at the ceiling. What a time for Sam to call. "I'm kind of busy here."

"Is Nathalyia with you?" came the tentative question.

"No." Rafael stripped off the other glove and tossed both toward the bench where he kept his equipment. "And she won't be."

"Talk to me, Rafael," Sam said.

"I don't feel like talking," Rafael said, shoving his hand over his hair and heading for the kitchen.

"Precisely why you should be talking. Helen and I both liked her," Sam went on to say. "We kind of hoped she'd be the one for you."

Rafael's hand paused while reaching for the refrigerator door. "We were just dating."

"You helped her with the carnival. I don't recall you ever volunteering with the other women."

"I like kids," Rafael said, and felt the tightening in his stomach.

"You brought her to the house," Sam pointed out.

"It just happened. I thought she didn't have family at the time," Rafael said. "Man, is that going to change."

"What's that supposed to mean?"

"I don't want to talk about it, Sam." Rafael reached for the refrigerator door.

"Talk to me or to Helen," Sam came back.

The refrigerator door closed again. All of the Dunlap brothers loved Helen. She fussed over them as much as she did Sam. And none of them would do anything to bring her one moment of worry. "That's dirty."

"She insisted I call you. She had one of her feelings, and it seems she was right," Sam said. "You know she loves and worries about you."

That was just it. He didn't want anyone, especially a woman, worried about him. They had enough in life to contend with. He also didn't want Helen to blow his reaction out of proportion because of her crazy theory. "It's complicated."

"Since I have a master's in criminology, the same as you and the others, I should be able to understand."

He was also as dogged as Patrick when he got something in his head. Helen had turned Sam down a number of times before going out with him. He'd always said he knew she was the one from the moment he saw her. He'd just had to wait until she accepted her fate.

"Come on, Rafael. Helen is waiting. You know she isn't patient and I don't feel like dressing and driving over there, but if you won't talk to me, you're going to have to face her whether you're ready or not," Sam warned.

"We broke up. End of story," Rafael said. "It's the first time a woman has dumped me, so I guess I'm entitled to be a little off."

"If that was all there was to it, you would have told me straight off, and your team members wouldn't have had to walk easy around you today," Sam said.

That's what he got for being in the same station as his brother. If he found out who had the big mouth, they were going to have a little talk.

"Helen just peeped her head in the door and she's wearing street clothes," Sam said.

"Tell her to grab the other extension." Rafael plopped down on the sofa.

"Rafael, we're butting into your business because we love you," Helen said. "Nothing has ever gotten you down like this since we lost Mother Dunlap. Even when Patrick was injured, you never doubted he'd pull through. You kept all of us sane. I like Nathalyia, but if she's hurt you, she's going to get a piece of my mind."

The fierceness of his sister-in-law almost made Rafael smile. She might be a little over five feet tall, but she'd go to the mat for those she loved. He told them everything about Nathalyia's pregnancy.

"Put the phone down for a moment, Helen," Sam requested, then waited a beat. "You're sure it isn't yours?"

"You and the others taught me to be careful, and I always have been," Rafael answered, although he had asked the same question. He hadn't wanted to believe she could be that callous.

"Can I come back on now?" Helen asked into the receiver.

"Yes," Sam answered.

"I'm sure Sam has asked the obvious question," Helen said. "But doesn't it appear convenient to either of you that she happened to have the procedure just before you started dating?"

Rafael's heart hammered against his ribs. "You think—" He couldn't go on.

"Seems a convenient coincidence now that I think about it," Sam said. "Good point, sugar."

"You were too close to think of it," Helen commented.

"You said she was upset," Sam commented. "If she'd planned the pregnancy, she'd be happy, even though it meant breaking up with you."

"Not if she really cared about Rafael, which I believe she does," Helen said.

Rafael told them about Nathalyia picking up the rose. "I don't know what to think."

"Women will mess up your mind worse than anything," Sam said.

"Since in this case you're right and I love you, I won't point out that men can work a woman's last nerve," Helen said.

"Since I love you, all I can say is, thank you," Sam said.

Rafael felt the corners of his mouth curve upward. "I think that's my cue to hang up."

"Sometimes things aren't the way they seem," Helen said. "And pregnancy makes a woman's hormones go crazy. I believe with everything within me that Nathalyia cares. Pregnancy, even when expected, can be scary. She just might need some time to figure things out, the way Brianna did."

Patrick had fallen in love with Brianna before either knew she was pregnant with another man's child. He'd claimed the child as his and none of them thought differently. Helen must really be worried about him if she'd brought it up.

"The difference is that Nathalyia and I were just seeing each other. We weren't serious," he said.

"I seem to recall Alec saying the same thing about Celeste," Helen said. "Don't you, Sam?"

"Exact same words, and now look at them." Sam chuckled. "One or the other is burning up the highway between here and Charleston until their December wedding."

"This is different."

Sam laughed. "I think he said that, too." Helen's laughter joined that of her husband's.

Rafael was not amused. "I have to go. Night."

"Night, Rafael," Helen said. "Just remember, I think we've established that women don't think as logically during pregnancy. Give Nathalyia time."

"I'm not sure I want to," he said.

"If you didn't, your gut wouldn't be doing somersaults. You'd be asleep in bed, which is where we're going," Sam said. "Night."

"Night." Rafael hung up the phone, his mind swirling. Could it be possible that Nathalyia was pregnant with his child? But if she was, why had she lied? And if it was her deceased husband's, did he still want to go out with her? The resounding answer came to him.

He still wanted her. He pushed to his feet. Lasting relationships weren't for him. That hadn't changed. No matter what Helen and Sam thought, whatever had been between him and Nathalyia was over. He'd just have to deal with it.

"Damn."

Jake saw Clarice's car the next morning at Nathalyia's house. She hadn't gone home last night. He didn't want to face her. She probably would have laughed off the kiss, but he'd had to go and put his hands on her hips.

He blew out a breath. He'd really stepped over the friendship line with that move. His only hope was that she'd just think he was trying to console her.

He took a deep breath and knocked on the back door. If there was no answer he'd go around the front and ring the doorbell. It was almost nine. Both women should be up. Nathalyia was usually at the restaurant by ten.

The door opened. Clarice stood there. Desire surged though him. Once unleashed, it was more difficult to control. "Morning."

"Good morning, Jake. Are you coming in or are you going to stand there all morning?"

He relaxed a bit. This was the teasing Clarice he was used to. He stepped inside, frowning as he did so because she didn't step back. He looked at her. "What—"

That was all he got out before she had her arms around his neck, her lips and body pressed against his. The kiss shattered his composure and his carefully made plans. He pulled her to him, feeding on her sweet mouth, his hands roaming freely over her voluptuous body.

She broke off the kiss. He had to fight not to pull her back into his arms. "I just wanted to see if last night was a fluke."

For once he couldn't read her. "And?"

She grinned. "Maybe after a dozen or so, I'll be able to tell you."

"It's about time."

Jake and Clarice swung around to see Nathalyia, then they quickly stepped away from each other. "I'm sorry. We're supposed to be here for you," Clarice said.

"Now wasn't the time," Jake added.

"I disagree," Nathalyia said, her mouth slightly curved. "In fact, it helps to see you two finally discover what's in front of you. And I have a restaurant to run."

Clarice frowned. "Jake, did a cab bring you?"

There was the briefest pause before he said, "I walked."

Clarice swatted him on the shoulder, then shook her hand. "Ouch."

He frowned and caught her hand. "You hurt?"

"I forgot how solidly you were built," she said, then smiled at him. "Maybe you can kiss it and make it better."

His eyes narrowed. "If I do—" He dropped her hand and jerked around to stare at Nathalyia. "I'll see you at the restaurant."

"Run, but I know where to find you," Clarice said to his retreating back.

"I never thought I'd see the day," Nathalyia said.

"To tell you the truth, neither did I." Clarice sighed. "The kiss last night surprised me."

"Last night?"

"We're not as callous as it sounds."

Nathalyia touched her arm. "I never thought that. You didn't have to stay with me last night."

"I didn't want you to be alone," Clarice told her. "It was after I came downstairs. He was trying to console me. I think it took both of us by surprise."

"Jake's a good man."

"I know." Clarice picked up her purse. "Who would have thought a man who didn't want to use me was right under my nose?"

"Clarice, go easy on him." Nathalyia continued through the kitchen and out the back door.

"Oh, I plan to . . . up to a point." Giggling, Clarice followed Nathalyia out the door.

Rafael arrived at work the next morning with a forced smile and a jaunty wave. He was determined to get on with his life. He'd thought about it a lot during a long restless night. No matter what Helen thought, Nathalyia wasn't carrying his child. He reasoned her tears, picking up the rose when she thought he wasn't looking, meant she did care about him and hadn't wanted to end the affair.

It took a great deal of soul searching and trying to see things from her perspective—which was damn difficult—to realize she'd probably been scared as Helen had thought. She might have even had second thoughts about the pregnancy because of him. Whatever else, Nathalyia cared about children. She'd want the best for her child.

In all fairness to both of them, she was right to end the affair. She'd gotten under his skin more than he had realized. She was slipping into his life as much as into his subconscious. As his team members and Sam had pointed out, he had changed his game plan with her.

He pulled out a chair, sat behind his desk, and punched on the computer. Perhaps that was it. He needed to get back in the game. A bit of hair of the dog, so to speak. He winced at the unflattering analogy and reached for his mouse. Yet the idea of getting back into the dating game had merit.

He heard the click of a woman's heels on the tile floor and looked up to see a leggy brunette headed his way. She wore a fitted navy blue sheath that showed off full breasts and a slim waist. While she wasn't beautiful, he liked the easy smile she wore.

Getting up from his desk, he smiled. "Good morning, may I help you?"

"Why, yes, thank you. I'm Lisa Sims." Her smile widened. "I'm looking for the public relations department. I'm doing research on a book, but I seem to have taken a wrong turn."

"I could show you, but why bother when I can answer all of your questions." He held out his hand. "Rafael Dunlap, lieutenant with the SORT unit."

A frown pleated her brow. "Sort?"

"S.O.R.T. Special Operations Response Team. I'm a negotiator," he told her.

"You're so young," she began, then rolled her eyes. "Forgive me. Age has nothing to do with it."

"That's all right. I'm kind of used to it." He admired a woman who could be so open. His thoughts went to Nathalyia and he quashed them. "Have dinner with me tomorrow night. Once I have clearance from the chief, I can answer any questions you might have."

"This is my lucky day." Reaching into her bag for a business card and a pen, she wrote on the back and gave it to Rafael. "My home address and cell phone number."

Rafael stuck the card in the shirt pocket of his uniform without looking at it. "I'll pick you up around eight. I know a quiet Italian restaurant where we can talk."

She beamed. "I'll see you at eight."

With a slight frown on his face, Rafael watched her walk away.

"The king is back on the throne." Diaz slapped him on the back. "I guess this proves to Cannon that she was wrong."

"No, it doesn't," Cannon said. "It just proves some men are in denial."

Diaz folded his arms in annoyance. "My money is on Dunlap. No woman can get the best of him."

"We'll see," Cannon said, walking off.

"She thinks she knows everything." Diaz slung his arm around Rafael's shoulders. "You'll show her."

Rafael wasn't sure about showing anyone. He just knew the thrill he usually felt at the beginning of a new relationship wasn't there. He definitely didn't like the feeling that he had somehow betrayed Nathalyia.

Clarice wanted to laugh aloud. She had made a man who could bench press three hundred pounds, a man who was a decorated war hero, nervous. Ever since they'd arrived at work that morning, Jake had been watching her as if he didn't know what to expect. A smile tickled her lips. Good. She didn't know what to expect either.

She just knew she enjoyed having self-assured and bossy Jake a bit wary of her. For the first time in a relationship—and there would be one—she wasn't the one unsure and afraid.

She also realized that his actions meant he cared. Just as she had cared about the clowns she'd dated who trampled her feelings. She'd never do that to Jake.

As if he were aware that she was watching and thinking of him, he slowly turned. She had time to school her expression to innocence. "One cosmopolitan for table seven."

Nodding abruptly, he went to fix the drink.

Clarice's lips twitched. You'd never know it by looking at those broad shoulders and that muscular build that he could be a pushover in some areas. In others, he was as bossy as they came.

"Here." He sat the order on the bar in front of her and immediately turned away.

"Thanks." Placing the drink on the tray, she started for the table, speculating on how long he'd cared for her. She might be flighty and make snap decisions, but she'd learned from working with him for three years that Jake weighed things, considered his options.

"One cosmopolitan." She placed the drink on the booth table in front of the attractive woman in a gray tailored business suit and red silk blouse. Anything else?"

"No, thank you. What's my tab? I just received a call and need to go back to work." She looked at the drink and sighed. "I was on my way home. That is definitely going on my office expense account since I can't drink it."

Clarice chuckled. There were a lot of businessmen and women who came in for lunch. The vast majority ordered alcohol, but stuck to only one. Clarice pulled out her pad and tabulated the woman's meal with dessert: "Thirty-seven dollars and seventy-five cents."

The woman reached for her brown-checkered purse and pulled a gold American Express credit card out of a matching wallet.

"I'll hurry and run this so you can leave."

"Thanks. My boss can be demanding, but I enjoy my job, and the pay is good."

"I know just what you mean," Clarice said, thinking of Jake. She turned and saw Theresa watching her. She didn't trust the woman. Continuing to the bar, she ran the credit card and returned. "Here you go."

Signing the bill, the woman grabbed her car keys off the tabletop. "Thank you and have a great day." Clarice gave her the carbon and picked up the drink to take to the bar and discard it.

"Is something wrong with the drink?" Jake asked.

"No. She had to return to work unexpectedly." Clarice waited until he reached for the drink. "So, you going to follow me home tonight so I can do some more testing?"

The tips of Jake's ears turned fiery red.

"I won't take no for an answer," she told him. "You know how persistent I can be when I want something." Picking up her tray, she started to go check on another table. Anger hit her. She quickly reached the booth the last customer had vacated and snatched the Louis Vuitton purse from Theresa.

"I just saw it when I walked by," Theresa quickly explained. "I was going to take it to Nathalyia."

"You—"

"Clarice, not here." Jake took the handbag from her. "Your customer is waiting, Theresa."

"You believe me, don't you, Jake?" Theresa asked, stepping closer to the bartender and looking up into his face.

Clarice reached for Theresa. Jake deftly stepped between them. "Theresa, table six is waiting."

Flipping her long black wig off her shoulder, Theresa stared at Clarice as if she wanted to push the issue, then swished away.

"That—"

"Clarice," Jake warned as he glanced over her shoulder.

"I see you found it," the woman said, rushing to them and reaching for the designer handbag. "I was in such a hurry. I had my keys out and didn't notice I didn't have my bag until I was in my car and needed my phone."

"You want to check the contents?" Jake asked.

The woman appeared surprised by the request, then sat at the booth, and went through the handbag. After a few moments, she looked up with a smile. "Everything's here. I didn't suspect otherwise." She made a face and came to her feet. "This isn't the first time I've left my bag behind. I wasn't as fortunate at the department store. Thanks again."

"You're welcome. Please come again," Jake told her. Once she was out of hearing distance, he said to Clarice, "Take a break and cool down. Nathalyia doesn't need to deal with this right now."

"She—"

"Don't." Grasping her arm, Jake didn't stop until he was outside and on the walkway. "Calm down. We'll discuss this tonight when I follow you home." Leaving her with her mouth agape, he reentered the restaurant.

This was a mistake. Jake kept telling himself that, but he continued to follow Clarice up the stairs to her second-floor apartment. He had planned to make up some excuse about not being able to follow her home, but had changed his mind after it had taken her three tries to start her car. He wasn't about to let her drive home at 1:35 A.M. by herself with her car acting up.

"Thanks for following me home," Clarice tossed over her shoulder as she unlocked her door. "Come on in."

He didn't move. "I should be going."

"I really need to talk to you." She stepped inside the apartment. She switched on the overhead light, but it was on dim, giving the room an intimate feel.

He should refuse. But there wasn't much he wouldn't do to help Clarice or make her happy. He followed her inside and kept his hands in his pockets to keep him out of trouble. "I can't stay long."

"We'll see." She closed the door behind him.

Her voice changed to a seductive purr and had every nerve ending in Jake's body on alert. He needed to get out of there and fast. He turned and came up against Clarice's lush body, felt the heat, the fire. He told his feet to move, but somehow it was his hands moving to draw her to him. His mouth greedily fastened on hers. Leaving became the furthest thing from his mind.

Pleasure rushed through him as she arched into him. She tasted sweet and wild. His tongue probed and teased. He couldn't get enough. Neither could his hands that swept up the curve of her back and around to cover her breasts. She moaned as his hands cupped her; his thumbs brushed across her rigid nipples.

"Oh, Jake." She moved restlessly against him.

He had the crazy thought that he wished he had more hands so he could hold her breasts and her hips at the same time. He wanted his hands, his mouth, all over her.

She jerked his shirt out of his pants, ran her hands over his muscled chest, then lowered her head and licked his nipple. He groaned and locked his trembling leg.

"My turn." Quickly removing her blouse and bra, he ran his

tongue over her distended nipple and caressed her. Her trembling hands clasped him to her, urging him on.

"Jake."

He loved having his hands on her, loved that he pleased her, loved that he made her hot and wet. He picked her up in his arms. He didn't think he'd make it to the bedroom so he placed her on the sofa, following her down, covering her body with his.

His hand reached for the hem of her skirt and slowly slid it up her thigh, enjoying the feel of her silken skin. He touched the elastic of her panties and groaned. His heart hammered so fast and so hard he felt light-headed.

"Don't stop." Her plea came out breathy and full of need. If possible, his erection hardened even more.

If he did as she asked, he wouldn't stop until he was buried deep inside her, until he had claimed her in every possible way. "No." He surged to his feet, his breathing harsh and labored.

He felt more than heard her move. "No," he ordered. Aware of how stubborn Clarice could be, he took four faltering steps away from temptation.

"Is—is it me?"

He whirled. His gaze was fierce. He saw her sitting up in the dim light holding her blouse together. "You're perfect."

"That's what I'd say about you. This." Her hands released the blouse. The sides parted to expose pale naked skin and the enticing swell of her lush breasts.

His hands clenched. "Close your blouse."

Grinning, she leaned back on the sofa and placed her arms on the back, causing the blouse to open even more. "I might need you to help me."

Despite the almost painful need for release, he wanted to smile. How he loved this unpredictable, sassy woman. "Behave."

"You started it."

"I kissed you. You pulled out my shirt first."

She tilted her head to one side. "You have a great body, Jake." She came to her feet. "You can't blame me for being anxious to get my hands on you."

"Don't come any closer," he told her, a hint of desperation in his voice. "We are not making love the first time I take you home or on our first date."

The teasing smile left her face. She blinked rapidly. "Jake," she whispered and launched herself into his arms, pressing her cheek against his. "You make me feel so special."

Clutching her to him, he closed his eyes and enjoyed holding her. In the next moment he realized her cheek was against his scarred one. Panicked, he started to push her away.

She held him tighter, rubbing her cheek against him. "Not yet."

As gently as possible he lifted her away. It had to be said. "I'm fifteen years older, have only a year of college, and have this scar that scares children."

Her eyes flared. "You're the smartest, kindest, most knowledgeable man I've ever met. I can look at you all day and never get enough. It's the person, not the degree, that counts. You're strong, with a body that makes me salivate. I don't see a scar. I see a man who makes every day more enjoyable, a man I can always count on." She grinned. "A man who makes me horny and happy."

She didn't care about the scar. The knowledge drummed through him. He wrapped the words around his heart along with the horny and happy part. He pulled her back in his arms and kissed her long and slow. As he felt himself reaching the breaking point, he lifted his head, kissed her cheek, and stepped back. "Good night. Call me if you have car problems in the morning. I'll look at it on my break."

She bit her lower lip and followed him to the door. "I have a confession to make. There's nothing wrong with my car. I was afraid you'd try to get out of coming over."

He shook his head. "I'm glad you're smarter than I am. Night."

"Nobody is that smart," she told him. "Good night, Jake. Drive carefully."

Unable to resist one last taste, he hooked his hand around her neck for a deep kiss, then he turned and went down the stairs. By the time he reached the bottom step he was whistling.

FIFTEEN

Nathalyia made up her mind during the sleepless night to stop feel-
ing sorry for herself and get on with her life. It wasn't going to be
easy, but she could do it.

Martin had taught her to believe in herself. Life sometimes
threw you a curveball; you either stepped up to the plate and
took your best swing or sat back and let the ball, and life, pass
you by.

She was stepping up to bat.

Closing the door to her office, she started for the main dining
area. She had given her staff enough to talk about by missing her
initial walk-through and her rounds with the lunch crowd.

Thankfully, the cold compresses she had put on her eyes since
early this morning had worked to decrease the swelling, and eye-
drops had erased the redness.

"Good evening, B.J. How are things going?"

The young man looked up from rimming a margarita glass. "Great, Mrs. Fontaine. Glad to see you're feeling better."

"So am I." She moved away from the bar and caught Jake's gaze. She smiled to let him know she was fine. He gave an almost imperceptible nod of his head.

Like she had told Clarice, he was a good man. He'd cared about Clarice for so long and had never told her. Nathalyia had never asked him why. She didn't pry into people's business, mainly because she didn't want them to pry into hers. She reached the end of the bar and saw Theresa and Clarice, standing close, their faces angry. She quickly approached. "In my office, now."

She didn't wait for them to answer, just returned to her office. She opened the door and waited as Theresa and Clarice entered. Jake appeared at the end of the hallway. She held up her hand. She'd handle this. She closed the door.

"Both of you were out of line just now. There is never any excuse for employees in each other's faces while on duty," Nathalyia said. "What I want to know is why." Silence. "I don't plan to ask twice."

"She's been stealing my tips," Clarice accused.

"She's a liar," Theresa defended. "Men just like me better, and why shouldn't they?"

"Any number of reasons. You have an hour so I can list them?" Clarice returned.

"You fat—"

"Stop it," Nathalyia said, stepping between the two women. Clarice looked ready to blow. "Theresa, stand over there. Clarice, there." Neither woman moved. "I'm not going to ask either of you again."

Clarice's lower lip trembled, but Nathalyia knew it was from anger. Theresa flounced to the other side of the room. After a few seconds, Clarice went to stand on the other side.

"Clarice, why do you think Theresa has been stealing your tips?"

"She—"

"Theresa, you'll get your turn. Now, I'm speaking to Clarice." Nathalyia held up her hand.

"Because I've seen money on my table, and when I've gone back to pick it up, it's gone," she said, her voice trembling. "I even caught her going though my receipts."

Nathalyia faced Clarice. There had been other waitstaff that had done the same thing and they'd been dismissed immediately. "How many receipts have you had thus far?"

"Nineteen."

Nathalyia spoke to Theresa. "How many? And before you say anything, rest assured that Jake will know."

"He'll lie for her." Theresa snatched her arms to her sides. "He's always looking at her. She's in his face every chance she gets. Maybe they're cheating you."

"Theresa, if you say another word about any staff member, I'll ask you to resign," Nathalyia said.

"You can't do that!"

"We both know I can," Nathalyia said calmly. "How many?"

She stared at Clarice coldly. "Nine."

"Empty your pockets," she ordered.

Theresa shoved her hand into the pocket of her black slacks, pulled out ten one dollar bills, and held them out. "See?"

"Now, what's in your bra?"

The smug smile slid from her face. "What?"

"You heard me." Her mother and sisters had always kept their money there.

"I got money, but it's what I earned from yesterday," she claimed. "I get off at five today, and I planned to do a little shopping."

"With my tip money," Clarice accused.

"You can't prove it's yours," Theresa taunted. *If she hits me, she's out of here.*

"Mopping up the floor with you will give me a lot of satisfaction," Clarice said. "You're a liar and a thief."

Theresa turned to Nathalyia. "Are you gonna let her talk to your—"

"Enough," Nathalyia said, cutting off Theresa's tirade before she mentioned she was her sister. She'd do it just for spite. "You're right. I can't prove the money you have is Clarice's. But hear this, Theresa. I'm going to ask Jake to watch you. If he has an inkling that you're stealing, you're finished."

"He'll lie for her," Theresa yelled. *Shit. She didn't want Baldy messing up her sideline, but she was too smart for him to catch her.*

"No, he won't. Take today off—with pay—and we'll see you tomorrow," Nathalyia.

"With pay?" Theresa said. *At least she could get something out of this besides Fatso's tips, since she couldn't push Fatty into hitting her.*

"Yes." Nathalyia knew Theresa thought she had won and didn't correct her.

Theresa untied her apron. Her nose in the air, she swished from the room.

"Are you all right?" Nathalyia asked.

Arms stiff at her sides, Clarice asked, "Why in the hell do you put up with that slutty woman? You know I'm not a liar."

"I gave her the day off because I know you were a heartbeat away from strangling the life out of her." Nathalyia approached an angry Clarice. "If that had happened, no matter how I might have wished otherwise, how it would have made Jake upset with me, I would have no choice but to fire you."

Clarice blew out a breath, then another. "It might have been worth it."

"At first, then you wouldn't have been here to tease Jake," Nathalyia said. "I think you'd choose him over putting Theresa down any day."

Clarice lifted her hand and held her thumb and finger a fraction of an inch apart. "I was that close."

"I know."

"Considering that fighting was the reason I had to resign from the school district, I guess you do." Clarice shook her head. "I was literally crying in my margarita when Jake offered me a job."

"Like I said, I don't want my best bartender, who is also a good friend, angry with me."

"It pisses me off that she thinks she got away with it," Clarice said.

"Only until she learns that I decided to give the two sections with the highest receipts a bonus at the end of their shift today." Nathalyia smiled. She often did unannounced bonus days. It kept the staff even more on their toes. "So you'd better get back to work."

Clarice grinned. "I can't wait to see her face."

Nathalyia went to sit behind her desk when Clarice left and saw the glass paperweight Rafael had given her. For a few moments she had forgotten. Picking up the orchid, she opened her lower desk drawer and placed it inside. If only it were as easy to close off the emotions and thoughts of the man who had given it to her.

Jake was waiting for Clarice outside Nathalyia's office door. "You're smiling."

She hooked her arm through his and kissed him on the cheek before he could admonish her to remain professional at work. But it was hard not to want to touch him at work after the way he turned her on at night when they were alone. "Nathalyia declared today a bonus day, and that thieving Theresa will miss out on a heck of a lot more than what she stole from me."

"We have to win first."

She laughed. "We're unbeatable together. You know that."

His hand lifted to her cheek. "You're impossible, and don't change."

"Let's go kick butt."

Rafael heard his fellow officers greeting Sam and looked up from his desk. It was a little after three P.M. Rafael had expected him sooner. His brother and Helen had dropped by last night. Today she'd called shortly after he arrived at work to tell him she was sending him some homemade pralines by Sam with orders that he not eat them all.

Sam's gaze, sharp and piercing, stared at Rafael before he sat the plastic container on his desk. Rafael realized that Sam had purposely waited to see how Rafael did later on in the day.

"Hi, bro," Rafael greeted, opening the lid of the rectangular container and reaching for a piece of candy the size of a baby's fist. His hand paused, then he closed the lid.

"Hi, yourself." Folding his arms, Sam crossed one leg over the other and leaned against Rafael's desk. "You're invited for dinner tonight. Pork chops."

"Thanks, but I have a date," Rafael said, then continued when he saw his brother's raised brow. "An author. She's doing research for a book and I volunteered to help her. I just received clearance from the chief an hour ago."

Sam simply continued to stare at him.

"We're going to Italiano's." Rafael didn't like it that he felt the urge to fidget. There wasn't a reason in the world why he shouldn't get on with his life.

"Not tonight you're not," the commander said, coming up behind Sam. "We're being placed on alert. An elderly woman being evicted from her home barricaded herself inside and refuses to come out. She's nailed the doors and windows shut. There's no indication she has a weapon, and her son has been called."

"My date isn't until eight. We might be clear by then," Rafael pointed out.

"You never know." Commander Coats nodded his graying head toward the container. "Helen sent you sweets again?"

Rafael nudged the candy over. "One piece."

His commander opened the candy and took the biggest cluster. "Thanks." He took a bite before he had taken two steps away.

Rafael didn't have to look around to know the rest of his team was waiting their turn. "One piece and no seconds, so don't ask."

Chairs rustled as those in the room rushed to grab pieces of candy. Amid mumbles of thanks, the candy dwindled.

"You know you just can't eat one of these," Henderson moaned, his candy half gone in one bite.

"Then don't eat one," Cannon said. "Give it to a fellow officer. Me."

"In your dreams." Munching, Henderson went back to his desk.

"Seems you have a phone call to make." Sam reached over and picked up a piece of candy.

"We might not have to go," Rafael said stubbornly, not liking the relief he felt that he had an excuse to cancel. He needed to get back into the dating game. He needed to try and forget Nathalyia.

"Make the phone call and refer her to someone else." Sam straightened. "Dinner will be waiting for you at the house."

Rafael sat there for a few minutes after Sam left, then pulled the woman's card from his shirt pocket. Taking out another woman wouldn't help him forget Nathalyia. He wasn't sure what, if anything, would. He picked up the phone and dialed a familiar number.

"Hi, Kurt, this is Rafael. I need to order some flowers for breaking a date."

A week later, wearing a bulletproof vest beneath his street clothes, Rafael and Barron strolled casually up the sidewalk of the small house in an older neighborhood that had seen better days. His unit had been tagged by the Narcotics Division to assist them in serving high-risk warrants. His team was to verify the address on the warrant, see if the suspect was there, and buy drugs.

This was the third warrant they had attempted to serve tonight. The others had been a bust.

His team members had traded off being the initial contact. Two patrol cars and their transport van were out of sight, waiting. You never knew how it would go down, and it was always best to be prepared.

"I heard you had to cancel another date tonight," Barron said.

Rafael let his gaze sweep over the front of the house, aware that Barron was doing the same. They were just two men coming to buy a gram of coke. "Yeah. I'm beginning to think the commander is doing it on purpose." At least Rafael was making the florist happy.

If he were honest, he would admit that he hadn't wanted to go either time. He'd finally accepted that it would take more than another woman to help him forget Nathalyia. He kept thinking about her, wondering if she was taking care of herself. Her sister hadn't seemed the caring type.

"There's always another night," he said doggedly.

"That's for sure. Let's do this." Barron stepped on the porch and knocked when he didn't see a doorbell. "Hey, man. I'm a friend of—"

The spat of an AR-15 fully automatic assault rifle drowned out what Barron had been about to say. The impact of the bullets knocked him off the porch. Rafael's hand closed around his secondary weapon as the next round caught him in his chest and knocked him backward as well.

Stunned, his hand clutching his weapon, his chest burning, Rafael lay on the hard-packed dirt and tried to draw a breath. It burned like hell. Beside him, he heard Barron moan, and the wail of a siren.

Thank heaven they had their mics on. Help was on the way, but it might be too late for either of them.

The front door burst open. A shirtless man came out with a pistol grip shotgun. He was grinning, his eyes wild. "You're going to hell tonight, pigs, and I'm the one who's gonna punch your ticket."

Laughing, the man lifted the gun. Rafael fired his .38, heard the blast, and wondered if the gunman had been right.

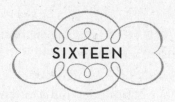

SIXTEEN

Nathalyia had gone over the order for the produce company three times and accepted she would have to go over it a fourth. Things kept slipping away. Each time she tried to concentrate, Rafael's face, hurt and angry, would invade her thoughts.

She'd hoped this aching loneliness would get better with time. It hadn't. She ran her hand though her hair, then took a long swallow of her bottled water.

Perhaps if she turned off the radio she could concentrate better. She usually liked soft music while she worked, but lately it was proving to be a distraction.

She reached for the remote control just as she heard a male reporter interrupt the program with breaking news. "Two members of the Myrtle Beach Police Department were shot tonight. Details are still coming in. Stay tuned."

Nathalyia's heart stopped, then pounded. "No. Please, no."

Clarice burst into Nathalyia's office. She took one look at Nathalyia's face and rounded the desk. "It's on the TV in the bar. We don't know if Rafael was involved."

Nathalyia was trembling so badly she could barely stand. "Please, God, let him be safe."

Clarice hugged her. "Rafael can take care of himself."

The reporter chimed in. "More information just came in. The Special Operations Response Team known as SORT was assisting the Narcotics Division, serving high-risk warrants when they were fired on. Two officers are down. The extent of their injuries is not known at this time."

"No!" Nathalyia cried. "That's Rafael's unit."

Clarice hugged her tighter. "Jake has contacts with some policemen. He's working on finding out more."

Nathalyia pulled away and reached for the phone. "His brother would know." She dialed Information with a trembling hand. "Sam or Helen Dunlap in Myrtle Beach."

"The number isn't listed" came the droll answer.

"Please try Alec Dunlap in Myrtle Beach."

The operator came back with the same answer for Alec, and later for Simon and Patrick in Charleston. Frantic, Nathalyia hung up the phone and reached for her purse. "He gave me his card." She found it in the card slot and dialed the main number of the police unit. The line was busy. She kept trying and kept getting the same response.

Jake came through the door, his face stony.

"I already know it's his unit." She swallowed, then swallowed again before she could go on. "Is he the one hurt?"

"I can't find out," Jake said. "As you can imagine, things are crazy at the station and at the house where the standoff is still going on."

Nathalyia's arm circled her churning stomach. "Please, God, protect them and keep them safe."

"They'll take the injured to County. The team will be there as well once this is over," Jake told her. "Do you want me to drive you?"

Nathalyia grabbed her purse and rounded her desk. "Let's go."

Rafael didn't think he was dead. He could see the revolving lights of the police cars flashing off the jagged windowpanes of the house, he could hear Nelson, the other negotiator, talking on the bullhorn, he could smell tear gas. He must have blacked out. He tried to move his legs and couldn't.

Panic hit before he glanced down and saw the gunman, sprawled halfway on top of him. Closing his eyes, he drew in a breath and found his lungs no longer burned as much.

"You try to come in here and you'll get the same thing the other two got," shouted a man from inside the house.

"Yeah, just try it and there will be more cops dirtying up the lawn," yelled another man.

Both voices were muffled. They had on gas masks. "Barron," Rafael said quietly. "Barron, you awake?"

Silence. There was only one course of action for Rafael; he had to get Barron out of there himself.

His vest had saved his life. He prayed the same was true for Barron. Bullets could ricochet once they entered the body, and on rare occasions they'd pierce an unprotected area of the body.

Inching his hand to his side, he felt Barron's arm, then moved upward to feel his carotid. The beat was faint, but it was there.

"You can't win this," Nelson said. "Come out with your hands up."

"Why don't you come get us?" yelled one of the men inside the house. The words were punctuated with another spat of gunfire. The men inside were well armed. The unit could use shields to try to come in and get them, but that would put more officers in danger.

"It's Dunlap," Rafael whispered. "Barron is wounded and unconscious. Kill the light. At the ten count, I plan to be up and moving with him to the left."

Rafael slowly worked one leg free, then used it to push the unconscious man off his lower leg. He began the slow count. He was taking a chance. There was no telling how those inside would react to the darkness, but he didn't know how badly Barron was hurt. He couldn't wait.

The lights went out.

Rafael rolled. Adrenaline pumping, he ignored the pain in his chest, came to his knees, and pulled Barron over his shoulder. He pushed to his feet as shots rang out from the house. He ignored the burning in his lungs and kept running.

Waiting hands took Barron from Rafael, and then grabbed his arm. He flinched. Pain shot up his left arm. He glanced down and saw a large dark stain. He touched the spot. His fingers came away wet and sticky. He'd been shot.

Jake couldn't find a parking space and Nathalyia hadn't wanted to wait. On the way to the hospital, they'd heard that one of the downed officers had carried the other to safety, and that both were on the way to the emergency room. Names weren't being released.

"I'll be fine." Nathalyia slammed out of the car. Clarice jumped out of the backseat and was right behind her.

"I've never seen so many policemen and media," Clarice said, hurrying to keep up with Nathalyia.

They were stopped at the emergency room by a policeman. "Do you have a medical emergency?"

Nathalyia opened her mouth to explain, but Clarice was already speaking.

"She's dating Rafael Dunlap and his unit was involved in the shooting. She wants to make sure he's all right."

The two policemen traded glances. The one who had spoken asked, "Do you have any identification?"

Nathalyia fumbled in her purse for her license and Rafael's card. "I tried to call his brothers, but their phone numbers are unlisted. Is he all right?"

The policeman handed back her license and the card. "We aren't giving out any information. You can go inside and wait."

"Are they here?" Clarice asked.

"On their way," answered the other policeman. "Please wait inside," he instructed as the first policeman who had spoken stopped three other women.

Clutching Clarice's hand, Nathalyia went inside. The area was jammed with patients, police, and reporters trying to set up cameras.

"Nathalyia."

She turned toward the sound and saw Helen. The other woman's eyes were red and swollen. Shaking her head, Nathalyia began backing away from the approaching woman.

Helen caught her. "He's been hurt, but there is a medic with his team. Thank God he had his vest on. They're bringing him in now. Sam and Alec went to the scene. The rest of the family are on their way."

Fear for Rafael almost buckled her knees, then she saw a woman crying softly. The two small children huddled close as a policeman with captain bars on his shoulders stood by her.

"The other policeman?" Nathalyia asked, her voice barely above a whisper.

Helen bit her lip. "The bullet missed the vest."

The senselessness of the shooting enraged her. She stared at the two children, their eyes wide and frightened. Guilt hammered her. Rafael might have died without knowing she was carrying their baby.

"This is Clarice Howard. Helen Dunlap. Rafael's sister-in-law."

The women nodded to each other. "He'll be here soon, Nathalyia," Clarice soothed.

"She's right," Helen agreed.

"Stand back! Stand back!" Several police officers pushed the crowd back. The emergency doors opened and paramedics rushed in pushing a gurney. The woman who had been crying came unsteadily to her feet.

"Al!" she wailed, rushing after the fast-moving stretcher that continued through the double doors. Several policemen kept the news media from following.

What-ifs hammered at Nathalyia. Regret and guilt swept though her.

"Stand back! Please stand back!"

The door opened. A paramedic pulled a gurney though the door. She saw Alec and Sam before she saw Rafael lying down, and when she did, her heart stopped, then beat wildly. His eyes were closed. There was a large white bandage on his left forearm.

Nathalyia clutched Clarice. Police officers began to applaud.

Rafael slowly opened his eyes, grimaced, and casually lifted his right hand a few inches from the gurney.

"Come on." Grabbing Nathalyia's arm, Helen rushed to Rafael. Once there, she gently hugged him on the right side. "I'm so proud of you."

He looked over her shoulder. His gaze clashed with Nathalyia's. Tears streamed faster down her cheeks. He'd always been so neat. His blue cotton shirt was untucked, the left sleeve cut up to his shoulder, and dark splotches were on the right shoulder and arm. It took her seconds to figure out they were bloodstains from the other officer. They could have been his.

He lifted his hand toward her and she ran to him, hugging him as sobs racked her body.

"Don't cry, Nat," he crooned. "Don't cry."

Nathalyia couldn't seem to stop crying any more than she could move away from him.

The sight of tears in Nathalyia's eyes, the naked terror he'd hoped and prayed never to see, made Rafael's chest tighten. Trying to hold her with his right arm as pain stabbed his left, the uncontrollable trembling of her body against his was almost more than he could bare.

"I'm all right, Nat. Shhh," he repeated, kissing her hair. He tried to lift her head, but she just shook it, burrowing closer. Helplessly, he looked to Helen. His heart turned over. She was battling tears herself.

"I'm all right," he repeated. "I'll be out of here in no time."

His teeth clenched, Sam pulled Helen to him. "Let the doctor check you out. Nathalyia can go with you. We'll wait here."

Since she didn't appear willing to let go, he didn't have a choice. He wasn't willing to let her go either.

"I'm glad you're all right. I'll wait here for Jake," Clarice said.

"Officer Dunlap, we need to get you into an exam room."

Rafael looked up to see a young woman wearing a printed smock. He looked down at Nathalyia, who showed no sign of letting go. "We're going to follow the nurse."

After a few seconds, she nodded and straightened. Her hand clutched his.

"We're ready." The paramedics followed the nurse, giving her a report of his injuries as they went. When they entered the patient area, he saw Barron's wife and several police officers outside an exam room. The door abruptly opened and out they came, pushing Barron on a gurney. They were almost running.

Nathalyia's hand flexed in his. There was no way she hadn't heard the doctor shouting that Barron was bleeding internally and they needed to get into surgery *stat*. Barron's wife was almost hysterical and had to be restrained from going to him. Rafael's heart went out to her and their two small children. Barron doted on his family and they loved him back.

Loving a policeman carried risks. There was always the possibility he wouldn't come home. Rafael said another prayer for Barron.

The nurse stood by a cubical holding the curtain back as he was wheeled inside and positioned next to the bed. "Excuse us, ma'am. We have to lift him on the bed."

Nathalyia released his hand and stepped aside. Her eyes bounced from his bandaged arm to his face. He tried to smile despite the throbbing in his chest, the pain in his arm.

"On the count of three, Dunlap."

"You don't have to—"

Ignoring him, they lifted him smoothly into the bed. "You did your job. Let us do ours," the paramedic at the foot of the bed said.

The paramedic who had been at his head stepped around to face him. "You did us proud, man. Get better."

"Thanks."

"Officer Dunlap, do you need help sitting up to get this gown on?" the nurse asked.

Rafael gazed up at Nathalyia, who had moved back beside him. Perhaps he should have insisted she remain in the waiting room. His chest was banged and bruised from the impact of the bullets.

The nurse glanced at Nathalyia. "Sooner or later, it will have to be dealt with."

Knowing she was right didn't help. Gritting his teeth against the throbbing pain, he tried to sit up. Nathalyia helped, then gasped on seeing the dark bruises on his chest.

The curtain moved aside and Alec peered into the room. Rafael knew he must have heard Nathalyia. "I'm all right," he repeated as the nurse and Nathalyia helped him put on the gown. Nodding, Alec let the curtain fall back into place.

Rafael had never wanted for them to go through this. Dealing with Patrick's injury was bad enough. The shivering woman beside him was exactly the reason he didn't plan to have a serious relationship. He didn't want to leave a woman with tears on her face and an ache in her heart that wouldn't go away.

"I'm going to take the dressing off so the doctor can examine you." The nurse positioned a tray beside him and began placing packages and gloves on top. "You can keep the gown on until he gets here."

His gut twisted at the misery and fear he saw in Nathalyia's wide eyes. "My vest protected me. Although it hurts a bit, the medic on the team said my arm just has a flesh wound. My chest is a bit bruised, but I'm going to be fine."

Her gaze slowly lowered to his chest. She lifted her hand, hovered. Closing his hand around hers, he held it to his chest.

"I was so scared," she whispered, the words barely audible.

That was exactly what he had never wanted to happen. "I would have done anything to spare you that."

"Somehow, I know that." Her eyes, glistening with tears, stared down at him. "You've always been so caring and protective of me. I should have remembered that."

He frowned. He wasn't following her train of thought. "Nat—"

The curtain whooshed back. A middle-aged man in a white

lab coat, with a stethoscope looped around his neck, entered. "I'm Dr. Freeman, Officer Dunlap." He extended his hand and briefly clasped Rafael's right. "I usually like family and friends to wait outside unless the patient is unable to give accurate information, but in this case we'll make an exception. Let's take a look. Please remove the gown."

Going to the sink in the corner, he began to wash his hands. Rafael grabbed the front of the gown to pull it down. Nathalyia reached to help. Her eyes widened on seeing the bruises again. Their gaze met. If he hadn't worn a vest, he'd be dead.

The nurse opened one of the packages on the tray, removed a pair of scissors, and cut away the bandage on his arm.

Gloved, the doctor probed the wound left by the bullet. "Looks like an in and out, but I want to be sure. I'm ordering an X-ray and CT scan." He moved to the bruises on Rafael's chest. "I bet your wound and this hurt like hell."

Rafael grimaced.

Unloosing the stethoscope, the doctor listened to Rafael's lungs and heart. "Take a deep breath and keep doing so until I tell you to stop."

Since Nathalyia's eyes were glued to his, he gritted his teeth and did as requested.

The doctor straightened. "Everything checks out. Let's get a temporary bandage on your arm, then send you to X-ray. If things check out there, you'll be out of here in no time."

"Thanks."

"Guess I don't have to tell you how lucky you are." The doctor glanced at Nathalyia, who was holding Rafael's hand again. "It seems in more ways than one."

"No," Rafael said.

"Thought not." Dr. Freeman went to the curtain. "That was a brave thing you did, helping your team member. You gave him the edge he needed. I'm glad we have men like you protecting us. See you after the tests."

"That goes for me, too," the nurse said. She redressed his wound. "I'll go see what's keeping X-ray."

"Thank you—for letting me stay," Nathalyia said.

"It never crossed my mind not to," he told her truthfully. She looked so lost and so terribly alone that Rafael reached for her without thinking. Perhaps she was frightened for herself as well. Her sister certainly wouldn't be any help.

"X-ray," a male voice called just before the curtain slid back to reveal a young bearded man pushing a gurney. "You ready to take a ride?"

"More than ready if it will get me out of here," Rafael replied, then slowly scooted over to the bed as the man directed.

The man put up the side rails and looked at Nathalyia. "You can come with us if you want."

She looked at Rafael. He reached for her hand. "Let's go."

In less than an hour Rafael, with his left arm bandaged and in a sling, eased off the exam table for the last time and got into a wheelchair. The X-ray and CT scan had come back negative. In the pocket of a clean shirt that Helen thought to bring were prescriptions for an antibiotic and pain pills.

When the nurse wheeled him into the waiting room, he saw Barron's wife with her head bowed, her hands clasped in her lap. Although people were with her, she appeared lost in her own hellish world.

As Rafael's family surrounded him, he knew they were all thinking of the night they had kept vigil for Patrick. He'd arrived earlier with Brianna, Simon, Maureen, Celeste, Brooke, and her husband, John, a short while ago. Now Brianna held on to Patrick as tightly as he held on to her. He might not have survived his injuries, and they would have never met and fallen in love.

Rafael glanced up at Nathalyia, who had been with him every second except when he was having the actual tests. Fear still shimmered in her eyes.

"I'm all right. I'm going to Sam and Helen's house. Thank you for coming. You need to go home."

She nodded, bit her lower lip. "If you need anything, just call."

"Thank you," he said, knowing he wouldn't call. Tonight he'd been selfish enough to want her with him, but for Nathalyia's sake it had to end. She was too loving and caring. "How are you getting home?"

"Do you need a ride?" Sam asked her.

Nathalyia blinked rapidly as the other brothers asked the same question. "No, Clarice and Jake are waiting outside." She looked at Rafael again. "Don't forget to have your prescriptions filled. Goodbye."

Rafael watched her go, his chest tight, an ache deep inside him that had nothing to do with his physical injuries.

Since Nathalyia knew she wouldn't sleep, she took home the checkbook from the office to pay invoices. She had an accountant, but Martin had taught her never to give anyone else authority to sign the checks.

She blew out a breath and reached for another tissue. She wished someone had taught her how to deal with the mess she had gotten herself into. If she had been truthful with Rafael, she'd be there with him now, making sure he took his medicine and that he slept. And if he couldn't sleep, she would hold him in her arms and just be there for him.

Her lie had prevented that. Tossing the tissue into the steadily growing pile in the wastebasket by her desk, she moved to another invoice. It was from the company that supplied their tea. Her lower lip began to tremble.

Getting up from her chair, she went to the balcony. The sun gently pushed away the night. The sky was beautiful in shades of blue and pink. The river behind her house stretched into an ocean that seemed endless.

She walked onto the balcony and ran her hand over the cushioned settee that she and Rafael had shared. She had lain in his arms on one of those rare occasions when she had been able to break away in the afternoon. They'd watched the sun set, then made love.

She wrapped her arms tight around her waist. How was she going to survive without him in her life? Her hands lowered. The baby. Their baby would help. Somehow she had to tell him. It was selfish and cruel not to. She'd come to the conclusion last night while looking at the ravaged face of Barron's wife. Nathalyia had called the hospital early this morning, but the hospital wasn't giving out any information on his condition. She prayed he was out of danger.

She hadn't thought last night to get Helen's number to check on Rafael. They'd probably had a big sleepover with the entire family, swapping tales and enjoying each other, celebrating that Rafael was all right—at least, that is the way she always envisioned a loving family.

The phone rang. She didn't move. It was probably a tele— She sprinted for the phone and saw an unknown name. Sam's phone was unlisted. "Hello."

"Good morning, Nathalyia," Helen greeted her. "I hope I didn't wake you."

"No. Is Rafael all right?" she asked, clutching the phone.

"He's resting now," Helen answered.

Now. Nathalyia's hand flexed on the phone. She should be

there, but he didn't want her. His asking her if she had a ride home had been telling. He appreciated her coming, but now leave and have a nice life, without me in it. It hurt, but she only had herself to blame.

"Everyone is going home after breakfast. We have to leave as well. Sam has a court case he can't miss, and I'm over at the senior citizen luncheon at the church."

"You're leaving him by himself?" Nathalyia asked, unable to keep the accusation from her voice.

"That's why I'm calling you. Would you mind bringing him lunch and perhaps dinner? Sometimes the luncheon runs late. So many seniors don't have anyone," Helen went on to say. "I realize you aren't seeing each other, but I could really use your help. I don't want to leave him alone, but the food we serve is often the only nourishing meal some of them get."

"He—" She took a deep breath and made herself say it. "He doesn't want me around him."

"Nonsense. He latched on to you the moment he saw you. He could have asked you to leave or for Sam or one of his other brothers. He didn't," Helen said. "After you left he ordered Alec to make sure you reached your friends safely—not that he needed to. As you probably already know, the Dunlap men are very safety conscious. Can you come? He needs to eat before he takes his antibiotics. He needs you."

There was only one answer. "Yes." She'd just drop off the food, check on him, and then leave. She'd done the same thing hundreds of times for the families of the children in her program.

"Wonderful." Helen gave her the address and her cell phone number. "If you could come anytime between eleven and twelve it would be perfect."

"All right."

"You're a lifesaver. Thanks again. Bye."

. . .

"*Helen, my love, you have* a devious mind."

Helen raised the bedcovers and slipped back into bed, placing her head over Sam's heart, her hand on his comforting chest. "I checked on Rafael before I called. He's restless, mumbling in his sleep. They love each other, and both are too afraid to admit their feelings and take a chance on the other."

"It's a complicated mess." He brushed his lips across her forehead. "You still think the baby is his?"

She angled her head to look at the only man she'd ever loved, the only man she'd ever given herself completely to. She never had one regret. "Nathalyia is a smart, successful businesswoman. It doesn't make sense to me that she would plan a life-changing event like a pregnancy and then go out with Rafael in a 'weak moment' like she said."

"If you're right, with the way he feels about marriage, it's going to make things worse for them, not better."

"I know. We just have to hope and pray their love is strong enough to get them through this."

"With your help, it will." His finger tilted her chin up. "Before everyone gets up, what do you say we concentrate on each other."

"I married a brilliant and intuitive man."

He grinned and lowered his mouth to hers.

Rafael woke up with dry mouth, a fuzzy brain, and a raging hard-on. He started to sit up. Pain lanced though his left arm. He suddenly remembered why his mouth felt like crap and why he had the erection. There was nothing he could do about either.

For the time being he needed the pain medicine. To stop

wanting to be buried deep inside Nathalyia's soft heat would be about as easy as moving his car with one finger.

When he'd needed one of those pills to help him sleep and forget the helpless fear in Nathalyia's face at around three that morning, he'd called the hospital and spoken to Barron's sister. He was in intensive care in critical condition. They'd removed the ruptured spleen the bullet had torn through. A bullet had nicked a kidney as well. "You can beat this, Barron," he said aloud. "You've got to."

Rafael scrubbed his hand over his face and gingerly scooted to the edge of the bed. He needed to brush his teeth, take a shower, and clear his head. Helen had said she would put on a waterproof dressing, but there was no way he was going to let her see him in this condition. It didn't matter that she'd been a nurse before she retired five years ago. He'd manage somehow.

"Rafael," Helen called, knocking on the bedroom door.

Rafael reached for the quilt at the foot of the bed. Helen could be a steamroller when she got something in her mind. "Morning. I think I'll stay in bed for a bit."

"Afraid not. Ready or not, at the count of three I'm coming in."

Rafael pulled more of the quilt across his lap just as Helen said "three" and entered. She placed the small tray that she held on the bed.

"Sorry, but I wanted to get this done before I leave." She opened a package and took out a bandage. "After breakfast everyone is leaving since you're doing so well. Sam and I will be gone all day. Don't worry. Someone will deliver your lunch so you can take your antibiotic."

She applied tape to the new waterproof bandage and stood. "After breakfast I'll change the bandage and you can sleep until lunchtime." She picked up the tray. "You want Sam to come in to help you adjust the water?"

"No," he said quickly. It would be almost as embarrassing if Sam saw what condition he was in. "Thanks for the bandage."

Her smile was tremulous. Leaning over, she kissed him on the cheek. "If you need help with the elastic pants, call."

He wasn't about to call. "I'll be fine."

Nodding, Helen left. Shoving back the covers, Rafael came unsteadily to his feet, then paused as his legs steadied. He just hoped the shower took care of his little problem. There was no way the sweatpants would hide his hunger and need for a woman he couldn't have.

SEVENTEEN

Thanks to Helen, Nathalyia had a new focus—helping to care for Rafael instead of worrying about him and feeling sorry for herself. Parking her car in front of Fontaine, she started for the door. Before she was three steps inside, staff members were coming up to her to ask about Rafael. The concern almost made her cry again.

"He's doing better. I plan to take him some food in a bit."

She went to the kitchen, put on an apron, and started cooking. She wanted to do as much as possible herself. The staff seemed to understand and worked around her as they went about food preparations for the opening.

"I'll have his iced tea waiting for you," Jake said from the kitchen doorway.

She glanced up from putting the bread pudding in the oven. "Thank you." She planned to take him everything he'd eaten at their first lunch together.

At 10:56 she pulled up in front of Helen and Sam's house. Her heart thudded with anxiety, but she refused to give in to her fear.

One of her pet peeves was serving warm or cold food that was supposed to be hot. Popping the Volvo's trunk, she got out and picked up the two large plastic-handled bags. Setting the food down, she closed the trunk, grabbed the handles, and went up the curved sidewalk bordered with white roses.

Again not giving herself time to get nervous, she rang the doorbell. The door opened and her heart rate went crazy. Her gaze clung to Rafael, noting the slight stubble on his face, the surprise in his eyes that she'd never tire of gazing into.

"Hi. Helen asked me to bring you lunch." She lifted the bags. "I can prepare you a plate so you can take your medicine and then be on my way."

"Yes. Sure." The frown on his face cleared. He stepped back.

"Glad to see you're doing better." She continued to the kitchen, glad she knew the way, since Rafael seemed to remain a bit stunned. "If you'll take a seat I'll have you a plate in a second. The plates and utensils are plastic, but that way Helen won't have to wash extra dishes. I brought you extra, so if you get hungry you can have a snack."

She clamped her teeth together. She was babbling. "How is Barron? I called the hospital, but couldn't get any information."

"He's strong. He'll make it."

Her heart went out to Barron and his family. "I'll keep praying." She pulled several containers from white plastic bags with a big red lobster with a knife in one claw and a fork in the other on the front.

"It smells good."

"It will taste just as good." She put a placemat she'd brought from her house on the table. On top she placed a plastic cup of iced tea, a small bowl of gumbo, and his utensils. "Please sit down. I'll put everything out so you can eat at your leisure."

She could feel him staring at her. "Aren't you eating with me?"

Was he being polite or did he really want her to stay? "You need to eat, take your medicine, and get back into bed." She busied herself with tossing his salad and tried to keep her mind off the enticing possibility of sharing that bed with him, and then chastised herself. The man had just been injured, for goodness' sake. She placed the Greek salad on the table, glad to see that he was eating.

"Where is your medicine?"

He looked at her. Her knees shook at the naked desire in his eyes. "In the bedroom. Second door to the left."

Ignoring the languid heat curling though her body, she went in search of the bedroom. The full-size bed was a tousled mess, just like hers had been after they made love. Swallowing, she straightened the covers, torturing herself by hugging his pillow, sweeping her hand over the sheet where he'd slept. Finished, she returned to the kitchen and set the medicine bottle by his plate.

He caught her hand. "I know how busy you are. Thanks."

Her throat clogged. No matter how busy she was, she'd always make time for him. "I—" She cleared her throat. "I'll get the rest of your food. It's a sample platter."

"Just like I had the first time we ate together," he said, watching her, still holding her hand.

He remembered. Was that what she'd hoped for? That the meal would bring back the memories of what they had shared afterward? Suddenly he released her hand and dug into his salad.

Nathalyia felt bereft. Had he thought of the baby he believed to be Martin's? She blinked away the tears and the guilt. As soon as he was better she'd tell him the truth. The doctor had said he should have the bandage off in a week to ten days. She could wait that long.

She placed the plate and the dessert on the table. "I'll put the rest in the refrigerator. All of the containers are microwavable."

"Did you eat breakfast?" he asked.

"No."

"When is the last time you ate?"

She frowned at the unexpected questions and tried to remember. "I think it was lunch yesterday."

A strange expression crossed his face. He stood and looked into the plastic bags. He pulled out a plate, took it to the table, and put a fried catfish filet and three shrimp on it. He placed the plate in front of the chair next to him, and pushed over the salad. "I'm not eating another bite until you do."

"Rafael, I'm not hungry."

"I guess I'm not either."

"You can't take your medicine on an empty stomach or you'll get sick."

"You need to eat." He repeated the same words she had earlier.

Aware she wasn't going to win the battle, she got another set of utensils from the bag, mumbled grace, and took a bite of fish. The first taste reminded her that lunch yesterday had been a small bowl of gumbo. She had to eat better for the baby's sake. She took another bite of fish, his salad. She thought of the times they'd fed each other, eaten from each other's plate. Her gaze lifted to his; yearning and regret stared back at her.

"Your food is getting cold," she managed, hoping he didn't see her unsteady hand.

Rafael took his seat and put another filet on her plate. "How are things at the restaurant?"

A safe topic. "Great. Three special events are scheduled for tomorrow, and of course people have already started booking for the holidays."

"I—" Air hissed though his teeth.

She was up in an instant. "What is it?"

"Nothing." His right hand lightly palmed the bandage on his left arm. "Guess the pain pill is wearing off."

She clenched her hands to keep from sweeping her hand across his furrowed brow. "When did you take the last one?"

He glanced up at her a bit sheepishly. "Three this morning."

"Three. That was eight—" She snapped her mouth shut and hurried into the bedroom to get his medicine. Returning, she shook two pills into the bottle cap, then added one of his antibiotics. "Open up."

"I can take them."

"Open."

He opened his mouth. She tilted the cap. Her fingers brushed against his upper lip as the pills tumbled into his mouth. This time air hissed though her teeth. His hot, hungry gaze locked on hers.

She grabbed his glass of tea and handed it to him. He simply stared at her. With a trembling hand, she pressed the glass against his waiting lips. "Do you want more?" she asked after he'd taken a couple of swallows.

His eyes flared, the heat hot enough to singe her. He'd once told her after making love that he'd always want more. Her entire body shaking, she set the glass on the table. "Do you feel like finishing or going to bed?"

"Bed," he answered tightly.

"Do you need help?"

He came to his feet. "I can manage."

She nodded abruptly. "I'll put the food away and let myself out."

"Thanks again. Take care of yourself."

"You do the same."

Slowly he turned and walked away. She wanted to go with him, watch him fall asleep. Instead she prepared him a fresh plate and wrote microwave instructions on top. Tidying up the kitchen, she started for the door and thought she heard a sound coming from the bedroom.

She was asking for trouble if she went to his bedroom. Yet she couldn't leave when he might still be in pain or need help. She went down the hall and peeped into the bedroom.

Rafael sat on the side of the bed trying to untie the laces of his tennis shoes.

"Let me help." She rushed over to kneel and quickly removed them.

"Thanks. Helen was afraid the pain medicine might make me clumsy and I'd trip over the laces. I can't stand house shoes or sandals."

"What about your loafers or deck shoes?" she asked, still kneeling.

"At my house. Sam is picking them up today."

She pulled the tennis shoes to her and threaded the laces so that they weren't dangling. "There. Some of my children feel strongly about wearing only their tennis shoes."

His gaze flickered to her stomach and then back to her. Shadows flickered in his eyes. "I can manage from here."

"Of course." Rejected. And it was her own doing. She swallowed hard and came to her feet. "Try to get some rest. Goodbye." Not waiting for him to answer, she turned to leave.

"Goodbye, Nathalyia."

She paused in midstep. Her breath caught. He'd finally said her name. Instead of the velvet lure she loved, his voice held a note of finality. She bit her lip, fought tears, and kept walking.

Rafael pushed to his feet when he heard the front door close softly. He wanted to see her one last time. Cradling his left arm, he went to the window in the living room.

His heart ached on seeing Nathalyia with her head down walking to her car. He forced himself not to go to her. This was for her. Caring about him would only bring her more heartache. She had enough to deal with. Once in the car she backed out of the driveway and drove away.

He turned away. Maybe he shouldn't have touched her, but he hadn't been able to stop himself. He hadn't known he could want this badly. The need intensified with every breath he took, but she wasn't for him. He just had to keep reminding himself.

Nathalyia entered the back door at Fontaine and quickly went to her office, closing the door softly behind her. The entire staff knew she had left to take food to Rafael. What would she say when they asked about the visit? *He appreciated the food, but he wanted no part of the person who delivered it.*

Yet there had also been those rare, wonderful moments when he'd been unable to hide his desire for her. But desire wasn't love.

Shoving her hand though her hair, she went to her desk. She'd drive herself crazy if she kept thinking about the situation she'd placed them in. She'd made a horrible decision and there was nothing she could do to try and fix it until Rafael was better. According to the doctor, that wouldn't be for several days. She just had to be patient until then.

Her office door opened behind her. Frowning, she turned to see Theresa. The surprise on her face was obvious. "Why were you coming into my office?"

"I thought you might have a comb," she said, her hand going to her wig, this one a sleek bob.

"Your hair looks fine."

"Really?" Smiling, she touched her hair again. "This is a new look for me, and I guess I'm kind of nervous. I'm trying to be the best waitress I can."

Her explanation sounded plausible, but Nathalyia wasn't sure she believed Theresa.

"You don't look too hot." Theresa folded her arms. "The cop didn't welcome you with open arms, did he?"

Nathalyia didn't want to talk about it, especially with Theresa, who never had anything good to say about the baby or Rafael. "I have an extra comb in the bathroom. I'll get it for you."

Theresa crossed to her and lightly touched her shoulder. "It's all right if you're ashamed. It sucks when a man turns his back on you, but I tried to warn you."

Nathalyia went to the bathroom and returned with the comb. "You should get back to work."

Theresa's lips, painted a bright red, tightened. "The sooner you accept that you're just like me and Paula, the better off you'll be. Men use us; they don't love us."

Nathalyia stared into Theresa's cold, calculating eyes. "You're wrong. I will never be like you, Paula, or Mama. I love the father of my baby. I didn't go out with him because I thought I could get something out of it, and I'm not running to another man hoping he'll make me feel better about myself. And when I have our baby, it will know that I love and want it. I won't teach it to hate its father, nor will I blame and hate it for the decisions I made."

"You can say that because you have money." Theresa lashed back, her voice trembling with anger. "You don't have to worry about food or rent like we did. You have that big house and never invited me over. Not once. It hurts when you care more for Jake and Clarice."

"Because they've proven they care for me. You've never asked how I felt since you've known about the baby. You just keep telling me what an awful mistake I'm making," Nathalyia told her.

"Because you are! Jake and Clarice are probably painting this rosy picture, but they've never been really poor like we have. You have it made, but if this restaurant fails, you and the baby will be on the street." Theresa shook her head. "You can't have both. I don't want to see you lose all this and end up with nothing."

"I'll have my restaurant *and* my baby," Nathalyia told her fiercely.

"But not the father of the baby," Theresa tossed in. "A man that good-looking wouldn't have stayed faithful for long anyway. He probably misses the sex, but once his old girlfriends hear he's been shot and how he played the hero, he'll be swamped with so many women he'll forget about you."

Not wanting Theresa to see how much her words echoed her deepest fear, Nathalyia turned toward her desk. She wanted Rafael to want to be with her because he loved her, not out of obligation and duty, once she told him about the baby. "Jake is probably looking for you."

"You never listened when you were growing up either. Just remember, we're sisters and I'll always be here for you and tell you the truth even when you don't want to hear it," Theresa said. "I know what it is to hurt like you're hurting because a man you care about has moved on. Clarice and Jake don't have a clue. I'll check on you before I leave tonight." Theresa closed the door, and took a deep breath.

That was close. Theresa had thought Nathalyia was still gone. *Good thing she didn't go in earlier or she might have been caught rifling through her desk for the petty cash box. It turned out good anyway.*

She was able to plant more doubts about the cop, but she had wanted to slap Nathalyia a time or two. She thought she was so much better than Theresa. She couldn't let her anger get the best of her. She had to play this cool and keep Nathalyia off balance. Marrying the cop would blow Theresa's plans to hell.

The moment Helen arrived home and saw Rafael's face she knew her plan hadn't worked. He looked lost and lonely. Standing beside him, Sam stared at his feet.

"I know you did it to help me, but please don't interfere again. She has her life and I have mine," Rafael said. "Sam is going to take me home."

"No." Helen quickly went to him. "Get mad at me, but don't do this."

"I'm not mad at you." He curved his right arm around her shoulders, held her close. "I just want to be by myself. Walk on the beach."

Fighting tears, she looked at him. The kind of pain that no pill could ease stared back at her. "Who will take care of you?"

"I'll be fine," Rafael told her. "I called a nursing agency and hired someone to change my bandage daily."

Anger flared in her eyes. She straightened. "You do that, Rafael Dunlap, and I'll never cook for you again. Plus it will break my heart."

"He wouldn't do that, would you, Rafael?" Sam said softly, but there was no mistaking the bite in his voice.

"Never." Rafael rubbed his forehead. "I can't be what she wants and needs. You have to understand that."

Helen opened her mouth, but Sam touched her arm and shook his head. "All right, now go lie down while I fix supper."

"She left food in the refrigerator," Rafael said.

She, not Nathalyia. "Would you like that or chicken tacos?" It was the quickest and the most opposite to seafood she could think of.

"Tacos."

"Go to bed," she told him. "I'll take you home myself in a few days when you're feeling better and can handle a can opener."

The corners of his mouth tilted upward slightly. He pulled a piece of paper from his pocket. "Will you cancel the nurse for me?"

"Yes, and thank you," she told him.

He hugged her again. "I know you did it because you love me, but no more interfering."

"All right," she said slowly.

Straightening, Rafael slowly went back to his bedroom. Helen went into Sam's waiting arms. "I made it worse."

"You made him see and realize what he's missing." Sam kissed her on the cheek, and curved his arms around her waist.

"I only hope she's doing better than he is," Helen said.

"From the frantic way she was last night, I wouldn't put money on it."

"I started this. I'll go into the kitchen and call her." Pushing out of his arms, Helen pulled her cell phone from her handbag and punched in Nathalyia's number. She answered on the third ring. Helen circled her arm around her waist. Nathalyia sounded as lost and as lonely as Rafael had looked.

"Nathalyia, this is Helen. I—I'm sorry."

There was a slight pause. "Don't be. I did this."

Helen's antenna went up. "Why do you think that?"

"Nothing. But could you please do me a favor and let me know when he's well?"

Helen reached out her hand to Sam, who had followed her into the kitchen. "Of course."

"I'd also like to send Barron's family some gift certificates to eat at Fontaine. Would you mind picking them up? I'll leave them with your name on the envelope at the hostess station."

"Not at all. That's thoughtful of you," Helen told her. "When

I went by the hospital before I came home, his wife said he's stable."

"That's good news. Thanks for the call."

Nathalyia was too polite to hang up first. "Good night, Nathalyia."

"Goodbye."

Helen turned to Sam. "It isn't over between them. Come on, help me cook. We'll talk later."

Sam went to the sink and washed his hands. "Good news or bad?"

Helen glanced toward the hallway. "Heaven only knows."

He was a weak man. Two weeks after he'd last seen Nathalyia, Rafael blew out a breath and climbed out of his car in front of her house. When she'd called that afternoon asking if he could come over later tonight to talk, he should have said no. But the slight trembling in her voice tugged at his heart, no matter how he wished otherwise.

She probably just wanted to see that he was well. His wounds had healed and the bruising on his chest had disappeared. The doctor had cleared him to drive, and he was returning to work in two weeks. He'd reassure her, and then he was out of there and going back home, where he hoped he'd sleep better.

Nearing the door, he saw her pacing in the entryway. The ability to see inside still bothered him, unbreakable glass or not. He stepped onto the porch. By the time he reached the door, she was there.

"I thought you might have changed your mind."

"I was talking to Barron. He's out of ICU and on a regular floor," he explained.

"I heard. Please come in." Stepping back, she waved him to a seat in the den. "That night the doctor said you made the difference."

Rafael shook his head and sat on the teal leather sofa. "There was no indication that things would go bad."

"Then how did they know you were the police?" she asked.

"Bad luck." Rafael blew out a breath. "We learned later from an informant that a friend of theirs happened to see the police cars and our transport and called them." His eyes narrowed dangerously. "I want to be there when they find and arrest him."

"I always thought being a policeman was more than just a job for you. You like what you do. You like helping people."

"Yeah. I guess it's in the blood. I have no intention or desire to do anything else."

"I guess not." She rubbed her hands on her pants, then stood. "I'm sorry. Would you like anything to drink?"

"No, thanks. You said this wouldn't take long."

"That's right." She looked at him, then away. "This is difficult."

"You said that before," he reminded her.

"Yes." She stepped away from him. "I also remember telling myself that you might hate me for what I was about to tell you. The same goes for this time as well."

Rafael came to his feet. "What is it?"

"You're the father of my baby. There was no procedure."

EIGHTEEN

"What?" Shock radiated though him.

"I lied. I thought it was the only way." She twisted her hands together. "We were just dating. Neither of us expected a baby. I didn't want to trap you, but the night of the shooting, I realized how wrong I was. You deserve to know you're going to be a father."

Rafael felt his legs tremble. He plopped back in the chair. His gaze locked on her stomach. "We were careful."

"It doesn't appear to have mattered," she told him and eased down on the sofa across from him. "I can understand you might have some doubt since I've changed my story, but the procedure to test for paternity is dangerous for the baby. We'll have to wait until the baby is born."

Baby. His hand scrubbed over his face. He stared at hers. There wasn't a doubt in his mind that she was telling him the truth this time. "I believe you."

Her shoulders sagged in relief. "Thank you."

"How—how far along are you?" he asked.

"About six weeks, as close as I can tell."

Lines radiated across his forehead. "You haven't been to a doctor."

She shook her head. "I took a pregnancy test."

He shot out of his chair. "Then you might not be pregnant."

"There are other signs." She twisted in her seat. "I'm pregnant."

Blowing out a breath, he looked skyward. "When do you want to get married?"

"I don't want to get married, and neither do you," she said. "You made that clear."

"We don't have a choice. Dunlap men take care of their responsibilities." He forged on adamantly.

"If I weren't pregnant, would you have asked me to marry you?"

She deserved the truth. "No, but then I didn't plan to ever marry. My job is too dangerous. The shooting proved I made the right decision. It wouldn't be fair to the woman or any children we might have." His jaw tightened. "I won't put any woman through what Barron's wife is going through."

"I understand." She came to her feet. "I'm your worst nightmare."

"Don't say that," he told her.

"It's been a long day. I'm tired."

He studied her, saw the dark smudges beneath her eyes. "Have you been sleeping all right?"

"I don't require very much sleep." She went to the door. "Good night, Rafael. Thank you for coming."

"Why don't you want to get married?" he asked.

"Because we don't love each other, and you just said you never wanted to get married. Good sex isn't enough to sustain a marriage, and the child would suffer," she told him. "I hope you'll want to be a part of the baby's life, but of course I won't ask for any financial support."

Her reasoning made sense, but for some odd reason her easy acceptance annoyed the hell out of him. Without a word, he went through the door she held open. He didn't stop until he was by his car. Instead of getting inside, he pulled his cell and dialed Sam's number.

"The baby that Nathalyia's carrying is mine," he said as soon as his brother answered. "Tell Helen she was right."

Laughter came through the phone. "Helen, get in here. Congratulations. Looks like you'll need a tux for yourself."

"There won't be any wedding."

"And why not?" Sam asked sharply.

"Like Nathalyia said, we don't love each other," Rafael said. "Marriage would be a disaster. I'll be a part of the baby's life."

"You know how we all feel about a man taking responsibility, especially if he's a father," Sam continued.

"Just let me handle this. I'd rather be grilled once. All of you can come over to my house in the morning around nine. I'm staying here tonight." Rafael stared toward the house. "She hasn't been sleeping. She will tonight."

"That's the Rafael we all know and love," Helen said. "Now, go take care of your family. Bye, and thanks for the call."

Your family. Rafael never thought those two words would have any association or connection to him. He'd planned his life. Nowhere in it was there a family.

Rafael started back up the walk. Through the glass door, he saw Nathalyia sitting on the bottom step of the stairs with her head in her hands. He'd caused that. He'd only meant to—what? His mind stumbled. What had he planned for them?

He knew from that first kiss she wasn't experienced. He should have walked away. In the past, he'd only dated women who knew what to expect—hot sex and short goodbyes.

With Nathalyia it had been different. Leaving never entered his mind. It wasn't a matter of making a conquest; he'd simply wanted to be with her and earn her trust.

Reaching over, he rang the doorbell, his gaze still on her. Her head came up sharply. He watched the smile form on her face, then saw it disappear. Standing, she quickly crossed the room.

"Are you all right?' Her searching gaze ran over him.

"I'm fine." He stepped inside, closing and locking the door before turning to her. "It's you. Tonight you're going to sleep." *Go take care of your family.* The words resonated in his head just as they had when Helen said them.

Grabbing her hand, he started up the stairs. "My turn to take care of you."

"You should be home resting."

Ignoring her, he continued up the stairs and pushed the bedroom door open. Memories hit him of the last time they were in this room, the wide bed, the pleasure. Shaking the thoughts away, he went to the bed. "Please sit down."

Sighing, she perched on the side of the bed. Bending, he removed her heels, thought of her doing the same thing for him. "I'll never understand how women can stay in these things all day."

"You really don't have to do this."

"Yes, I do. Tonight, you sleep." He rose to his feet. "Which drawer is your gown in?"

"In the middle drawer of the dresser. but I don't think it's a good idea for you to undress me."

His mouth quirked. "Pity."

Her lips almost curved upward.

He went to the dresser instead of leaning down and kissing her as he wanted to. Tonight wasn't for him. Opening the drawer, he picked up the first gown he saw. Thankfully, it was long and made of cotton. He handed it to her. "I'll step outside for a few minutes."

"Thank you."

Nathalyia lowered her head as soon as the door closed. Her emotions were all over the place. She had been so wrong. She'd thought he'd insist on marriage. He had proposed, but it had been because of duty, not love. Despite her being concerned that he'd think she was trying to trap him, she couldn't push aside the feeling of hurt.

"Nathalyia."

She started. "Just a minute." Standing, she headed for the bathroom, the gown in her hand. Quickly undressing, she put on the gown and hung up her clothes. Removing the pins from her hair, she placed them on the vanity, brushed her hair, and then her teeth.

"Nat."

"Almost there." Rinsing her mouth, she hurried back to the bed, pulled the duvet to the foot of the bed, and climbed in. "Ready."

The door opened. Rafael's gaze swept the bed. "Where are your clothes?"

"I hung them up," she said, then hurried on. "Habit."

Something hot flared in his eyes. Both knew there had been times when she had cared less about her clothes. "I'm in bed, so you can let yourself out."

"If I leave, how can I make sure you're sleeping?" He picked up a small chair by the fireplace and placed it a few feet away from the bed. He paused before sitting. "You kept the rose."

"It was the last thing you gave me," she told him.

"Have you made an appointment to see the doctor?" he asked.

"No." She played with the top bedsheet. "Although I know I'm pregnant, sometimes it's like, if a doctor doesn't confirm it, it might be a mistake."

He leaned forward and took her hand. "The past couple of weeks haven't been easy for you."

She almost lied, but if they were to develop a friendship beyond the bedroom, she had to be honest. "I worried about what kind of parent I'll make. How I'll manage the restaurant later on and take care of the baby."

"I'll help in any way I can."

"I know."

"Enough talking." Standing, he lifted the covers so she could scoot down farther. He tucked her in. "Close your eyes and go to sleep. I'm here."

She wished he were in bed with her, holding her. "Good night."

"Night, Nat."

Nathalyia turned on her side away from him, but she didn't close her eyes. She glanced over her shoulder and found him looking at her. "You should be in bed."

"I'm fine. Go to sleep." The light went out.

She closed her eyes briefly, then opened them. Gradually her eyes adjusted to the darkness. The full moon and drawn drapes allowed her to make him out. "You can't sleep in that chair and I won't be able to sleep knowing you're uncomfortable." She scooted over, keeping her back to him. "This bed is big enough for both of us."

Seconds stretched into minutes. She looked over her shoulder. Sitting up, she snapped on the lamp on the night table, then picked up a magazine.

"What are you doing?"

"Either we both sleep or we both stay awake." She went back to the restaurant industry magazine. "I've been meaning to read this article for a week."

"You know you're just being stubborn."

"I could say the same thing about you," she said and began reading.

"Move over."

Placing the magazine back on the table, she scooted farther over in bed. She felt the bed dip. The light went out. "Good night."

After a long moment, she heard him say, "Night."

Closing her eyes, she clasped the pillow under her head, wishing it were Rafael.

Rafael lay on top of the sheet. He'd removed his shoes. Anything else was asking for trouble. He stared up at the ceiling, trying to keep his mind from thinking about the woman he wanted and how close to him she was. He wasn't afraid of his own death. He couldn't be and remain effective. Yet he knew the possibility was there, just as every policeman did. He hadn't counted on a family, but he had one anyway.

He heard a whimper from beside him. His heart squeezed in his chest. Nathalyia was turned toward him, her body huddled in a fetal position, her eyes closed. Throwing back the sheet, he pulled her into his arms.

"Shhh. It's all right," he kept repeating, rocking her, kissing her hair. She burrowed into him. The trembling of her body gradually eased and so did the death grip she had on his shirt.

Finally, her even breathing told him she was asleep. He could release her. He told himself he didn't want to because she might wake up. He pulled the cover over them. If a raging hard-on was the price he had to pay to ensure she had a good night's sleep, he'd gladly pay the price.

· · ·

Nathalyia woke up in Rafael's arms. She smiled to herself, feeling the bulge against her hips, and snuggled closer. He stiffened. At once the night came crashing back.

She shut her eyes tighter to keep the stinging moisture at bay. Moving away, she got out of bed and went to the bathroom, shutting the door behind her.

Not giving herself time to dwell on her unhappiness, she took a bath. When she came out in her robe, he was gone. Swallowing the lump in her throat, she dressed and went downstairs.

She entered the kitchen to find him sitting at the large breakfast table, which looked out to the east gardens. On the table was a glass of orange juice and two slices of toast.

"Good morning. I can go get you something, but I didn't want to leave until you came down."

"I'm not very hungry, but thank you." She rubbed her hand on her slacks.

"It's important that you eat," he said.

A stiff smile on her face, she said, "I know. I'm fully capable of taking care of my baby."

His dark eyes narrowed. "It's mine as well. Maybe we should get married."

"We had this conversation last night. You don't love me, do you?" His silence wounded her just as much as his words had last night. She tried not to let it show on her face. After all, she'd known what his answer would be, but she realized that deep in her heart she thought that after last night he might have realized he loved her.

"Neither one of us expected this," he finally answered.

"Of course." She dragged her hand though her hair. "It's better this way. A child shouldn't grow up feeling unloved or in the way." Her hand fisted on her stomach. "I couldn't stand that."

He looked at her for a long time. "Is that how you grew up?"

Her eyes widened. His accurate assessment caught her by surprise. She started to retreat from the truth as she'd always done, then decided the truth might help him accept and understand her decision.

She took a seat in one of the chairs. "I have a confession to make. Both of my parents aren't dead, and I'm not an only child." She frowned. His expression didn't change as he took a seat beside her. "You don't seem surprised."

"I'm not. You have a very open face."

Her frown didn't clear. "Yet you said nothing."

"It wasn't my right to dig," he replied.

She understood. "And since neither of us planned for this to last, it didn't matter."

"No."

The pain deepened. She glanced away. "I guess I'm like them just like she said."

"They who? Like whom?"

She squared her shoulders and lifted her head. "My mother never even came close to marrying any of the three men who fathered her three different children. My two older sisters each have children by two different men." She clasped her hands tighter.

"I made myself a promise that I'd never be like them, being passed from one man to the other, hoping for 'the big score' as they called it." Her head lowered. "They saw the baby as a meal ticket, and when that didn't materialize, a nuisance."

"You're nothing like that, could never be," Rafael told her, anger in every line of his body. "You would never see your child that way. You have an amazing capacity for love. You care about people."

But very few adults love me in return. She stood. "I need to go to work."

"You need to rest." His brows knitted.

"Thanks to you, I did." Leaving the kitchen, she went to the front door. "Goodbye, Rafael."

He didn't move. "I don't want us to be polite strangers."

"Then we won't be." She glanced at her watch and opened the door. "I don't want to be late."

He stopped when he was even with her. "What happens now?"

"I don't know."

He nodded. "I'll call you tonight."

"You don't have to do that," she said, her eyes bright with unshed tears.

"I'll call."

"All right."

He started out the door again, only to stop and look back at her for a long moment before continuing to his car parked at the curb.

Refusing to cry, Nathalyia closed the door and started toward the stairs. She'd cried enough.

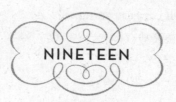

NINETEEN

Rafael got into his car and just sat there. What had he done? He'd seen the sheen of tears in Nathalyia's eyes that she refused to give in to. She was hurting. Hell, what decent, honest woman wouldn't be in her situation?

It didn't do any good reminding himself that he should have walked away. He hadn't and now she was going to have his baby.

A baby!

He rubbed his face and felt the tightness in his chest. He'd never thought of being a father. Yet there was no way he wouldn't be there for his child and for Nathalyia. To do that, he had to somehow get his desire for her under control. Continuing the affair would be selfish and irresponsible. He never wanted a family to worry about him. Yet whether he was married to Nathalyia or not, that was going to happen.

He pulled away from the curb and headed home. He wasn't

looking forward to the conversation with his brothers, but knew he'd have no choice.

Twenty minutes later, he turned onto his street. Several houses away, he saw the metallic gray truck in his driveway. He parked on the other side of Sam's truck in the double driveway of the detached garage.

They'd all had keys since he'd never changed the locks on the house, but his four brothers sat on the rattan furniture his mother prized. He winced and got out. She'd be ashamed of him. His father even more so. They'd been taught from an early age to honor and take care of women.

He hadn't.

Rafael wasn't feeling too pleased with himself at the moment either. He'd prided himself on swaying people to his way of thinking. He'd failed last night and this morning with Nathalyia. The hard question he had yet to answer was: Had he tried hard enough to get her to marry him, or subconsciously had he thought that if they were married and something happened to him, it would be harder for her?

He slowly went up the wooden steps and unlocked the front door. "Anyone want coffee?"

"No, thanks," came the response from his brothers.

Rafael continued to the kitchen, the place where many of the family decisions were held. He pulled out a chair that allowed him a view of the marshes and ocean beyond. Before she became pregnant, he had begun to toy with the idea of bringing Nathalyia here. He could easily visualize them walking along the beach holding hands or sitting on the back porch relaxing, just as his parents had done.

"Did you change your mind about getting married?" Sam asked. His big brother was never one to shy away from the tough subjects.

"No."

"Why?" Again Sam spoke. Apparently Patrick, Simon, and Alec were content at the present to let Sam handle things.

"Lots of reasons." Rafael watched a seagull glide on the wind above a sailboat. He and Nathalyia had planned to go sailing the week she'd told him she was pregnant.

"Rafael?" Sam pressed.

"We care about each other, but we don't love each other," Rafael finally answered. "She thinks we'd end up hating each other if we got married. More important, it would ruin the child's life."

"It doesn't have to be that way," Patrick said. "Women get moody sometimes when they're pregnant."

"Her home life growing up wasn't like ours, and that's all I'm going to say." It still made Rafael angry to think she compared herself to her mother and sisters.

"You're a persuasive man, Rafael. You proved that by pursuing Nathalyia when she didn't seem interested," Alec pointed out. "So, what's the difference this time?"

"I never planned to get married." Rafael looked at Simon sitting across from him. "I don't want an officer knocking on her door to tell her I won't be coming home."

"You're sure that's the only reason?" Sam asked.

"I'm sure," Rafael said. "And before you ask, I plan to be a part of the baby's life."

"From a distance?" Patrick commented, his displeasure obvious in the stern set of his mouth.

"If she needs me, I'll be there." With Patrick's wife pregnant, Rafael understood his brother's annoyance with him. He wouldn't let Nathalyia or his baby down.

Patrick looked at Sam, then Simon. "Does Helen or Maureen always tell you when they're bothered or not feeling well?"

"No," the brothers answered.

"Add Celeste's name to the list." Alec shook his dark head. "She's as independent as they come, and thinks she can take care of everything herself. Her reasoning is that she doesn't want to worry me. I worry about her anyway."

"Exactly," Patrick continued. "When Brianna is at work, knowing she'll be home later makes my day better. Since she's pregnant, I don't relax completely until she is home, until I hold her, and know she and our baby are all right."

"No matter how many times I tell Celeste not to drive up here at night from Charleston, she continues to." Alex grimaced. "I worry about her driving back in the morning. My transfer can't come soon enough."

"Phone calls aren't going to do it for you," Sam predicted. "I don't mind saying, you wouldn't be the man I'm proud to call my brother if they were."

Rafael turned to Sam. "Even after what's happened?"

Sam affectionately clasped him on the shoulder. "Things happen for a reason. You and Nathalyia just have to figure out, once the shock wears off, what happens next."

"You think that's marriage?" Rafael didn't have to look at his brothers to know they all felt the same way.

"Honestly, yes." Sam stared at Rafael. "But that's a decision for you and Nathalyia."

"There won't be a wedding," Rafael said.

Sam stood. The other brothers followed. "I've lived long enough to learn that life has a way of changing people's minds."

"Not this time," Rafael said.

"We'll see." Sam continued out the door with his brothers. They all climbed into his truck. Backing out of the drive, Sam drove away.

Rafael went back inside to shower. He loved and respected his brothers, but this wasn't going to turn out the way they wanted.

He just wished he didn't have this unsettling feeling in his gut that he was missing something.

Clarice walked from the parking lot early the next morning with a huge grin on her face. Jake hadn't left her apartment until almost four. She should be tired, but being with him was exhilarating. They hadn't made love, but they had come close. As usual, Jake had been the one to pull back. He'd said he wanted her to be sure. Telling him that she was hadn't convinced him.

She finally realized why she sought him out while they were at work, why she liked to tease him. She cared deeply for him. She was on the brink of falling in love for all the right reasons—not just to have a man—and it felt wonderful.

If possible, her grin widened. It was fantastic being able to tease the man who held your heart in the gentle palm of his hand, as well as to get him so turned on that he forgot everything except pleasing each other.

Jake was still a little hung up on the difference in their ages and, despite his being one of the most self-confident men she'd ever met, he worried that his scar bothered her. Her smile faded and she had to stop.

Tears mixed with anger clouded her eyes. Tears for what he had to go through, tears for him thinking he was less because of the scar, anger at the ignorant people who had made him feel that way.

"Did Theresa mess up?" Clarice turned to see Nathalyia staring at her. "Or did you and Jake have an argument?"

Clarice still didn't understand why Nathalyia kept a troublemaker like Theresa, but she had more important things to think about—like driving Jake to the edge again tonight.

"No, I can handle her." Jake was right, Nathalyia had enough on her mind. Clarice looped her arm through Nathalyia's and continued toward the back door. "As for Jake and me, we're doing fine. How about you?"

"Hopefully getting there, but I'm tired of talking about me," Nathalyia said. "I'm glad about you and Jake. A good man deserves a good woman."

About to punch in the code, Clarice straightened. "Thank you."

"Just telling it the way I see it." Nathalyia punched in the code and opened the door. "You ready for the private party?"

"Yes." Clarice stepped though the door Nathalyia held open. "Thanks for selecting me."

"I always want the best for private parties. That's you. Besides, you're doing me a favor by coming in on your day off." Nathalyia closed the door. "Serving thirty women, as you know, can be challenging."

"I'm up to it." She glanced over her shoulder toward the bar. "Besides, there are certain perks."

Nathalyia smiled. "Go on. He probably can't wait to see you."

Clarice was already moving. "Later." She stepped around the corner and saw Jake immediately. Her heart did a little dance. His back was to her as he reached up to place bottles of liquor on the display above the bar. His jeans cupped his rear, his white shirt stretched over his chiseled back and broad shoulders. He was built, and all hers.

He turned, saw her, and stopped. From thirty feet away she saw the flare of desire in his blue eyes. Her body reacted; her nipples hardened. Somehow, she made her legs move and went around the bar. All the while, he watched her like he wanted to strip her naked and do wild erotic things to her. "Hi," she managed, when she could draw enough air into her lungs.

"I thought I could handle this," he said. "It's getting harder and harder."

"What is it?" she asked, reaching out to brush her hand down his arm.

"I see you and I want you," he growled.

She smiled provocatively at him despite the desire surging through her, the need. "Same here, and, in spite of that, I want to be near you, have you chew on me."

His eyes seared her. She sucked in her breath. "There's something on the shelf in the storage room I can't reach. Maybe you can help me." Without waiting for an answer, she turned and walked away. She heard him following and smiled.

"I don't see why I wasn't asked to work the party," Theresa said, her hand planted on Nathalyia's desk.

"Because you haven't shown me yet that you can take the demands of thirty women and remain cordial and efficient," Nathalyia answered. She hadn't been in her office thirty minutes before Theresa had knocked on her door. She was in no mood for this.

"How would you know?" Theresa asked. "You're gone almost every evening with that dude. At least you were until you got knocked up and he walked out on you."

"He didn't walk out," Nathalyia snapped.

"I didn't mean anything," Theresa said, trying to backpedal. "I just don't want you to forget that men can talk sweet, but all they want is one thing."

"Perhaps you went out with the wrong men." Nathalyia leaned forward and picked up her pen. "Any luck in finding work at home?"

"Ah. No."

"People should be happy at work," Nathalyia went on. "I don't think you are here."

Theresa's eyes widened. "Yes, I am. Just because I heard them talking about the great money in tips you can make and I wanted to earn some doesn't mean I'm unhappy."

"You're thinking about the money. I hope the other servers really enjoy what they do," Nathalyia told her. "Therein lies the difference between you and the ones who are working the party."

Theresa's lower lip began to tremble. "Maybe because they've never had it as hard as I have. There haven't been many days in my life when I've gone to bed really happy. I'm trying, for you and for Mama."

Nathalyia didn't feel the familiar guilt. Perhaps because Theresa always brought up how bad she'd had it, or their mother when they talked. Nathalyia had tried to please her mother in so many ways while growing up, until she had learned it was impossible.

"Your shift is about to start. You don't want to be late on the floor."

Theresa looked as if she wanted to hit Nathalyia. When she was younger, Theresa had. "I'm doing my best."

"That's all I ask." Nathalyia wasn't falling for the "poor me" look again. Looking as if she was still a bit unsure, Theresa left.

Nathalyia leaned back in a chair for a moment, then pushed to her feet. She wanted to do a walk-through again of the private dining room before the engagement party arrived.

The woman's sister had been rather demanding. She'd wanted extra waitstaff—at no cost—assigned parking spaces, and shrimp at wholesale prices. If the future bride or the guests were anything like the hostess, Nathalyia might have actually done Theresa a favor.

Theresa stared at Nathalyia with pure hatred as she went to the private dining room. *Put that fat sow over your own sister, will you? Thinking about firing me, are you? We'll just see about that.*

She fingered the small device in the pocket of her apron. She was making good money using the decoder to steal customers' credit card information, but it was no longer enough. She planned to strip Nathalyia of everything and leave her with nothing and no one. *Before I'm through with you, you'll wish you'd never been born.*

Clarice, as the lead waitstaff member for the private party, finished her walk-through with Nathalyia, then went to stand by the hostess booth to wait for Mrs. Ford, who was giving the engagement party. Nathalyia had said the woman had a lot of demands, but that was all.

The doors swung open and three women came though the double doors being held open by two waiters. Clarice couldn't believe it. *Please no.*

One of the women stopped, stared at her. Hate shone back at her from dark green eyes, thanks to contacts. The other two continued.

"Welcome to Fontaine," one of the hostesses greeted them.

"I'm Alice Ford. I have a private room reserved for my sister's engagement party," the woman said. Middle-aged, thin-faced, she had the same fake blue eyes as the younger woman with her. Both were slender with fair skin. Their mousy brown hair was dyed blond.

"Certainly, Ms. Ford. We're expecting you." Marilyn turned to Clarice.

There was no help for it. "Welcome, Mrs. Ford. I'm the lead waitress, Clarice Howard. We're happy to have you and will do everything to make the day memorable."

"That remains to be seen," Mrs. Ford said. Then she said to the elderly woman next to her, "Come on, Mama."

"Alice, I don't want her anywhere near me," said the younger woman, who had stopped on seeing Clarice.

Clarice gritted her teeth to keep from saying she felt the same way.

"What's the matter?" Alice asked, looking back at her sister.

Her sister whispered in Alice's ear. Her head jerked up. "I want to see the manager immediately!"

Since the day had just begun, many of the waitstaff were in the front to greet guests, hold open the door, or just hang. All were glued to the obviously tense situation.

"She's in her office," Clarice said. Neither she or Nathalyia would want this discussed in front of the arriving guests or employees. "I'll show you."

"I don't want you anywhere near us," Alice Ford snapped.

"I'll take you," Theresa volunteered, a gleeful expression on her face. "I'm sure Nathalyia would want to know there's a problem."

Alice threw a hateful look at Clarice, then with her mother, followed Theresa. Her sister stalked after them.

Clarice could think of only one thing, getting to Jake. He met her a few steps away. "Don't you dare buckle."

Clarice clamped her lips together and clenched her fists. Anger made her tremble.

Jake caught her arm. "B.J., take care of the bar." In the storage room, this time there were no heated kisses. "Talk."

"The intended bride is the woman I hit. She's the one who made me lose my teaching job."

Nathalyia looked up as her door swung open. Seeing Theresa, she started to ask her if she had forgotten how to knock when she saw the three women with her. Two looked angry. Since Theresa was practically dancing with glee, Nathalyia was sure she wasn't the cause of the problem.

Nathalyia came to her feet. "Mrs. Ford, good morning."

"I want that woman fired," she said.

"Who and why?" Nathalyia had dealt before with irate customers who wanted people fired.

"Clarice. She attacked my sister." Mrs. Ford pointed to the tight-lipped woman standing behind her.

Nathalyia knew Clarice had a quick temper, but she also valued her. "Theresa, please ask Clarice to come in here, and close the door behind you."

Theresa glared at her, then left. Nathalyia hoped the subtle reminder to close the door would keep her from eavesdropping. With Jake probably watching the door once Clarice entered, Theresa wouldn't have a chance to spy.

"I don't want that woman near me," the sister said.

"I'm sorry, but I have no intention of discussing this without Clarice here." She indicated the sofa. "Why don't you sit your mother there. You and your sister can have a seat in front of my desk."

"I knew I should have selected another place for the engagement party," Mrs. Ford said, then helped her mother to sit down.

Nathalyia felt like saying she wished she had as well. The door opened and Clarice came in. Behind her, Nathalyia saw Jake.

The woman's sister sneered. "He's the only type of man she can get."

Nathalyia came around her desk. "What is your name?"

The woman blinked and looked uneasy before she said, "Evelyn Hill."

"Ms. Hill, if you want to continue this conversation, I suggest you respect everyone in this restaurant and keep your unwarranted opinions to yourself," Nathalyia said, clearly seeing why Clarice had hit the obnoxious woman.

"My sister has a right to say what she wants," Mrs. Ford said.

"Yes, she does," Nathalyia said. "Just not in Fontaine. Your decision."

The women traded looks. Mrs. Ford relented. "Let's get this over with. Our guests will be arriving soon."

"Clarice, please come in. Jake, I know you'll see that we're not disturbed. If guests for Ms. Hill's party arrive, please section off a part of the Cajun private dining room, and offer them complimentary soft drinks or tea," Nathalyia said.

"Yes, boss." He touched Clarice's shoulder briefly and closed the door.

"Now, Ms. Hill, repeat your claim," Nathalyia said.

"It's no claim," Mrs. Ford's sister snapped. She pointed a finger at Clarice. "She hit me."

"You hit me first," Clarice said. "I let you get away with putting your finger in my face then. I should have put you in check long before that."

"You were jealous. Stephen only took you out to make me jealous," Evelyn shouted. "We're engaged now. Like I would be jealous of anyone like you."

Clarice moved. Nathalyia was faster. She placed her hand on Clarice's chest and felt her tremble. "You provoked her. Just as you're doing now."

"She hit my sister with a closed fist!" Mrs. Ford announced. "She almost broke her nose. You can't compare that to a slap."

Nathalyia kept her hand on Clarice. "If you can't take a lick, don't give one."

Both women gasped. Mrs. Ford's nose shot up in the air. "I will not stay here. I want a full refund."

Nathalyia fully faced her. "That will be impossible. Food has been prepared and extra staff hired. You signed a contract."

"You can't possibly expect us to stay," Evelyn said.

"Whether you stay or go is your decision. In either case, there will be no refund," Nathalyia told them.

"I don't want her serving," Evelyn insisted.

"We certainly don't," Mrs. Ford agreed.

"That's not your decision to make. You requested the most efficient waitstaff to be in attendance and that is what I've provided," Nathalyia said. "Changes at this late date are impossible and will not provide your guests with the high level of service Fontaine is known for."

Mrs. Ford's lips pressed together so tight, she probably cut off circulation. "I will never come here again, and I'll tell everyone I meet not to either."

"That's your right. But, to tell the truth, my lawyers and I take a very dim view of slander." Nathalyia looked at her watch. "It's two minutes until your guests are scheduled to arrive. Should I have Clarice show you to the private dining room?"

"Bitch."

Nathalyia heard Evelyn mutter the remark and caught Clarice's arm. She looked straight at the other woman. "You really shouldn't feel that way about yourself, even if it might be true."

Clarice burst out laughing.

"Your decision, Mrs. Ford."

"The service and food better be everything I paid for." She marched over to her mother. "I'm not scared of you."

"Enjoy your party." Nathalyia turned to Clarice. "Please escort our guests to the Cajun room and show them what it means to be a guest at Fontaine."

Clarice smiled. "This way, ladies, and might I say again, welcome to Fontaine."

Heads high, Evelyn and her sister left, pulling their elderly mother with them.

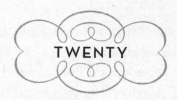

TWENTY

Clarice escorted the women to the Cajun room and then went to the adjoining room for the women who had arrived early. There were three. None had gifts. After showing them to where Evelyn and her sister waited, Clarice went to find Jake.

"Is everything all right?" he asked.

She came around the bar. "Nathalyia was brilliant. She showed them that she wouldn't be dictated to."

"I knew she would. If you didn't let your temper get in the way," he said. He drew a beer and served a customer before returning to her.

She made a face. "I almost hit Evelyn again. My brothers taught me how to fight."

"Fighting isn't always the answer."

Clarice folded her arms. "I just wish I could show her up."

"With me, you can't do that," he said quietly.

Clarice was taken aback. She put her hands on her hips. "That is so idiotic I won't even address it." She caught a signal from the hostess that more guests had arrived. "I'll be back."

Showing the women to the Cajun room, Clarice checked on the guests and ignored the glares and snide comments of the sisters. "Ladies, Holly and Marie are here to ensure you have everything you need to make this occasion a memorable one for Ms. Hill. If you need anything, please don't hesitate to let us know."

Amid thank-yous Clarice left and went straight to the bar. "Are you through being idiotic?"

Jake looked up. Misery stared back at her. His hand lifted toward his scared cheek before dropping to his side. "I'm older and the bartender. Maybe we made a mistake."

If he hadn't looked so miserable, Clarice might have thought he was using the incident to break up with her. He wasn't. He was still unsure of her. She had no such qualms. She cared for him. He steadied her, made her happy, content, and horny.

"Jake Sergeant, you're stuck with me. You better grin and bear it." She kissed him on the cheek.

"I'm not surprised she can't do better." The words were followed by nasty laughter.

Clarice looked around to see Evelyn with a couple of her cronies from the elementary school where they had worked. Evelyn looked at Jake, then at Clarice, as if they were nothing.

Clarice started around the bar. Jake caught her hand before she could punch her again. "She's trying to get back at you anyway she can. Think."

"I'd like to follow her into the bathroom and hold her head in the toilet," Clarice muttered.

"Then you'd be arrested and fired, and she will have won."

"She's mean."

"I don't care what she thinks, I only care about you." Jake

waited until she turned to him. "Now, go show her you're dating a man who would gladly give up his life for you."

Clarice fought back tears. Squeezing his hand, she returned to the dining room. There were nowhere near the thirty women expected, and there was only one gift on the gift table. It seemed as if Clarice wasn't the only one Evelyn had ticked off.

Two very long hours later, Evelyn, her sister, and her mother left. Thirteen women instead of the thirty came. When it was over there were only two gifts. Clarice didn't gloat. Her mother had taught her that gloating would often land you in a similar position. She was too happy with Jake to want to mess up.

"All done," she told Jake as she stopped at the bar.

"I'm proud of you."

"You can show me when you come over tonight." Grinning, she continued to the kitchen with a stack of dirty dishes.

"You can do this, Nathalyia. You're strong." Nathalyia blinked, refusing to cry or to put her head down on the desk as she wanted to. The pep talk wasn't helping.

Throughout her life, as far as she could remember, she had relied on herself to get through bad times. Even loving Martin, she had kept a part of her to herself. Somewhere along the way with Rafael she'd begun to look at him as more than a lover, as the man to whom she could finally give her heart, her love, and, more important, her trust.

She'd made a horrible mistake, but she wouldn't blame the baby as her mother had blamed and mistreated her. Nor would she wallow in self-pity. She'd seen the disastrous effects of that on her mother and sisters.

She'd tried to help Theresa, but Nathalyia didn't think it was possible. It might be too late. Perhaps if their mother had shown love instead of disinterest, her sisters might have had a chance to turn out differently. She didn't know.

She was just thankful that she wasn't all about herself, or always trying to get over on other people. While growing up, and even into adulthood, Nathalyia had wondered why she was the one who'd been picked on and left out. Now she was glad.

She could be like Theresa or Paula, "working her way" across the country. Her pregnancy scared her, but they'd make it. Her baby would know that he or she was loved, no matter what.

A knock sounded on her door. She put her head in the palm of her hand.

She didn't want to see anyone or deal with a problem. She wouldn't let herself think it was Rafael and he'd changed his mind. One thing her hard life growing up had taught her was to face reality, not hide from it. He'd called last night to check on her. The conversation had been brief.

The knock came again.

Her head lifted. Martin had taught her that, regardless of what was going on in their lives, Fontaine came first, because not only was the restaurant the source of their livelihood, it was a source of pride.

"Come in." The door opened. Nathalyia's mouth gaped.

"Hello, Nathalyia. We thought we'd say hello before we sat down to lunch," Helen said. With her were Maureen, Brianna, and Celeste.

"When we asked for you, a waitress named Clarice said we should come on back," Maureen said.

"This will be my first time eating at Fontaine," Celeste said. "I'm looking forward to it."

"I already know I want the bread pudding—without the bourbon sauce—if it comes that way," Brianna commented.

Nathalyia's lashes blinked, her mouth opened, but nothing came out initially. She came unsteadily to her feet. "Did Rafael send you?"

Helen's face saddened. "No."

Nathalyia pushed aside the hurt. "I don't understand."

Helen and Maureen came around the desk, easing Nathalyia back into her chair. "We're here to let you know that we care. You have four new friends who will be here for you regardless."

Nathalyia shook her head. They didn't know. "Rafael—" She had to stop before she continued. "Rafael and I aren't getting married."

"Even more reason for us to be here for you," Brianna said. "You don't need to be alone during this. I don't know what I would do if I didn't have my family."

Nathalyia bit her lip. Deep down she wanted someone she could count on. "Thank you."

"Your baby will have aunts and uncles who love him or her." Helen smiled down at Nathalyia. "We hope you'll let us be a part of your life now."

Nathalyia looked at the four women surrounding her. She couldn't recall anyone other than Martin reaching out to her so clearly to be her friend. Except Rafael. Tears filled her eyes.

"They're the real thing," Celeste said. "There are good people in the world. You can trust us."

"I can understand why you'd want to be a part of the baby's life," Nathalyia said softly. "Thank you."

"Yours, too." Celeste draped her arm around Brianna's shoulders. "I'm new to the sisterhood of Dunlap women, but they welcomed me with open arms."

"But you and Alec are getting married." Nathalyia looked at Brianna. "You're having Patrick's baby."

Brianna's eyelashes fluttered. "Yes, I am, but not in the way you think. If I didn't see you loved the stubborn man, hadn't seen how impatient he was to see you, and feel despite what's happening now, that you two would end up with each other, I wouldn't tell you this."

"Patrick is very touchy on the subject, Brianna," Helen warned.

Brianna's tilted her head to one side. "As I said, I know how to put him in a good mood." Her beautiful face grew serious. "Patrick is not the biological father of our baby. He has always known it, and yet it has never made a difference to him or his family." Her arms curved protectively around her distended stomach. "This is Patrick's and my baby."

Nathalyia stood and gently hugged Brianna. "You didn't have to tell me your story. The baby is blessed to have such great parents." She looked at the other women. "My baby is going to have wonderful aunts. Thank you."

The women hugged, brushed away tears. "Lunch is on me. I'll have the cook hold the bourbon sauce for you, Brianna."

"I love desserts," Brianna said, moving with the other women to the door. "My doctor's appointment is tomorrow, so please only serve me a small portion or I'll eat the whole thing."

"When is your appointment, Nathalyia?" Helen asked.

Nathalyia stopped, moistened her lips. "I haven't made one yet," she confessed and waited for them to berate her.

Brianna nodded in understanding. "It's a shock initially. My best friend made me an appointment."

Nathalyia felt she had to be just as honest as they were. "Seeing a doctor will make it real."

Maureen hugged Nathalyia again. "A baby is a huge adjustment. My son is an obstetrician and Brianna's doctor. If you'd like, I can ask him if he can recommend a doctor in Myrtle Beach."

"That would be wonderful. Thank you." Nathalyia led the women into the restaurant. She was so pleased and happy that they cared, but she was unable to stop wishing that Rafael did as well.

Rafael was having a miserable day. The endless blue ocean, the cry of the seagulls, the gentle wind as he walked on the beach in back of his house no longer soothed him. He couldn't put out of his mind Nathalyia's announcement that she was carrying his child and that she might as well be alone for all the help Theresa would be to her. The calculating woman was all about herself. He'd always known he had family who loved and supported him.

He pulled his cell phone from the pocket of his shorts and called Nathalyia on her cell phone. When he couldn't reach her, he called the main number of the restaurant. He hung up a short while later. Nathalyia was walking the floor.

He continued down the beach trying to tell himself that she must be all right if she was greeting customers, but it wouldn't hurt for him to keep checking until he spoke with her.

Exactly sixty-one minutes later Rafael reached her on her cell phone from his house phone.

"Hello."

Rafael didn't expect just hearing her voice to make the need to see her almost painful. "Hi."

"Are you all right?" she asked.

"That's the question I called to ask you."

"I'm fine now."

He tensed. "Now? Were you sick?"

"No. Please don't worry," she told him. "I have to go. Thanks for calling."

Rafael looked at the silent phone in his hand. She hadn't wanted to talk to him. The restaurant was more important. Even as the thought formed, he knew he was being selfish. She'd taken off more to be with him than she probably had done in all the years since her husband died.

A terrible thought struck him. What if she had told people the same story she'd told him, that her deceased husband was the father?

He jerked up the phone in the kitchen and pressed in two numbers before sanity returned. She had told him the lie because she hadn't wanted to trap him. People would talk when her pregnancy became obvious. Nathalyia favored fitted clothes. People could be nosy and cruel. He pressed in the other numbers.

"Hello."

"What are you going to tell people when you start to show?"

"Frankly, Rafael, I haven't thought that far. I'm surprised you have."

"I don't want people in your face, bothering you," he told her, just the idea making him angry.

"I learned long ago that you can't let what people think affect you or dictate how you run your life. I would have thought you had, too."

He had . . . until the possibility of her being hurt or embarrassed entered the equation. "Maybe we should get married." The words only marginally stuck in his throat. He wished he could figure out the answer to their problem.

"Trying to escape gossip is no reason to get married," she told him. "Rafael, I really have to go."

"What's so important?" he asked before he caught himself. He wasn't jealous, he was annoyed—which still was uncalled for. "I'm sorry. Don't answer that."

"I didn't intend to. Goodbye."

She hung up again, and this time he couldn't blame her. He'd acted like a jealous kid. She had a business to run that was important to her. He rubbed his hand over his face, silently admitting to himself that despite his best intentions he was beginning to wish he was just as important.

Nathalyia stared at the cell phone on her desk. Rafael's call had been a complete surprise. She'd cut the conversation short because it had been too painful. She wished he felt love instead of obligation. He cared about them, but he wanted to maintain his distance.

Which might be for the best. Seeing him all the time would be a constant reminder that he was only there because of his responsibility.

The cell phone rang again. She tensed until she saw Maureen's name. The four Dunlap women—for Celeste the wedding was only a matter of formality—had left a little over an hour ago. They'd had a wonderful lunch in the private dining room so they could talk freely. By the time she waved them off, they'd felt like old friends.

"Hello, Maureen," Nathalyia said. "Are you still here?"

"Celeste just crossed the city line into Charleston. It's a wonder we didn't get a ticket," Maureen said.

"Radar detector," Celeste said loud enough for Nathalyia to hear. "Alec has threatened to have it taken out. He worries."

"So does Patrick. He won't even let me drive anymore because I've gotten so big and was having trouble getting out of my car," Brianna said with a laugh.

The Dunlap men worried about the women they loved. Nathalyia wouldn't feel sorry for herself.

"I finally got Adam on the phone," Maureen went on to say.

"Here's the name of the doctor he recommended. He's going to call him and let him know to expect your call, and get you in tomorrow."

Nathalyia, reaching for a pen, went still. "Tomorrow?"

"Tomorrow. Adam thought it best for you to get in ASAP. It's better to have a doctor to call if you start having morning sickness or other normal symptoms," she explained.

"Oh." Nathalyia picked up the pen and opened her day planner. She hoped she wouldn't have to deal with morning sickness. "Ready." She took down the information. "Thank you again, and please thank your son for me."

"You're more than welcome. Call the number as soon as you hang up," Maureen instructed.

"I will."

"Goodbye, and call if you need anything or just to talk. You have our phone numbers," Maureen said.

"Goodbye, Nathalyia," Celeste said loudly.

"Goodbye, Nathalyia," Brianna called. "Adam has high standards, so the doctor he's referred you to will be top-notch."

"Thanks. Goodbye, Maureen, Celeste, Brianna." Nathalyia put down the cell phone and reached for the phone on her desk to call the obstetrician. After giving her name, she was immediately given an appointment for one o' clock the next day, with instructions on what to bring with her.

Hanging up the phone, she leaned back in her chair. The pregnancy was becoming real. She couldn't stop the spurt of fear that she wouldn't be a good mother.

The cell phone rang. "Unknown" popped up on the caller ID. She answered. "Hello."

"Hi, Nathalyia, it's Helen. You have your appointment yet?"

The Dunlap women made a good team. "Tomorrow at one."

"I'd like to go with you, if you don't mind."

"I would appreciate it," she said. She hadn't wanted to go alone. "Rafael called to check on me."

"As well he should," Helen said. "I'd be angry with him if I didn't know he'd eventually come to his senses."

"He asked me to marry him again so people wouldn't gossip about me when I began to show."

"Men! Even the smartest ones can be a bit dense at times. What woman would accept a marriage proposal like that?" She snorted. "He'll get it right and ask you because he loves you, just like you love him."

Nathalyia couldn't deny it. "How do you know I love him and that he doesn't love me?"

"This might be hard to hear but, for him, it's easier thinking this was another affair. Making it permanent scares him."

"Because of the dangerous work he does," Nathalyia said. "He told me."

"There's more. Until he faces it, he won't see that love is worth any risk," Helen said.

Nathalyia frowned. "More like what?"

"I'd rather not say for now. Just don't give up hope. Like I said, he's a smart man. He's going to figure out his true feelings. He wants to be there for you. He just has to get his heart and head aligned."

Nathalyia's hand flexed on the phone. "It's hard hearing his voice and not being able to tell him how I really feel. He was upset with me when I had to hang up."

"Good. He had to work to get you. He'll have to work to keep you and your child," Helen said with feeling. "He'll want to know what is going on, and when he can't, he won't be able to stand it."

"You and the others make this easier." Nathalyia's voice trembled. She brushed away tears.

"We're the sisterhood of Dunlap women. We stick together,

and don't you dare say you're not included," Helen said strongly. "Just because Rafael is running from his feelings is no reason for us not to be there for each other. Now, what time should I be there to pick you up?"

Nathalyia felt her lips curve upward. "How about eleven thirty and we can have lunch? Sam is a lucky man."

"I'm a lucky woman, but it hasn't been easy getting to where we are today. Relationships are a never-ending work in progress."

"I wonder if Rafael and I will have the chance one day," Nathalyia mused.

"One day is already happening."

TWENTY-ONE

At 11:30 A.M. the next day Rafael parked in Fontaine's parking lot and shut off the motor. He was going to talk with Nathalyia and make sure she was all right.

Pocketing the keys, he strolled casually to the entrance. He had purposely arrived early so he wouldn't spend time searching for a parking slot. A good thing. The lot was filling up already.

In his hand he carried a manila envelope with the employee parking placard. He planned to use it as an excuse for being there if Nathalyia questioned why he'd come.

Following a young couple who were holding hands into the restaurant, he waited for his turn to be seated. The man kissed the woman on the cheek.

"This way," the hostess said to the young couple. They moved to follow her. When they did, Rafael saw that the woman was visibly pregnant. His thoughts immediately went to how Nathalyia would feel when she saw the loving couple.

Betrayed. The word leaped into his mind. His gut twisted. He had never wanted to see her unhappy.

"Good morning, sir. Welcome back. Glad you're better," another hostess greeted him.

Rafael turned his gaze from the couple. "Thanks. I'd like a quiet table in the main dining room. I'm expecting a guest."

Her eyes twinkled. "Certainly, sir. This way."

Rafael followed her as she wound her way though the tables. He saw them before they saw him. Somehow he wasn't surprised.

The hostess stopped at the table where he and Nathalyia had first eaten. "Your other guest is here."

Nathalyia and Helen glanced up. Nathalyia's beautiful face registered stunned surprise. He was glad to see the smudges beneath her eyes didn't look so dark.

Helen looked pleased. "Hello, Rafael."

"Hello, ladies." He pulled out a chair across from Nathalyia and sat down. He just wanted to look at her, breathe in her scent. If he were lucky, he'd touch her. It was rude not to ask for permission, but he wasn't taking a chance she'd say no.

The hostess's smile faded at Nathalyia's continued silence. "Is this all right, Mrs. Fontaine?"

"Certainly, Marcie." Nathalyia finally smiled. "Please ask James to bring an iced tea."

Marcie looked uncertain, then gave him a menu. "Enjoy your meal."

"I definitely will." He held up the manila envelope. "The parking placard. I'd like to keep it for the time being, if you don't mind."

She was caught off guard again. She glanced at Helen, who sipped her strawberry lemonade. No help there.

"If you need me, I want to be able to be here quickly and not have to worry about a parking space," he told her, letting her know that he had no intention of fading from the picture. He still didn't have all the answers to how they were going to work this out given his stance on serious relationships and marriage. He just knew not being there with them wasn't an option.

"I suppose it's all right."

She really knew how to deflate a man's ego. He wasn't giving up. "Thank you."

"Here's your tea, sir." The waiter placed the tea and flatware setup rolled in a white cloth napkin on the table. "Anything else?"

"Please give me a minute," Rafael requested. Nathalyia had looked panicky when the waiter posed the question.

"Certainly." The waiter moved away.

"I'd like to stay, but if it's going to make you uncomfortable or have you not eat, then I'll leave."

"Excuse me." Helen picked up her purse and headed toward the ladies' room.

Rafael moved to the seat next to Nathalyia. "This didn't work out the way either of us planned. I might not have been at my finest when you told me, but I'm trying the best way I know to be there for both of you."

She looked at him. He thought he saw a glint of tears in her eyes.

"Please, if you cry again, I'm not sure I can take it," he said. Not caring who might be looking, he tenderly touched her cheek, then took her hand in his, felt it tremble. "Don't shut me out."

She blinked, then slid her hand from beneath his. Now he was the one who was panicky. There was no easy solution for them, but he knew he wanted her to trust him, wanted her to know that he would be there for her and their baby. "Tell me what it is I'm doing wrong."

"Answer one question," she finally said.

"Anything." At least she was talking to him.

"Are you here because you see this as your responsibility or are you genuinely concerned?" she asked, her lips trembling. "Please be as truthful as you've always been with me."

He took her hand again. "Responsibility wouldn't have kept me up most of last night. I was prepared to wait here all day until you made rounds to see you."

She bit her lip, glanced away.

He searched his mind for something to say, some way to persuade her even as some part of him whispered that it might be better if he didn't. *If you were apart or estranged it would be better for her.*

Rafael looked into Nathalyia's sad brown eyes and dismissed the voice. She was hurting. The thought that he had caused that hurt and was unable to fix it cut deep.

"You can always depend on me."

She kept looking over his shoulder. Almost before he turned to follow the direction of her gaze, he knew he'd see the pregnant woman. She came from the back of the restaurant where the restrooms were located and retook her seat. The man with her leaned over and kissed her.

When Nathalyia looked back at him, he saw the yearning in her eyes. She wanted a family. She wanted a man she could count on. "You will never be alone or have to wonder where I am," the words were out before he could stop them. At that moment he hadn't wanted to.

"All I have to do is call, right?"

"Right," he answered, hoping the shadows would leave her eyes. They didn't. He thought of what Sam and his brothers had said about needing to be there in person and not on the phone. He was fighting for his family. His family. The words echoed in his head, his heart. "Even if you don't call, I'll be there. Just trust me again."

She picked up her glass of water and took a sip. "We've probably given my staff enough to talk about. Please move your chair back."

He wanted to shake her. Kiss her. This cool woman wasn't Nathalyia. He wanted the passionate, fun-filled Nathalyia back. He'd worry about the consequences later. It scared him spitless that he might have lost her. He moved his chair back.

Helen returned and took her seat. "I took the liberty of ordering for you, Rafael." The waiter must have been standing nearby because he began serving the table.

Rafael waited until the man withdrew and Helen said grace before pulling out his wallet and placing a twenty and a ten on the table. He didn't want the Greek salad. "I won't be staying."

Nathalyia shared a look with Helen, then she picked up her spoon and took a bite of her crawfish bisque. "So, what you just said was all talk?"

Rafael had started to rise but sat back down. "I meant every word."

Nathalyia placed her spoon on the plate beneath her bowl and met his direct gaze. "My doctor's appointment is at one. I'd like you to come if possible."

The heavy weight compressing his chest lifted. "Thank you. I'd like nothing better."

Nathalyia filled out the patient information forms at the doctor's office with Rafael looking over her shoulder. He'd been that way since she had paused over the baby's father's information. He'd taken the clipboard from her and written in his name before giving it back to her. He was letting her know that he was accepting his parentage.

She just hoped and prayed that Helen was right, that he loved her, and that she was making the right decision in letting him be a part of this. Being near him and not being able to touch him, to tell him her fears, her love for him, was a delicate balancing act. She wasn't sure how much longer she could keep up the cool façade.

She'd allowed him to drive her, but Helen had come with them. She'd kept the conversation going so Nathalyia hadn't felt so tense. She wished she didn't feel that way now. Helen sat on the other side of Nathalyia, flipping through a magazine.

"Mrs. Fontaine."

Nathalyia glanced up and came to her feet. "Yes."

"The doctor will see you now."

Her damp hands gripped the clipboard. Her body trembled.

A strong arm circled her waist. "Is it all right if I walk back with her?" Rafael asked.

The sandy-haired nurse in a light blue smock smiled in understanding. "Yes. The doctor will see you first and then do the exam."

With Rafael's assistance, Nathalyia followed the nurse to the doctor's office. The first thing she noticed was all the degrees on the wall. A tall, thin attractive woman with short black hair in her midforties entered behind them. She wore a white lab coat and a smile.

"I'm Dr. Waters, Mrs. Fontaine," she greeted, extending her hand to Nathalyia and taking the clipboard.

"Rafael Dunlap, the baby's father."

Nathalyia's head snapped around at the possessive sound in Raphael's voice.

"Mr. Dunlap. I sort of figured that out." Still smiling, she waved them to matching Queen Anne chairs in front of her cheery writing desk, then took her seat. "I want to go over a few things with you and then do an exam. I'll tell you up front that I'm a stickler for my patients getting exercise, plenty of rest, and eating properly."

"I own and run a restaurant," Nathalyia told her. "Food and exercise won't be a problem."

"I know. I've eaten there. You probably work long hours. Am I right?" Dr. Waters asked.

"Yes," Rafael answered. "She's there by ten and is one of the last to leave at closing."

Nathalyia glared at him. "She was asking me."

"Would your answer be the same?"

There was only one answer. "Yes."

"I thought so." Dr. Waters placed her clasped hands on top of the forms Nathalyia had filled out. "Your reputation for high standards precedes you. Before too much longer your body and your baby won't let you keep up that hectic schedule. It's best that you work toward a compromise now rather than taking a chance on damaging your health or the baby's."

"I'd never hurt our baby," Nathalyia said, her arm curving possessively around her waist. Unconsciously she edged closer to Rafael's solid warmth.

"Not intentionally, but I can say, after years of practice, I've seen women try to maintain the same all-out frantic pace they had before they were pregnant, and the results weren't good."

"What—what happened?" Nathalyia asked.

"Since it's not going to happen to you or the baby, it doesn't matter," Rafael said.

Nathalyia felt his arm tighten a fraction. He was just as concerned as she was. "Please tell me."

"It has varied from threatening to deliver prematurely and being put on restrictive bed rest to actually miscarrying or resenting the baby," Dr. Waters answered frankly. "Be prepared for your life to change, but I hope you'll see it in a good way."

Nathalyia didn't know what to say. She wanted the baby. She wanted to run the restaurant the way Martin had taught her—hands-on. She didn't want to choose.

. . .

On the way back to the restaurant, Helen's talking hadn't helped ease the tension in the car. Nathalyia knew Rafael was thinking about what Dr. Waters had said, and her silence afterward. He probably thought she would make a terrible mother.

Her hands gripped her purse. Maybe he was right.

He turned into the parking lot and stopped by Helen's car, which was parked near the front. Nathalyia opened her door.

"Nat, wait," he called, grabbing her arm.

She didn't want to look at him. She didn't know how she'd go on if there was censure in his eyes when she prayed to see love. "Please."

His fingers uncurled. "We'll work though this somehow."

Shaking her head, she got out of the car and headed inside the restaurant. She didn't want to see anyone. She hurried to her office.

A few steps away, she heard her name. She kept going. Inside her office, she closed the door and leaned back against it. Martin had entrusted Fontaine to her. He'd always been very hands-on, and never missed a day until he became ill. She'd tried her best to have the same practice and high work ethic. She couldn't let him down, but neither could she endanger her baby.

A knock sounded on the door. Her first instinct was to ignore whoever it was. She straightened, wiped the tears from her lashes instead. She'd find a way. She stepped away from the door. "Come in."

Rafael came inside. "Just listen if you don't want to talk. I know you're scared. You want to take care of the baby, but you feel torn. In a way, Fontaine is your baby as well. You worked hard to ensure the success of Fontaine and you're afraid if you're not here, things won't get done."

He stepped closer and gently closed his hands around her arms. "I don't know squat about running a restaurant, but I can learn, and on my days off and after work I can come in and help out. I can get you a longer sofa so you can stretch out and rest. Together we can make this work out so you don't have to choose."

Her lips trembling, she went into his arms and held tight. "I thought—"

He held her closer. "That I wouldn't understand?"

She nodded.

He kissed her hair. "Fontaine is as much a part of you as my being on the force is part of me. The difference is that you haven't learned to completely rely on your team. I couldn't survive if I didn't."

Her head lifted. "I had a dream that I was holding our baby and we had no place to go. You wouldn't help us."

His hands speared though her hair, tilting her face upward toward his. "That will never happen. As long as there is breath in my body, I'll be here for you and our baby."

"I want to believe you," she whispered.

His eyes shut briefly. "You will." He gently brushed his lips across hers. "I'll be back at closing. Lock the door when I leave, and prop your feet up." He kissed her again.

She caught him by the arm before he turned away. "I'm almost seven weeks. It must have happened the first time we were together."

He pulled her to him, held her as if she were the most precious thing in the world. "You're going to make a great mother."

I hope so, she thought, then stepped back. "I have a restaurant to run."

"I'll see you later."

When the door closed, Nathalyia went to her desk and sat down. Rafael was right about one thing. Fontaine was not only a source of pride, but also her income. The restaurant might be paid for, but the expenses to keep it running were enormous. The house had a hefty mortgage. Her dream that she and her baby were homeless wasn't too far-fetched.

She studied the accolades, honors, and awards on the walls that Martin and she had received for community service and for the restaurant. She'd come from nothing. They'd validated her worth when she had been looking for a place to belong. She'd been so proud of her accomplishments. She'd achieved more than she had ever imagined. There was only one decision she could make.

There was a quick rap on the door, then Theresa barged in. "I just saw that cop. He walked out of here as if he owned the place. I hope you weren't stupid enough to take him back."

"My life. My decision."

Theresa's eyes hardened. "He's just after your money."

Nathalyia tilted her head to one side. She didn't for a second think Theresa cared about her. It hit her. "You're jealous."

Her sister jerked back. "I'm just trying to keep you from making mistakes like I did."

"I won't." Her sister had always been happiest when Nathalyia was miserable. She bent to put her handbag away. "Please close the door on your way out."

Nathalyia expected the door to slam and wasn't disappointed. Perhaps it was time that Theresa moved on. The confrontation wouldn't be pretty. It couldn't be helped. She wasn't working out. Nathalyia would just have to face the fallout. No matter what, Fontaine always came first.

Nathalyia picked up the time sheets just as someone knocked on her door. "Come in."

The door opened and Jake slowly came in. She'd never seen him look so downcast. She came from around her desk. "Clarice?"

He swallowed, rubbed the back of his neck. "I love her."

Nathalyia's heart went out to him. "Then tell her."

His blue eyes were haunted. "She's all I want. But . . . but . . ." He looked away. "I'm afraid if I tell her everything, I'll lose her."

Nathalyia touched his arm gently. "You only have to look at

the mess I created to realize that telling the truth is your only option. Clarice cares about you. Don't let lies destroy that love."

"My wife was never faithful to me even before this." His finger jabbed in the direction of his scar.

Nathalyia's eyes flared. "You're not being fair to Clarice to compare her to your ex. Some people can't be faithful, but for others it's the only way."

"Dunlap?"

"If we can work through this, I'll never worry about another woman," she said, praying she'd have that opportunity. "He's an honorable man."

Jake's mouth tightened. "I'll reserve judgment on that."

"I love him, Jake. I caused this situation, but he's trying," she told him. "Love, I'm finding, isn't always so easy to grab when the opportunity presents itself."

"I want her in my life forever," he said, his voice strained.

"Then tell her. Let love, not fear, guide you."

He stared at Nathalyia for a long time, then hugged her for the first time since she'd lost Martin.

"Martin couldn't have picked better to entrust Fontaine with." He stepped back. "I'd better get back to the bar."

Nathalyia watched him go and wished he and Clarice luck. They both deserved happiness. She wouldn't give up hope that she and Rafael would find their way as well.

Rafael walked along the beach behind his home as the sun slowly descended. Hands in the pockets of his jeans, he stopped and stared out as the waves crashed against the shoreline and receded. He thought of his parents doing the same thing. They were always in each other's corner. Their love had been unshakable and undeniable. Anyone who saw them knew it instantly.

"I thought I'd find you out here."

"She's scared, and I can't help her."

Helen touched his arm. "You're dealing with a lot yourself."

Rafael blew out a breath. "I'm so mixed up. In my head I know I need to push her away, but it tears me up inside just thinking about not being there for her. I don't want her hurt."

"Look deep into your heart and you'll find the answer," Helen said. "Your brothers love just as deeply as your father did. Love carries risks, but the rewards are far greater. Despite Barron being wounded and his wife almost losing him, she wouldn't hesitate to marry him all over again. Neither would I hesitate to marry Sam. Maureen would say the same thing about Simon. Celeste is counting the days."

He blew out a breath. "I know. It's just . . ."

"You remember the pain of losing the one you love," Helen said. "You saw what the misery of losing your father did to your mother, but you've forgotten the deep love they shared."

"Sometimes she'd cry in her sleep," he said, his voice strained. "No matter what I said, I couldn't make it better for her."

"And because you loved her, you felt as if you failed her and your father," Helen said softly.

"Dad told me to take care of her, and I didn't." A muscle leaped in his jaw.

"Rafael." Helen stepped in front of him and took both of his arms. "There was nothing you could have done to change things. Your mother died of a broken heart. She simply gave up, but she loved you and knew you had your brothers to watch over you."

"I wanted her."

"Yes, you did, and it hurt you deeply when she slipped away from us. From that day on you changed," Helen told him.

He shrugged his shoulders. "I was about to go into the police academy. I knew then that I didn't want to leave a wife and kids behind."

"You were also afraid to love someone and have her leave you. Nathalyia has to face her fears, but so do you."

"I already told you you're wrong."

"Search your heart and you'll see that I'm right. But I wouldn't wait too long," Helen warned.

"What does that mean?"

"Nathalyia is a beautiful, successful, caring woman. Her pregnancy is not going to deter a man from wanting her," Helen pointed out. "How will you feel if another man is there to care for her, love her, and take care of your child?"

Rage swept through him. "No other man is going to do that."

"I hope not, Rafael. It would be tragic if you discovered you loved Nathalyia and wanted your family and it was too late," Helen said.

"No man is taking my family," Rafael told her fiercely.

Helen touched his stiff shoulder. "For all of your sakes, I hope you're right. Goodbye, Rafael."

Rafael watched his sister-in-law walk slowly back to the house on the wooden walkway. He wasn't afraid to love, and no man was taking his family.

But all Rafael had to do was think of Patrick, who would fight the devil for his family, to know that, at least in this, Helen was right.

Rafael recalled the tears in Nathalyia's eyes. She didn't believe he'd be there for her and their baby. Her lack of trust in him stung his pride and wounded his heart.

Hands in his pockets, he started back to the house. Maybe a drive would clear his head. Grabbing the car keys, he got into the Mustang. Helen was wrong about him being afraid to love. But what if she was right?

He had no idea where he'd end up until he saw the entrance to the cemetery where his parents were buried. After all this time he still felt a catch in his throat, a tender ache in his heart.

After parking his car, he got out and walked to the rose marble headstone. Just beyond it water ran down a stream in front of a small white chapel. Rafael sat down at the foot of the grave site and crossed his legs.

"I let you down." He didn't know if he was talking to his father about not taking care of his mother, or to his mother for not helping her get over losing his father, or to both of them for his getting Nathalyia pregnant.

"You were always so proud of me. I don't know if you would be now." He scrubbed a hand across his chest because it felt tight. "That's a lie. Dad, you'd blister my ears, and, Mama, you'd be ready to let me have it, too."

He hung his head. "Helen thinks—" His head lifted and he glanced away. "She's wrong. I'm not—" He swallowed the lump in his throat, swallowed again.

He stared at the inscription on the marble: *forever united in love.* He tried to push the words down, but they burst free. "Mama, why did you have to go? Losing Dad was hard enough."

His fists clenched. His chest heaved. "Watching you grieve, come out here to see Dad every day, made me feel helpless. And angry and ashamed."

He swiped his hand across his face, felt the wetness and pulled his handkerchief from the pocket of his jeans to wipe his nose. He thought of all the handkerchiefs his mother had ironed for her "men" and all the hundreds of other things she'd done for her family and not once had he ever heard her complain.

"You always took such good care of us. I wanted to take care of you."

Just like he wanted to take care of Nathalyia. "I can't fail her. I can't." The notion of failing tied him in knots. "Mama. Dad. Nathalyia is the best there is. She's as beautiful on the inside as she is on the outside. You would have loved her.

"She's terrible at most sports, but she's not afraid to try. Can you believe she doesn't know how to play dominoes? But she can cook. She helps children with life-threatening illnesses. They love her and she loves them back. Her friend Clarice says Nathalyia put the children before Fontaine, her restaurant, which always comes first."

The last words had no more than passed his mouth when he recalled all the times Nathalyia had left Fontaine to be with him. She was a wealthy woman, but she had shared a corn dog for breakfast with a smile. She'd rushed to the hospital when he'd been injured and stayed with him despite her fear because she thought he needed her. She'd brought him food and saw that he took his medicine.

What had he done for her?

Rafael closed his eyes. He'd enjoyed the sweet pleasure of her body, gotten her pregnant, and tried to figure out a way to keep her at arm's length. Despite everything, she was willing to let him be a part of her and the baby's life.

She was truly an extraordinary woman. He'd missed being able to see her, talk to her, touch her. No matter what he did, the ache never left.

His eyes flew open. His parents had been married fifty-five years and had spent only a handful of those days apart before his father passed. Naturally his mother had missed him. There was nothing Rafael or anyone else could have done to fill the void.

"Mama, I finally understand. Forgive me." He came to his feet. "I have some shopping to do, but I'll be back soon." His steps lighter, Rafael headed for his Mustang.

TWENTY-TWO

At half past one in the morning, Rafael straightened from leaning against the trunk of his car when Nathalyia came out of Fontaine's back door with Jake and Clarice. As usual, they were the last to leave. There was only one other car besides Nathalyia's. Since Jake and Clarice were holding hands, it appeared that Jake had finally made his move. "Hi, Clarice. Jake."

"Hi, Rafael. Bye, Rafael," Clarice said, tugging Jake toward a black Trans Am.

Jake resisted. Rafael waited for some cutting remark. "I expect you to take care of her."

"I will." Rafael stuck out his hand.

Jake clasped it, looked at Nathalyia, then continued with Clarice.

"Why didn't you come in?" Nathalyia asked.

"I wanted to think, and it was quieter out here." Taking her arm, he walked her to the Volvo. "I'll follow you home, then I want to take you someplace. It won't take long."

She hesitated for a moment. "All right."

Closing the door, Rafael went to his car and pulled out behind Nathalyia, hoping tonight would work out the way he'd prayed it would.

Jake was taking a chance, but it couldn't be helped. Nathalyia was right. If he waited any longer, Clarice might never forgive him. If he lost her, he'd lose everything. He pulled up to the manned gate at the entrance of the Navarone Estate. The guard waved. The gate began to swing open.

"Jake, you turn this car around," Clarice demanded. "I can't believe you're actually following Rafael and Nathalyia home."

"I'm not following them." He drove through the gate.

"Well, what are you doing here?" Clarice asked.

"You'll know in a bit." Jake pulled into a circular driveway of a two-story French-manor-style house. Lights shone from every window.

"What are you stopping here for?" Clarice tugged on his sleeve. "Come on, before the owners come out or call the police."

"The owner won't call the police." Getting out, he opened her door. "Come on. It's all right. You know I wouldn't get you into trouble."

Clarice got out of the car. "Gosh, it's fabulous."

"Wait until you see inside."

Wide-eyed, she followed him up the stone steps. "Are you house-sitting or something?"

Instead of answering, he opened the door. Reaching back for her hand, he stepped inside and closed the door after him.

"Oh, my!" Clarice looked up at the soaring entryway, then at the double staircase. She stepped farther into the house. Three arches framed the entrance to the living room and lined up with the three sets of French doors at the other end. "What lucky person lives here?"

"I do."

She swung toward him, then laughed and slapped him on the shoulder. She frowned, shaking her hand. "I'm going to have to remember not to do that. Seriously, who lives here? They did it in my favorite colors of blues and greens."

"I know."

She stared at him. As comprehension dawned, anger swept across her face. She started for the door.

"Clarice," he called. She kept going. He grabbed her, holding her to him.

"Turn me loose!"

"I was afraid you wouldn't go out with me if you didn't think I was poor!" He felt her trembling with anger and talked faster. "You're so tenderhearted. I knew you felt a little sorry for me because I don't date and have this face. I didn't tell you so I could keep you, not to hurt you."

"That's so stupid. Are you calling me stupid?"

"No. No. You're smart, funny, and caring. Please don't be angry."

"If a woman did the same thing to you, what would you do?" she asked, anger still shimmering in her voice.

This time he was ready. "If she cared about me as deeply as I care for you, I'd consider myself a lucky man." Slowly releasing her, he stared down into her face. "I love you, Clarice. I've loved you for so long. I'd never do anything to hurt you."

"Do you have any other secrets?" she asked.

"Besides the custom motorcycle, I have a sailboat, a couple of rental properties, stocks, bonds," he answered. "Martin and several of the customers who came in to Fontaine helped me invest."

"And you never said anything."

He pulled her closer. "It wasn't important. This, you, is what I value."

Her face tender, she sighed and touched his cheek where the scar was. "I suppose I can be a bit gullible, but thank goodness this time I picked the right man."

He kissed her, then picked her up and started for the stairs.

"I want to see the rest of the house."

"How about we see the bedroom first?"

She grinned. "Works for me."

Jake increased his pace, laughing when Clarice laughed. Entering the bedroom, he didn't stop until he was by the bed. He placed her on her feet. "I've dreamed of this for so long."

"Me, too." Her body moved against his in blatant invitation.

Jake tumbled her into bed, his hands reaching for her blouse while trying to kiss her. Finally he freed the last button. Lifting his head, he stared down at her lush body.

"You're beautiful."

"When you say it, I believe."

"You'd better," he said gruffly, emotions clogging his throat. With trembling hands, he unclasped her bra. "Perfect," he murmured, his head lowering to nuzzle and kiss the sides of her breasts before fastening his lips on a pouting nipple.

She moaned beneath him, her unsteady hands clasping him to her. He wanted, needed to see all of her. He sat her up to pull off her blouse and bra, then reached for the buttons of her skirt. She batted his hands away.

"I get to look, too." She jerked his shirt out of his pants and reached for the snap on his jeans.

Too slow for him, he pulled the knit shirt over his head. "Since

I don't want to stop again." He took off his shoes and jeans. His eyes on her, he unbuttoned her skirt, then inched it down over her hips, taking her panties with it.

He stared up at her, his heart thundering. He was a starving man gifted with a banquet. Rising, his mouth brushed against her quivering stomach and worked its way up to her tempting mouth.

"I love the way you're built," she whispered, her fingertips grazing over his broad back, his muscled chest.

His eyes darkened. "I want you so badly. I don't know where to start loving you first."

Her breath quivered over her lips. No man had ever looked at her with such longing, such naked desire. She'd always felt self-conscious about her body shape, her large breasts. The hungry, intense way Jake stared at her made those feelings disappear.

"Then we'd better get started." She kissed him, her teeth nipping at his mouth.

His mouth and hands loved her. In the core of her body she felt the heat and pleasure of him. He was gentle and demanding.

Her legs wrapped around his waist as he drove into her moist heat. She clenched around him, quivered with the pleasure and rightness of it.

"Mine," he murmured, and began to move, slowly at first, then with increased speed, taking her higher and higher until they shattered together.

Pressing a kiss to her cheek, he rolled to his side and hugged her possessively to him. "Better than any dream or fantasy."

His softly murmured words touched her deeply. She angled her head up to find him looking down at her. She felt loved. The thought caused tears to crest in her eyes. She loved him.

"Did I hurt you? What's the matter?"

Despite the lump in her throat she managed to say, "I've never felt this cherished before."

His lips tenderly brushed across hers. "I wasn't lying when I said I'd give up my life for you."

"I know." She sniffed. "And there isn't anything I wouldn't do for you."

He smiled. "There is one fantasy."

"If you'll tell me yours, I'll tell you mine."

Laughing, he pulled her to him, kissed her deeply, and said, "It's a deal."

Rafael opened the door to his house and stepped back for Nathalyia to enter. It wasn't anything like the elegant house she lived in. It was filled with comfortable furniture and wonderful memories. He watched her face closely.

She went directly to the pictures on the end table in the family room. She picked up one of him on his bike when he was about ten. "I bet you were a handful."

"Adventurous. Can I get you anything to drink?"

"No, thank you." She put the picture back and faced him. "Why am I here?"

He stuck his hands into the pockets of his jeans. "You've never shied away from the tough questions. I've always liked that about you."

She waited.

His hands came out of his pockets. "Don't look at me as if I don't matter," he said.

Her eyes widened at the harshness of his voice, but she remained silent.

"I'm sorry," Rafael said, worry creeping though him. "I'm messing this up. Please sit down. You should be sitting down." When she didn't move, he went to her and urged her to sit down in an overstuffed chair. Instead of moving away, he knelt.

"I want you to look at me the way you used to, as if you couldn't wait to be alone with me." His hand moved over his head. "I know I ruined your life."

"What?"

"You had everything, and then I came along, thinking I knew all the answers." He came to his feet, turned away, then went back to her. "I knew you weren't experienced, but I went after you anyway. I wanted what I wanted."

She folded her hands in her lap.

He knelt by her again and tilted her head up. "I didn't realize that it went far beyond wanting until I was faced with the possibility of never having you in my life again." He blew out a breath. "When you told me about the baby, I was shocked, then glad. I acted like a jerk when you said it wasn't mine."

"I'm sorry about that."

"My fault again. Nothing used to bother me for long, but I couldn't get past the fear that I was losing you and our baby. I never felt so helpless or afraid in my life," he confessed. "I've made mistakes. I even tried to forget you by trying to date."

She snatched her hands from his. Chuckling, he reclaimed them. "I made two dates, canceled both because my unit went out on calls, and never thought about the women again. I was miserable without you. I finally accepted that you're the only woman for me."

Her lips trembled.

"No crying," he said desperately. "I'm going to keep working on you until you look at me the way you used to because I finally realized you're my life. Without you in it, I'm just going through the motions."

"Exactly how do you propose to do that?"

"I thought you'd never ask." Catching her around the waist, he leaned backward, taking her down with him, his lips finding hers.

She felt good in his arms. "I've pictured you here with me—walking on the beach, sitting on the back porch, just like my parents used to."

Her head came up, her face softened. "Your parents loved each other very much."

"Yes, they did." He came to his feet, pulling her with him. "I'll take you home. You need to rest. But if you're free tomorrow evening for an hour, I'd like you to go with me. Barron is coming home and some of us plan to drop by for a small homecoming party."

"I'd like that."

"Great. I almost forgot." He went to a drawer and pulled out an oblong wrapped box. "You'll need this."

She frowned at the pink wrapping paper and white silk bow. He grinned. "Open it."

She slid the ribbon off. Her eyes widened. "Dominoes."

"It was on your list, remember? You can play when you come for Sunday dinners. This Sunday Helen and Maureen will draw straws to see where we're having Thanksgiving dinner. Cooking for all of us would be too much for Brianna, and Celeste is busy planning the wedding. If Maureen wins, I'd like for you to go to Charleston with me. We can ride up with Sam and Helen. If Helen wins, I can pick you up."

"You want me to have Sunday dinner with you and spend Thanksgiving with you?"

"Not just this Sunday, but every Sunday you can make it. We're flying to Houston for the wedding. I checked flights this afternoon," he told her. "I know the restaurant is closed Christmas Eve so we could go up on the twenty-third. The rest of the family will already be there. We all want you there with us."

"You want me to be a part of your family celebration?"

"You *are* a part of the family. One more thing. Wait here." He returned from the kitchen with a bag of cotton candy. "This is for you."

He was telling her and showing her that he wanted her to be a part of his life. He'd be there. Opening the bag, she bit into the confection, tasted the sticky sweetness that evaporated almost instantly on her tongue.

"Want a bite?" she asked, feeling absolutely giddy.

"Always." His mouth nibbled on hers, licked, teased, then nudged her hand with the cotton candy to her mouth. She took another bite, aware of the slight tingling in her breasts that radiated downward. His tongue swirled over her lips, exploring and tasting. By the time she finished eating the cotton candy and he finished licking it away, her body hummed and burned.

"I planned to take you home," he said, his breath loud, his gaze boring into hers.

He was giving her a choice. She studied his face, then her hands went to the buttons of his shirt. "I'd rather stay here and you can work on me."

"Nathalyia." Picking her up, he carried her to his bedroom. He rained soft kisses over her face. She leaned into him and circled her arms around his neck. His mouth settled over hers again, his tongue thrusting deep into her mouth, wanting her to feel the passion, the pleasure.

With a soft moan she opened for him. He hungrily took her offering. Need pulsed though him. His nostrils flared. He breathed in her unique fragrance and felt at peace for the first time since she'd told him she was pregnant.

The kiss deepened. Her heart pounded. Her breasts grew heavy and ached for his touch, his mouth.

She had missed the warmth and security of his arms. His tongue teased and tangled with hers. Excitement and need ran hot though her veins. She heard the rasp of the zipper at the back of her skirt and shivered with anticipation. How she had missed him, missed this. The skirt pooled at her feet and she stepped out of it. Her black lacy bra fell next.

Kneeling before her, he kissed her quivering stomach and laid the side of his face over the place where their child was growing. "I'll always be here for you and our child."

Tears crested in her eyes. "I know." He didn't know any other way. He was giving her all he could. She'd try not to be greedy and want his love as well.

Leaning back, he stared up at her. His gaze was tender and hungry. Her shivering grew worse. Lowering his head, he kissed the part of her that ached for him. Her feminine core clenched with burning need. She gripped his shoulders to steady herself.

His thumbs hooked into the top elastic of her lace panties and drew them down and over her feet. His hot, possessive gaze slid over her. He came to his feet. "You're all that I desire."

Her breath caught in her throat. He meant every breathless word. She felt loved and wanted. It was enough. Her hand touched his cheek. "You're all that I desire."

His breathing turned harsh. He quickly dispensed with his clothes, all the time his searing gaze on her. "Let me show you."

His mouth fastened on hers, his tongue gliding over hers as his hands did the same with her body. They were skin to skin, heart to heart. His fingers caressed the arch of her back, the slope of her shoulders, the roundness of her hips. Everywhere he touched, she wanted more. He brought pleasure and need.

Lifting his head long enough to toss back the bedcovers, he lay down with her, his mouth and hands intent on loving her. He didn't plan to leave one inch of her silken body untouched, unloved.

Nudging her legs open, he moved over her and stared down into her desire dazed eyes. "You will always come first with me."

With one sure thrust he joined them. She clenched around him. Nothing had ever felt so perfect, so right. She met him thrust for thrust. Wave after wave of exquisite pleasure rippled through them. The tempo built. She spasmed. He followed.

Murmuring his name, she pressed a kiss to the side of his neck. He felt her even breathing and knew she had gone to sleep. Rolling over, he kissed her face and her hair and then fitted her precious body against his. His family. He was going to keep them exactly where they were.

Nathalyia woke up in Rafael's arms. For a moment, she thought she was dreaming until she felt his erection nudging her stomach. She giggled. "I see you plan to work on me some more."

Laughing, he rolled on top of her. "You know I believe in practice, practice." He ran his fingertip over her lower lip. "For a while I didn't think I'd see you smile, hear you laugh, or make love to you again."

Her hand palmed his cheek. "I didn't either. You were right. I was scared. After you left, I figured out what's important. I love Fontaine, but I love the baby and you more."

He tensed. His eyes closed.

"It's all right. I won't ask for more than you can give me," she told him despite the hard knot in her throat.

He rolled from her. She had to clench her hands to keep from pulling him back. She sat up to get out of bed. Naked, Rafael knelt in front of her. He had a printed sheet of paper in one hand and a diamond solitaire ring in the other.

"You're everything I want. I printed out an application for our marriage license."

She shook her head. "I won't marry you unless—"

"I finally realized after I left you yesterday that I love you. I can't imagine life without you. You aren't my worst nightmare. You and our baby are my life, my salvation."

Tears misted in her eyes. "If you're just saying that . . ."

"I'm not." Picking up her left hand, he slid the heart-shaped diamond ring on her finger. "Having you in my life is everything. Helen helped me face my own fears. It might sound crazy, but so did talking to my parents. I realized that, despite everything, you love me and that you are a courageous woman.

"I always thought my mother gave up. I needed her in my life, but she left anyway. I didn't want to go through that pain and heartache again." He kissed her hand. "It wasn't just about my fear that I'd leave a family, I was afraid the woman I'd love would leave me. You'd never do that."

"No, I wouldn't. I've always known that if you were my man, life would be richer, fuller." She kissed him and came to her feet. "I need to get to work, hire an assistant, then come back here and continue letting you work on me."

Nathalyia couldn't stop smiling—or looking at the ring on her finger or at the man walking beside her. They were only thirty minutes late, which was a miracle considering they'd lingered over breakfast at his house and in the shower at hers.

"If you keep looking at me like that, we're going home and you're not leaving for a long, long time." Rafael punctuated the threat with a quick kiss.

"Your fault." She kissed him back as they paused at the bottom steps leading to the back door of Fontaine.

The smile slipped from his face. "I'm glad I didn't lose you or our baby."

"Never." She hugged him. "Now, I have to go inside and work."

"I'll be back for lunch."

"We'll eat in the private dining room so I can be as naughty as I want," she said.

"It's good having my Nathalyia back." His fingers brushed across her lips. "Don't forget to rest, or that we're going tomorrow to look for a longer sofa."

Smiling, she pushed him toward his car. "Go."

"Bye, honey." After kissing her again, he went to his car.

Nathalyia waved and blew Rafael a kiss as he drove away. Staring at her ring, enjoying the play of light in the diamond, she didn't notice anyone approaching.

"What are you looking at?"

Nathalyia jumped and whirled, then pressed her hands to her booming heart. "You scared me."

Theresa didn't appear to care. She stared at the glittering diamond. "You bought a ring so people will think you're engaged?"

Nathalyia was in too good a mood to let Theresa ruin it. "Rafael and I *are* engaged."

"You're letting him con you. The money is all he's after," Theresa said.

"He's after me and our baby, and he has both." Nathalyia punched in the code and entered. Theresa brushed by her. "We need to talk when your shift is over."

Theresa turned with a frown. "What about?"

"We'll discuss it then." Nathalyia was putting off the confrontation for as long as possible.

Her sister studied her for a long time, then continued down the short hall.

Nathalyia entered her office, put away her handbag, picked up the phone, and dialed. It was answered on the second ring.

"Hello."

"We're engaged," Nathalyia blurted, unable to keep the sparkle of tears from her eyes. "Helen, I'm so happy."

"Oh, Nathalyia. He called just before you did, saying he was coming over to tell us something. He sounded so happy."

"I keep staring at my ring."

"I want to see it."

Nathalyia laughed. "Rafael is coming for lunch around noon. Why don't you come? Sam and Alec, too, if they can make it. It will keep me out of trouble."

"I'll call them. Congratulations again, and welcome to the Dunlap sisterhood."

Dunlap sisterhood. She belonged. "I'll see you at noon. Bye." Nathalyia replaced the receiver and then went to find her new assistant.

Clarice was exactly where Nathalyia knew she would be, working with Jake to get the bar ready. Hearing him tell her to behave, Nathalyia's lips twitched. They were good for each other.

"Good morning, Jake. Clarice. Clarice, can I please see you for a moment?"

They faced her. Jake actually looked a bit embarrassed. "Good morning, boss."

"Morning, Nathalyia." Clarice whispered something in Jake's ear that put a grin on his face before following Nathalyia to her office.

"Please have a seat." Nathalyia went behind her desk.

Clarice didn't take the seat offered. "What is it? What did she say I did?"

Nathalyia immediately knew who "she" was. "This isn't about Theresa. It's about what a wonderful employee you are. I'd like to offer you another position that I'm hoping you'll take."

Clarice sat down. "Another position?"

"Because of my pregnancy, the doctor has advised me to cut back on my schedule. I'll not only need someone personable and smart, and who cares about Fontaine, to be my executive assistant, but someone who can also pitch in with staffing needs." Nathalyia mentioned a salary that doubled Clarice's current income.

"You'll have a desk in here with me, and work directly under me. I know you'll want to think about it, but I'd like an answer by tomorrow so if you decline, I can look at other staff members before going outside Fontaine."

Clarice shot up from her chair and rounded the desk to hug Nathalyia. "I'll take it!"

Nathalyia laughed. "You had me worried for a moment."

"I thought you were going to take me out of the bar because of what happened," she said. "Jake is going to be so proud of me."

"He certainly will."

Suddenly Clarice screamed and jerked up Nathalyia's left hand. "Oh, my goodness! Oh, my goodness!"

The door burst open, and Jake stood there. "I heard you scream."

"She's engaged to Rafael!" Clarice shouted.

Several employees crowded in the door behind Jake. Nathalyia came to her feet. "I guess this is the official announcement that I'm engaged, and my fiancé and perhaps his family are coming for lunch."

Employees applauded and cheered as they surged into the room. The women oohed and aahed over the ring.

"Thank you. Now, please return to your stations," Nathalyia said. "We open in fifteen minutes."

Clarice and Jake were the last to leave. She told him about the position she'd accepted.

"I told you how smart you were," Jake said proudly.

Clarice leaned her head on his shoulder. "I guess you know he lives in your subdivision."

"Actually, I live in his." Nathalyia folded her arms and leaned back against the desk. "He moved there six months before I did. Martin visited him and liked the security of the estate."

"Man, can you two keep a secret!" Clarice said. "We'd better get to work. I don't want you to change your mind and hire someone else."

"Not a chance. You'll be perfect. We'll start training tomorrow," Nathalyia said. "With you and Jake, I won't worry about not being here."

"We'll always be here, except when we're on our honeymoon," Jake said. "If Clarice will have me?"

Clarice screamed, then launched herself at Jake. "Yes! Yes! A thousand times yes!"

Grinning, he caught her. "We'll pick out your ring as soon as possible. I'm letting everyone know you're mine."

"Always."

Employees rushed back in. "We have another engagement," Nathalyia announced. Jake and Clarice were well liked, so the congratulations were just as profuse.

"Come on. Let's get to work." Clarice pushed people out the door.

Rafael was barely out of his car when the front door of Sam's house flew open. He and Helen rushed out. Both were grinning. "How did you know?"

"Nathalyia called me." Helen hugged him. "She sounded so happy."

"So am I." He shook Sam's hand and hugged him with the other. "Thanks, Helen, for helping me get my head straight."

"She's invited me to lunch with you along with Sam and Alec." Helen hooked her arm though his, and they started inside. "I haven't told him yet. I wanted to leave that to you, but do it now, because I can't wait to tell everyone and plan a celebratory dinner."

Rafael stopped and hugged her. "Thanks for being there for her when I couldn't."

"That's what families do," Helen said as they continued into the house.

Nathalyia had planned on making rounds early, but suppliers kept her on the phone longer than anticipated. Thank goodness she'd been able to get the private dining area ready. She planned to serve them herself and since they were family, they could help.

Family. She had what she'd always desired and had been so afraid she'd never have. Smiling, she entered her office and came to a dead stop.

Theresa was taking credit cards from Nathalyia's billfold. Dollar bills were already on the desk. Incensed, Nathalyia slammed the door. "Put everything back! And get out!"

Theresa's head snapped up. Hatred stared out of her dark eyes. Grabbing the money, she stuffed it and the credit cards into the pockets of her slacks. "This is no more than I deserve. You promoted the blimp over me. I'm your sister."

"No, you're not. Not in the ways that matter." Nathalyia stepped in front of her. "A sister is someone who cares. You never did and you never will. You're all about yourself. Now put it back, and get out. You're fired."

"I'm not going anywhere," she sneered. "What will people think when they learn the well-respected Nathalyia Fontaine is knocked up and had to get engaged, let her mother die in poverty, and won't help her sister?"

Theresa turned back to the purse on the desk, upended it, and snatched up the car keys. "On second thought. I'm tired of taking the bus, and working here. I'll be around to get my paycheck, but I want triple unless you want people to know a few things. Get ready to pay and pay big."

Taking off the apron, she threw it down. Theresa passed Nathalyia, intentionally bumping her as she did. All the nasty things Theresa would say about her ran through Nathalyia's mind. The people who loved her wouldn't believe them, and the rest didn't matter.

Out of habit, she picked up the apron on the way after Theresa. She felt something heavy and looked into the pocket. A credit card reader. Theresa had been stealing credit card information. Enraged, Nathalyia sprinted out of her office after Theresa. She saw the back door swing shut and hurried outside and saw her sister walking toward her car. "Theresa!"

The other woman stopped, then hurried to the Rolls. Nathalyia pounded down the steps after her.

"Nathalyia!"

She heard Rafael call her name, but she kept going. Her sister was not getting away with this. She reached her sister just as she opened the door. Nathalyia slammed it shut and held up the credit card reader. "This time you're going to jail."

"Nathalyia," Rafael called.

Her eyes wild, Theresa shoved Nathalyia backward, then reached for the door handle. Nathalyia staggered back, regained her balance, jerked the door open and grabbed Theresa's arm. "You're not leaving!"

"Let go of me, bitch."

"Nat!" Rafael caught Nathalyia around the waist with his left arm, set her out of harm's way, then reached for Theresa with his right. He had to drag her kicking, screaming, and cursing out of the car.

Rafael twisted her arm behind her back when nothing else quieted her. "Calm down."

"You bastard! I'll have your badge. Just because you knocked her up, you're hassling me."

The altercation had brought some of the staff members out. Customers had stopped to watch. Sam, Helen, and Alec were there as well. Nathalyia wanted to cringe until she looked into Rafael's eyes. The love she saw there steadied her. "I want her arrested. She was trying to steal my car. You'll find money and my credit cards she took out of my purse in her pocket. And this was in her apron pocket."

"I never saw that before." Theresa kicked at Sam when he reached for her pocket. "She gave me the money and credit cards to keep me quiet! She didn't want anyone to know I'm her sister or that she deserted my mother and she died poor, begging for her! She tried to get me to do a threesome with her husband. She's pregnant and I had to talk her out of getting rid of the baby."

Nathalyia could feel the eyes on her. She couldn't look at anyone.

"Sam, take this before I forget I wear a badge," Rafael said. His arm slid protectively around Nathalyia. "Your lies won't save you, and they won't discredit Nathalyia. She tried to help you."

A police car with lights running and siren blaring pulled up. Two uniformed officers jumped out. "Commander Dunlap."

"Book this woman on suspicion of theft and forgery. I'll be down to file a report later on." Sam handed Theresa to the police officers, then stepped behind her and removed the money and credit cards from her pockets and put them into a plastic bag that Alec gave him.

"Sorry, Nathalyia, I'll have to keep these as evidence for the time being." Sam gave the bag to one of the policemen. "Take her away."

"Come on, Nat, let's go inside," Rafael said. "I hope you rested this morning."

"Watch out, Nathalyia. He's going to be as bad as Patrick," Helen warned.

"No one could be that bad." Alec came up the steps behind them.

"I'll remind you of that when Celeste becomes pregnant." Sam slapped Alec on the back.

Rafael keyed in the code and opened the back door. "A man has to take care of his family."

Inside, Nathalyia finally had the courage to look at them. The disappointment and disgust she'd feared wasn't there. "You didn't seem surprised that she's my sister."

"No, I wasn't," he answered. "I heard you two talking shortly after you hired her. I figured I'd respect your privacy."

Nathalyia glanced away. "You didn't believe what she said about me?"

Rafael frowned. "If I didn't know how upset this has made you, I would scold you. I might do it anyway. What in hell were you doing trying to wrestle her out of the car?"

"She made me so mad. She stole from me after I tried to help her, then threatened to tell all of those lies."

"A lot of us have relatives we'd rather forget," Helen said with feeling.

"People will talk," Nathalyia continued.

"Let them. We have more important things to think about and plan." Rafael kissed her, then continued walking. "Like how are we going to divide our time between our two homes, and does that mean we'll need two nurseries? I've been thinking that I might have to get another car. I'm not sure the backseat of the Mustang will be comfortable enough for the baby in the car seat."

Nathalyia gazed up at him. "You must love that car."

He kissed her. "I love you and our baby more."

Tears sparkled in her eyes. Yes, she had it all. He pulled her to him and kissed her hair.

"First we have to decide on a time for the engagement party with just the family," Helen said. "Nathalyia?"

She looked at the people who would become her family. "Whatever time works best for everyone. I'm going to start training my new assistant tomorrow."

"Now that that's settled, I want to see your ring."

Leaning into the shelter of Rafael's arms, where she'd always feel loved and cherished, Nathalyia proudly stuck out her left hand. She had a family and a man who would love her forever.

She finally had it all. She was going to enjoy every precious, wonderful second.

READING GUIDE QUESTIONS

1. Rafael wanted Nathalyia from their first meeting. Do you think a strong sexual attraction initially draws most couples together?

2. Nathalyia was wealthier than Rafael, yet money was never an issue between them. Would you date a man less successful than you? How important is income in a relationship?

3. Nathalyia was ashamed of her family and denied their existence. The decision came back to haunt her when her sister showed up at Fontaine. Is there ever a valid reason for turning your back on your family? Can anyone, no matter how dishonest or deceitful, be redeemed? Could Nathalyia's sister?

4. Clarice had a quick temper, a caring heart, and a record of going out with losers. Why do you think some women have

trouble finding good men? Do they settle? Are they impatient and just get tired of being alone, or are some men, especially the no-good ones, very persuasive?

5. Jake loved Clarice, but he didn't speak up because of the scar on his face and their fifteen-year age difference. Have you ever cared for someone, but were afraid to tell him/her? If you didn't speak up, do you regret your decision?

6. Is there ever a good enough reason not to tell a man he's the father of your baby?

7. The road to happiness was not smooth for Nathalyia and Rafael or Clarice and Jake. Lies, secrets, fears, and insecurities all played a role in keeping them apart. When do you know you love a person and that the love is worth the risk? Is it a feeling? Something he/she says or does?

"The best storyteller of the century. From the first page to the last, I fell in love with Francis Ray."

—Mary Morrison, *New York Times* bestselling author of *Unconditionally Single*, on *And Mistress Makes Three*

Don't miss these other Francis Ray titles:

I Know Who Holds Tomorrow
Somebody's Knocking at My Door
Trouble Don't Last Always
Like the First Time
Any Rich Man Will Do
In Another Man's Bed
Not Even If You Begged

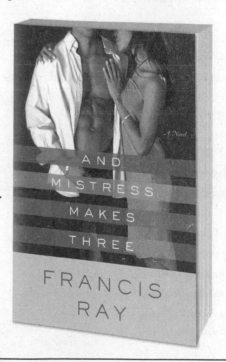

Visit www.thc-blackbox.com and sign up to receive "Dare To Love," a never-before-released short story by Francis Ray.

🦁 **St. Martin's Griffin**

"A story that tugs at the heartstrings."

—Romantic Times BOOKreviews on *Nobody But You*

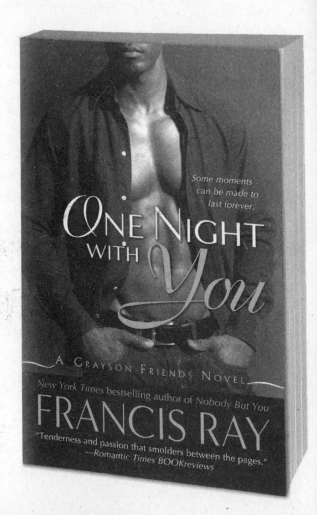

Don't miss these other Francis Ray titles:

The Turning Point
Someone to Love Me
You and No Other
Dreaming of You
Irresistible You
Only You
The Way You Love Me
Until There Was You
Nobody But You

Some moments can be made to last forever.

ONE NIGHT WITH You

A GRAYSON FRIENDS NOVEL

New York Times bestselling author of *Nobody But You*

FRANCIS RAY

"Tenderness and passion that smolders between the pages."
—*Romantic Times BOOKreviews*

St. Martin's Paperbacks